New York Times bestselling author Molly McAdams grew up in California but now lives in the oh-so-amazing state of Texas with her husband, daughter, and fur babies. When she's not diving into the world of her characters, some of her hobbies include hiking, snowboarding, travelling, and long walks on the beach . . . which roughly translates to being a homebody with her hubby and doing out movie quotes. She has a weakness for crude-humoured novels and fried pickles, and loves curling up in a fluffy comforter during a thunderstorm . . . or under one in a bathtub if there are tornadoes. That way she can pretend they aren't really happening.

Want to keep up with Molly and her upcoming releases? Subscribe to her newsletter: **www.mollysmcadams.com/newsletter**, find her on Facebook: **www.facebook.com/MollyMcAdams** or follow her on Twitter: **@MollySMcAdams**.

Get swept away by Molly McAdams's spellbindingly powerful love stories:

'I'm in awe. This is writing. This is romance'
Rachel Van Dyken, No. 1 *New York Times* bestselling author

'McAdams delivers another devastatingly satisfying
page-turner . . . that is sure to please her fans and all
devotees of searing contemporary romances'
Booklist

'This story has all the usual McAdams elements: It's funny, sexy and
twisty – not to mention the scenes are wickedly hot . . . And, remember,
McAdams loves to throw major curveballs, so plan accordingly'
Romantic Times Book Reviews

'A story that will undoubtedly touch on every single
emotion. No one can paint each page with equal parts
triumph and tragedy the way Molly McAdams can'
Jay Crownover, *New York Times* bestselling author

'Consuming. Enthralling. Sexy. MIND-BLOWING . . .
A mustall
your emot'
A.

D0227812

Firefly

MOLLY McADAMS

HEADLINE **ETERNAL**

First published in Great Britain in 2017
by HEADLINE ETERNAL
An imprint of HEADLINE PUBLISHING GROUP

1

Cataloguing in Publication Data is available from the British Library

ISBN 978 1 4722 4753 7

Typeset in 10.75/14 pt Garamond MT Std by Jouve (UK), Milton Keynes

Printed and bound in Great Britain by CPI Group (UK) Ltd, Croydon, CR0 4YY

Headlin   yclable
                                                                            to
The l

For Sarah.
For finding beauty in the darkest times.

Firefly

Prologue

Lily

A crippling acceptance washed over me in the split second that seemed to last forever and pass within a beat of my heart.

Because I knew it would end this way, and I'd been foolish to think it wouldn't.

But given the chance, I'd do it all over again.

Chapter 1

BREATHE IN. BREATHE OUT.

Lily

I woke with a grave sense that something was wrong. My mind and ears were alert, but I kept my eyes closed and my body as relaxed as possible. I focused on each breath that filled and fled from my lungs, but as the seconds went on, my breaths turned shallow and started coming faster.

Someone was in my room.

Breathe in. Breathe out.

Breathe in. Breathe out.

It was dark behind my eyelids, too dark for anyone to try to wake me.

Kieran.

The name floated through my mind for merely a second before it was shoved aside by that overwhelming sense of wrongness.

Kieran was silent as the night.

If I'd woken to him, I knew my heart would have been beating wildly in my chest, calling out to the guy who had stolen it at some point in my life. It wouldn't have been slowing, as if even my heart knew it needed to be silent in those moments.

If it had been Kieran, his dark, complicated presence would've filled the room, pressing against me in a way I'd spent years recognizing. Instead, electricity danced across my skin in warning, as if I was standing in the path where lightning was about to strike.

Whoever was *in the room with me was attempting to quiet their steps . . . and failing.*

The warm summer air blew strands of hair across my face, tickling my lips and nose, but still I didn't move. Fear flooded my veins as that ominous feeling grew stronger and stronger, my breaths halting when I realized I hadn't opened the large windows in my room.

"One of the other rooms?" a harsh, masculine voice asked from across my room, the hushed whisper floating over to me on the breeze.

"No," another deep voice responded. "He said it was in here somewhere."

My body shook as I fought with myself over what to do. Before I could decide on screaming for someone or remaining silent, a third intruder made my decision for me . . .

Rough, thick fingers trailed from my cheek to jaw, and a raw scream burst from my lungs as my eyes flew open.

The same hand that had gently caressed a split second before promptly slammed down over my mouth, muffling my scream and allowing me to hear the curses and demands now flying from the strangers.

"Shut up!"

"You fucking idiot—"

"We need to go."

"Goddamn it, I said shut up!"

"—what the fuck did you do?"

"Let's go!"

Footsteps could be heard pounding down the hall seconds before my door was flung open. The light to my room was turned on, revealing Aric and the three men in my room.

They were in dark jeans and jackets. Their hoods were drawn over their heads and held in place by dark bandanas that covered their chins to just below their eyes. The two standing near the foot of my bed immediately began yelling what sounded like accusations at my brother, but Aric didn't seem to be hearing them.

He didn't seem to notice them at all.

A flurry of emotions passed over his face: shock, worry, hesitation, and fear . . . but as his eyes narrowed on the man standing above me, fury replaced all the rest.

I screamed for him against the large hand covering my mouth, but I didn't know what I was screaming.

Screaming for him to run and get help.

Screaming for him to save me.

Just screaming.

"I said shut up," the man repeated again, his growl splitting over the shouts in the room.

The hand covering my mouth left briefly, but then connected with my face hard. The force made me bite my cheek and stunned me for long seconds as the metallic taste of blood met my tongue.

My brother tore into the room, shouting for me and shouting at the men, not even stopping when the man closest to him calmly pulled out a gun from the back of his dark jeans.

But he didn't point it at Aric or at me; it just remained at his side in warning.

My world tilted as a high-pitched ringing filled my ears.

A stain spread rapidly on Aric's shirt as he finally stumbled to a stop. It was blood red. And it didn't make sense, and someone was screaming, and they needed to stop.

They needed to help Aric.

Something was wrong with him, but there was so much screaming, confusing my already flooded senses as my world continued to tilt. And Aric was staring blankly at me as I was ripped off my bed by the man who had hit me—a gun in his free hand, raised in Aric's direction.

Why wasn't anyone helping him?

The screaming finally stopped, but someone was holding me back—pulling me away. Away from Aric and the safety of the house, toward the large windows. That rough hand was back over my mouth, the arm it was attached to completely oblivious to my clawing at it.

A wet choking noise sounded in the room, and I fought harder—except, I wasn't sure my arms worked anymore.

Aric.

I couldn't move.

I couldn't get to him, and I needed to get to him. He was going to fall!

Aric's lips moved one last time, but I couldn't decipher his words as my world darkened.

His knees hit my floor, and suddenly a pair of familiar green eyes were directly in front of my own. Rage and something so terrifying filling them as they locked on the man dragging me away.

Kieran.

Relief slammed into me as darkness wrapped its arms around me like an old friend and pulled me close . . .

I jolted awake, my arms reaching to catch someone who wasn't there. A sound between a sob and a scream tore through the room before I could choke it back.

My hands slammed down onto the mattress, barely keeping my torso up as my arms shook. My head fell between my shoulders like a dead weight as my breaths rushed from me mercilessly. Each strained breath sounded like an inverted scream as I tried to force the memories from my mind.

Within seconds the door to the bedroom burst open, slamming against the wall. The sound followed Beck's frantic voice. "Lily!"

I opened my mouth to respond as my best friend rushed around, looking for a threat, but I only managed another pained cry as everything crashed into me again and again.

Hooded figures that used the dark to their advantage.

Red stains on his shirt and my carpet.

Lifeless eyes.

Lines and circles. Always lines and circles.

"I'm fine," I finally forced out, my words shaky and directed at the bed. "I'm . . . I'm fine."

"Jesus fuck, Lil." Exhaustion crept through his tone. "You scared the living hell out of me." He sat near me on the bed and placed a hand on one of my arms, but I jerked away from his touch.

"Don't," I pleaded. "Don't . . . just don't."

"Lil," he began softly but didn't try to reach for me again. "Do you need me to get in touch with Kiera—?"

"No, don't." It felt like I'd shouted my plea, but I wasn't sure if Beck had even heard my whispered words. "He's working. He can't— just don't contact him."

"You think work would keep him from you if you needed him?" Beck asked with a hint of amusement, but worry was still in his tone.

Kieran had been saving me for as long as I could remember. Whether from spiders and other crawling insects, or from men who tried to steal me in the night . . . saving me had been his life's mission. It was in his blood.

It was one of the many reasons I'd fallen in love with him.

But my favorite trait of his had become his biggest flaw over the last few years, and I hated that it had come to this. Hated that I now resented him for being who he was.

Because he loved me, and my heart ached for the love we'd had, but he was a warrior through and through. And ever since that night Aric died, those instincts had slowly enveloped Kieran's love for me, until they were all he knew.

Save Lily.

Protect Lily.

Hide Lily.

Cage Lily.

And one word from Beck would have him running home to save me, but I needed this time alone.

I needed to process the grief and pain the nightmarish flashbacks always brought with them, and process the piece of that night I'd remembered. And I couldn't do that with him here—not when his presence felt so suffocating.

"One of the other rooms?"

"No. He said it was in here somewhere."

A chill crept up my spine, adding to the trembling of my body as I remembered the men's words.

"Lil?" Beck prompted.

I gritted my teeth against the pain that felt so fresh, and instead of answering his question, whispered, "It's been four years."

He didn't need to ask what I was referring to. Every year, the anniversary of Aric's death hung like a dark, menacing cloud above the Holloway Estate as the date loomed closer.

"Four years . . . Christ. I still remember it all like it just . . ." Beck shifted on the bed and was silent so long I didn't think he would continue. When he did, his tone was hesitant, as though he wasn't sure he should say what he thought. "If you should be thankful for anything in your life, it's that you weren't there to see Kieran the day they lowered those two caskets in the ground. It didn't matter that your casket didn't hold your body. It didn't matter that we all knew you were safe . . . hidden. You hadn't said a word in nearly five days, and no one could get you to eat. To Kieran, you *were* in that casket, because the girl he loved was gone. He lost it. I have no doubt he would've killed every single one of us to get to the Borellos and avenge your deaths if your dad hadn't grabbed a shovel and knocked Kieran out cold."

My grief was momentarily replaced with shock from his words. My gaze snapped to Beck, but he wasn't looking at me. His stare was distant as his head shook.

"I've seen men who have nothing left to live for, but I've never seen anything like that. Never seen a man lose it the way he did. He looked wild, completely out of control as if he would take the entire world down with him without blinking. But for that to be *Kieran*?" Beck blew out a slow breath that bordered on a whistle.

I understood why Beck was having such a difficult time grasping what had happened those years ago, even if he'd been there to witness it.

Kieran was calm. Kieran hardly reacted to anything.

He'd slit your throat with a blank expression and then walk away as though you'd just finished a pleasant conversation.

Then again, you couldn't expect anything less of the man who'd trained to be an assassin from the day he took his first steps.

The only time I'd witnessed any form of fear and anguish from him had been on *that* night . . .

"Why didn't you tell me before now?"

"What, you expected me to tell you when it happened?" He huffed. "By the time you could've handled knowing, there was no point bringing it back up. But now?" He hiked a shoulder up before letting it fall. "With the day here, and you waking up screaming . . . I don't know. I guess I wanted you to know that you aren't the only one who still struggles with what happened."

If I hadn't felt so physically exhausted, I would've laughed. But the thought of Kieran struggling with anything was still enough to make my eyes roll as I sat back so I could rub my head.

Beck suddenly caught my chin in his fingers, pulling me close. "Do you blame Kieran? Is that why you don't want me to get hold of him?"

My shoulders hunched. All the air in my lungs rushed out as if his words had been a physical blow. "Of course not."

"Because *he* does, Lil. Every fucking day."

"What?" I asked, the word nothing more than a breath.

"He lost his best friend, and a huge part of the girl he loved, all because he wasn't fast enough that night."

"But—but Kieran hadn't even been in the house when everything began," I argued. "You *know* that! He heard—"

"It doesn't matter. What actually happened and whatever you might say . . . it doesn't matter to him. And to the rest of us? To your dad? It doesn't matter that Kieran was able to save you. Nothing matters when the Borellos still killed and tried to abduct the last remaining O'Sullivan kids."

"I know what happened, Beck," I gritted out. "I was there."

He grimaced, letting silence stretch between us before he gently continued. "You're the goddamn princess of the Irish-American mob, Lil. You're the last chance your dad has to keep O'Sullivan blood running through the Holloway Gang. We had to fake your damn death. And, yeah, you're still here, but you're different now. You've changed. I see it . . . he sees it. Because of that? Kieran's going to blame himself for not being able to stop them that night. You can't expect him not to."

A flash of longing and resentment flared inside me, and I wanted to say that I wasn't the only one who'd changed. Instead, I nodded subtly as I climbed off the bed, squeezing his hand as I did. "No, I guess I can't. Go back to bed, Beck. Sorry I woke you."

I turned toward the large bay window and walked over to sit on the window seat where I spent most of my time when trying to escape the world I'd been born into, or the nightmares that plagued me because of it.

I hugged one of the throw pillows close to my body and rested my head against the cool glass as I looked across the grounds toward the house I'd grown up in. The massive structure looked haunting in the grey, pre-dawn sky. My eyes automatically found the window of my old room, and their voices played through my mind again . . .

"One of the other rooms?"

"No. He said it was in here somewhere."

"Lil?"

I glanced over my shoulder to see Beck's brow pinched as he studied my position. "You sure you don't want me to get him?"

"I'm sure."

He nodded slowly, and I knew he was trying to decide whether or not to listen to me. "See you in a few hours."

I lifted the corners of my mouth in a faint smile before looking back to the windows of my old room, replaying the memory over and over.

Every time, wondering who *he* was.

Every time, getting caught on the fact that my brother hadn't looked surprised to see the Borello men there.

And every time, wondering why I had never noticed that before.

Chapter 2

HEARTLESS BASTARD

Lily

Walking into that room hours later was the worst homecoming I'd ever experienced. I hadn't set foot in there since the night I'd woken up to find members of the Borello family standing inside it.

I'd stayed in different rooms for a while . . . Kieran's. The library. If Beck or Conor were working, I snuck into their rooms in Soldier's Row on the other side of the property to sleep. Anywhere so long as I didn't have to be in the room that had been the source of my nightmares until Kieran, Beck, and I had moved into the guesthouse.

Nothing had changed except for the carpet, and an odd sense of nostalgia filled my chest before I began trembling violently.

Because not three feet from where I was standing was where Aric had fallen to the floor.

And just across the room was where I had been. A man dragging me away before Kieran had ended his life.

All of it played out on a twisted loop as I watched from the doorway. And I couldn't stop it.

"One of the other rooms?"

"No. He said it was in here somewhere."

I swallowed thickly, forcing down the bile that rose in my throat, and shut my eyes as I tried to remember those words over and over again.

So many places something could be hidden, and I had no idea what they'd been looking for.

Half an hour later, I was sitting on the floor of my closet, somewhat relieved that I hadn't found anything in my room for the Borellos to find, despite wishing I had.

I'd wanted to find a reason for that night to have happened at all. To know they hadn't been there by mistake, and he'd died for absolutely nothing.

Their words had felt so crucial when I'd woken to them early this morning, like I'd *needed* to hear them. But I was starting to wonder if that little piece I'd been given had been real at all. If *any* of the new pieces during my nightmares were real, or just what my subconscious created over time.

I climbed to my feet and took one last look inside the empty closet, then turned to leave.

My gaze shifted to my feet as I shut the closet door, desperately trying not to linger on places that triggered a cold sweat and images I saw far too often.

I took quick steps away from the closet and had just reached the dresser when something caught my eye, and I slowed.

Backing up a few steps, I looked behind the dresser from my new angle, studying the way the baseboard seemed to be hugging the wall instead of attached to it.

I pushed the dresser a few inches away so I could drop to my knees behind it, and quickly reached for the piece of baseboard.

My heart thundered when the wood easily fell away at my touch, and I forced myself to take steadying breaths when I saw the sheetrock had been cut out from behind it.

I knew from the chill that gripped at my spine *this* was what they'd been looking for that night.

And I hated him—whoever *he* was. For putting me in danger by using *my* room. For leaving something there for those men to find. For letting Aric die.

I hated all of them.

"One of the other rooms?"

"No. He said it was in here somewhere."

My hand shook as I reached inside, but my hope died and heart sank as I searched and searched and came up empty.

I sat back on my heels and stared at the empty hole in my wall as that night continued to torture me—silently begging for something to appear. When minutes passed and nothing in the room changed, I placed the baseboard back and stood. After shoving the dresser back into its place, I quickly left the room, my eyes closed tight in a vain attempt to shut out the never-ending nightmares playing in my mind.

I'd only made it down a few halls when I heard my name called out, and I reluctantly stopped. Forcing all of my hatred for the man who belonged to that voice away from my expression, I turned to face my dad.

Mick O'Sullivan. *Mickey* to those closest to him—to those who used the darkness of the world to conceal their sins.

CEO of an empire.

Boss of the Holloway Gang.

Heartless bastard.

"What are you doing coming from the rooms?" Before I could respond, he stalked toward me. "Let's go. Meeting is starting."

"But I—"

"Come on, Princess," he said as he passed me. He turned, his million-dollar smile on display.

A smile that could charm almost anyone. Almost.

He was in his early forties—my parents had been teenagers when they'd had the twins, and then me—but you wouldn't know it looking at him. Men Mickey's age only looked the way he did when they were on the silver screen.

Or if they'd sold their souls to the devil.

With his looks and smooth words, he could lure the purest hearts to do the darkest deeds, all with that smile on his face.

It was why no one had batted an eye when he'd killed the old boss and taken his place twenty years ago. People fell over themselves to work for him.

"This is all going to be yours one day," he continued, his deep voice booming throughout the large hall, as if he was trying to sell me on the idea. "You need to sit in on as many of these as you can. You can't expect Kieran to run it all by himself."

But Kieran wasn't supposed to run this world.

Then again . . . neither was I.

We'd had plans and made promises—promises he'd broken years ago.

My dad's smile abruptly vanished when I didn't move or respond, and a look entered the ice-blue eyes identical to mine. "Lily," he demanded in a low, even tone.

He was done being nice. Done pretending to care.

I walked in his direction without a word, then followed him to the meeting.

Of the dozen or so men that worked for Dad and Kieran and still spoke to me, only a few mumbled quiet hellos as I walked into the room behind my dad, still unsure how to handle being near me on this day even after four years.

If I was allowed to come and go around the property, I was sure it would be different.

There wouldn't be weighted silences that fell over rooms when I walked into them, or the worried stares that accompanied it. Wondering if I was okay but too afraid to ask.

There wouldn't be the uncomfortable waves of tension from the rest of the men—the ones who would rather I'd actually been in the ground than locked away on the back of the property. Some because they felt my presence was a risk to their lives. Others because they would've followed Aric to their deaths, and they blamed me for living just as my mom had.

There wouldn't be the slanted glares as their anger boiled just beneath the surface, waiting for a time when they could repay me for the unfair card they felt had been dealt to them.

But to touch me would evoke a wrath not one of them could survive.

And they respected Kieran as much as they feared him.

I took a seat between Beck and his younger brother, Conor, as they spoke to the guys next to them, and looked blankly ahead waiting for the meeting to start.

"No girls allowed," someone jeered from the other end of the room.

A few of the other guys laughed mockingly, but not nearly as many as usual when I sat in on the meetings.

Even the ones who had come to hate or fear my presence couldn't forget what today was. Couldn't forget they'd lost the man they'd readily followed—some even above my dad.

Both Conor and Beck tensed beside me but didn't say anything. They knew not to after all these years.

I gave no indication that I'd heard them at all. They liked it when I responded, and I didn't want to give them anything to like.

"Ah, give it a rest. That got old years ago," one of my dad's men said with a groan. "She doesn't know where she is anyway. Lily." He exaggerated my name, smacking the table in time with the syllables. "Look at her . . . Nightshade's fucked her stupid. Her pretty little head is so full of air she doesn't even know her own name anymore."

Beck's chair shot back as he stood, his hands fisted as he slammed them on the table. But before he could say a word, my dad laughed long and loud.

"Well, fuck me. I'm gonna have a hell of a time replacing you when Kieran catches wind of that comment."

I let my eyes flit in the man's direction for only a second to see him pale and sink into his chair before I looked blankly at the wall again.

Bailey. He'd been with Holloway nearly as long as Mickey, and was just as devoted to the gang and what they stood for.

But Aric's death had changed so much more than some would ever understand.

With Mom turning into a shell of herself after the death of Aric's twin, Aiden, and then leaving to live with her family about a year ago, a couple of the families who had been in the mob for generations thought Mickey was losing his hold on the gang. Now Bailey and his son Finn were just waiting for one more thing to go wrong. One more thing to loosen the grip my dad had on Holloway before they could slip in and try to take it from him.

Their greed had grown too great over the years for them to realize that Mickey was three steps ahead, just waiting for Bailey and Finn to present the perfect opportunity to be taken out.

And with that one comment, Bailey had started a ripple effect that couldn't be stopped. Now he was being held above open water, dripping blood, and Mickey was going to let him bleed before he attacked.

"Anyone have a problem with Lily being here?" Mickey called out.

His tone rang with false concern. Something about the sincerity called out to them, begging them to tell him their problems. It was one of the reasons he was such a good leader. His ability to be anyone they needed him to be. But there was a razor edge to his voice that warned what would happen if they ever gave him the wrong answer, ever disappointed him.

When he spoke again, that razor was all that was left, and it sliced through the room like a threat. "That's what I thought."

I could feel every one of the men's stares as my dad began the meeting, but I forced myself to maintain my façade. Forced myself not to show any hint I'd been paying attention or knew their eyes were on me.

Truth was, my mom and I were the only women allowed in this

room. But she'd been so lost in bottles of whiskey even before Aric died that she'd stopped coming long before I was old enough to sit in on the meetings.

As it was, I only came when I wasn't given an option, and I did the same thing every time.

Maintained a blank stare. Never let a word leave my lips.

Dad had called me out a few times afterward, telling me I needed to start paying attention and participating if I wanted to gain the men's respect before I took over.

Beck often elbowed me to make sure I was awake.

And whispers floated around the room whenever Kieran was out—which was most meetings.

"You think they drug her?"

"Fucking zombie."

"How much you wanna bet she'll drool?"

"Why's she here at all?"

"She should go back to her fucking sanctuary."

But it didn't matter what they said. It didn't matter what they thought. Because people often said things they normally wouldn't when they thought you weren't listening, and I knew I'd heard more than I was ever supposed to.

Like Bailey and Finn's plan.

Every bit of information kept tucked away for when I would need it.

"Be strong and relentless," my mom had always said. *"Look fragile, but never act it. Be a viper disguised as a lamb, and you'll never lose their loyalty."*

If only she were around to see me now.

Mom had trained me from a young age . . . not just how to be the princess of the mob, but how to rule it. Because I hadn't just grown up in this life, I'd been groomed to *stay* in it.

Kieran and I had been inseparable for as long as I could remember, and everyone had known we would remain that way. To them, it couldn't have been a more perfect match.

Before his death, Kieran's dad, Georgie, had been Mickey's advisor long before Kieran became the hired assassin, and earned a revered reputation all on his own. And it had never been a secret that Kieran would be Aric's advisor when he finally took over.

When Aric died, Mickey had forced Kieran to take his place as Underboss.

With his title and mine, we were supposed to be the unstoppable couple.

Except I'd always hated this life and had wanted to get far from it. Something only Kieran had known.

Late at night over the years, he'd slid soundlessly into my bed and pulled me close, his lips at my ear as he built our future with words and dreams, promising a life away from this place—far from the mob.

But those promises to run kept getting delayed until they were broken, and I watched as I slowly lost Kieran to the same world that had stolen my brothers from me.

Ever since, all I'd wanted was to take this world and watch as it was destroyed.

So I'd ignored every piece of advice my mom had given me, and I waited for my chance.

Blank stare. Lips closed.

The air in the room grew heavy seconds before my dad laughed, low and threatening. "Well, if my day wasn't just made because you walked in. Wasn't sure if you'd make it. Wasn't sure if some people wanted you to."

I didn't need my dad's words. I didn't need to look. I'd already known he'd walked into the room.

He was silent as the night, but I *knew* the man who had just slipped into that room.

I'd spent most of my life trying to match my heartbeat to his, trying to memorize the way the room felt when he was in it, all so I would know when he was near.

He settled himself against the wall opposite me, and I fought back the surprise and heartache that threatened my bored expression at seeing him there.

At seeing him at all . . .

But his light green eyes never once met me, and they were so, so cold as he stared down at the man sitting just two feet in front of him.

Kieran folded his arms across his chest, the picture of ease. But the heaviness in the room and the look on his destructively handsome face gave away everything he was feeling, everything he was thinking, as he glowered at Bailey.

He dipped his chin, his tone lethal when he ground out, "Continue."

I allowed myself a quick glance at Beck to see him fight back a smile just before my dad burst out laughing.

"Someone had your days numbered," Mickey taunted. "Pray Nightshade doesn't find you . . ." He let the haunting threat trail off, not attempting to hide his enjoyment watching the man squirm.

I forced myself to stare at the wall, but I could hear the nervousness in Bailey's voice when he stuttered, "Didn't mean nothin' by it, Kieran."

Mickey feigned a sigh. "Like I said . . . gonna have a hell of a time replacing you. Let's finish this so we can enjoy the show that's sure to follow."

Chapter 3

TRUTH OR DARE

Dare

I stood still as I studied the man tied to the chair, watching his every move.

Every twitch.

Every hitched breath.

Every jerk of his gaze around the warehouse.

With a drawn-out sigh, I rolled up the papers he'd slipped my sister the night before, hitting my palm with them as I started walking in a slow circle around him. "Lie."

His head snapped up and tried to follow me. "No! N-no, I did-I didn't. Swear to God, Demitri. I wouldn't."

I waited until I was in front of him and bent to eye level before I spoke again. Lifting the papers slightly, I asked, "You expect me to believe that Holloway's now selling to law enforcement? That they're getting their supply into prisons now?"

I knew for a fact that Mickey O'Sullivan had drugs going to people in the government, but not law enforcement.

He was stupid—just not *that* stupid.

The paperwork this guy had sent my way had all been fabricated, and I knew Mickey was behind it. Knew the Holloway snitch in front of me had probably let slip to Mickey that we were watching every move and he was trying to lead us in false directions.

I wasn't so easily led.

"Swear to God. I've been taking it myself. Every week I make the drop off." Sweat ran from the man's brow and dripped down his nose, and his voice grew shallow as he continued to ramble and bullshit.

Lie.

I held out the papers until Johnny took them from me, slanting my eyes at him in a look that had his mouth twisting into a crazed smirk as he backed slowly away.

Johnny and I had grown up together. Been best friends for as long as I could remember, and worked together for most that time. We worked together well. He knew what I would do as soon as I decided on it, and I knew how to calm his homicidal tendencies.

Unfortunately, I'd just unleashed that manic need inside him to watch someone's life slip from their eyes because people couldn't be allowed to live when they threatened everything.

And a snitch who started playing both sides undeniably threatened everything.

I slid my arm around my back, curling my hand around the grip of my gun and pulling it out of my waistband.

The man thrashed in the chair as understanding and fear filled his eyes. "It's the truth, I swear! I swear to God—I'll do anything. I'll—"

"Truth or dare," I said in a calm, dark tone, and waited for his answer when he started sobbing.

"T-t-truth. *Truth.* I'm telling you the truth. What do you want? I'll work for you—*only* you. I'll tell you anything. I'll f-feed you any information from Holloway you want. Just don't fucking kill me," he cried out. "It's the truth. I'll tell you anything."

I clicked my tongue and tilted my head to the side. "If you were telling the truth, you wouldn't—"

"Lily O'Sullivan is still alive."

My taunt died in my throat.

It felt as if all the oxygen was sucked from the large space, then replaced with a fire so hot it was agonizing.

Rage burned deep inside me, spreading through every inch of my body until I was consumed with it—until all I could see was *her*. Until all I knew was the pain of holding her limp in my arms, blood covering us both.

"The fuck you just say?" My voice could barely be heard over the inferno in the warehouse, but the man shakily looked up at me.

His voice leveled out and his eyes held mine. "Lily O'Sullivan is still alive."

I glanced at Johnny, but wished I hadn't.

My normally stone-faced friend's expression was a mixture of the same rage and shock I felt.

Looking back at the man, I staggered a step away. My body felt heavy. Wrong.

He was wrong. He had to be. Because otherwise—I forced the thought from my head. He was wrong . . .

Clearing my throat, I bit out, "You should've picked *dare*."

Lifting my arm, I aimed at his head and pulled the trigger.

Chapter 4

SAVE US

Lily

As soon as the meeting ended, I left for the guesthouse without giving anyone the chance to stop me. I didn't want to stay for the *show*, as Mickey had called it. My throat tightened and stomach churned at his excitement over what was to come . . . at *who* it involved.

As soon as I was inside, I headed for the kitchen to make coffee, and the water had just started boiling when Conor began a perimeter check around the house.

No sign of Beck or Kieran.

Then again, I doubted I'd see them anytime soon. When I'd snuck out at the end, Kieran had still been leaning against the wall with a calm, lethal expression as Bailey gripped at the arms of his chair, too afraid to move.

As I waited for the coffee to finish brewing in the French press, I wondered how long Bailey would stay in that chair if Kieran never moved from his position, and how Kieran had happened to show up after Bailey's comments when I couldn't remember the last time he'd been on the property during the day.

Before he'd been forced to take Aric's place, Kieran had only worked when Mickey needed someone silenced. I'd spent all my days and nights with him and had hated the few hours when he was gone.

Now, everything had changed. Mickey had him working constantly. Two or three nights a week, I'd wake up to Kieran slipping into bed only for him to be gone when I woke.

Yet I'd never felt more suffocated or hurt by him.

And somehow, the only person who noticed was a breathtakingly captivating guy who had stolen my thoughts, one by one, and crept into my dreams, unbidden . . . until I'd found myself falling asleep, praying he'd meet me there. He had a relaxed smile and an easiness about him, while still managing to remain intimidating.

And he saw straight through me.

Whoever's the cause behind that sad smile will never deserve you.

I'd been sitting on the bench at the kitchen table, mind on an intriguing stranger's words, coffee long since cooled, forgotten, when I noticed it . . .

The change in the house.

The charge pressing against my ribs and stealing my breath, growing stronger by the second.

The only way I could ever have known Kieran was there, moving closer with each stuttered beat of my heart.

I hadn't even heard the door open or shut.

Silent as the night.

His hand suddenly covered my own, pinning it to the table. My body stilled and I slowly turned my head to look at our overlapping hands until he removed them both from the wood.

There, below where my hand had rested, was a symbol smudged onto the surface of the table that chilled me to my core.

Lines and circles.

A symbol I'd been taught to fear growing up.

A symbol I drew without meaning to.

My subconscious conjured it up in ceilings and clouds and woodgrains. I saw it inked onto a forearm when I closed my eyes . . .

Even if I never knew why the men were in my room that night, the man who'd shot Aric and tried to take me with him had revealed enough secrets once he was dead.

By way of this symbol tattooed on his arm.

I'd always known what it meant—known who wore it with pride. But I'd never seen the symbol on a person before that night, and I hadn't since.

That didn't mean it had stopped haunting me.

Four horizontal lines, each shorter than the one above it, with one vertical line slashing through, longer than all the others. All centered in an outline of a circle.

The symbol that a mafia family had adopted long ago.

A family that the Holloway Gang had been at war with since long before my father was born—the Borellos.

But that war between our families had led to an immeasurable amount of death throughout the years and to my dad faking my own.

"Protect the princess at all costs," he'd told every one of his men.

I still hadn't been found. Then again, I was well guarded.

I needed to be kept hidden from the world. I knew that.

But Kieran wanted me hidden to keep me alive and with him.

Mickey wanted to keep me alive so O'Sullivan blood would stay in control of Holloway.

Neither realized this couldn't last.

If Kieran became Boss and we had a child, it wouldn't matter if the world still assumed I was dead or not. That child would be the Borello's newest target, and I refused to put my child through the life I'd lived.

The moment I found out I was pregnant, I would be gone—whether Kieran came with me or not.

Kieran tightened his fingers against mine, bringing me back to the present as his mouth brushed along the back of my neck.

Just as he started to release my hand, I clasped our fingers tighter. "Bailey?"

I felt his anger slam into me, but he gave no hint otherwise. His voice was still the same dark warning it had been since we were kids. "He won't say anything to you again."

"What'd you do, Kieran?"

"Nothing."

"Kieran . . ." I released his name with a sigh, and slowly untangled our fingers.

I would've loved to watch Kieran knock Bailey out for what he'd said, but hitting someone wasn't Kieran's way.

It wasn't how he'd been raised. It wasn't who he was paid to be.

The assassin wasn't who he'd *wanted* to be.

I felt him move away from me, and knew he was going to shower and try to sleep before Mickey sent him away again.

Not taking my eyes from the smudged symbol on the table, I hurriedly whispered, "Take me away from here."

I didn't hear him stop walking but knew he had.

Glancing up at him, I watched him slowly turn, those pale eyes giving away his need to do anything for me.

"Take me away."

"You know I can't."

"Yes, you can. *We* can. Don't you remember everything we planned? Everything you promised?"

His head listed to the side as his brows dipped low, his eyes now cold. The beast inside him instinctively awakening and reacting to being challenged.

But I held his stare, knowing his reaction was as involuntary as breathing. Knowing he was fighting it and would never willingly hurt me.

He had the mind of a monster and the heart of a dreamer.

He'd never hidden either from me, and long ago I'd fallen in love with both.

"You think I'd ever forget, Lily?" A hint of the softness he only ever used with me laced through his words. "But I have a job to do."

It'd been obvious what he'd chosen, but he'd never stated that he held the mob over me before. Hearing it now felt like a physical blow.

"A job you never wanted," I reminded him, trying to hide the pain in my voice. "A job *we* never wanted. We were supposed to get away from this, I wasn't supposed to lose you to the mob."

Despite his guarded expression, I knew my last words had hurt him. Could see it in the way his hand twitched like he was about to reach for me or for one of his blades—anything that brought him comfort.

"Is that what you think's happening?"

My shoulders sagged as I studied him . . . studied the distance between us. Before everything had happened, we couldn't be in a room together without touching in some form—it didn't matter that we'd already been together for years. Now, it was as if there was a force slowly pushing us farther apart, and neither of us would try to fight it.

Planting my elbow on the table, I dropped my head into my hand, staring down at the smudged symbol as I whispered, "It's just what *is*, Kieran."

"Because we never left. Because I took Aric's place." He didn't word them as questions, so I didn't respond.

Because you broke your promises. Because you've turned into someone else. Because you're letting this life destroy what we could be.

I inhaled quickly when he suddenly appeared on the bench beside me, pulling my back flush against him. One arm wrapped around my waist, the other around my chest so he could press his hand firmly between my breasts.

Holding me the way he had all those years before.

Protective and gentle, powerful and loving.

Something deep inside me ached. Ached for what Kieran and I'd had.

"This," he said in a gruff tone. "This is my job."

Save Lily.

My chest rose and fell roughly as I waited for him to continue.

"All I want is for you to keep breathing. All I want is for you to let me keep you alive."

Protect Lily.

"Leaving?" he asked as his lips brushed against my neck. "Christ, Lily, I would've taken you away years ago if I could've. But you're the target they've been waiting for. If I go, they'll know. They'll follow. That's why we've stayed."

Hide Lily.

"I understand staying hidden, but you don't know they're waiting for *me*," I argued gently. "You can't know they would follow us."

Kieran's mouth paused just above my skin for a few moments before he said confidently, "They're waiting. And I won't hand you over to them."

Cage Lily.

"You can't kn—"

"They're waiting, Lily. Trust me." The hollow tone of his voice had a chill creeping into my bones, and for a few seconds, I forgot how to breathe as I wondered what information Beck or one of the other guys may have heard on the streets.

"What do you know?"

He hesitated before speaking. And when he did, the words were soft and tortured, and pulled a pained breath from me. "Things that don't matter if I'm already losing you."

"Kieran . . ." I glanced over my shoulder and was met with something I never thought I'd see from the man behind me.

My hardened, unemotional assassin. Green eyes full of defeat and fear. Every emotion lain bare.

"I love you, Lily. I would give my life for yours." His eyes searched mine for an immeasurable amount of time before he said, "I'd give you the world if you asked for it, but not at the expense of your life. Don't ask me to stop saving you, because I don't know how."

If only Kieran could understand I'd never asked him to.

If only he could see what I'd been begging him for all along.

If only he knew he'd pushed me so far away that my heart was sure we'd never find a way back to who we'd been. And in that, I felt more torn in this moment than I ever could've imagined.

Unbidden images of secret, written words and dark, mysterious eyes entered my mind. Guilt ripped through me as I desperately tried to focus on the hope I'd clung to for so long . . .

That one day the Kieran I'd fallen in love with would come back to me.

"Then give me the boy who fought my imaginary battles. Give me the man who crept into my room to plan out a future with me in the dark. Because one day something will happen that you won't be able to save me from. And when that day comes, I want to cling to every moment with you. I want a reason to be selfish enough to ask time to stop so that my last breath, and my last moment with you, will never end." I reached up to brush my fingers over his lips, and licked my own as an old, familiar warming entered my chest. "I won't ask you to stop saving me, Kieran, if you'll just save us."

Less than a second passed from the time the words left my lips to when his mouth crashed onto mine.

Wrapping his arms around me, he pulled me off the bench and turned us toward our room. His mouth never once left mine as he effortlessly found his way in there and laid me on the bed, tearing at my clothes as he did.

A flutter of anticipation filled my stomach and heat coursed through my veins. Both as foreign as the feeling of his mouth on my own.

I pleaded with my lips alone for him to show me we could have a connection like we used to. That we could have the love I'd been longing for. That we could have the kind of intimacy I so desperately needed. *Missed.*

I nearly started begging right then for those things, but he straightened to strip out of his clothes, then roughly forced me onto my side.

I turned my head, my mouth searching for his again when he slid onto the bed behind me and pulled me close. A moan slipped from my mouth as his hardened length pressed against me.

"Kier—" His name cut off with a hiss when he suddenly gripped my hair and yanked back, forcing me to stare at the headboard instead of him.

The hand on my hip went to my thigh to spread my legs, and before I could beg him to slow down—beg him for any of the things I'd just been thinking of—he roughly pushed into me. Again and again, each roll of his hips more forceful than the last until he released my hip and gripped my shoulder to force me down onto him harder still.

I clung to my pillow, gritting my teeth against the pain in my shoulder and on my scalp, and tried to focus on the feel of him moving inside me.

Just once, I wanted him to *crave* my touch during this.

Just once, I wanted him to *need* to kiss me like a man dying as he moved inside me.

Just once, I wanted him to *want* to look at me as he fucked me.

Kieran growled in approval when my sharp cry broke free, and his fingers dug into my shoulder so deeply that tears pricked my eyes as his hips jerked powerfully once . . . twice . . . and then he finally came with a low roar.

He released me just as suddenly as his body left mine, but the lingering pain in my shoulder and my heart caused me to forget I'd been aching for more from him.

Gentleness. Tenderness.

I blinked quickly, forcing the wetness in my eyes away, and took slow, steadying breaths.

Breathe in.

God, Kieran, what have you done to us?

Breathe out.

I could feel the wall between us grow wider, could feel it start to solidify. And I didn't know how to stop it.

His arm slipped over the dip in my waist, but before my mind could hope that his touch was meant to be comforting or loving, his hand hit the mattress in front of me and quickly snaked across it until he was hovering over me and reaching over the side of the bed.

Just as I opened my mouth to ask what he was doing, the muscles in his forearm tensed and twitched, and my heart rate slowed as I took in the rapidly changing tone in the room.

Dark.

Lethal.

So silent that the lack of sound felt heavy in my ears.

I knew what I would find when I glanced up, had seen the image so many times before, but the sight of his eyes somehow still shocked me.

He was staring off toward the edge of the bed, seeing nothing as he listened to something I couldn't hear. His eyes lacked any of the warmth I'd seen before, and even with the distant look in them now, were filled with a hollowness that terrified me.

Nightshade.

Even though I was prepared for it, a scream tore from my chest when Kieran's arm snapped back and he let the blade in his hand fly. The sound of one of his knives embedding into the wall was closely followed by a familiar voice.

"Jesus fuck! You almost got me, you asshole. Jesus." Beck was bent at the waist as he dragged in ragged breaths, not even noticing Kieran had already gotten off the bed and had another knife ready to throw before he'd realized who was walking in.

I scrambled for the comforter to cover myself before Beck straightened, my eyes widening when I saw the handle of the knife less than an inch from his ear.

"You—" Beck paused when he took in Kieran's naked body, his face pinched. "That's not any way to greet someone, dude. You don't need to brag." His eyes darted to me, then back to Kieran, his eyebrows lifting when he finally understood what he'd walked in on. "That would explain the near-death experience."

"You coming in unannounced would explain it," Kieran growled. "Leave."

Not seeming to care about the demand or that Kieran was still naked, Beck pointed to the opposite side of the guesthouse. "I live here, in case you forgot. Your orders, if I remember correctly."

"You still announce yourself so you don't die, Beck. *Leave*."

Beck threw his arms out to his sides and then let them fall. "I didn't know you were here. Conor said he hadn't seen you since the meeting, and I didn't think I needed to announce myself to Lily. Mickey's looking for you."

Kieran tensed, then slowly forced himself to relax by flipping the blade with a flick of his wrist over and over again. "What does he want?"

Beck shot out a hard laugh. "What . . . I could've asked him that?"

Glancing over his shoulder, Kieran's hardened eyes took me in as he spoke to Beck. "Get out so Lily can get dressed. Don't leave the house."

The door had barely clicked shut before Kieran was stalking to the bathroom to clean up. He didn't acknowledge me in any way when he came back in the room, grabbing his discarded clothes. He didn't look at me at all until he was dressed and I was sitting on the edge of the bed.

Stepping up to my side, he gently grasped my chin in his fingers and lifted my head so I would look at him.

His eyes were now etched with worry, but I could see the warrior in him slowly taking over. I knew it wouldn't be long until the moment where I'd thought I was breaking through to him would just be a memory.

His fingers slipped from my chin as he turned and left the room, ripping the knife out of the doorframe as he did.

No words.

No assurances.

No empty promises.

No murmurs of love.

Less than a minute later, I was stumbling from the bed to the bathroom when Beck walked back in with wide eyes and an apology already on his lips.

"I didn't know what I was walking in on. I'm so—" His brow pinched when he saw the wetness gathering in my eyes. "Lil . . . ?"

Unable to hold them back any longer, a sob tore from somewhere deep within me and the tears fell free.

"Lily, what happened?" Beck rushed toward me, his hands moving to my shoulders to keep me in place when I tried to wave him off. His eyes were wild and panicked as he took in my tear-streaked face. "Did—did he—fuck, did he hurt you?" he finally asked between gritted teeth.

I shook my head as another sob broke free, and pressed my hand to my chest in an attempt to ease the aching there.

"Jesus fuck, Lil. Give me something before I go get myself killed. Because I know I'll at least get one good hit in before he comes after me with a—"

"No. Beck, *no!*" I choked out as I tried to force the tears back. "I'm fine, it's just—it's this day, you know? This stupid day." My chin trembled, but I forced myself to continue on. "I'm emotional, and it's all just getting to me. I need a shower, and I need to sleep, or something." I forced out a strained laugh. "I'm being such a girl."

Beck looked lost. He looked like he didn't know if he should still risk his life by going up against Kieran or believe me.

After a few moments of staring at me with a dumbfounded expression, he hesitantly asked, "Is this one of those times when I need to send someone out for chocolate?"

A real laugh tumbled from my lips, soggy from my tears. And despite being so wrong, I nodded. "Yes, this is one of those times."

"Okay. Okay, I'll send Conor." He released me and took a step back, but paused as he searched my face. He was trying to force himself to believe me, and I knew he was worried about getting this wrong. "Okay, yeah. Chocolate."

"You're the best."

I waited until the door was shut behind him before heading into the bathroom and stripping out of the shirt I'd pulled back on. Once the shower water was on and steaming up the bathroom, I stepped in and let the hot water mix with the tears that were slowly falling again.

I rubbed at my chest as I felt the growing distance between Kieran and me become a living thing inside me, and grieved what had become of us.

Every one of our firsts had been together. And knowing him the way I did, they had gone as expected.

He was ruthless in everything, with moments of tenderness reserved for me. Making him lethal with his knives and on my heart.

The touches, the kisses . . . they all came from the same place. They all came from the dreamer who knew how to be soft and melt me with words. They'd come from *Kieran*.

Sex with him had always been rough and intense and full of power. It had been exhilarating, unrestrained passion. I'd craved it. Craved *him*. Every dark fantasy came to life, prompted by the monster inside. Pure Nightshade.

But there was never anything more. There were only those nights I could remember in flashes of slick skin, the sweetest kind of pain, and body-numbing tremors as he'd push me to the edge. There was never intimacy, there was never the tender love I knew he felt for me. And as the years went on, the *more* had been necessary. I'd wanted and needed Kieran in my bed too, not just Nightshade.

But that force between us that threatened to push until we couldn't find our way back to each other? It had been born from broken promises, and fueled by every rough and disheartening sexual encounter over the last years.

Because when Aric died, I'd needed Kieran. *Only* Kieran. And each time I was met with Nightshade, it broke something inside me, hardening me to the man I loved.

Maybe it was my fault for believing he could be someone I knew he couldn't. For believing one of those times, he would see what he was doing to me . . . how he was breaking me. *Us.*

Maybe it was my fault for forgetting the complexity of the man I loved. For forgetting why I'd fallen in love with him in the first place.

Maybe it was . . .

But those glimpses of his heart would always make me foolishly hope for things he couldn't give me.

Would always make me foolishly hope he could save us. That he *wanted* to save us. But that hope was dwindling every day.

Chapter 5

DECLARING WAR

Dare

Everyone at the table was talking loudly, trying to be heard over the others as they all reacted to the news that Johnny and I had been given just hours before.

Lily O'Sullivan was alive.

Motherfucking *alive*.

I gripped my head in my hands as I stared at the table, trying to block out their voices.

Because she couldn't be. I knew in my gut that she wasn't.

But if she was—I would stop at nothing to steal Lily's last breath the way *he* had stolen *hers*.

"Dare!"

I glanced up when my older sister shouted my name, my eyes already narrowed on her.

"I've been calling your name for, like, a minute," Libby said, her eyes full of concern. "What are we going to do?"

"Nothing."

Everyone except Johnny erupted in shouts of displeasure.

He didn't have to say a word for me to know he didn't agree with my decision. If someone had asked him—I had no doubt he'd leave right now and go massacre everyone on the Holloway property.

I waited until the table quieted before saying, "Nothing until we know for sure. I can't be sure that piece of shit wasn't lying to me today. He said her name and I forgot where I was and what we were doing. All I knew was what he'd said and what I wanted to do to a goddamn *name*."

"But you said he'd been looking right at you. You said he had no tells," Maverick, one of the twins, said.

I shrugged.

"It doesn't matter. I wanted him to be telling the truth because I want a chance to take from them what they took from me. But when I look back on it, I can't be sure that he wasn't forcing that stare. We need to make sure."

I looked every member of my team in the eye to make sure they understood it wasn't just a suggestion—it was an order.

The twins, my sister, Einstein, Johnny.

Once I received nods from all of them, I looked at Johnny.

"Aric and Lily's funeral," I began, bringing up that day we'd sat in the shadows, watching to see if it was true. If Johnny's cousin Joseph had really killed them both before Kieran had gotten him. "Kieran lost it. He wouldn't have if she hadn't—"

"He could've faked it," Johnny said, cutting me off. "Or it could've been because of Aric. Everyone knew they were like brothers."

I lifted a brow. "You gonna lose your shit the way he did if someone kills me, Johnny?"

The bastard smirked. "I might consider shedding a tear."

"But you can't know that until it happens," Einstein said, giving Johnny a meaningful look.

Einstein was a genius. If she didn't know something, she had ways of finding it out that Google couldn't dream of. She was my hacker.

She was also the only person who had ever touched Johnny's cold, dead heart.

And from the way Johnny's face was suddenly an unreadable mask again, I knew he wasn't considering what she'd just said—he was considering what would happen if he had to watch Einstein be lowered into the ground.

I knocked my knuckles on the table to get his attention. "That's what I mean. No ruthless killer like Kieran Hayes is going to do what he did that day over his best friend. You're made of stone, Johnny? That guy is made of fucking steel. And you watched him break that day. Lily was in that casket. You know it. I know it."

Of anyone at the table, *I* knew it.

That rage from earlier threatened to consume me again, but I forced it down.

It had been nearly four years—and about half that since I'd wanted to make every member of the Holloway Gang pay for what they'd done. But in that moment, it was as if no time had passed.

I couldn't trust myself to walk away from the table and not go unleash hell on all of them.

But if I did that?

Well . . . retaliation was a very real thing in our world, and I wasn't willing to lose another person from this table. I wasn't willing to lose another member of my family—blood or not.

"I'm with Johnny."

I glanced up, my eyebrows raised at the other twin's words. "Come again?"

"I think Nightshade could've been faking it."

My head was already shaking. "No. N—"

"No, wait a second," Diggs began. "You're gonna hear me out, man."

The room fell silent as they waited for my response to his demand.

Demands weren't allowed from people in the twins' positions, especially at the table. But this was my team, and I'd been trying to lead the entire family in a different direction for years . . . starting with this generation.

So instead of throwing around a title I didn't want—instead of staining the wood floor and adding to the blood from years past—I sat back and pushed out a heavy sigh.

"Listening."

"Nightshade killed Joseph. Right?" Diggs's gaze darted between Johnny and me as he waited for a response.

Johnny's head dipped in acknowledgment, but I answered, "He came in as we jumped out the window."

"And you heard one more shot after you jumped out," he recalled from our stories. "That shot could've been aimed at Nightshade. It didn't have to be for Lily. And you know it didn't take more than a few seconds for him to figure out who Joseph was once he was dead—just like you know they'd expected you to be watching and waiting for them to hand over his body. It isn't hard to think they'd expect you to follow them to the funeral the way you two did, to see who actually died. It could've been one big setup to pin us with their deaths so we wouldn't try to retaliate for Joseph."

I slanted my eyes at him. "That's reaching. And whether or not Lily O'Sullivan died that night, I didn't need to check Aric's pulse to know that he *did*. There's no way he survived that."

Johnny nodded.

"Joseph got what was coming to him for it."

"What the fuck, man, come on," Diggs grumbled. "Four years ago he was at this damn table."

"Dare's right," Johnny muttered.

"A lot of people would still be alive if he hadn't come with us that night. Have you forgotten he wasn't even supposed to be there? And he not only fucked everything up, he killed one—maybe two—O'Sullivans, and *they* retaliated for it. They took everything from me because he couldn't keep his hands to himself, or follow the goddamn rules." My voice dropped to a dangerous level when I repeated, "He got what was coming to him."

You could've heard a pin drop once I finished talking, and I couldn't take it. I couldn't take the silence or the sympathetic looks at the reminder of what else happened nearly four years ago.

As much as I was afraid of what I would do if left alone—I knew I would chance it rather than staying in that room.

I stood but didn't turn to leave. "If she's ali—" The word choked me, picturing her alive and well. Living in the world when mine was gone. "If it's true," I began again, working my jaw, "then we aren't taking it at the word of a pathetic excuse of a man who knew he was about to die and would've said anything not to." I looked to Einstein. "Search for proof. Can't find it? Then find someone who can give it to me. Until then, we go on like nothing's changed."

When I turned to go, Johnny mumbled under his breath, "What's the point? I say we go in there now and kill as many Holloways as we can. It's not like they don't all need to go to ground."

I leveled him with a glare when I faced him again, but forced a low laugh.

Because this was Johnny—and I knew him just as well as he knew me.

Johnny was old school.

Illegal games and ways to make ends meet, and taking out the enemy with a bullet to their head.

And if I took him seriously, or even seemed to, there'd be no containing him.

Johnny unleashed would be complete devastation, but he was the closest thing I'd ever had to a brother. I would do whatever it took to keep him alive—even if that meant saving him from his own rage and darkness.

"Why?" I asked him with a teasing hint to my tone. "So the rest of them will come to our homes and do the same? Don't forget this isn't a kill *or* be killed world we live in, Johnny. It's a kill *and* be killed world. And I'm fucking tired of burying my family."

He waited until I was at the door to speak again. When he did, anticipation laced his words—because he knew he had me. "You gonna worry about a little retaliation if Lily O'Sullivan is alive?"

I paused with my hand on the doorknob, sure that the metal would give beneath my grasp as I embraced every dark thought when it came to that girl.

Every dark want.

Every dark need.

"If she's alive, I'm going there in the dead of night, and I'm ripping Kieran's world out from under his feet the way mine was from me. And then I'm declaring war on every person connected to Holloway until there's nothing left of them."

Chapter 6

BURDEN

Lily

I pulled my arms through a kimono as I walked from the bedroom to the kitchen half an hour later. My hair was still wet from the shower, but after how long and exhausting the day had been, I needed coffee just to get through drying it.

My pace slowed when I rounded the corner out of the hallway into the main area of the house and found Beck and Kieran talking in low tones.

There was no point in turning around and pretending I hadn't noticed them. Kieran would've already known I was on my way out there long before I'd ever seen or heard them.

Wrapping the material of the short kimono around my waist so it would cover my bare thighs, I stepped closer to the guys but didn't interrupt them, and they didn't say a word to me even when they glanced at me.

Their hushed conversation didn't stop until Kieran finished giving Beck his orders. Everything was said quickly, words and sentences clipped, names in code.

Codes I knew, of course. Words I could've caught if I'd actually tried to pay attention.

But there at Kieran's feet, taking all of my focus, was his dad's old military backpack. The bag that had been stashed in our closet for years, waiting for the day we ran from this life.

After what had just happened between us, I wasn't sure how much more pain my heart could take before I finally started tearing at my chest.

I'd known that something irreparable had happened before Kieran had left to meet with Mickey. But that didn't mean I was ready to finally accept that the future we'd planned would never happen.

"You're leaving," I said as soon as they finished talking, and forced my gaze away from the faded green pack to his piercing eyes. Kieran reached for me but I took a step away. "You're *leaving*?"

Kieran loosely encircled my wrist with his long fingers, and waited to make sure I wouldn't pull away from him. "I'll be back after I sort things out in Texas."

The pain in my chest eased as his words sank in. "Texas?" I shook my head as I wracked my brain for any mention of the state before then. "What's going on in Texas?"

For the first time ever, Kieran hesitated in telling me something about the business. His brow pulled low and his mouth tightened in a hard line as he stared at me, indecision clear as day in those eyes.

And it hurt.

All I could think of in that moment were the times Kieran and I had told each other our darkest secrets—things we'd never shared with anyone—and now he was keeping something from me. He'd *been* keeping something from me.

I wondered what else I didn't know, but couldn't ask because I was keeping a world of things from him . . .

The nightmares and an old friend.

Disguises, cherished notes, and an intoxicating bond I tried not to make sense of.

Is it weird that I dread these mornings as much as I'm eager for them? My weeks drag waiting to see you, but then it's always over too soon.

Guilt sat low in my stomach like acid.

"Our contact didn't pick up a shipment, and no one has been able to get in touch with him for a week. I'm gonna check on him."

There wasn't a need to ask why Kieran was the one going to Texas even though it wasn't his job to check on contacts. If he was going, he was going to make sure the contact wouldn't have a way of talking. "I didn't know we had a contact in Texas."

"Well, we might not anymore." Beck's wry grin abruptly fell when Kieran set his cold glare on him.

"Why didn't I know about this?"

Again, that hesitation from Kieran before he finally said, "There isn't a need for you to know."

"Since when isn't there—" I began, but stopped when he picked up his bag and turned toward the front door. "Kier—"

"I'll be back when I'm done."

"*Kieran.*"

He paused and ran a hand through his shoulder-length, dirty-blond hair. A heavy sigh left him when he turned to look at me again. "I'll be back when I'm done, Lily." His tone was softer, his eyes now pleading with me to drop the issue.

As much as I wanted to stand my ground and demand to know why there was a contact in another state that Kieran would hesitate to tell me about, I knew if I mentioned it again, he would do what he'd been about to.

Walk away without looking back.

I swallowed thickly and started to step away from him, but at the last second rocked forward and hurried toward him. "Take me with you."

A look of horror flashed across his face so fast I almost missed it before his cold, emotionless mask could replace it. "No."

"Please," I said soft enough that Beck wouldn't hear me, and hated how weak it made me sound. I glanced quickly at Beck, then looked back to Kieran as I continued toward him. "It doesn't have to be forever. All I'm asking is for you to take me to Texas with you."

"No—"

"I can keep myself safe. You can lock me in a hotel room if it'll ma—"

"I said no, Lily," he snapped, his booming voice echoing off the walls in the house.

I jolted back, stumbling over myself to get away from him when he suddenly stalked toward me.

One of his arms shot out to block Beck from coming between us, but his stare never left me as his large hands grasped my shoulders and pulled me close.

Everything about him was magnificent and terrifying. The strength in his body and his grasp. The chilling combination of love and promised death that poured from him as he looked down at me, that beast inside him crying to be freed. And yet, all I wanted was to stay in this moment for an eternity. It didn't matter what led to us being in this position, I'd never been in his arms this way . . .

I'd been waiting for this—*begging* for this—for as long as I could remember.

Kieran's entire body was vibrating and his eyes were on fire, but his voice was hushed and pained when he asked, "Why do you keep fighting me when all I want is to keep you safe? Can't you see what you mean to me?" His eyes bored into mine, desperate and begging for me to understand. "I won't let a Borello within seeing distance of you. Now try to imagine the kind of men our contact in Texas and his associates are if I'd never let you in the same state as them. These men steal women. They *buy* multiple stolen women and keep them. If you were there, even hidden away, I would be too dis—"

"What?" I asked under my breath, jerking in his hold. "They *what*?"

There was no response, but I didn't need one. Kieran's expression told me more than I wanted to know.

An image of a woman, kicking and screaming as she was hauled into a van flashed through my mind. And then the image morphed to the woman standing in front of a room full of perverted men, leering at her as she shook and cried for someone to save her.

I felt sick.

"And you knew? They do this and you knew when you started working with them?" The bliss of being in his arms had vanished, and suddenly I wanted nothing more than to get away from him. I tried to pull from Kieran's grasp but he pulled me closer.

"You don't understand."

"Don't tell me I don't understand, Kieran. There's nothing *to* understand," I said with an incredulous laugh.

"Lily . . ."

"How could you let that continue?"

"I tried to sever the ties with Texas. I've tried dozens of times," he said in a rough tone.

"Oh, have you?" Disbelief dripped from my words.

His jaw ticked, but he didn't respond as that beast inside him fought to be unleashed.

"You just met with my dad . . . so, on his orders you're now going to Texas to silence this guy if he isn't already dead. Right?" I asked, but didn't wait for his response. "And all because he didn't accept a shipment and has been missing for a week."

Kieran blew out a harsh breath through his nose, his mouth forming a tight line.

"Whoever this *contact* and his *associates* are, you know who they are, and you know what they do. You've known." Leaning closer, I whispered, "You're an assassin, Kieran. If you'd ever really tried, he would've been silenced years ago. They all would've."

His mouth twitched into a frustrated grin that bordered on a grimace as he released me, one of his hands moving to rub at his jaw. He started to take a step away, but stopped. "I had an important job here." His questioning stare quickly ran over my body before meeting mine. "At least I thought I did."

That same crushing pain from earlier came on so strong and fast, it nearly knocked me back.

I couldn't take in a deep enough breath, and I couldn't speak as he turned and left.

That force between us set into a thick, reinforced wall as I watched him go. As I understood exactly what he'd given us up for.

The mob would've been bad enough. But Texas? Knowing about it and allowing it to continue when he could've put an end to it?

It was unforgivable.

There was no saving us. Not anymore. Not from the resentment that now burned deep within me.

I flicked my gaze to Beck when I turned to go back to my room, but he was staring at a spot on the floor and didn't bother with any excuses as I went.

Nearly an hour later, Beck came into the room with a tentative knock, his face wary as he looked at where I sat on the window seat, staring out at the property, seeing nothing.

Holding up a bag, he attempted a grin. "Conor brought these a while ago, but I wasn't sure if you were ready to see me."

"You knew."

"About Texas?" he asked, then dipped his head in confirmation. "Yeah, Lil. I knew."

"Does everyone?"

"No. Your dad's advisor is the only other person who knows."

I nodded for a few seconds then shook my head. "If it's been going on so long, why is Mickey keeping it a secret? Why have the two of you been keeping it from me?"

Beck seemed to search for the right words for a while before he huffed and walked deeper into the room to sit on the bed. "I think you already know why, Lil. Mickey can shut a lot of people up about his business, and the guys in Texas can too. But the more people who know, the more risks they all take, so it's not good to go around letting words fly about other people's business. And for Mickey . . . this is big money. This is cocaine for the entire southern part of Texas. He doesn't want to fuck it up."

That sounded mostly right. Mickey liked to have control of people and places, and liked to make sure money was constantly flowing in.

But Mickey wasn't humble about anything in his life. He didn't know how to remain tightlipped about money and power. Especially about jobs as big as this.

I waited for more, but when there was none I asked, "And you?"

He let out a slow breath, his eyes finally meeting mine. "Because it's a burden knowing what we do."

"It doesn't have to be. It could've been ended years ago." A hard laugh forced from my chest. "*Kieran* could've ended it years ago."

Instead of arguing, Beck just sat there for a while staring blankly ahead. Finally, he lifted his shoulders in a brief shrug. "Maybe there's a lot more going on than you realize. Maybe there're things involved that Kieran's trying to protect you from, and he can't protect you if he kills dozens of men in Texas."

"Then he should tell me what's happening. He should've told me all of it when he found out." I gestured out the window like he'd be standing there then pressed my hand to my chest. "He used to tell me everything, Beck."

"You used to tell him everything too," he countered gently, the slight challenge in his tone emphasized with a lift of a brow. "But you don't tell him about whatever has you waking up some nights, screaming. You don't tell him about the shit the men say to you when they see you."

Beck's grin when Kieran entered the meeting that afternoon flashed through my mind. My eyes widened as suspicion hit me swift and deep.

"You told Kieran about Bailey, didn't you?"

His mouth twisted into a wry smirk before falling. "Someone had to."

"You didn't . . ." My stomach twisted at the thought of what Kieran might have done after the meeting. "Beck, I told you to stay out of it."

"Lil, something had to be done. You're not standing up for yourself, and you won't let us. Kieran had to get the guys in line."

"Not by hurting or killing them."

Beck rolled his eyes. "He didn't, I was there the whole time. Kieran knows things that Bailey doesn't want getting out. That was enough to make Bailey nearly piss himself and swear to never look in your direction again."

As much as I couldn't stand Bailey or his son, I was glad that for once, Kieran had kept the beast in check. The men already knew what he could do—knew how lethal he was. He didn't need to make enemies within Holloway by killing off members because they'd said something to me.

"But like I was saying, you're keeping things from him. I don't know why, but I know you have your reasons, Lil. Maybe try to understand that he has his reasons for doing things."

I steeled myself, gritting my teeth against the resentment I felt. "Women are being kidnapped and sold, Beck. There's no excuse for what's going on in Texas, or that Kieran hasn't put an end to it."

Beck suddenly went still, his expression solemn. "Sometimes we have to do what we don't want to," he said softly. "And sometimes we hurt people because of it. I've been selling on the streets for your dad for as long as I can remember. With every year that passed, I hoped he'd put me somewhere else—doing anything else—because I hated selling. I destroyed the only girl I think I ever really loved because of it, and I continue to on a daily basis. I watched her transform into a shattered shell of herself, selling herself just so she could pay *me* because her mom keeps herself pumped full of our supply. And she fucking hates me for it."

"Beck . . ."

I'd heard about her, the girl he used to love. He'd talked about her often before he'd stopped talking about her at all. I'd thought she'd died. To Beck, she had. He'd wanted to take care of her forever, and to spite him for continuing to control and ruin her mom's life, she'd started selling herself.

It had nearly destroyed Beck.

"I didn't put an end to it, Lil. I could've, but I didn't because I knew if her mom didn't come to me, she'd go to another dealer. One who would take advantage of both of them like her previous ones had . . . and I wouldn't have been able to live with myself."

He shifted uncomfortably on the bed, his eyebrows drawn tight as he thought about what could've been.

He looked so exposed. So completely unlike the broad-chested, thick-necked drug dealer who'd been my best friend for so long.

"And now? I'm who Kieran trusts most, which means Mickey trusts me. So now I know all this shit I wish I'd never heard about. Wish I'd never seen. But there's not a damn thing I can do about it. All I'd wanted was to stop dealing on the streets, but now I'd give anything to *only* be dealing on the streets. For my only job to be out there every single night so I can check on the girl I destroyed by saving her. You understand?"

I could, but only because I'd been raised in this life.

But I wasn't sure Beck could understand me. Wasn't sure he could understand the girl he'd destroyed or the women being sold in Texas.

"Kieran might know about things you don't, and, yeah, he might not be putting an end to it. But there might be bigger things at work. If you fight him—if you fight what the two of you have and the way he's trying to protect you—it's going to destroy you."

He stood to leave and had just gotten to the door when I called out his name.

"Knowing what you know now—seeing what she's become," I added, hinting at the girl he'd loved, "would you still do it all over again? Or would you try to find a different way to put an end to it?"

"There was only one way to end—"

"There's always another way."

He swallowed thickly and gave me a sad smile, his eyes dulling with torment. "I told you, Lil . . . it's a burden. This whole life is."

Chapter 7

ELLE

Lily

It never stopped being disorienting—glancing in a mirror, expecting to see the same person you saw every single day . . . and seeing someone different. My reflection was as strange to me as my relationship with Kieran had become, even though I'd been catching glimpses of this stranger in mirrors for nearly two years now.

My ice-blue eyes were what people noticed first, and were a dead giveaway to anyone who knew Mickey or had known me. To pass as anyone other than Lily O'Sullivan, I hid them by drawing attention to them.

Hidden behind non-prescription thick-framed glasses and hazel-colored contacts, my normally bare eyes were now accentuated with shadow and liner, my lashes dark and full. My blonde hair that usually sat high up on my head in a messy knot was falling to my waist in waves.

In just over half an hour, I was a different person. One who would be gone with some makeup remover.

I'd only glanced in the mirror long enough this morning to acknowledge the stranger looking back at me before I'd ducked my head, grabbed my old purse filled with some cash, as well as everything required to create and erase the stranger in the mirror, and hurried out the bathroom window since it faced away from the main house and Soldier's Row.

I hadn't lingered.

I never did.

And I'd left Holloway property . . . as I did every Monday morning.

Now as I sat in a café booth downtown, a twenty-minute walk from Holloway, I found it hard to look away from the stranger staring back at me in the wall of mirrors off to the side.

The makeup alone was a big enough change since I never wore any . . . but the eyes and the glasses. The length of my hair. All of it combined was fascinating and horrifying to look at.

Whether ordering it under Beck's name and card or having Conor buy it one item at a time . . . I'd spent the better part of six months stashing money and gathering everything I would need to slightly change my appearance for when Kieran and I ran from Holloway and North Carolina.

But when that dream had become nothing more than shattered promises, everything had remained untouched until two years ago when someone came looking for me . . .

And then I'd been thanking God for the plans that had led to what was hidden away in the crawl space in our closet, because it'd created this familiar stranger who found herself in this same diner every Monday morning.

Kieran may have decided he wanted us to stay here. That didn't mean *I* didn't plan to leave.

In order to continue on with my life and to prepare for a future with or without him, I had to leave the property.

So I did . . . I *do.*

There's something thrilling in sneaking away unnoticed from a property filled with mob members, many who are sworn to keep me hidden from the outside world.

Something exhilarating in breathing air that doesn't feel tainted with every bad memory from my life.

Something addictive in possibly putting myself in proximity with my biggest nightmares, and hoping I'll be as invisible to them as they've always been to me.

The first time hadn't felt nearly as gratifying as I'd thought it would. In fact, it'd been terrifying. I'd been so sure the moment I set foot on the road outside the main house that a Borello would be waiting for me. Or at any moment, Beck would wake up and realize I wasn't there.

That fear hadn't vanished over the last two years, but it had lessened . . . morphed into excitement thrumming in my veins each time I slipped out of the house and crawled back in without alerting anyone.

Sneaking out at night would've been easier since Conor guarded the outside of the house and rarely came in, but Kieran was too unpredictable. He knew the dark made it easier for people to move around undetected, which was why he tried so hard to get home at night. He needed to assure himself I was still alive and safely hidden away.

Save Lily. Protect Lily. Hide Lily. Cage Lily.

That never-ending, maddening cycle.

Even though Beck was inside the house with me during the day— unless he was sent somewhere—he typically slept until noon. That came with the territory of selling on the streets until early hours of the morning. Therefore, mornings were my chance to leave.

Most importantly . . . the person I left Holloway to see only had a small window of time each week to meet up with a girl who was supposed to be dead. And Brooks Street Café in Wake Forest was where we met without fail.

I looked around expectantly for her, then realized a few moments later that my gaze had left the front door and was slowly working across the diner, lingering on the places I usually saw him . . .

My heart betrayed me by increasing in speed at just the thought of him.

His knowing eyes and unrestrained smile.

The way he seemed to demand attention so casually . . . just as he had demanded mine for two years, even spilling over into dreams.

The current of energy that hugged my skin whenever he was near, a feeling so intoxicating and foreign . . . and, yet, there was a hint of familiarity. So much so I had to restrain myself from closing the distance between us to see if it grew. And I couldn't help but wonder if I knew him, because that buzz had remained constant over the years rather than fading.

He looked at me as if he could see straight through to my heart, and see every hope and fear that lies there. He seemed to understand me even though we'd never spoken a word to each other. And this connection . . . it felt as if my soul was screaming—*begging*—for me to recognize its mate was within reach, and I was keeping myself from him.

But soulmates . . . they couldn't be real.

And though his written words were exhilarating and I was dreading when they would end, I spent so much of my time consumed with guilt for being intrigued by someone who wasn't Kieran.

"My future ex-wife has returned."

I jolted, pulled away from my musing by the booming voice.

"God, Ethan." I huffed, a breath of a laugh tumbling from my lips as I finally regained some of my composure. "You scared me."

Ethan gave me a wounded look and sighed exaggeratedly. "How could I scare you? I am your love. You are mine."

Ethan was the kind of guy who kept up an endless stream of teasing words, just waiting for someone to smile back at him—to laugh at his jokes.

Like a golden retriever waiting to be petted. In a way, it was almost endearing.

"My lovely lover," he continued when I didn't offer anything, "I haven't seen you in years. Where have you been? I thought you'd decided to leave me."

"It's been a week."

He gave me a dopey smile. "A week can feel like a lifetime, future ex-wife. So, what can I get you on this now perfect morning?"

"Um, I . . ." I shook my head, trying to clear my mind. "I'll just have a coffee for now."

He stared at me with wide, unblinking eyes for long seconds before murmuring, "If I knew you were boring, I wouldn't plan our entire future every time I see you."

"Ethan . . . I start off with the same thing every time."

"And it kills me every time." He clutched his chest as though my order was literally killing him. "I'm waiting for the day when I walk up and ask what I can get you, and you say, 'You, Ethan. I've been waiting for you.' My heart can't take that you aren't here for me."

I rolled my eyes at his dramatics but forced a smile. "Sorry to disappoint you."

"I'm divorcing you before we can get fake married."

"Is the divorce taking place before or after coffee?" I asked warily.

"Depends," he mused, then leaned down so he was closer to my level. "Let me take you out to dinner sometime, and maybe I'll reconsider divorcing you."

I started to smile for his sake but froze halfway. I was dumbfounded when I realized that—*for once*—Ethan wasn't joking.

It'd been Kieran and me for as long as I could remember—since long before either of us knew how to flirt.

None of the other guys of Holloway had ever flirted.

None of them had ever crossed a line with me sexually.

If any of them had ever been remotely attracted to me, I hadn't had a clue because they all valued their lives.

The most attention I'd ever received from another guy had been Ethan's jokes and a stranger's notes . . . so I didn't know how to handle someone asking me on a date, when I'd never expected another man to have the nerve to.

"I'm sorry . . . but I—"

"What do you say?" he asked, cutting me off. "I know a place that—"

I shook my head and hurried to stop him. "I'm sorry, I can't. Thank you for the offer, but I have a boyfriend."

"Oh." Ethan stared at me, then dropped his gaze to the table. He shrugged and forced a smile that wasn't nearly as charming as usual. "Well, hey, coffee's on the house today . . ."

"That isn't necess—"

"I insist." He held up a hand as he began backing away and gave me a look that made me once again think of him as a golden retriever. "Boyfriend or not, I have to take care of my future ex-wife."

Unsure of how to respond to him, I mumbled, "Thanks, Ethan."

I sucked in a quick breath when electricity trickled over my skin like a dance. Everything I'd been hoping and waiting for earlier but knew I needed to avoid. As if compelled, I turned toward the source of that addictive, unexplainable feeling, but stopped when I saw a girl walking toward my booth.

Teagan.

The corner of her lip curled in a smirk when she saw me, but she didn't speak until she got closer.

"Sorry I'm late."

"You're not, I just finished ordering coffee. How are you?" I asked as my eyes darted over her face and arms, my words getting lost in the noise of the café.

She lifted a shoulder in a nonchalant shrug. "Hungry."

I sent her a look that she ignored, but really, I didn't know what other response I expected from her.

Teagan was as tough and stubborn as Kieran, but as caring as Beck. She was the one who found me hidden on the back of the property two years ago, and the only reason I continued to risk leaving it. She was also the source of half of my information on Mickey, Bailey, and Finn, and vice versa . . . and the day I left Holloway, she was coming with me.

She'd been one of the very few friends I'd had growing up, her dad being a member of Holloway, but we'd wanted different lives.

Teagan had wanted all the mob had to offer, and was terrified of being pushed out when she got older . . . so she'd made sure that wasn't a possibility by marrying Finn a year after they'd faked my death. A marriage that became her biggest regret when she discovered how cruel the family she married into could be, and how abusive her husband was.

Something she'd finally confessed to me a couple months ago when a bruise had been too hard to explain away, and only because she knew I couldn't share the information with anyone else since I wasn't supposed to have seen her in four years.

Like all the women and children within Holloway, Teagan had been told I'd been killed the night of Aric's death. While the men swore to protect me and I mourned Aric's death and my relationship with Kieran, she'd grieved my death.

But Finn had a drinking problem and loose lips, and one day during a meeting I'd managed to evade, she'd shown up at the guesthouse with tears streaming down her cheeks, screaming accusations and grabbing me in a hug that lasted forever and ended too soon.

It was in that short time with her I realized nothing about Teagan had changed, yet everything was different.

She was still stubborn and tough and loving . . . but I could see something was breaking her from the inside. I could see something was making her hate the mob as much as I always had.

I snuck out for the first time the next morning to meet her, and I hadn't missed a week since.

We traded secrets learned from Holloway men. We plotted. We reminisced. And we spent countless mornings pouring over a memory in the form of a nightmare, trying to figure out what I was missing from that night.

Teagan's attention caught on the journal resting on the table before sliding back to me, her mouth forming a perfect O.

Ever since the first nightmare, I'd written down what I remembered, adding to it as more of it came to me.

"Was there more?"

I gently placed my hand on the journal before she could snatch it away, my voice uncertain. "Do you think maybe my mind is just adding more? That I'm not actually remembering more of that night?"

"No." Her response was immediate and sure. "I wondered that a long time ago, but *if* it ever changes, it's when you get a new piece. I've researched it, it's common for people's minds to block a traumatic event and for them to regain pieces over time."

My mouth twisted with doubt, but I nodded and slid the book toward her, waiting patiently while she opened it to the page where I'd rewritten the dream while I'd waited for her, adding the new parts.

"One of the other rooms?"

"No. He said it was in here somewhere."

Teagan slanted me a glare as she reached across the table for the pen. "Someone must've zoned out while writing again . . ."

I swallowed thickly, looking away when she began furiously crossing out the Borello symbol I must've drawn. "Sorry."

The book slammed shut less than a second before Ethan crooned, "Well, fancy meeting you here again."

I glanced up as he slid the coffee onto the table, his eyes never swaying to Teagan or even acknowledging her presence. Shaking my head, I grabbed the mug and creamer Ethan had just set down. "I think I'm ready—"

"Finally. My love. I've been waiting for you for an eternity."

"—to order."

Teagan snorted and slid her menu Ethan's way, never once having looked at it since we already had it memorized.

Once we'd both ordered, Ethan grabbed the menus and took a step back. "Offer still stands," he said coolly. "Boyfriend never has to know."

"Ethan . . . I'm sorry, but—"

"Sorry, future ex-wife. Didn't catch that. You're gonna remember that the offer stands?" He winked, that charming grin making another appearance on his face as he backed away. "Perfect."

Knowing it was pointless, I just lifted my cup at him in thanks, and looked at Teagan.

"Ethan," we murmured at the same time.

"He asked me on a date today." Teagan began laughing, but stopped abruptly when I added, "A real one."

"So that was what . . ." She nodded to herself, and tried to bite back a smile. "Got it. Better not let Kieran know."

"Ha. Right." I glanced around the café, searching without realizing until Teagan cleared her throat.

"I know what you're doing. You need to stop."

My eyes snapped to Teagan, shamed heat filling my cheeks. "I'm not—"

"Elle," she began, her voice low as she used the name we'd agreed on two years ago. "I'm not stupid. Whenever he's in here, your eyes drift to him. Whenever he's not, you look for him. It's one thing to let Ethan fall in love with you every week because he's pathetic and harmless. But this guy? You're walking a dangerous line—"

"I've never even spoken to him," I hissed.

She lifted a brow, studying me. "Yeah? Then tell me something. Imagine your life wasn't what it is and you were allowed to be out having breakfast with me. If Ethan was standing at our table and the guy you can't stop staring at—"

"I don't stare at him," I interjected softly.

"—was sitting in his booth, and Kieran walked in . . ." Teagan's mouth pulled into a knowing grin when my head jerked back and eyes widened. "That's what I thought. You were afraid of Kieran seeing either guy, and I'm going to take a wild guess it wasn't Ethan."

"You're making this into something it's not," I finally said, even as my hand slid to rest on my bag beside me on the bench. As though to hide the notes I'd pored over too many times to admit to even myself. "He's just a guy who is consistently here. Like Ethan. It's weird when he's not."

"Elle . . ."

"Kieran came for Bailey at yesterday's meeting," I said quickly, trying to change the subject.

From the way Teagan's eyes widened to the point of looking comical, I knew I'd accomplished what I'd set out to. I hurried to tell her all that had happened, thankful to take her mind from the mystery guy in question.

But his absence felt physical, and I hated that—hated that I noticed at all.

"He left him whole?" Teagan whispered once I was finished, barely concealed rage dripping from her words.

"According to Beck, and he doesn't have a reason to lie about this. There has to be a reason Kieran didn't touch him. You know as well as I do Bailey's going to get himself a grave."

"Yesterday should've been the start of it," she replied through gritted teeth as she opened up the journal again.

"Mickey's biding his time. It'll happen."

Bailey and Finn's greed was one of the reasons Teagan wasn't running from Finn or his family. She knew if she left, Finn would just find another wife to hurt. She also knew Bailey and Finn were going to get themselves killed trying to take over Holloway—and she wanted to be there when it happened.

After a few minutes, Teagan closed the journal and slid it toward me. "All this time we've been trying to figure out why they were there . . . only for whatever it was to be gone."

"I know."

"And you still don't know what Aric was saying to you before he fell?"

I straightened after I slid the journal into my bag. "No, but there's something else I noticed this time and have been trying to figure out, and I forgot to mention it in there. Aric didn't seem surprised the men were there."

Teagan's brows pinched, her head shaking subtly. "That doesn't make sense."

"I know, trust me." I worried my bottom lip, lifting a shoulder in a shrug. "But the way they were yelling at him . . . it was like they were accusing *Aric* of something, and he didn't bat an eye at them until he noticed the guy touching me."

"Elle." Her face pinched, like she was worried about me. "That's—that can't be right. Maybe you just saw it wrong that night because you were panicking."

I grabbed for my coffee. "Yeah, maybe."

A slow shiver raked over my skin again, the feeling so sudden and exhilarating that my lips parted with a shaky exhale.

It felt like that first anticipated touch that finally comes in the dark.

Soft and powerful and sensual.

If I hadn't been surrendering to this sensation for two years now, I would've been sure someone had just stepped up beside me to gently caress me. Even still, my gaze darted to the mirrored wall, looking for the source . . .

My eyes locked on a pair of dark ones as he walked through the café, and my heart thundered mercilessly.

Everything faded away when he was near—the café, Teagan, Kieran—and I knew Teagan was right. I was walking a dangerous line.

My breath caught in my throat and I sank back against the cushioned booth when I realized he didn't stop at his normal booth and was coming toward us.

In all the times he'd slipped me notes, it had only ever been before Teagan had shown up or if she was in the bathroom.

But Teagan was here. And I didn't know what to say or where to look when my body was calling out to him, begging to touch the man who'd silently tormented me for years.

I finally forced my stare down in time to watch Teagan's mouth slowly fall open when the guy stopped at our table and wordlessly placed our food in front of us.

I chanced another look at him and found his dark eyes piercing mine, that perfect smile I'd thought of so often playing on his lips as he backed away to the booth not far from ours.

And then my stomach sank when I noticed the girl sitting opposite him.

I'd seen him alone, working away on books.

I'd seen him with a guy around his age.

I'd seen him with a group of men Mickey's age and older.

But I'd never seen him with a girl.

I tried to force my disappointment away, but it lingered and grew, making me more confused than I'd ever felt before.

Because I'd been with Kieran my entire life, and this man was a stranger I'd never spoken to.

I felt like an idiot for spending so much time reading and re-reading his words to me. For spending countless hours . . . *years* . . . thinking of him.

"So, your ogling boy is a waiter here?" Teagan asked softly as she dug into her food.

"No, I don't think so," I responded absentmindedly. "He's sitting in a booth now, and some weeks he's walking around in the back, talking with people. But I've never seen him actually do any work like that. Sometimes it looks like he's doing bookkeeping though. Maybe he owns the café. Or someone in his family . . ."

I eyed Teagan when she didn't respond, and felt myself shrink at the look she was giving me.

"Do you have any idea what you're doing . . . how stupid you're being?" she whispered, her tone a mixture of fear and disappointment.

"Teagan, nothing is going on. Again, I've never said a word to the guy." I leaned across the table and dropped my voice so it wouldn't carry. "Maybe you should focus on keeping yourself safe and what

you're going to do once we leave instead of worrying about my relationship. We're not you and Finn, but Kieran and I have our own issues."

"So what, you're counting down the days until he's six feet under?"

"God, Teagan. No. Of course not."

"Are you still planning on leaving with him?" she asked, the challenge clear in her words.

I hesitated, then clarified, "I'm planning on *leaving*."

"With him?" she asked again, her tone harder.

"It's complicated, and you know that."

"But if Kieran asked you to leave with him today, you would."

I studied the frustrated set of her features for a few moments before I shrugged and leaned away. "I've spent my life loving him and planning a future with him away from here. But the last few years I've been clinging to a fraying rope, hoping he'll change. And no matter how I try to repair it, it's like he's doing everything to make that rope snap. Doesn't mean I'm not holding on until it does."

Teagan nodded after a second then gestured to our plates. "The way you look at him doesn't seem like you're trying to hold on very hard."

I ground my teeth so I wouldn't lash out at her.

Growing up as one of my closest friends meant Teagan had been friendly with Kieran—and I use the word *friendly* loosely because Kieran didn't let many people into his life. And although she now hated the mob, I think some part of her still saw Kieran and me as the future of what she'd always considered her home—of *Holloway*.

For me to be shattering that vision in any way, when all of Holloway thought that was what the future held, would be difficult for her—I knew that. But Teagan didn't understand what had happened to our relationship, how resentment had formed and wedged itself between our love.

She knew he was always gone. She knew he'd broken promises. She didn't know about the work he was doing or what loving a man

like Kieran really entailed because I didn't think it would be fair to tell her of our problems. Not when she was determined to stay with an abusive husband just so she could have a hand in his demise, to be present the day he was lowered into the ground so she could spit on his grave.

So she couldn't understand this . . .

Hell, I didn't.

There was no understanding or explaining this electricity that rushed over my skin whenever *he* was near—whenever I found those dark eyes fixed on me. There was no understanding or explaining the way he could weaken every defense I'd ever built with one look, begging me to expose my soul to him . . . and those looks felt more real and intimate than anything I'd ever had with Kieran.

And I didn't even know his name.

"If that's how you see it," I finally mumbled.

That too familiar shiver raced down my spine. I automatically reached for the back of my neck to feel the lingering effects, and I couldn't stop myself from looking toward him from beneath my lashes.

His brow was pulled tight as if he was trying to figure something out—trying to figure *me* out. But I forced myself to ignore that current dancing along my skin . . . forced myself to ignore him. Because a part of me was still clinging to that rope, and he was here with a girl.

That energy that always surrounded us buzzed. Awareness prodded, begging to search out those dark, knowing eyes.

But I never looked toward him again.

And I ignored the slip of paper peeking out from underneath my plate.

Chapter 8

TRIGGER

Dare

That girl.

Something about those eyes promised every truth wrapped in the sweetest deceit. Flames ignited in my veins every time I was near her, my blood roaring with the need to uncover every one of those hidden truths. She felt familiar in an inexplicable way—something about her tugging at my memory, haunting me.

And, Christ, if I didn't want her to haunt my every thought.

Libby suddenly hit my arm and hissed, "Are you even listening to me?"

"No."

She scoffed. "Dare, I need you to talk to—"

"Libby, look at this girl," I said quickly, keeping my voice low. "A couple booths back and to the side. Who is she?"

My sister finally stopped talking and turned in the booth to look. She took a long sip from her drink as she eyed the girl, not bothering to be subtle.

"Am I supposed to know the answer?" she asked before looking over her shoulder at me.

"She comes in here on Mondays. I thought she looked familiar."

"Well, she doesn't," Libby huffed as she sat back in the booth. "But I'll ask her who she is if you'll talk to Mom."

"Why are you even here if you and Mom are fighting? I can't remember the last time you actually came to Brooks with me to check on things."

She looked around guiltily for a few seconds before taking another long drink. "Einstein and I forgot to get groceries. Needed breakfast. I hate the store. It's free here. Feed me," she said on a rush, each sentence getting softer and faster until it was too hard to hear her.

I spared an annoyed glance at my sister before looking back at the girl.

I twitched with the need to go to her. To lift her head so I could look at those eyes again. To lay bare every secret within them.

For years it'd been like this. Silent. Charged. On the edge of igniting.

We were like the resistance before a trigger breaks. The world around us had fallen into a silence so unnerving and intoxicating, and with each passing week we inched closer to when that silence would explode into chaos.

"You notice when she comes in," Libby suddenly mumbled, catching my attention. "How long have you noticed her? Or cared?"

"Libby . . ."

She looked at me curiously, like she'd just realized she was sitting with a stranger. "It's been . . . it's been years. And after finding out that Lily O'Sullivan might be alive—"

"That's enough, Libby."

"You're more concerned with some girl you don't know than avenging your—"

"I said *that's enough*," I growled, the warning and demand clear.

I let my head fall into my hands as memories assaulted me. My chest moved exaggeratedly as I tried to force my breathing to slow— tried to force every want I'd just had away.

It was like the entire universe was mocking me by placing this girl in my life, week after week. *Taunting* me with a torrent of emotions I'd never wanted to experience again. *Daring* me to make a move.

I had . . . and I'd been slammed with the cruelest memories ever since.

Being captivated by someone for any reason was something I couldn't afford. Something I couldn't allow.

My obliterated heart couldn't take it.

Kicking at Libby's foot, I ground out, "Let's go," and stood to leave.

I kept my head down as we walked, but was unable to stop myself from glancing over my shoulder—searching her out—one last time when we reached the door.

The warning glare from her friend said what I'd already told myself dozens of times—I needed to forget about her. But that would always be impossible. The need to move closer, the need to beg her to let me be someone who deserved her, told me as much.

Chapter 9

SEE ME

Lily

"I gotta get out there, Lil. Need to get on the street," Beck mumbled the next night as he walked into my room. "You need anything before I go?"

I glanced at him from the window seat, but went back to looking outside without responding.

The only thing I wanted was to know more about Texas ... something Beck knew since I'd already tried to get additional information out of him a handful of times over the last two and a half days.

He'd stayed firm on his decision not to give me anything.

Rather, he'd stayed loyal to Kieran by not giving me anything.

"I told you, Lil, this life's a burden. Be glad you don't know," he'd said repeatedly. *"Fine, you wanna know somethin'? Kieran loves you and would do fucking anything for you. Think on that. Know and be content with that. Stop digging because that's gonna get you nowhere, except maybe dead, and we've been working our asses off to keep you breathing."*

As if I didn't already know that.

But that was the last time I'd asked. It was the last time I'd spoken to Beck at all.

"Look, you wanna be pissed? Then be pissed. But don't fucking take it out on me or Kieran."

A disbelieving laugh punched from my chest, my head shook slowly. "Who should I be mad at?" I gave him a wary glance. "Mickey? What's going on disgusts me . . . but when I think about it, it doesn't surprise me he would do something like this. It surprises me that the two of you *would*—that you wouldn't put an end to it. It disappoints me. It hurts to be so ashamed of the two of you that I can barely look at you, Beck. At least with the drugs, people are seeking you out. They're making a conscious effort to seek you out so they can put something in their bodies . . . so they can harm themselves. But those girls they're taking? They're innocent. They don't want what's happening to them and they don't want to be ripped from their lives."

His shoulders fell and his mouth opened, but no response came.

"You want to know what hurts more than knowing you both kept this from me and that you're a part of it? It's that *this* is what Kieran chose over me."

"He did—"

"And it kills me that if Aric were still here, none of this would be happening," I continued, my voice getting louder and louder. "He would've put an end to this as soon as he found out about it."

A dark laugh rumbled deep in his chest, but there was no humor behind it. A muscle in Beck's jaw ticked, his eyes were filled with frustration. "That so, Lil?"

"He was never afraid to challenge Mickey when he went too far— that's why people followed and trusted him. He would've seen this put to an end years ago, not done whatever Mickey demanded. Kieran and I would've been—" My words ended with a sharp inhale as the air in the room changed, grew heavy.

I stood from the window seat, my eyes searching just before Kieran ground out, "You should be headed to Raleigh, Beck." His tone and expression were detached if you didn't know him.

But Beck and I did.

There was an edge that warned Beck not to say anything else. And after everything I'd found out the other day, it suddenly reminded me of Mickey.

I turned back to the window, unable to look at him anymore when that thought made my stomach roll and eyes burn with unshed tears.

The front door slammed shut seconds later, but in that moment, I couldn't feel bad for fighting with Beck before he went to work. I still wanted to scream at both of them and hit them until they felt the pain I experienced when Kieran had slipped up about Texas.

But I knew it wouldn't do any good. If they'd been working with Mickey on this for so many years—and all behind my back—nothing I said would make them stop now.

"Beck's under orders, Lily. You can't question what he's doing. You can't yell at him for doing what he's told."

Pain speared my chest, making it difficult to breathe. "Is *that* an order?"

The only warning I had before Kieran was slipping up behind me was the sound of his bag dropping to the floor just before his fingers curled around my arms and he pulled me against his chest. His hold soft but unyielding. All Kieran.

"When have I ever given you an order?" he asked, his voice a low growl.

I didn't answer, because I knew I couldn't without being hurtful.

There had been so many times over the years when Kieran had told me not to do something in order to keep me safe, and I'd known in most of those moments he'd been right. But right then I wanted to hurl every one of those occurrences back at him.

"Is he dead?" I asked instead. When Kieran didn't respond, I looked over my shoulder and searched his stoic eyes. "The man in Texas . . . is he dead?"

"No."

"W-what? Why? I don't—I don't understand why you would be sent—"

"Mickey wants him alive," he said simply, firmly. The conversation was over.

I hated knowing what Kieran did for Mickey . . . for Holloway. I hated knowing he'd been trained his entire life to be this person, so much so that he *was* Nightshade and Nightshade *was* him.

In all the years I had known him, I'd never wanted him to come home, knowing he'd just ended someone's life.

But over the last days I'd been anxious for the time I'd wake to him slipping into bed, anxious to have the confirmation that the man in Texas was no longer living—no longer taking and hurting stolen women.

Knowing that Kieran had left him alive left a sinking feeling deep in my gut.

I tried to turn in his arms to fully look at him, but his grip tightened, preventing me from facing him—as he always did. Tearing out of his hold, I whirled on him, my voice a soft rasp as I tried desperately to hold back the tears. "*Mickey* wants him alive? And you just do whatever Mickey wants, don't you?"

Kieran's eyes hardened. His jaw clenched. That monster inside him flickered to life.

"What about *me*, Kieran? What about *you*? What about what we want?"

He slowly backed up to lean against the dresser, his shoulders lifting slightly. "It's not that simple."

"It is. It *can* be. But you refuse to let it be." Tears burned my eyes and my throat tightened when I reminded him, "That man *buys* stolen women. You had a chance to end him, and you didn't take it."

I studied his cold, unapologetic expression as he watched me from across the room. My anger and resentment built as he continued to stand there without a hint of remorse. Without a hint of regret for pushing us further apart with each passing day.

Then again, he couldn't regret what he didn't know . . . what he didn't understand.

It didn't matter that our relationship had been straining—*cracking*—under the knowledge of his deceit when he'd left just days before . . . Kieran didn't linger on arguments or tears once they ended.

He loved me. Fiercely. But he couldn't see what was emotionally broken because he wasn't wired that way—because he was too focused on keeping me physically safe.

I laughed, but it sounded pained. "I don't know why I'm surprised," I whispered as I stepped to the side, nearly crumbling from the weight of my agonizing pain and grief. "Why wouldn't you keep him alive? You've had years' worth of chances to get us out of here, and you've chosen Mickey every time."

I caught sight of Kieran's hardened façade falling just before I turned for the bathroom, but I hadn't made it past the bed before his strong hands grasped my arms to haul me back into his embrace.

"Chosen Mickey?" Kieran asked roughly, his lips brushing my ear. "I'd choose a grave before I ever chose him over you."

"And yet, he's who you answer to," I said through my tightened throat, my words soft and laced with pain. "He's why you do what you do. He's why we're here."

"Lily . . ." My name was agony as it climbed up his throat. A strangled noise followed before he dropped his forehead to my shoulder and tightened his grip on my arms. "Why can't you see?" he asked, the words nearly too low to hear.

"Why can't *you*?" I choked out as the tears slipped free. Once again, I tried to turn in his arms but was unable to move.

A lifetime of knowing Kieran. A lifetime of loving him. And throughout all those years, there had been one thing he'd always refused to give me—refused to *tell* me. One thing I still silently begged for.

For him to hold me while looking into my eyes.

"See *me*," I begged. "See what you're doing."

"I'm protecting you. Ev—"

"You're breaking my heart," I cried. "You're destroying *us*."

"Lily," he said on a harsh breath. His hands loosened but didn't release me. We stood like that in silence for long moments until he whispered, "Everything I have ever done has been for you. Everything."

I didn't hear him leave. I only felt the emptiness of the house once he was gone.

I usually went to sleep alone, and stayed that way unless Kieran was able to come home. But he'd never walked away from me for any reason other than work, so I'd spent the night pacing the room, waiting for him.

He hadn't come back.

It'd made for a long night and was the reason I was in the kitchen waiting for water to boil for coffee when Beck got home at four.

Beck's and Conor's laughs were unmistakable, and caused a smile to tug at my mouth, despite my frustrations with Beck. But the third laugh that joined in a second later made me pause.

Rough and low, foreign—almost as though he didn't laugh often and wasn't sure how. But that sound was my childhood. That sound was everything before Aric's death. That sound was something I had fallen in love with.

I found myself walking closer to the front door, trying to keep my steps as silent as Kieran's in hopes I would hear another laugh before he realized I was on the other side of the wall.

But when I finally got close enough to hear their conversation, the humor was gone.

". . . no one else I can trust with this," Kieran said.

"But Lil," Conor said after a few seconds, his voice hesitant. "We've never—"

"You think I don't fucking know that?" Kieran growled, his tone toeing the line between Kieran and Nightshade. "But if this meeting is happening tonight, it can't be missed."

"It's happening," Beck confirmed.

"I'm working with Mickey tonight," Kieran said after a few seconds, sounding defeated. "Beck's with us before he hits the streets—and that's during the time of the meeting. There's no one else."

There was a heavy sigh then Beck said, "Lil never comes out here. She only talks to you if you go inside. She won't realize you're gone."

"Can't I tell her I'm getting her ice cream or something?" Conor asked, pleading.

The silence that followed his question was answer enough for both him and me.

"I'm not going to be able to look at her today," he said with a groan. "I'll tell her if I do. I don't know how to leave her unprotected during my shift."

"It's not your shift," Kieran said. "It's mine. It's always mine. I'm the one leaving her unprotected."

The guilt in his voice slammed into me, stealing my breath.

I grabbed at my aching chest, but when Beck started talking again, a low, warning whistle began in the kitchen.

I rushed through the living room into the kitchen as quietly as possible, and turned off the stove just as the kettle's scream sounded through the house—alerting the guys that I was awake.

Forcing myself to breathe slowly, steadily, I scooped coffee into the French press, then poured water in to let it brew.

I'd just grabbed a mug a few minutes later when the door opened and Beck's heavy steps filled the house.

I glanced up to ask if he wanted coffee, but paused, sucking in a sharp breath when strong, familiar arms wrapped around my waist.

"Why are you awake?" he asked in that rough tone as he rested his forehead on the back of my head.

"Couldn't sleep." I set the mug down to grip the edge of the counter. "Where were you?"

Why didn't you come back?

Where did you sleep?

Why did you let the mob get between us?

Why can't you see that it is?

"Outside with Conor."

His answer surprised me. I was sure he would've gone back to his old room in the main house. Or Conor's room in Soldier's Row. Anywhere to sleep after such a long job.

"All night?"

"Where else would I go?" I didn't need for him to say the rest. I'd heard it for years. *I need to make sure you're safe.*

What Kieran was saying, and what he had done last night, made the conversation I'd just overheard that much more confusing.

Since that night, I'd never been without one of the guys watching me, guarding me. And now there was a meeting happening tonight that was so important Kieran would pull Conor away from watching me.

But not important enough that Mickey would go.

Or *could* go . . .

And in that moment, I knew that whatever this meeting was—wherever Conor was going—I needed to go there too.

"You could've done that from inside the house," I mumbled as I grabbed the mug and reached for the French press.

Kieran released me only to grab and still my hands.

"I plan to. From our bed."

As I said, Kieran didn't linger on arguments or tears once they ended . . . because he couldn't comprehend emotional damage.

"Kieran," I began warily, but paused when his hands tightened around mine.

"Everything, Lily . . . *everything* I do is for you. See that," he pleaded hoarsely. "Fucking *see* that."

"How can I when you refuse to see what you continuously do to us?"

He was silent for so long that if he hadn't been holding on to me, I would've been sure he'd left the room. "I told you last night, it's not that simple. Things aren't that simple anymore. You see what I'm doing *to* us, maybe one day you'll see what I'm doing *for* us."

But we were already crumbling, and if that day comes, there might not be anything of us left.

Chapter 10

JUST OUT OF REACH

Lily

The street fair in our tiny town was just how I remembered it . . .

Except it wasn't.

The smells were still strong and enticing. The music was still loud and begged you to move to its beat. There was still that sense of ease and contentment as soon as you walked onto the main streets of downtown Wake Forest.

But there were essential elements to these nights that were missing from it now.

I wasn't there with my friends. Like Teagan, the other few friends I had grown up with had mourned my death.

I felt an odd mixture of fear and determination rather than the freedom and rebelliousness that had always slid through my veins when I'd snuck out under my mom's nose.

And instead of the giddy feeling deep in my stomach as I waited for my green-eyed hunter to find me, I was terrified he would.

But though that fear grew, the need to know where Kieran had sent Conor pushed me forward even as I lost his massive, familiar frame in the crowd and got turned around more than once.

I paused near a cluster of tables, contemplating whether I should stand on one of the chairs to get a better view or turn around and go home.

My hand had just touched the back of a chair when a booming voice sounded behind me.

"Future ex-wife!"

I whirled around, hand to my chest in a vain attempt to calm my racing heart.

Ethan held his hands out in front of him apologetically. "Hey, hey, hey, hey now. Didn't mean to scare my love, I was just so surprised to see her." His mouth curved into one of his charming grins, but it seemed off. "You sure do seem to scare easily, you know."

"Uh, well you kind of just yelled from behi—"

"Offer still stands," he reminded me boldly as he stepped closer.

And it was then that I got a better look at him.

His eyes were glazed. The *charming* grin he wore so often seemed off because it wasn't charming at all. It was a mixture of his grin and a sneer.

"Are you drunk, Ethan?"

"I'd like to buy you coffee," he responded, then lifted a shoulder in a shrug. "Or everything. Let's start with everything and then move to coffee."

I took a step away to put some distance between us, but a step from him brought him closer than before.

"I really can't. I told you, I have a boyfriend."

He cocked his head to the side, seeming to wait for something. After a few seconds, he laughed mockingly. "Well, wouldya look at that? No boyfriend," he said in a whisper, as if he was telling me a secret. His lips twisted, that grin of his fighting to hold on. "If you ask me, Elle, he doesn't exist."

I'd started shaking my head, ready to explain I did have a boyfriend even if he wasn't there with me, but the words died on my tongue as I took another step away. A guy like Ethan or not, I wasn't stupid enough to let him know I was alone.

"I'm sorry you don't believe me, but—"

"Where you going? I wanna take you out. I wanna show my future ex-wife a good fucking time before she escapes me."

My eyes narrowed and jaw clenched. "And I think you've had too much to drink."

"If you wanna look at it that way. Or we could look at it this way . . . maybe you just need to get on my level. And, guess what? I can help with that, because I'm just so handy." His bleary-eyed gaze swept my body. "If you want, I'll show you just how many ways I can be *handy*. Whatdya say, milady?"

His hopefulness at Brooks Street could have been seen as endearing if I'd wanted to be pursued by him . . . if I wasn't the last girl he should ever try to pursue.

But this was different.

Alcohol distorted his charm, causing his words to give me the feeling like bugs were crawling beneath my skin. Being drunk had turned him into someone like Bailey and Finn.

But I knew men like that, and I knew Ethan. And I had a feeling Ethan wouldn't drink again if he knew this was what he turned into.

"Go home." I took another two steps away from him and wanted to scream in frustration when he matched them.

"Care to join?"

"Ethan, *listen* to me," I pleaded. "You need to stop. You wouldn't be acting like this if you hadn't been drinking, but if you don't stop, I *will* make you. So back away before . . ." My words trailed off when a large hand slid around my waist possessively, and my eyes fluttered shut as a whispered curse fell from my lips.

In the second before he spoke, my heart stopped as the dread that had filled my stomach spread through the rest of my body like thick oil.

But the deep, gravelly voice that came from behind me wasn't Kieran's or anyone else I knew.

"There you are."

I didn't have time to catch my breath. Didn't have time to comprehend the rush of relief or newfound fear that surged through me when I realized Kieran wasn't there, or that a stranger was gripping me and pulling me toward him.

I was turned quickly, only giving me enough time to see the darkness of his eyes and hear his hushed, "*Easy*," before his mouth descended upon mine.

His lips were firm, the kiss hard and fast and completely unmemorable . . .

At least it should have been.

Because that's where it should have ended.

It never should have happened at all.

But when I thought he'd pull away, his fingers left chills in their wake as they trailed along the soft skin of my throat to gently curl around my neck. His mouth relaxed against mine and his thumb pressed against my jaw, tilting my head back to deepen the kiss for just a moment.

It *should* have been unmemorable, and some distant part of my mind knew that it needed to mean nothing.

But it felt like that kiss had freed me.

And it didn't matter that I was completely unaware of what I was being freed from. All that mattered was the moment it ended . . .

Because the breath I took following that kiss felt so deep and so pure, and like I'd been waiting hundreds of years for it.

Awareness hummed beneath the surface. Prodding at my memory like a gentle reminder just before I opened my eyes as he slowly lifted his face from mine.

Those eyes . . .

Recognition slammed into me, and I was sure I would have staggered back if he hadn't been holding me so tightly.

"You . . ." Surprise and confusion and a need to feel free again made my voice nothing more than a breath.

Dark, dark eyes were staring down at me, studying me as they had every week during the last two years. But his brow was drawn together like he was trying to comprehend what had just happened. As if *he* hadn't been the one to initiate it.

The hand gripping my waist tightened, and his thumb moved from my jaw to brush against my bottom lip as that same energy that always danced across my skin in his presence seemed to come alive with his touch.

"What are you doing?" I asked, my words still soft as a whisper.

"Think that's obvious." The corner of his mouth pulled up in a quick, lopsided smile before his expression fell into a mesmerizing combination of wonder and frustration.

Oh God, his voice. As long as I'd dreamt of him, I'd wondered what his voice would sound like . . . and it was everything I'd imagined and more. Smooth and warm, and able to create a whirlwind of fire in my belly with just a few words.

And he was now looking at me as though he was holding the greatest mystery he'd ever come across—one he was trying to talk himself out of solving.

After a few moments in weighted silence, an amused huff punched from his chest. "Think I've been looking everywhere for you." It sounded like a confession and a denial, and it was murmured so low it should've been lost in the noise around us.

But it was only him . . . only me.

Those words felt like they were wrapping me in their warmth as the need and the pain within his declaration resonated in my mind.

And I knew from the way his eyes seemed to demand to know my secrets, and offer to share every one of his, that I wanted to stay in that place for the rest of time.

Only him. Only me.

"I've been right here."

And then my world caught fire when his mouth suddenly fell onto mine again.

My eyes fluttered shut and knees weakened when he parted my lips with his, and I became painfully, blissfully aware of the pounding of my heart for the first time in so, so long.

Alive.

I was alive.

The hand on my waist slid around my back, pulling me closer against his firm chest as his tongue teased mine.

"I've been looking everywhere for you."

My body stiffened against his when his words replayed through my mind.

"I've been looking everywhere for you."

Oh God . . . Kieran.

I quickly shoved away from him, ripping from his hold before he had a chance to let go.

"Wait!"

My gaze went everywhere. I pressed my hand to my mouth as I fought back a wave of nausea.

He was suddenly at my side, the tips of his fingers grazing my forearm before I could yank it away.

"Look, I'm sorry. I shouldn't have . . ." He roughed a hand through his dark hair, gripping at it as he released an edgy laugh. "I shouldn't have kept kissing you."

I shouldn't have let him. Yet in that moment, with him so close after years at a teasing distance, I wanted his touch and his kiss more than I wanted my next breath.

"I took it too far, I get that." He suddenly gestured off to the side. "But he wasn't getting the fucking hint. And then—"

"What?" I looked in that direction, staring at the mass of faceless bodies walking by for long seconds before I remembered.

Ethan . . .

How could I have forgotten everything so completely the moment this man had touched me?

And then it hit me. What he'd meant . . . why he'd kissed me at all.

Why, after all this time, he'd put an end to our silent misery.

A flash of hurt and embarrassment flared in my chest, and I prayed the darkness of the night would hide the blood rushing to my cheeks.

I felt like such an idiot.

"I had it handled, he wasn't bothering me," I said, my voice tight.

His eyebrows rose in disbelief. "He told anyone who would listen that you turned him down the other day. That should've been enough. Tonight he kept coming after you while you repeatedly told him to stop or leave . . . that's not bothering you?"

I looked at him blankly as I thought through the encounter through someone else's eyes.

A guy repeatedly coming after a girl who's by herself. A way to save the girl.

But Ethan had never been anything more than an endearing, hopeful, eager puppy. There wasn't a malicious bone in his body. He might turn into an overly confident jerk when drunk, but in the end, he wouldn't end up harming anyone but himself.

And the man in front of me knew that.

Because the man in front of me? There was something dark and dangerous that radiated beneath his enticing surface and enchanting grin. Something easily noticed when you'd been raised in a similar life. A darkness easily identified when you'd embraced and loved it for so many years. And it only added to his appeal.

Kieran had the same darkness. Only he wore his like armor.

Men like Kieran and the one in front of me could take one look at Ethan and know any woman wouldn't need saving from him.

And this man had made me feel alive and free. He'd made me want so many things as long as they were with him. All with some words and kisses that never should've happened—because he'd thought I'd needed to be *saved* for a minute or two.

I already had enough men saving me.

"I have to go."

He snatched my wrist in his grasp as soon as I took a step away, and hauled me back to him. His dark eyes were dancing, the corner of his mouth pulled up in amusement. "Where are you going?"

"Ethan never stopped me from leaving." I meant for my voice to be hard. I meant to sneer at him. But my tone was soft and breathy as my traitorous heart silently begged him to kiss me again.

"No," he agreed, his eyes boring into my own. "But he hadn't just found what he hadn't even realized he'd been looking for."

My chest tightened from the ache in his words. "But I've been here."

When he spoke again, his tone was gruff, his words dripping with need and regret. "Right in front of me, and just out of reach."

As much as I wanted to deny everything he was saying, I understood.

Just as there was a force pushing Kieran and me farther apart, there had always been something keeping me from this man. Keeping him at looking distance . . . keeping him an idea, a fantasy. A boundary I'd pushed at and tested . . . one I'd thought he'd attempted to get past every day he'd left me notes.

But my life at Holloway and with Kieran was what had always kept that invisible force secure. Until tonight.

And now, being in his arms, it *was* like I'd finally found him.

As right as it felt, it was impossible to ignore the crushing force that was my struggling relationship.

I needed to get home. I needed to get away from this man before I forgot who I was and let myself believe this constant thrum that danced between us was real.

His free hand found that place at my neck again, his thumb gently sliding along my jaw before he was guiding my head back.

"I have to go," I repeated, but couldn't force myself away from him.

His eyes searched mine for a few seconds as he nodded, then dipped his head closer. But just when I thought he would kiss me again, his lips went to my ear. "If I let you go, how do I know I'll find you again?"

My brow pinched as confusion swam through me. "You know where I'll be, just as I know where you'll be."

A low rumble of a laugh sounded in his chest. "There's something in your eyes that makes me wonder every week if it will be the last time I see you. But after tonight . . . what happens when you disappear?"

"When that day comes, then maybe I won't want to be found."

My entire body trembled when his lips grazed my jaw. "I think your answer might change if I'm the one looking for you."

Oh God . . .

My body and my heart and my mind rebelled against each other. All wanting and screaming for different things.

Just one more taste of his lips.

To beg him to look for me.

To realize this was a game. To run home before Conor made his way back and realized I wasn't there—before Kieran would be the one looking for me.

"I have to go."

He moved so his lips were hovering over my own, and pleaded, "Don't."

I wanted to feel that rush. I wanted to feel my heart race. I wanted to feel alive again—if even for a second.

But I couldn't.

"Please stop touching me." The words were barely a whisper leaving my lips, but from the way his dark eyes snapped to mine, he'd heard them over the crowd and music.

A sharp huff forced from his lungs. And after a moment, he released me and took half a step back.

I'd just turned to leave when he called out, "Truth or dare."

I stopped, but didn't look back at him for a few seconds as I told myself to leave. Against my better judgment, I looked over my shoulder—my confusion plain in my expression.

"Truth or dare," he repeated in that deep, rough tone. His expression pleading.

My head shook absentmindedly before I finally shrugged. "Truth."

"Why did you come out tonight?"

My chest tightened, and it suddenly became hard to breathe as I wondered who this man was—if he was somehow connected to my family.

"I was bored," I said tightly and stared straight ahead as I began walking.

I hadn't made it two steps before his hands wrapped around my upper arms, and he pulled me to a stop so my back was pressed to his muscled chest. "*Lie*," he whispered against my ear.

The mixture of his lips brushing my ear and his hushed tone made me shiver. The feel of him pressed against me stole my focus so completely I didn't catch that he'd called me out on my lie until moments later.

I quickly thought of his face, trying to place it somewhere along the men who worked for my dad or Kieran—but came up empty.

"Truth or dare," he said again, causing my stomach to drop.

"Why are you doing this?"

"Because I felt your reaction to me. Saw it."

My breath rushed out and knees shook with relief when he didn't call me out, and I knew he couldn't have been with my family—couldn't have known who I was. If he had, he would've taken me back to the property any one of the mornings he'd seen me at the café.

"And now you're trying to leave . . ." His words were a rumble from deep within his chest, the sound so primal that I wanted to shut my eyes and get lost in his voice and the intoxicating current that hummed where he touched me. "So, truth or dare."

My heart was racing. Each pounding beat so forceful I was sure he felt it from being pressed against me.

"Truth," I whispered.

His hands trailed down my arms until his fingers were loosely encircling my wrists. "Do you really want me to let you go?"

I swallowed thickly before answering, "I need you to."

Before he could respond in any way—by word, by releasing me, by pulling me closer—I jerked against his hold when loud voices suddenly came from behind and beside us.

"Dare!"

"Where'd you go?"

"We got so much food. It's time to feast. Oh, *oh*."

"Why are you just stand—?" The girl's voice cut off abruptly when she rounded us, her eyes widening with unabashed disbelief as she took me in, standing where I didn't belong.

The girl from Brooks Street on Monday.

As I had so often this week, I wondered if she was his girlfriend, fiancée, wife, his *anything* . . . but there wasn't an ounce of jealousy or anger dripping from her.

My familiar stranger released his hold on me, his body disappearing from behind my own just before two guys came up behind the girl, carrying plates of fried foods and desserts.

Another girl followed behind them as she tapped away on a phone, a third guy trailing close to her side.

"Well, well, well. Who do we have here?" one of the first guys asked, a wicked smirk and gleam in his eye as he sauntered closer and hooked an arm around my neck.

I was too stunned from the loss of that tormenting energy that kissed my skin whenever *he* was near to try to prevent this new man from getting too close.

"Who are you?" the girl who was still staring at me asked.

"No one," I answered immediately. "I was leaving—"

I tried to maneuver out of the new guy's hold, my gaze darting around, looking for the man who had just shifted my entire world with a kiss.

"Einstein!" the guy holding on to me called out, turning us so we were facing the rest of his group as they pushed two tables together. "Pull up an extra chair. This one's staying."

My eyes widened in horror as I found the stranger I'd been looking for. Those dark eyes were locked on mine as he stood behind a chair, his hands gripping the back of it tightly. Too tight. As if he was forcing himself not to move from that spot.

"I'm not," I whispered, then glanced back at the girl now standing directly in front of me again. Her curious stare bounced over me like she was trying to figure me out. "I'm not," I assured her.

The man holding me laughed as he tightened his arm, giving my neck a gentle squeeze. "It's just food, darlin'," he said as he led us toward the tables. "It won't bite you. Doesn't mean I won't."

I glanced at the tables, my gaze searching out *his* again. The look in his eyes as he locked onto the man touching me was one I knew so well.

Because I had fallen in love with that look when others would have run.

That darkness—that had nothing to do with the color of his eyes—pulsed just beneath the surface, begging to be freed. Teasing that the man standing in front of me was dangerous.

I'd grown up surrounded by powerful and dangerous men, hating the monsters those traits turned them into. I'd wanted to put an end to every horrible thing they were involved with before I escaped them completely. And yet the danger that lay barely concealed in this man was just as enticing as the rest of him. As if the dangerous side within him called to me, begging me to touch.

"How do you know Dare?" the girl in front of me suddenly asked.

I blinked quickly as I focused on her, noting that she never once looked behind her as she took confident steps backward.

"Excuse me?"

"Dare." She pointed behind her, directly at the guy in question. "How do you know him?"

"I don't."

"Uh-huh. So you were just standing there in his arms for no reason?"

The guy with his arm around me tensed. "Wai—you—I might've missed, uh . . ." As we came upon the tables now littered with food and people I didn't know, he looked toward Dare for the first time and quickly released me as he murmured a low "Shit" and walked to the other end of the table.

"He ju—"

I jerked, my attention darting to see Dare's hard glare set on the girl in front of me when he said a name—a name I would have sworn was my own.

"*Libby*," he snapped again. "Leave her alone."

Relief surged through my veins, the feeling so great my body wanted to sag now that the moment's fear was gone. But with so many eyes on me, I stood still, expressionless.

I didn't watch her turn to go sit down.

I couldn't stop looking at Dare.

He was still leaning against the chair, gripping it as though it was a lifeline. And he was waiting to see what I would do.

I wanted to stay. I wanted the steady hum in my veins to turn into that addictive spark when he touched me.

Despite whatever was happening between Kieran and me, every time my head cleared enough to remember that I needed to get home, I felt sick for letting another man touch me at all.

I needed to go.

From the way Dare's expression hardened and brows pulled together, he knew I'd made my decision.

I rocked back to leave but was suddenly pulled down.

I tripped over my feet as I tried to land in the chair instead of on the ground, and found myself less than an inch from the girl who'd had her face buried in her phone.

"Einstein!" Dare barked from behind me.

Like Libby, she looked to be maybe thirty, give or take a couple years. But she could've passed for barely legal with her doe-eyed look and small stature.

But those eyes locked on and studying me gave her away. Calculating, wild, and a little crazy. There was nothing innocent about her.

"Do I know you?" she asked once she was done studying me.

I was so thrown off by her and the way Dare tensed beside me that I didn't have the chance to be worried about why she would ask. "No."

"Your mouth."

My eyebrows shot up. "Excuse me?"

"Your mouth looks familiar."

I stared at her, dumbfounded, as I tried to think of what to say to her, but she'd already released me and was tapping furiously on her phone again—as if the odd exchange had never happened.

A laugh that was rich and full of frustration burst from Dare as he sat next to me, filling me and making me want to beg to hear it again and again.

"Jesus Christ, Einstein," he mumbled, then reached into his pocket. Pulling out a phone, he tossed it onto the table. "Phones."

Four phones quickly followed with dull thuds, and all eyes went to the girl sitting next to me, who still had her face buried in her screen.

"Einstein." Dare's tone was a mixture of annoyance and humor as he scrubbed his hands over his face. "Phone."

"I've almost got it," she said on a rush. Eyes wide with excitement. "Just a little bit more."

"Whatever it is, you could've had it if you hadn't wasted time trying to rip peoples' arms off. Phone." When he said her name again, all traces of humor were gone from his voice. "Einstein."

She blew out a frustrated sigh as she tossed her phone on the table. "This close, Dare," she said, pressing her index finger and thumb close together. "*This* close."

"You know the rules."

The guy who had led me to the tables jerked his chin in my direction and asked, "What about the nerd?"

"She's a—"

"I don't have a phone," I said, interrupting Dare.

A short laugh left Libby but died quickly when she took in my blank expression.

"Doesn't matter anyway. She's a guest." Dare gestured toward the plates of food littering the tables, and mumbled, "Eat."

I watched in confusion as Libby passed around a stack of paper plates—one short since they hadn't been expecting me—and everyone started serving themselves as though it was a family dinner.

Because that's what it felt like—from what I remembered of family dinners—but that wasn't what was confusing.

While everyone at the table looked to be around thirty, I was sure Dare was the youngest, and he was clearly the one they all looked to. The one they all listened to and respected.

Something about it felt weird. Wrong in the sense that it felt all too familiar.

Or maybe it was the nagging voice inside telling me I needed to get back to the house—that I'd already spent far too long gone.

I quickly scanned the area, looking for any familiar faces, but found none.

"Here," Dare mumbled, and I looked back as he pushed a plate between us.

I glanced at the plate for only a second before looking away. "I'm not really hungry."

Dare caught my chin between his fingers, his dark stare holding mine for a few seconds. "I'm sure you're not," he said with a smirk as he released me, then pushed the plate closer in my direction.

"You met my sister, Libby," he said suddenly as he took some food off the plate and popped it into his mouth, nodding toward the girl I'd spoken to earlier. "She has a thing for playing twenty questions without letting the other person ask anything."

Sister.

I tried to ignore the relief pulsing through my veins, but it was nearly impossible. She was his sister.

But I didn't know if I felt better or worse that she wasn't only that intense with me, because now I knew the intensity wasn't over—and neither were the questions. Questions I couldn't answer.

"The twins. Diggs," Dare continued, pointing to the guy who had brought me to the tables, and then another on the opposite side of Einstein, who I hadn't noticed. "And Maverick."

Now I wasn't sure which one had had his arm around me. They were identical.

"You're next to Einstein, and this is Johnny," he finished, gesturing to the guy seated directly across from me.

A guy that I'd seen with Dare at Brooks Street plenty of times . . . and a guy that made me regret allowing one of the twins to lead me toward the tables.

The way he was looking at me sent a chill up my spine, and set off every warning inside me to run.

He hadn't touched any of the food on the table, his plate was clean, and his cold, calculating stare was unyielding as he glared at me from across the table.

That look? It was nothing compared to the eyes of the assassin I'd shared a bed with for years. But I knew Kieran and knew his heart . . . and I knew I would never have to fear those piercing eyes.

This man? It was as if he was taking every ounce of his hatred and anger and pushing it onto me with one look.

And I was trapped in his stare.

I needed to get away, now more than ever.

Johnny jerked suddenly. His gaze dipped to the table then over to Dare, releasing me.

I let out a shuddering breath and shrank into the chair, trying to ward off the lingering bone-deep chill as I fought the urge to run, and tried to come up with a reason to leave.

After a few seconds, Johnny straightened and started grabbing food, his cold eyes only glossing over me when he asked, "What'd you say your name was?"

His voice matched the rest of him. Cold and hard and unforgiving.

A shudder had started from deep within me, but stopped, and I froze when I realized he'd been talking to me.

I thought back over his words, and tried not to panic when my mind blanked. "I didn't," I finally said, my words soft but bold.

Everyone stopped moving.

Johnny's cold glare was back, but the rest of the table had mixed expressions of surprise and amusement.

I didn't look at Dare, but after a few tense seconds, a low, dark laugh left him. "This girl just might give you a run for your money, Johnny." His eyes slid to mine, and a devastating smile pulled at his lips. "I've never met anyone who's as untrusting as this guy right here. But you might have him beat."

My head shook quickly. "I'm sorry, I just . . ." I trailed off, not knowing how to explain.

I have to go.

And like I was drawn, I looked behind me, then all around us.

Nothing. No one.

Dare was studying me when I finished, and leaned forward until his face was just a breath from mine.

I knew I needed to lean away, but I couldn't move.

Those chocolate eyes held mine, and a hint of something warm and spicy that clung to him made me want to lean closer.

"Are you waiting for someone?" he asked low enough that his voice wouldn't carry to the others, who had gone back to eating and talking.

"Excuse me?"

"You've been looking around ever since I first saw you backing away from Ethan. Are you waiting for someone?"

"I'm not. I—"

"Do I need to be worried about a boyfriend showing up?"

If only you knew that was exactly what you needed to be worried about.

I sat there with my lips parted for a few seconds before I repeated my earlier words, "I need to go."

From the way his brows drew together and he leaned away a bit, he'd expected a different answer. "So I should take that as a yes?"

"Please—"

"No one's keeping you here." His once warm eyes were now as cold as Johnny's. "If you really want to go, then go."

Without another word, he went back to eating and effortlessly joined into the conversation Johnny was having with Einstein.

I studied his strong profile for only a moment, committing it— and the way he made me feel—to memory, before I slipped out of my seat and turned to go.

I hurried through the crowded street fair, but tried to force myself not to walk too fast . . . not to draw attention to myself. All the while my eyes never stopped moving—never stopped looking for anyone who might be looking for me.

My chest felt both tighter and looser as I got closer to the end of the blocked-off streets that held the fair, and closer to home.

I *needed* to get there—to get back to the safety it provided.

But all I *wanted* was to experience the way Dare had made me feel again. And again.

Those knowing eyes. That mouth that could make me feel free . . .

Guilt ripped through me as I thought of the way I'd betrayed the only man I'd ever loved tonight. But I knew that the betrayal wouldn't end. Not when I wanted another man's kiss and touch the way I wanted Dare's.

Tears pricked at my eyes. I gripped at my churning stomach as I pushed through another group of people.

I'd almost made it to the end when a hand clamped down around my wrist. My blood ran cold as I was hauled back against a tall, hardened body.

Oh God.

Chapter 11

LIGHT UP THE DARK

Dare

I didn't watch her go, but it was impossible to miss the shift in the air once she was gone.

Something in me called to go after her. To chase her down and beg for her name. To ask what she was doing to me with those wide eyes and those lips I'd wanted to claim again and again.

This was no longer about just revealing her truths.

This was so much more.

Everyone stopped eating to look at me as soon as she left, but I refused to meet their questioning stares.

"Well, I'll go first," Libby stated after a minute of silence. "What the hell?"

"Who the fuck was that?" Johnny growled in a low tone that earned him a glare.

"I think she's pretty." Einstein shrugged, then fixed me with a wild-eyed stare I'd come to recognize meant there was a code she wanted to crack.

She would be nearly impossible to be around until she had.

"But there's something about her mouth, I'm tellin' ya, Dare," she went on, her words now rushed at the thought of having something new to work on. "I know her, and I'm going to figure out how."

An addict looking for their next fix. That was Einstein when it came to codes.

I now knew the feeling.

Two years of keeping a distance. Then ten minutes and two kisses with the girl, and I'd been reduced to a restless junkie. Muscles twitching as I forced myself not to jump out of my chair so I could find her and get another taste.

I was ready to beg Einstein to help me figure out who the girl was when Diggs huffed. "I'll tell her what she can do with that mouth . . ."

I launched the first phone I touched at his face, but he caught it in time.

"That was mine," Einstein yelled and kicked me from under the table.

"I don't know her," Johnny muttered, his attention on Einstein before drifting toward the direction the girl had gone. "But there's something not right about her."

"Back to my question," Libby interrupted. "What the hell, Dare? She was just suddenly there? And after what happened the other morning?"

"What happened the other morning?" Johnny demanded, but Libby continued on.

"And you were—you were . . ." Her shock and irritation with me were replaced by hurt and sadness. Her voice dropped when she said, "It's been almost four years and you were—"

I shoved away from the table and took off after the girl before Libby could finish.

Because it *had* been almost four years.

Since my world had gone to hell. Since I'd wanted someone the way I wanted this girl. Since I'd struggled to keep myself from touching a girl—kissing her.

And I couldn't let her walk away now.

I found her rushing through the crowd, and hurried to get to her before she could slip away.

I reached for her, grasping her wrist to stop her and turn her toward me. The jolt that went through her body felt as if it had gone through my own.

"I'm sorry," she cried out, her next words falling from her lips on a rush. "I'm so sorry. I—" Her eyes widened in horror when she looked up and saw me there, her body still trembling violently.

From her outright panic when she first turned, I wondered if there *was* someone she'd been waiting for—someone she'd expected to show.

Someone she'd been afraid would.

"Dare." She swayed toward me for a moment before blinking quickly and trying to pull away. "*Please.* I told you . . . I have to go."

I looked away for only a second to see where we were, then pulled her down a little alley between two shops.

"No, no, no. I need to go. I need—"

I pressed my mouth to hers to stop her hurried plea, and because I couldn't imagine going another minute without feeling the rush when I did.

Fucking ecstasy.

She gripped at my forearms to steady herself, a soft moan sounding in her throat and getting lost in the kiss as I pushed her gently up against the wall of one of the buildings.

"Dare," she whispered when her back settled, my name sounding like a hesitant invitation.

I forced myself to remember where we were—to remember she'd had me chasing her in the short time I'd let myself be around her—when all I wanted was to hear her say it again.

Hear her scream it.

One of her hands moved down to grip at my shirt, pulling me closer, but the hand clinging to my arm was straining, as if she was trying to force herself to push me away.

"Truth or dare," I murmured against her lips, then kissed her again.

Her breaths were heavy when I pulled away so she could answer, indecision playing in her eyes. "Why . . . *why* do you keep asking me that?"

"Because people who are scared always pick *truth*, and I need to know if you're lying to me."

"If you know what I'm going to choose, why give me an option?"

My mouth lifted in a smirk. "It's what I do. Truth or dare."

Her head dropped and voice lowered, but not enough that I didn't hear her when she said, "If you already have me so figured out, then ask your question."

I leaned back and pressed my knuckles under her chin so I could search her eyes. "Are you in danger?"

Instead of the immediate response I expected, she studied me for a few moments. "What do you think?"

"Yes."

A shudder ran through her body as she nodded absentmindedly, her breaths slowly growing more exaggerated as my answer hovered between us. "Then you should probably let me go."

She was skipping around every answer, but it didn't matter. I'd spent the last two years trying to understand her expressions. I'd seen her fear earlier, and I'd seen it again when I'd caught up to her.

I tried, but couldn't contain the smile that stretched across my face. She didn't know me—didn't know anything about my life. But the thought that I'd let her go because she was in danger was ridiculous. One of the most dangerous men in the state, and probably the most dangerous man she would ever meet, currently held her. Nothing would happen to her as long as I continued to.

"Nothing's getting past me," I assured her.

Her breath washed over my lips as I leaned in to kiss her again when she whispered, "I thought we were talking about you."

I paused for a few seconds, then looked up into her hazel eyes. "What?"

"I think I'm in danger from you."

My brow pulled tight, and I forced out a low, frustrated laugh. "Me."

She nodded again, the movement of her head so slow as her eyes explored mine. "I *need* you to let me go for so many reasons, but I easily forget why when you don't. I think there was a reason neither of us crossed that invisible barrier before today. Because being in your arms?" She hesitated, her tongue quickly darting out to wet her lips. "Trust me, it's dangerous."

A weight pressed down on my chest, making it hard to breathe. Because damn it if she wasn't right.

There were dozens of girls over the years who'd meant nothing more than a night. Maybe two. Not one could I remember the name of, most I couldn't remember their face.

Then there'd been one who I would've sold my soul for if I could've had one more night with her.

My days with her had been everything. A slow burn that had built over time until I hadn't been able to get enough of her. Until she'd meant too much.

And there hadn't been a girl since.

Not a second glance. Not a thought. Nothing.

Until one morning at Brooks a few years ago.

But there was nothing *slow* about the thoughts and needs for the girl pressed against me. There hadn't been since the very first morning I'd found her staring at a mirror like it had the power to destroy her world. Like that possibility fascinated her.

Fuck, if I didn't need to find out why.

Dangerous was exactly what we were. Only she had no idea just how much.

My gut twisted as unwanted thoughts entered my mind, but I pushed them away. Because I knew what I needed to do. I needed to let her go and force myself not to follow.

But when there's a flicker of light in your life after so much darkness, it's impossible to stay away.

And this girl burned so damn bright.

Calling to me and beckoning me toward her, and I knew no matter how many times I let her slip away, I would follow her just to catch her again.

I brushed my thumb across her full lips. "Goddamn firefly."

She'd started leaning into my touch, but stilled when I spoke, her eyebrows pulling together in confusion. "What?"

"Tell me why you left."

"What?" she repeated, then blinked quickly as she pulled away from my hand, as if she'd just remembered she didn't want me touching her. "If you've forgotten, you told me to leave."

"You wanted to go, I wasn't going to force you to stay. But I thought you would've because you and I both know you didn't *want* me to let you go."

She sucked in a quick breath at the reminder, her mouth stayed slightly parted like she wanted to deny it. But when no denial came, her eyes pleaded with me to understand. "I *needed* you to."

"Why?" I begged. "What did you keep looking for tonight?"

Her head was already shaking, an excuse or evasion on her lips.

"Who did you think I was when I came after you just now? You were apologizing before you even turned around and looked fucking terrified. Most girls would scream if they were grabbed—not do what you did."

"It's complicated."

"Boyfriend?" I asked, my tone harder than I meant for it to be.

Ethan also told everyone that this girl had claimed to have a boyfriend. Something no one had believed since we'd all witnessed his pathetic attempts to get her attention over the years. Something *I* hadn't believed until just before she'd left the table.

"It's complicated," she began again.

"It doesn't have to be," I argued. "But I'd like to know what I'm up against, and I'd like to know if you're in danger from someone other than me."

A sad laugh tumbled from those lips and her eyes met mine. "Of course not."

True.

She let loose a slow breath. "You know, most girls would probably scream when some stranger grabs them and kisses them too. If not the first time, then the second. Or third."

She was trying to change the conversation again, but I had a feeling she would continue to no matter how many times I pushed to understand what had happened with her tonight.

So instead of trying to get inside her mind one last time, I let my mouth pull into a smirk. "I'd hardly say we're strangers, Firefly."

That same confusion from before settled over her face. "Are you calling me—*why* are you calling me that?"

Because it's exactly what she was.

I dipped my head closer to hers and asked, "Have you ever tried to catch a firefly?"

"What? No."

I lifted a hand to cradle her face, and tried to contain the urge to pull her closer when she relaxed into my touch. It'd been so long since I'd had this, and the sickening sense of fear that crawled through my veins almost made me wish I'd never found it again.

I was afraid of losing the electric hum I felt everywhere I touched her. I was terrified of losing the only person who had made me feel in so long. But I didn't know how to keep it. How to contain it.

Goddamn firefly.

I swallowed roughly as I forced that unwanted fear back. "You wait for them to light up in the dark, then try to catch them before they stop glowing," I explained. "You're the first light that has appeared after many very dark years. After tonight, I know I would chase you, just for you to keep slipping away week after week. But I also know I would willingly do it just to keep seeing you light up the dark."

She stared at me in awe for a few moments before realization settled over her, and she tried to pull away from my hold. "I have to go."

"My point exactly."

"Right," she huffed, her hazel eyes narrowing on me. "And how many girls have you used that 'firefly' thing on before?"

Her question stunned me for a second, but before I could give her a response, Johnny was suddenly there.

"Dare."

I whipped my head toward him, ready to make him leave, but my demand died on my tongue when he said, "Time to go."

There was nothing special about his words, but it was the tick of his eyebrow that meant everything, and a sudden surge of adrenaline and hatred pounded through my veins at the possibility of what was waiting for us.

I dipped my head in a nod. "Coming."

Looking back at the girl in front of me, my sudden aggravation poured through my tone. "Before tonight? I'd never said those words to anyone. Before tonight? I hadn't kissed anyone in *years*. I told you, my life has been dar—"

Her head was shaking and she hurried to speak over me. "You're someone who kissed a stranger for all the wrong reasons. You can't tell me it isn't something *you* do."

I met and held her stare, noting the hurt she was trying to cover with pride.

I saw it, and it was adding to the frustration that Johnny's arrival meant for us all.

"Think what you want," I said on a low growl. "Tell yourself all of it was just a way to get you into my bed. Try to forget what *this* felt like." I pressed her body closer to mine for emphasis. "Try to make yourself believe you *wanted* me to let you go. Tell yourself you didn't lean into me when I kissed you."

"Those kisses meant nothing." Her voice was a whisper, but she wasn't able to cover the tremble in her voice. "We'll forget about them by morning and go back to not speaking next week . . . and you know it."

Lie.

"Got it." I released her and took a couple steps away, then stopped and looked back at her. "Truth or dare."

She clenched her jaw and didn't say a word.

"Truth then," I murmured, choosing for her, and closed the distance between us again. "You want me to kiss you again."

She didn't answer, and she didn't need to. The longing that flashed through her eyes was the only answer I needed.

I couldn't have fought the smile that spread across my face if I'd tried.

I leaned close to brush my lips against her jaw. "Looking forward to chasing you, Firefly."

I turned and followed Johnny out of the alleyway, ignoring his hardened stare.

"Libby told me about her. When were you gonna tell me you've been watching this girl at Brooks, and why didn't you point her out before?" When I didn't respond, he said, "I don't like that she's always there on Mondays. There's something about her, Dare. I don't trust he—"

"I don't care," I said firmly. "What's going on?"

He blew out a harsh breath and ran a hand through his hair as he spoke, his words nearly lost in the noises from the street fair. "Lily O'Sullivan."

Just hearing her name made me see red. Made my entire world go dark again. Nothing but ice-cold rage roared through my veins, so different from the heated moments before.

But I'd already known that was why Johnny pulled me away. What I needed to know was what new leads we had in regards to this supposedly dead princess. "Right, what do we have?"

"Got someone waiting for you who has information—says he has a recent picture."

I stopped dead in my tracks for all of two seconds before I began walking toward where we'd left the cars, this time faster than before. "Libby stays with the twins . . . Einstein comes with us. If there *is* a picture, it goes to her so she can make sure it's legit and test it against other pictures of Lily. If this bitch is still alive, her breaths are numbered."

Chapter 12

HEADSTONES

Lily

Once I'd gotten away from the busy streets of town, the weight on my chest began easing. My feet started slowing until I was walking at a normal pace, and then strolling.

I'd been in a rush to get home so I'd taken shortcuts to make sure I got back before Conor. But with Holloway now just minutes away, I would've given anything to stop time and live in that moment.

Some part of me knew once I returned to Holloway, what happened between Dare and me would fade away as that invisible barrier formed between us again. Until he was nothing but a memory I confused as a dream. Until the idea of even speaking to him was nothing more than a fantasy.

It had to.

And I wanted to live in a world where that barrier didn't exist for a little longer, where the possibility of touching him and kissing him was as real as every breath pushing from my lungs.

His words that I so badly wanted to believe were sincere. His hold that had been possessive and gentle. His kisses that were both demanding and pleading. The way his eyes had begged and danced. Most importantly, the way he'd tried to save me . . . and had let me go.

"After tonight, I know I would chase you, just for you to keep slipping away week after week. But I also know I would willingly do it just to keep seeing you light up the dark."

My chest warmed at the memory of his deep, gravelly words. My heart thudded so hard it hurt.

But I welcomed it. I welcomed the hurt because it was such a sweet reminder that I was alive. That he'd set something inside me free.

The warmth fled my body, leaving a sickening chill when I glanced to the side as I started to cut across another street. I came to a stop in the middle of the road, and stared at the cemetery down the road.

I hadn't been there for years—long before Aric had been murdered. And I'd ached to visit his grave. To say goodbye. To say I was sorry.

Kieran had always stopped me from going.

No matter how many times I'd told him I'd *needed* it to grieve the other brother I'd lost, he'd stopped me.

"You don't know who will be watching the graves, Lily," he'd always said. *"I can't let you go. If they thought for one second you were still alive, there's only one place they know you would go. You're staying here."*

But whether or not they *were* sure I was alive, I couldn't stop myself from walking in that direction—as if I was being pulled toward the headstones that marked numerous O'Sullivans and other men and women who had pledged their loyalty to the Holloway Gang throughout the generations.

My fingers trailed over the tops of the stones of the names I knew, and lingered on Georgie's for a few seconds before I turned toward the row I'd come for, and found three marble slabs lined up.

I faltered for only a second when my mind couldn't immediately process the extra two headstones there, but my steps became slow and unsure as I got close enough to make out the names and dates etched into the stones.

Each movement I made was suddenly difficult as I realized I'd been wrong . . . all of this was wrong.

I looked at the slab on the left, marking my brother's grave, and felt an old ache deep in my chest. It was one I'd seen dozens of times—had visited so often growing up.

Aiden and Aric had been ten, I'd been eight, when two members of the Borello Gang had slipped into one of our parties and started shooting.

They were taken out, but not before six of our own had died—including Aiden.

Both Kieran's dad and my dad had left immediately, and hadn't come back until the morning with news that the mafia's leader was dead.

Retaliation. It was what happened between the Borellos and us.

Guess it was naive of me to think that someday the killing would end.

The two marble slabs next to Aiden's that I'd never seen before should have told me that.

Because I'd thought it was over until the night Aric had been murdered twelve years later.

I took a shuddering breath in and finally looked at the other headstones.

My breath rushed out and my knees threatened to give from under me.

The ache in seeing Aric's name made the hurt feel too fresh—too new. I wanted to apologize a hundred times for what happened to him. Why it happened.

If only I hadn't screamed that night . . .

But no words came. And no tears fell. Because I couldn't take my eyes off the headstone on the right.

The one that made my head light and the world spin.

The one that made me feel all wrong.

Because I was still alive. But a living person should never have to look at what I was seeing then.

HERE LIES LILY O'SULLIVAN
BELOVED DAUGHTER AND SISTER
SLEEP SWEET PRINCESS
FEB 1992 – AUG 2012

Deep down I knew I should've been there with my brothers—I should've been there in Aric's place.

Kieran had said he was trying to prevent someone from recognizing me at the cemetery . . . I should have known he was lying. Should have known he was protecting me from the shock I now felt.

Because he'd known saying goodbye was something I would never be prepared for—not when this was what I would be met with. Not when seeing a headstone meant for me made me feel so lost. *Displaced*.

Not when I was now desperately struggling to find the cord that kept me tethered to earth.

Forcing my stare away from the headstone, I rushed through the cemetery and back to Holloway Estate.

I pulled the glasses off my face and prayed I wasn't seen by anyone, shoving them into my bag as I ran. But as soon as I crossed onto the property line near my house, the night with Dare and the pain in my chest from the cemetery was quickly forgotten.

Something wasn't right.

The hair on the back of my neck stood on end and my heart rate slowed. Everything seemed so loud, but there was no sound.

It felt so much like when Kieran slipped away and Nightshade took over, but this . . . there was no way to explain *this*.

I slowed as my eyes darted everywhere, looking for anything that might explain what was making the night air feel so off. A loud crash suddenly came from the guesthouse, and I slipped, landing roughly on the grass when I tried to quickly change my direction.

I crawled back a few feet before rolling to my knees and pausing as I strained to hear anything or see anyone in the windows. And that's when I remembered . . .

I'd left the lights off.

Something so much greater than terror slid through my veins, paralyzing me for long, torturous seconds as I waited—praying I would see Kieran walk past one of the windows.

But as I waited, hopelessly praying while someone destroyed my house, I realized what else was missing. What else was *off*.

Conor would've been the first to realize I wasn't home. Mickey would've been the only way to get in touch with Kieran. Both would've had all of Holloway searching for me . . . and I couldn't see one member on the grounds.

Another crash came from within the small house a second before Kieran's words from last weekend drifted through my thoughts. *"They're waiting, Lily. Trust me."*

And suddenly it was the hooded figures that used the dark to their advantage that I saw, as I struggled to get up.

Breathe in.

Breathe out.

Don't let them know you're awake.

A harsh finger stroking my cheek.

Red stains on a shirt and my carpet.

Lifeless eyes.

Lines and circles.

My body began violently shaking.

This can't be happening again.

Another crash sounded as I turned and ran.

Chapter 13

FIND HER

Dare

I stared vacantly ahead as Johnny grabbed a lamp from one of the nightstands and casually tossed it into the bathroom. The sound of it shattering on the marble floor was dull . . . subdued.

Everything was compared to the roaring in my ears.

Rage, deep and pure, burned hot in my veins as my eyes slowly made another pass around the room. As though maybe I'd hallucinated the first dozen times, and everything would be different that time.

But nothing had changed other than the new destruction Johnny had caused.

There were still clothes and other touches that boasted a woman lived there, in a place that should have only been occupied by men. One man—an assassin.

"Wrecking the place is only going to alert people that we're here," Einstein said from where she rested against one of the bedroom walls.

When Johnny's response was to stalk down the hall, a crash coming from the front of the small house soon after, she clicked her tongue in disapproval.

"Well, you're certainly letting them know who *was* here if they don't come rushing in before we leave." Her tone was laced with frustration as she endlessly tapped and swiped on her tablet.

Trying to make a connection . . . trying to gain answers.

Her face had become more pinched as the last half hour had worn on—I knew she wasn't getting anywhere with the picture.

"Nothing," she said after another minute, her irritation noticeable as she dropped her arms, letting her tablet slam against her legs. "It's too far away . . . too blurry. I wouldn't be able to do facial recognition anyway because her face is mostly hidden by her arms, but I can't even get a lock on any of her features. She has blonde hair. Maybe. That's all I know."

I glanced at the phone in my hand and forced myself not to throw it through the window as I studied the picture we'd received from our snitch tonight.

The girl was sitting on the window seat, just inches from where I now stood, her head resting on her arms as she looked outside.

I clenched my teeth. "It doesn't matter. It's her. I know it is."

"But I don't know for sure." Every word from Einstein was clipped, telling me exactly how badly it was grating her to not be able to confirm the girl's identity.

"We do," I disagreed, the rumble in my chest hinting at the rage I was trying to keep hidden.

"I know what you're thinking, Dare, I do. But there are countless blondes in the world. The girl in the picture could be anyone. You said you wouldn't do anything until you had proof. This isn't proof."

"Look around, Einstein." I raised my arms to gesture to the room as I lost my fragile grip on my composure and seethed, "This is all the fucking proof we need. Not just *anyone* can handle an assassin. Men like Kieran Hayes don't allow just *any* girl into their lives. They fuck women then move on to the next, keeping them as far away as possible so they can't destroy them. Do you honestly think if Lily O'Sullivan had died that night, he would let another girl close enough to that kind of danger? Close enough to *him*?"

Einstein blinked slowly, her wide, wild eyes assessing me. "You can't force your hurt to be Nightshade's hurt."

I jerked back, caught off guard by the unexpected assault hurled at me. "I wasn't—" I ground my teeth, the muscles in my jaw ticking when Johnny slowly entered the room, his eyes narrowed on me as he put himself slightly in front of Einstein—as if I would ever hurt her.

But Einstein just stepped around him, placing a hand on his arm when he tried to stop her, and walked slowly to me. Her large eyes were full of wonder and sadness. "You're afraid of losing everything again, Dare. I know. I get it. We all do. But that doesn't mean everyone else would do what you've done the last four years."

"Ein—"

"It also doesn't mean you'll be able to keep doing it if you find someone." She arched a brow, then dropped her head to mumble, "If you haven't already."

Hazel eyes and seductive lips flashed through my mind—quieting the need to devastate the Holloway Gang for brief moments before the room came back into view. Before I remembered why we were here.

I shook my head, an argument on my tongue that I couldn't make myself voice.

I glanced at Johnny, but dropped my stare when I found him watching Einstein intently.

No, not everyone would do what I'd done . . . but I knew Kieran.

I knew what he'd lost, and was starting to get an idea for how well protected he kept the tiny house that was supposed to only be his.

I held up my phone as I turned to leave. "She's alive. Find her."

Chapter 14

LITTLE BIT OF CRAZY

Lily

My gaze darted everywhere when I found myself back on the crowded streets of downtown, unable to comprehend what I was seeing—what I wasn't hearing.

The street fair was still in full swing, but that couldn't be right.

That night—the passionate kisses with Dare—felt like ages ago.

But even as I took in the people walking around, talking and laughing as they remained utterly clueless to the world around them, I heard nothing.

Only that deafening silence that promised death and destruction.

I clutched the wall beside me as I tried to calm my racing heart. My eyes never resting on one person for long as suspicion pricked at my spine.

They found me.

They came for me.

And I wouldn't know if the next person who passed by was one of them too.

I shoved away from the wall once I'd caught my breath, and tried to keep my outward appearance calm as I looked for an open store . . . but most of the small town was shut down for the fair.

Digging into the bag I held close to my body, I snatched the glasses

I'd dropped in there and put them back on as I walked, knowing full well the disguise could be useless to anyone who might be searching for a dead princess.

I slipped inside the first open place I came across—wanting nothing more than to get off the street that was getting louder and louder as the deafening silence faded away—and nearly groaned when I realized I'd stepped into a bar, filled wall to wall with people.

So many voices. All trying to be heard over the others and the live music coming from the stage, which was like a beacon in front of a mass of dancing bodies.

It was too loud.

I resisted the urge to go back outside, knowing the noises wouldn't be any easier to handle out there on a night like tonight, and forced the same blank stare I maintained around the Holloway property as I made my way to the bar.

A man and two women stood behind the large wooden bar, the women dressed in tight pants and revealing shirts. Men from my side of the bar followed their every move with lust-filled eyes as the women made drinks, while girls tried eagerly to catch the man's attention.

But his eyes found me, narrowing as he pushed away from the bar to stalk over to where I was standing.

Before my fear could take hold at the thought of being recognized, he stopped in front of me, his lips twisting into a sneer as he gave me a once-over.

"You old enough to be in here?"

I opened my mouth to tell him I was twenty-four, but paused. It wouldn't have mattered right then if I was thirty or an eighteen-year-old trying to pass off as legal. I'd only ever driven a handful of times when the boys had snuck me out to teach me, so there'd never been a reason for a driver's license. And my parents had so rarely let me off the property growing up that Mickey had used it as an excuse to stop me from getting an ID.

I'd been well hidden and protected even before they'd faked my death.

Instead of trying to convince the man of my age, I hurried to tell him exactly why I was here. "I just want to use the phone."

"Sure you do. And I just need a million dollars."

I didn't let my emotions slip through. I didn't scream at him, begging for the phone because it was an emergency.

There weren't emergencies in our world.

There were tragedies that were repaid.

Despite the raw terror still pushing shards of ice through my veins. Despite the flashbacks from four years ago assaulting me again and again . . . I simply gripped my bag like it would give me the strength to continue on, and forced myself to stare blandly at him.

Lifeless eyes.

Lines and circles.

I blinked, chills skated across my skin, and I sucked in a calming breath as the bartender and bar came back into focus once again.

"Well?" he asked when I didn't say anything or move. "Unless you've got ID or a million dollars on you, you might as well get on out."

"I just want to use your phone."

"Look, I don't need cops in here because I served underage kids. Get on out of here."

"All I want is to use—"

"Jesus Christ, Zeke. Let the girl use the damn phone," a girl huffed as she stalked up beside him and slammed a phone down on the bar in front of me. She gave me a tight grin. "Keep it short, then head out unless you plan on showing some ID and buying something. 'Kay, sweetheart?"

I nodded as I murmured my thanks and reached for the phone. I eyed the man as I hurried to punch in Kieran's number but looked away when his glare found me again.

When the call went straight to voicemail, I quickly hung up and dialed Beck, the only other number I had memorized. Then called again. But he never answered.

I started punching in his number a third time when the phone was ripped from my hands.

"All right, that's it," Zeke grumbled. "Whoever you're trying to get hold of isn't there. I don't need you keeping my phone busy all night."

"I—"

"Now I told you to get on out . . . so turn that underage ass around, and get the hell on out. You hear me?"

I grit my teeth to keep from saying anything more, to keep from begging to let me stay there and call the guys until someone answered, and turned to leave.

And that's when I felt it. That weight that slowly pressed down on me, making me aware of every breath I tried to take.

Someone was watching me.

If I hadn't spent years learning to know when Kieran was in the same room with me, I might not have noticed it.

But this wasn't the same. My heart wasn't slowing from the overwhelming and terrifying chill that accompanied Nightshade . . . and it wasn't steadily increasing from being in the presence of Kieran.

I struggled to keep my face impassive as I let my eyes scan the crowded bar, and stilled when I found vaguely familiar eyes locked on me and closing in.

She didn't pause as she neared me, just grabbed my wrist and hauled me back in the direction she'd come from.

As we got closer to the corner of the building, I found two more familiar faces waiting expectantly on a plush couch.

"Oh, oh! Knew you'd come back to me, nerd," one of the twins called out as Libby forced me to sit.

She rolled her eyes. "Don't be an idiot, Diggs, she's not for you."

"You never know. The newbie might want a night of this," the other said. "Fuck if we didn't all see her dismiss Dare."

"She's not for you either. Both of you go. I'll find you when I'm done."

Libby's eyes stayed focused on me, darting over me questioningly as she waited for the twins to grab their drinks and leave with groans of protests.

"You look like hell," she said unapologetically as soon as they were a few feet from us.

"Thanks," I said tightly.

"Thought I remembered you speaking." Her tone was the same as it had been earlier that evening. Curious . . . something like awe driving everything she uttered to me. "Who are you? And why is it I've never seen you before this week, but suddenly you're everywhere?"

I'd wondered the same thing when she'd grabbed me.

"I also remember you not answering much . . . kind of like now." She sighed when I glanced around the bar. "He's not here."

I wasn't looking for him.

Once I'd seen Libby, I'd focused in on every nerve ending. But the comforting buzz that meant Dare was near had been absent.

I was trying to gauge if there was anyone I didn't recognize looking for *me*.

"What do you want me to say?" I licked my lips, my eyes darting across the people in the bar again. "You're the one who keeps showing up where I am, but I haven't asked why you're here."

Surprise crossed her face for only a second before the corner of her mouth lifted in amusement. "Trust me, sweetie, you don't want to play that game with me. I'll play all day long and I'll win."

"What game?"

"My mom owns Brooks Street, and I've been here with the twins ever since you went running off. Not to mention The Jack is my home away from home," she said with a satisfied smile, lifting her hands to gesture to the building we were in. "Which means you keep showing up in *my* places. Not that I mind. Not that Dare minds. Speaking of, you never told me how you know my brother. The other day he led me to believe that you don't, but I find that kind of funny because tonight it sure as hell looked like the two of you know each other really well, if you know what I mean."

I shook my head and tried to ignore the rush that spread through me . . . tried to ignore the need to feel his lips on mine again. "I didn't even know his name until you said it tonight."

She studied me shamelessly, her head tilting as she did. "He's intrigued by you, you know. And Dare doesn't get intrigued by anyone."

Excitement flared deep inside, and I fought to push it back.

"He's smart and he's cautious, but from what I've seen tonight, I'm worried he won't be concerning you. Which means someone has to be for him."

"There isn't a need to be cautious when there's nothing going on between us."

Her smirk was back and broader than before. "I doubt that."

I looked to the door, trying to mask my conflicting feelings. My need to find Conor was fighting with my need to hide. "Libby—"

"Why did you look so scared when you walked in here?" she suddenly asked, her voice dropping to a whisper. When I glanced at her again, her brow was furrowed.

"I wasn't."

"Yeah, okay . . . and my boobs aren't fake," she countered with a dry look. "I'll talk to you all night to keep you distracted until you forget whatever's happened to you . . . but I can't help you if you keep running from everything."

"This is your idea of helping? It comes across as borderline interrogating. And I never asked for your help." With that I stood and walked quickly out of the bar and back onto the busy streets of downtown.

But I hadn't even made it past the building before my wrist was grabbed and I was yanked backward.

"Answer one thing," Libby begged.

God.

If one more member of this family grabbed me tonight, the

Borellos wouldn't have a girl left to hunt down. I'd be dead from heart failure before they could find me.

I blew out a shuddering breath as my heart painfully started back up, and pressed my hand roughly to my chest in an attempt to ease the aching. "*What*, Libby? Let it be enough for you to know that there is nothing going on between your brother and me. I'd never spoken to him before tonight."

She held up her free hand, waving her fingers at me. "Totally not what I was going to ask you, or any of the dozens of questions I want to. Earlier you said you had to leave, but now you're right back here. It's only been about forty-five minutes. Why did you have to go?"

Forty-five minutes?

No, it felt like it'd been hours . . . *lifetimes*.

My head shook, the motion sluggish as I fought my exhaustion from the night. "I just needed to leave."

One of her eyebrows ticked up. "Earlier you seemed anxious and kept looking around. When Dare came back from running after you, he told me that you'd been afraid when he'd caught up to you—that you'd thought he was someone else. But you're still in town, asking to use a phone at a bar."

I stared blankly at her as she spoke, trying to figure out where she was going with this, and worrying what her next question would be.

"Where are you going right now?"

"It's none of your business."

Eyes as dark as her brother's dragged over me repeatedly before she insisted, "Then you're coming home with me."

A startled laugh escaped me. "What? No, I'm not."

"So then you have a home? You have somewhere you can go?" she asked, challenging me. "Because I feel like if you did, you would be *there* instead of *here* trying to contact someone. I feel like you wouldn't have so perfectly replicated what Dare described to me earlier when I just stopped you from walking away from me." Libby glanced at her nails and gave a noncommittal shrug. "But what do I know . . . right? I'm not observant or right or anything."

I stared at her with my mouth open, unsure how to answer her. Because I did have a home, but I couldn't go back there now. I didn't know if the Borellos were still there. I didn't know if they were waiting for me.

They'd hit on the perfect night.

Mickey and Kieran were out, Beck and most of the other men were working as well. Conor had been called off for the first time. Only a few men remained on the property, and I didn't know if any of them were alive.

Libby eyed me carefully, the haughty expression suddenly gone. "Look, I might not know a lot about everything, but I do know women. Because, well, duh. You were breathing fast when you first walked into The Jack, and your fear was enough to make everyone in there think the cops were about to come charging in."

"That's an exaggeration," I whispered, but she just held her hand up again.

"You've refused to give me or any of my friends your name at least a thousand times now—"

"Another exaggeration . . ."

"—and while I may not be a human lie detector like Dare, you have these looks that keep flashing across your face at random that show everything you're trying to hide. And like I said, girl-with-no-name, I know women. You're running from someone, and if I had to guess, I'd say you're running from a man."

I watched her in shock, unable to say a word.

"Am I right?" When I still didn't respond, her tone filled with compassion. "Husband?"

I quickly shook my head. "No."

"Boyfriend? Parents?"

My head never stopped moving, and she dipped hers to try to look into my eyes. "Is your answer going to be *no*, no matter what I say?"

"I just . . . I can't." There was no explaining.

I *was* running from the Borellos.

And if I was being honest, the last four years I'd been running from Mickey and Kieran's broken promises. Tonight, I'd been challenging Kieran and Beck's deceit. While not all of those were the kind of situations she meant, not one of those would someone like Libby understand.

She offered me a sad smile and gently squeezed my wrist before releasing it. "If I've learned anything in my life, it's that girls need to be there for each other. Especially during the hard times." She took a step back and looked up at the bar. "Well, to be honest, this place is boring if I'm not working—especially if it's just me and the twins because they scare off any potentials. And there's a couch at my apartment that's actually pretty comfortable that could easily sleep two of you on it."

I thought of Dare, of the way he could make me feel just by looking at me, of the guilt that followed . . . "I don't . . . I don't think that's a good idea."

Libby sent me a knowing smirk that slowly faded. "It's just Einstein and me there. Look, our place is free. There's food and a huge shower. You can borrow some clothes to sleep in while you wash what you're wearing. It's better than running around the town, terrified. And tomorrow, if you need anything, Einstein and I can help you with that too."

I didn't know how to turn down her help, but I also didn't know how to accept it.

There was something about Libby that spoke to me, drawing me in and making me want to give in. Her strength. Her kindness. But I'd never slept anywhere away from Holloway.

I couldn't go home. There was no point trying to find Beck. I only knew he was in Raleigh—where most of the Holloway Gang worked in order to avoid conflict with the Borellos—a thirty-minute car ride away. And Kieran . . . well, I never knew how long he would be working or when he'd come home.

"I really just need to try to get hold of someone."

"Will they be able to pick you up?"

I hesitated, and that pause was enough for Libby.

"Then you're coming with me for now. You can use my phone if you need to. Come on," she said, jerking her head back toward the entrance of the bar. "Let's go get the twins so they can drop us off."

She turned and began walking without waiting to see if I would follow, but after a few seconds, I did.

Once I caught up with her, she said, "If you plan on running right out of town, make sure my brother knows you don't plan on sticking around."

My eyes shut, and in a moment of weakness, I welcomed the memory of his lips ghosting along mine. Of the current that bled from his skin to my own.

Forcing my eyes open, I said, "I don't want him finding out about this."

Libby lifted a shoulder. "I won't tell him. Doesn't mean he won't find out. He has his ways."

I just hoped for my heart's sake I would be gone before he did.

Glancing at Libby, I cleared my throat and murmured, "I'm Elle."

Her eyes drifted toward me and rested there for a second before looking straight ahead again. "You look like an Elle. It's been . . . different meeting you."

"I could say the same."

A soft laugh sounded in her throat. "Yeah, well. I'm a little bit of crazy, and a whole lot of drama. Get used to it."

Chapter 15

THEY'RE ALL PUZZLES

Lily

I woke, my heart already racing and arms tensed before I ever opened my eyes.

Someone was watc—

"*God.*"

Einstein was sitting on the edge of the coffee table just feet from where I lay on the couch, leaning so close to me that I could've counted the freckles splashed across her face.

"Your mouth," she mumbled quickly as she sat back to take a bite of the cereal next to her on the table. "It looks so familiar."

"So you've said," I choked out, automatically shooting a hand toward her chest to keep her from coming too close when she began leaning forward again.

"Have you had any kind of fillers?"

"What? No, are you ser—*no!*" The hand not keeping her at arms-length swatted hers away when she tried to touch my lips. "What are you doing? People have boundaries."

Her stare was unapologetic and mixed with the lingering confusion from whatever continued to plague her about my lips. "I don't have those."

"I've noticed," I said through clenched teeth. "Could you respect that other people do and give me some space to breathe?"

A feminine laugh sounded from the other side of the room before Libby came into view. "Be happy you didn't wake up to find her curled against you. Einstein likes to cuddle."

"Only because I'm so great at it," Einstein added as she lifted another spoonful of cereal to her mouth, her eyes still fixated on me.

She seemed excited almost, like she was having trouble sitting still as she studied my lips like she'd found something so rare. But there was something behind the excitement in her eyes that had my heart racing as I waited for it . . .

Waited for whatever she was silently worrying over.

"Only because you're always freezing," Libby countered.

"Yeah, that too."

I looked between the two of them, then settled on Einstein. "Please let me sit up."

As soon as she straightened, I pulled myself up into a sitting position and scooted back into the corner of the couch—away from Einstein. She followed my every move.

"Something about you," she muttered softly, as if to herself, but Libby snorted.

"Don't worry about Einstein. She thinks there's something about everyone." Tapping her temple twice with her middle finger, she rolled her eyes and whispered, "Poor girl. Her brain works so much faster than the rest of ours that she just can't figure out how to be normal for five seconds."

Einstein smiled as she took another bite of cereal, and lifted her shoulders in a quick jerk that said she wasn't going to deny what Libby was saying. "I don't think there's something about *everyone*," she argued around the mouthful of food and hurried to wipe milk as it dribbled down her chin.

Libby huffed. "Name one person you haven't tried to study and pick apart in a way that only you can."

"Well, I probably wouldn't know their name, so how could I?"

"She practically grabbed our UPS delivery man every time he

showed up so she could stare at him," Libby informed me with a dry look.

Einstein pointed her spoon at Libby, but never lifted her stare from my mouth. "But I was right, wasn't I? I told you I knew his eyes and the shape of his eyebrows . . . and I did."

Libby shook her head, her tone apologetic. "We went to school with the poor guy's nephew. He no longer delivers here. I can't imagine why."

I swallowed twice, trying to relieve the dryness there from sleep. "So, you have a thing with faces?"

Einstein's eyes darted up to mine, her mouth curling up in a knowing smirk. "I have a thing for locks and codes and puzzles." Her tone growing more eager as she spoke, her eyes now burning with excitement. "And that's all people are. Their minds, their bodies, their features . . . they're all puzzles."

And she was fascinated with my mouth . . .

One of my most noticeable features that I couldn't attempt to alter for a quick, simple disguise.

For a moment, my pulse spiked until Libby flopped onto the couch opposite me with a loud groan.

"Good Lord, Einstein. Show a little normalcy before you bring out all the crazy. We've talked about this." She kicked up her feet to rest them on the table and turned her attention on me. "I put some makeup remover and another outfit in the guest bathroom. There's already stuff in the shower if you want to take one. We can talk about whatever you've decided once you're done. And in the meantime, I'll explain to this one why you're here," she said with a jerk of her chin in Einstein's direction.

Right. Because I was just running from a man . . . trying to figure out my next move.

I had a feeling Einstein wouldn't believe the story as easily as Libby had.

And although every instinct told me to get as far away from her too perceptive stare, I'd passed out within minutes of arriving at the house the night before, so I still didn't know what I was going to do . . . and a shower sounded like heaven.

"Thank you. I, uh . . . I really appreciate it." I avoided Einstein's eyes as I scrambled from underneath the blanket, off the couch, and hurried to grab my bag.

"You shouldn't be here," Einstein said, her tone suddenly subdued.

I looked over my shoulder in time to see Libby kick Einstein's hip and glance up at me. "Don't listen to—"

"Johnny didn't like her. If he finds out she's—"

"If he finds out what?" Libby challenged with a raised brow. "She needed help, and we're helping her. By the time Dare finds out, she'll either be gone or we'll have a plan. Let it be his decision if Johnny finds out."

"So you want me to keep it from him?" Einstein asked, frustration lacing her words.

"I'm *telling* you to let it play out how it's supposed to. She didn't ask to come here, I brought her. When you find out why, I know you'll agree with my decision."

Einstein regarded me silently, her wild yet intelligent eyes darting over my face. After a few seconds, she nodded. "Fine."

From Einstein's frustration and disbelief at Libby's insistence that she not tell Johnny about me, I knew Johnny meant something to her . . . knew she meant something to him.

I wouldn't have been able to accept the task easily if I'd been told to hide something from Kieran—something I knew he wouldn't be happy about. There was an underlying tremor of panic deep in my stomach just at the thought . . . and it wasn't even happening to me.

"I don't . . ." I swallowed thickly under Einstein's heavy scrutiny. "I don't want to put Einstein in that position. I don't want to put either of you in this position. I'm gonna go."

Libby met my stare, then rolled her eyes and waved a hand in

Einstein's direction. "You're fine. She'll understand once I explain last night." When I still hadn't moved, she said, "I promise."

I took a few hesitant steps, then turned and quickened my pace when Einstein finally looked away from me.

I wasn't out of the living room yet when she mumbled, "I know her mouth."

"Oh my God," Libby groaned. "Get over yourself."

I hurried into the guest bathroom and shut the door behind me, resting my forehead against the wood as I took deep breaths to shake off the lingering feeling of being interrogated by a look alone. Finally pushing away from the door, I walked over to the sink and hefted my bag onto the counter next to everything Libby had left for me.

Another pair of sleep shorts and a fitted tank—like the ones I was already wearing from her—makeup remover, and everything to dry and style my hair. Glancing up at the mirror, I grimaced at the stranger I found there.

The contacts were still in and my hair was wild, but that wasn't the worst of it. The hours of running and sleeping had smudged and smeared my makeup, creating thick, dark circles around my eyes. I looked like I'd kissed death and had lived to see another day.

Lines and circles.

Images from the night before slammed into me, nearly knocking the air from my lungs as it all came rushing back.

They'd come for me, and if I hadn't followed Conor, they would've had me.

If Conor had been there, who knows what they would've done to him.

Had they known? Had they known I was supposed to be there alone . . . unprotected for the first time?

I pushed the thought from my mind. They couldn't have. But the threat was still as real as it had always been, and I wondered how this would all end.

I hurried to turn on the shower when my eyes started burning with unshed tears, then grabbed for the makeup remover while waiting for the water to warm up. But despite how hard I tried to choke back the tears, despite how hard I tried to wait until I was under the cover of the streaming water, they continued to fall as I scrubbed at my face and stripped out of the borrowed clothes.

A sharp sob escaped my lips as soon as I was under the hot spray of the shower, my chest heaving from the force of it.

My heart couldn't handle the fear. It couldn't handle the pain of what I'd learned over the last couple days.

I clawed uselessly at the tile wall to keep myself standing as each agonizing beat of my heart threatened to destroy me. Threatened to bury me under my grief and uncertainty and pain so that I'd never be able to find my way out again.

My emotions flared and ebbed while I dried and styled my hair, but by the time I was finishing applying my makeup, I was overcome with resentment.

I needed to continue contacting Kieran or Beck until one of them answered to let them know I was okay. I knew that.

But as I shoved my makeup into my bag, all I could think of was their lies and the work they'd been doing for Mickey—their decision to pull Conor off last night for that work—and I didn't care.

I didn't care if they thought I'd been captured by Borellos or if they thought I was dead.

Their pain . . . their fear . . . I wanted it.

I wanted them to experience a fraction of what the families of the women who were kidnapped and sold in the human trafficking ring felt. I wanted them to understand what they already had their hands in.

I shoved the glasses on my face and tensed at my next bitter thought, my chest immediately aching.

I want Kieran to never have been involved with this at all . . .

I tried to swallow past the sudden tightness in my throat, and blinked quickly when my vision blurred.

I needed to hold on to my anger.

I needed—

"Damn it," I murmured when my hand caught on the strap of my bag, knocking it off the counter and spilling the contents across the floor.

I dropped to a crouch, quickly tossing everything back inside.

My head snapped up when the door to the bathroom opened, confusion and annoyance flooding me when I realized I'd never locked the door.

But every emotion and every thought I'd been battling in that room over the last hour abruptly vanished when the person walking through the door wasn't Libby or Einstein.

A man who looked just as surprised to see me as I was him.

A man whose stare quickly turned cold and cruel as recognition hit.

And just as it had last night, the calculating look in his eyes made it feel like ice-cold fingers were slowly trailing up my spine.

Chapter 16

LOSING CONTROL

Dare

Libby and Einstein immediately stopped talking to watch Johnny and me walk toward where they stood in their kitchen. Something was off about the way they were staring at us. They were worried. I could practically feel it. If I hadn't been so focused on keeping Johnny calm, my steps might have faltered.

But as it was, I *was* focused on keeping Johnny calm.

I'd passed out sometime early this morning once my adrenaline had finally died down and woken up not long ago. By then, my rage had faded enough for me to realize what Johnny had done last night . . . what Einstein had tried to warn us both of.

I'd watched as he wrecked that guesthouse on the Holloway Estate and hadn't once tried to stop him. They would know it had been us, and we hadn't even gotten Lily O'Sullivan out of it.

Now because he'd fucked up, I had to make sure my family was safe— had to *keep* them safe—and I needed to make sure Johnny never once felt my anger or fear. If he did, if he knew I was truly afraid for our family, for Einstein, and it had been his fault . . . he'd be uncontrollable.

"Morning," I said with a practiced grin.

Libby scoffed. "I hear last night was a bust. I could've told you it was going to be. Oh, wait, I did tell you."

Einstein cut her a look before quickly dropping her stare to the floor. I tried to study her face and hands, but Johnny blocked my view of her when he slipped up to kiss the top of her head, quietly talking to her as he did.

I looked back at Libby, but she was staring at her nails.

Typical of her, but it was obvious in how tense she was holding herself that she was deliberately avoiding looking at me now.

Their unease was making me edgy, but I wondered if the girls had come to the same conclusion I had this morning. Maybe they already knew Johnny needed to remain calm.

Einstein didn't know him as well as I did, but she knew him well enough . . . and she'd been there last night for the destruction.

Trying to ignore the way their worry magnified my own, I clapped my hands and kept my voice light. "All right. Time to pack."

Libby finally looked at me, but her eyes darted twice to Einstein before holding mine. "For what?"

"Well, if you heard about the bust, then you heard that this dumbass destroyed the house." I sent Johnny a grin when he looked over his shoulder to glare at me. "Don't act like you didn't. Anyway, we have to take precautions now. Need everyone in one place in case they want to know why we were on their property destroying their shit."

"I told you they would know," Einstein said softly. Too soft. Too *anxious*.

I couldn't remember a time in all the years I'd known her that she'd shown nerves.

Johnny tensed and took a shuddering breath.

Shit.

"If they know, then they know. If they decide to do something, that's on them. That's why we take precautions." I shrugged then drummed my hands on the counter. "So pack and do it fast. Twins are already headed that way, and I'm starving."

Johnny had his head dropped low so he could whisper to Einstein, and then he was leading her out of the kitchen toward her room. My sister started following after them, but I gripped her arm and held her there until they'd gone down the hall.

"Tell me what's going on," I demanded in a low tone as I turned her to face me. Her blank stare shifted to something in the kitchen to avoid looking at me.

She huffed, but there was a slight hitch in it. "Well, I would've thought that was obvious. You're making us pack so we can all have a stupid camp out at the house, clearly I'm annoyed."

"Don't lie to me, Libby. I could see it when we walked in . . . I could *feel* it." I paused when Johnny started walking back down the hall, and lowered my voice when he ducked into the bathroom. "Neither of you would look at me once I came into the kitchen, and you're *still* refusing to look at me. Tell me what's going on."

"Nothing. I'm just going to pack and meet you at the house."

"No. You're driving with me. Johnny's driving with Einstein."

She sighed and finally met my stare. "Dare—"

"Don't," I warned, cutting her off. I opened my mouth to continue just as a loud thump came from the bathroom. I started to look in that direction, but stopped when I noticed Libby.

Mouth set in a tight line, an anxious look in her now wide eyes.

Exactly how she'd been when we'd walked in.

"Libby . . . what's wrong?"

She was already shaking her head before I'd finished asking, and when she responded, the snarky tone she usually dealt held a hint of panic. "This is bullshit. Not only do you not give us the option of staying in our place, you and Johnny came in here, forcing us to pack while you breathe down our necks. Some space would be appreciated."

I lifted my shoulders in an apologetic shrug. "That's not going to happen."

"All of this is pointless, and you're overreacting because you made a bad call last night."

"You and I both know what Johnny did puts everyone in danger,"

I said in a grave tone. "Einstein knew that last night, and he still did it. And I'm not letting you, or any member of the family, wait around for a Holloway to decide to return the favor. If they do, they'll find us all together and waiting for them."

"Where's Johnny?"

I glanced up to where Einstein was standing halfway down the hall, and jerked my head in the direction of the door just feet from where she was standing. "Bathroom."

A look of dread covered her face. "Shit . . . *shit*." Her voice started as a whisper and ended with a yell as she ran for the bathroom door, pounding her fists against it when it didn't open. "Johnny!"

Libby's hand shot out to grip at my arm. "Johnny's in there?" she asked, her voice rising with panic.

"Yeah, what's—"

"Oh God . . . *Elle*." Libby whirled around, her expression morphing into horror as she rushed toward the bathroom with me behind her.

"Who the fuck is Elle?"

"Open the door," Einstein pleaded as Libby yelled, "Johnny, he'll kill you."

"I told you," Einstein cried out between pleas and banging on the door. "I *told* you, Libby. She shouldn't be here."

I was already trying to push the girls away from the door when Einstein's voice—her tears—cut through all the chaos, stunning me.

Einstein never cried.

I knew in that second I'd had it all wrong. The girls hadn't been worried about keeping Johnny calm after last night. They'd been worried about him finding whoever they were hiding in this bathroom.

And now two of the strongest girls I knew were crying because he had.

There was a deep yell from inside the bathroom, quickly followed by Johnny cursing.

"Dare, *stop him*," Libby screamed as she grabbed for my arm again. "It's the—"

But I was already pushing her from me and yelling, "Fucking *move*, Einstein."

As soon as she was away from the door I charged into it with my shoulder, slamming all my weight into it and stumbling into the bathroom when the door gave.

I looked up as I fought to gain my footing and found Johnny pressing someone up against the wall, his large frame engulfing the other person and blocking my view. Their arms were outstretched, a knife between their clenched hands where Johnny had them pinned to the wall . . . blood dripping down their arms.

I glanced in the mirror, and my world stopped turning.

Ice surged through my veins when I saw my firefly struggling with a man who was so close to losing control.

Chapter 17

KNEW YOU WERE TROUBLE

Lily

Johnny's mouth twisted in a sneer as he took another step into the bathroom and shut the door behind him. I slowly stood from my crouch, setting my bag on the counter so I could easily search for what I'd tossed in there just before he'd opened the door.

His gaze darted from my bag to my face to the window behind me—the window I'd opened after the shower to let the steam out— then back to my face. And I knew . . . I knew as his eyes filled with rage he was assuming the worst.

"Wanna tell me what the hell you're doing in here?" he asked as he twisted the lock and slowly started toward me.

My body begged to respond, to match his steps with ones of my own, but I stood at the counter and held his stare, searching for the knife Kieran had given me and trained me to use so many years ago.

"I asked you a question, bitch," he said through gritted teeth.

"It's not—" I'd just grasped the knife when he grabbed my throat and barreled me back into the wall, my shoulder smashing into the edge of the towel rack and forcing a cry from me.

His other hand slammed down onto my mouth to mute the cry, and for a few moments he didn't move or speak. He finally released my throat to press his forearm against my chest and his hip to my stomach, pinning me to the wall and preventing any obvious attempt to fight back . . .

All the while I was struggling to reposition the knife I'd almost dropped so I could flip out the blade as pain pulsed from my shoulder to fingertips.

"I'll ask you again, but this time you're gonna answer. Got it?" His voice was hushed but no less menacing. "What are you doing in here?"

I clenched my jaw against the pain when he removed the hand from my mouth, forcing out, "It's not what you think."

"Isn't it?" His eyebrows pulled low over his eyes, and like last night, it looked like he was taking his hatred and forcing it on me. "Knew there was something from the first second I saw you. Knew you were trouble. Knew Dare was a fucking idiot for not listening to me. And now here you are . . . in a place you shouldn't be, near *my* girl." His free hand slowly moved down, his lip curling as he tightened his fingers around my wrist until I no longer had control of my hand. "I'll snap your fucking neck for even thinking about hurting her. Drop the knife."

Someone yelled just before there was a loud smack against the bathroom door. "*Johnny!*"

Johnny tensed against me and looked over his shoulder. The hand clutching my wrist loosened and his chest heaved as he blew out a ragged breath.

One of the girls yelled as she banged against the door, and soon the other's voice joined in.

I watched Johnny carefully as they yelled for him to open the door, and saw the war that raged within him. The way he responded to Einstein's distress, as if hearing her caused him pain . . . the way his hatred and suspicions overcame that pain and concern every few seconds.

I waited for his hesitation and finally flicked the blade out.

Johnny growled as he swung his frustrated glare back on me, his forearm shoving harder against my chest. "Who the hell—?" His pained roar filled the bathroom when I jammed the knife into the wrist where his hand now barely circled mine.

He tore his arm away, but before I could swipe at him again, he rammed his shoulder into my chest. "You fucking bitch!"

The air flew from my lungs as the towel rack dug into my back, but I somehow managed to tighten my grip on the knife when Johnny grabbed my hand and bashed it against the wall over and over again.

Everything ached as I struggled to suck in air to cry out for help.

Blood was steadily dripping down his arm and transferring onto my own as he attempted to pry my fingers loose one at a time, his movements sloppy as his hand trembled against mine.

"Knew not to trust you," he rasped out again as he stepped back.

My legs threatened to give out without him keeping me against the wall. But just as soon as my knees weakened, Johnny's shoulder collided with my chest once . . . twice.

A hint of a breath wheezed from my lungs.

My vision darkened.

I no longer heard the voices outside . . . I no longer heard anything.

But Johnny was there—unfurling to his full height as his hand moved to my throat, the other gripping mine to once again drive it against the wall.

My mouth opened on a soundless cry.

There was so much pain. I wanted to close my eyes, but knew I needed to stay awake. Knew I needed to hold on to the knife.

I needed to breathe . . . and I couldn't.

All I remembered was the feel of his fingers tightening around my throat and the crazed look in his eyes before he was suddenly gone, and I was collapsing to the floor.

An eternity made up of seconds passed as I struggled to make my lungs work.

Someone reached for me. I swung. My hand moving across the floor sluggishly.

And then eyes . . . those eyes.

Dark, knowing eyes.

Truth or dare.

"Firefly."

Chapter 18

FUNNY

Lily

The pulse-pounding fear I'd experienced when I'd woken that morning was absent when my heavy eyelids slid open to an unfamiliar room. But I knew I wasn't alone. If a man silent as the night could no longer hide from me, the one watching me in that moment didn't have a prayer of catching me unaware.

Besides, I'd been prepared for this.

Dark eyes were the last things I saw before everything went black and somehow, I'd known they would be waiting for me when I woke. Only now that I was awake, I didn't know what to expect.

I'd been determined to have our lives go back to how they'd been—a silent, longing dance along an invisible wall. The memory of his mouth, the ache for another taste, it was all so dangerous in ways he couldn't begin to imagine. For my sanity, for my frail resolve, for Dare's life if Kieran ever found out . . .

But now it was all so much more complicated than seeing the man who had freed me with a kiss and pretending I wasn't trying to resist a pull unlike anything I'd ever experienced—a pull I wasn't sure I *wanted* to resist.

Because I'd been hiding from him at his sister's apartment. I'd stabbed his friend. And now he was waiting for me.

I'd been raised in a world of rival mobs. In that life, shed blood came with retaliation. I hadn't been so sheltered to think the rest of the world lived the same way, but even during the short time around Dare last night, I'd known—I'd sensed it. There was a lethal darkness about him that buzzed just beneath the surface. Behind that easy smirk, he was dangerous. It wasn't hard to imagine his life might mirror my own in some ways. Ways that currently caused me worry because it was Johnny's word against mine.

Taking a deep breath, I steeled my nerves and pushed up on my elbows.

My body ached everywhere. From Johnny's hands, from the wall and towel rack, from the adrenaline crash . . . but every ache was abruptly forgotten, and I paused in my attempt to sit up when I found one of the twins and Einstein sitting on a couch to the left of the unfamiliar bed instead of Dare, talking in hushed tones.

The twin was watching Einstein intently, but she was eyeing me expectantly; her stare solemn.

"Maverick," she murmured without looking at the twin.

After a few seconds, he let loose a sigh and reluctantly left the room.

"Hi," I said once he was gone. The word was a rasp; the short syllable painful as it slid up my throat.

The corner of her lips tilted up. "Your mouth . . ."

"So you've said."

What felt like minutes passed without either of us saying another word. I wanted to ask where I was. I wanted to ask where Libby and Dare were and why Einstein was the one in the room with me—why she wasn't with Johnny.

But when I finally spoke, it wasn't to ask any of the questions filling my mind. "I'm sorry." When one of her eyebrows ticked up, I said, "I know Johnny is your boyfriend, or something like that, and—"

"And he should've never been in that bathroom with you," she finished for me. "He told me he was going to get a drink. I didn't know . . ." She took a shuddering breath. "I didn't know he would see you. I was *hoping* he wouldn't see you. He has problems with his anger, and when he doesn't trust someone, he sees them as a threat to his friends."

I started to nod but stopped when the movement hurt. "I had the window open. He saw it and . . ." I wavered, remembering the rage that had burned in his eyes. "I'm pretty sure he thought I snuck in here."

"*There*," she corrected.

"Excuse me?"

"We're at a different house. Dare and Libby brought you here."

I stilled, then slowly let my eyes touch on everything in the room as I pushed myself the rest of the way up. It was large and had masculine tones, but otherwise held nothing to hint at where I might be.

"Where is *here*?"

"Libby and Dare's family home," she responded coolly. "We all stay here from time to time."

"I don't . . . I don't think I should be here."

"Really?" she asked, sounding more curious than was necessary. "Why?"

A strained laugh forced from my chest. "Because your boyfriend tried to kill me. Because I stabbed him. Because I don't know any of you and I just—I need to leave."

Einstein watched me in silence as seconds slipped by. "A long time ago we tried to be there for my sister when she ran, but she was too proud to accept the help. Maybe a little afraid," she added softly, a sad smile touching her face. "We can be a little intimidating. But she should've accepted the help."

"Wait, what—?" I started when she rose from the couch, my bag in her hand.

"Dare told Johnny never to touch you again. If that wasn't enough for him, Johnny knows why you're here now, and he knows I'll leave him if he goes near you," she said as she dropped my bag onto the bed near my feet.

I studied her intense stare to see if there was anything there—anything that might let on she had gone through the bag and seen more than she should've—but there was nothing.

"I don't understand anything you're telling me," I said when she began turning toward the door.

She stopped, her eyes dropping to my mouth before searching my face. "Libby told me about you before the guys showed up at the house. Was she right . . . are you running from someone? Hiding from them?"

I hesitated then nodded.

"And Dare . . . why him?"

I blinked slowly, trying to absorb her question. "I don't—" Another breath of a laugh left me, the sound laced with my aggravation. "I don't understand your questions or your rapid change of direction in this conversation."

She didn't respond, only continued to watch me as she waited for my response.

"There is no *why* Dare—I can't even say I know who Dare is. I meet a friend at Brooks Street Café every week, so I see Dare there. But we've never spoken before last night, and I planned on never speaking to him again once I left. Then I ran into Libby at the bar, and she refused to let me leave without her. I thought I would be gone from your apartment before Dare ever knew I was there."

Einstein not only seemed to accept that answer, but was relieved by it. "Then all you need to know is you're safest here," she said as she once again turned to leave.

"What—*no*. After what happened today, this is the last—I *shouldn't* be here," I reiterated, stumbling over my words.

She paused, but didn't turn around. "I'll never forget how paralyzing the grief was when Johnny found my sister's body hours after she left us, because she'd been so determined to run from her ex. It's something I live with, and will continue to. It's a past that made me who I am now." Looking over her shoulder, she held my stare and whispered, "She should've accepted our help. You're safe here . . . trust me."

I watched her go, stunned into silence, then dropped my head into my hands.

A moment from the night before flashed through my mind.

Libby's hand squeezing and releasing my wrist. "If I've learned anything in my life, it's that girls need to be there for each other. Especially during the hard times."

Her words and her worry for me now made sense, and my chest ached for a girl I didn't know.

I couldn't imagine Einstein's grief because what happened to her sister was so different than my brothers, but in a way, I felt like I knew her better than any of the people I'd met last night.

But what I was going through . . . it was nothing like what her sister had.

Kieran would rather kill himself than hurt me. Beck and Conor would die for me. Aric *had*.

I was Mickey's only source of ensuring the O'Sullivan blood in Holloway. He'd do anything to keep me safe—keep me hidden.

I needed to get home.

I needed to let them know I was okay.

I snatched my bag from the foot of the bed as I climbed off it, and hurried out of the bedroom into an unfamiliar hall.

I rubbed a hand over my arm as electricity spread across my skin. I tensed, my breath catching just before he spoke.

"You planned on never speaking to me again, huh?"

I spun around, my heart rate taking off in a violent rhythm seeing him standing there, leaning against the wall with his arms folded over his chest. But the smile that had haunted my thoughts for years was nowhere to be seen now.

"It's for the best," I whispered, my words shaking from the chaos whirling inside me.

As always, every cell in my body was responding to his presence. How can the need to feel his touch . . . his lips . . . just to hear him speak again be nearly overwhelming?

He pushed away from the wall, his steps slow and calculated as he closed the distance between us. "Why is that, Firefly?"

Because you evoke feelings I've never experienced—never expected—and it doesn't make sense.

"Because I can't do this." My admission was nothing more than a breath, but it felt heavy falling from my tongue.

I bit back a whimper when he reached me, the tips of his fingers finding my lower stomach to guide me back until I was pressed to the wall.

His forearms framed my head, leaving his lips and body close enough to tease me with the memory of his touch, but far enough to torment me with the space still between us.

Space I knew I needed so I wouldn't lose my mind in his presence. *Again.*

"Can't do what, exactly?"

I searched his hypnotic eyes, trying to remember what it was he was asking—what I'd said.

I sucked in a ragged breath and had to force my eyes not to shut when the movement pressed my breasts against his muscled chest.

This wasn't sane.

Nothing could be this addictive. Nothing could be this consuming. And yet, Dare was.

"I can't be near you like this," I finally managed to say, "for so many reasons . . ."

He dipped his head, his nose trailing down the side of mine until his lips were hovering just a breath above my own. "Funny," he murmured, the word somewhere between a growl and a bite. "Because I don't want you anywhere near me or my family."

The air in my lungs rushed out when he suddenly shoved away from the wall, a scowl on his beautiful face.

"Get out," he demanded between gritted teeth.

I blinked quickly, trying to gain my bearings. "What?"

He jerked his head toward the right. "Get out. Don't come near my family again."

I'd had every intention of leaving before Dare had stopped me. If I'd found my way out of the house before I'd seen him, I would've done exactly that.

I'd just said I couldn't be near him like this . . . and I'd meant it. I had a life that was complicated enough without mixing in this man who left me feeling intoxicated and aching to be closer to him. But I'd also felt lost not knowing how I was supposed to be apart from him.

But I couldn't comprehend what he was saying. Couldn't register what he meant or the anger radiating from him and directed at me. Couldn't look at him and see the same man who saved me with his words.

Do you know how many times I've imagined your laugh?
One day I'll hear it. Maybe that day I'll be the one making it happen.

"You were supposed to be an easy fuck. You were supposed to be someone I ignored after last night—but I couldn't even get you back to my place," he said with an aggravated laugh. "All those people you met last night? They're like family. And you somehow inserted yourself in the middle of them like you had a right to fucking be there, and created chaos."

His words stole my already shallow breaths. They pierced at my chest . . . at the shattered parts of me he'd pieced back together.

"I didn't . . . I didn't mean to. I'm sorry for hurting Johnny," I whispered, honesty dripping from my hollow words. "I'm so—"

"Walk away before I drag you out of the house."

I jerked back, stunned by the hate in his tone. It was like listening to Johnny's words coming from Dare's mouth. It sounded wrong . . . *felt* wrong.

But then again, I didn't know him.

Like he said, I wasn't supposed to be here—I was never supposed to see him outside of Brooks Street. For all I knew, the Dare who'd lit my world on fire could've been an act . . . and the man in front of me was who he truly was.

I turned, but I wasn't sure if I was hurrying away from him or barely moving. I was too stunned to know. Too stunned to hold my emotionless façade as I followed the hall into a larger room.

It took a few seconds to realize there were other people in there, and that I recognized most of the faces. I caught glimpses of an older woman glaring at something—or someone—behind me, Einstein's worried expression, and Libby attempting to cover her shock with her hands, but I didn't stop to acknowledge them.

I was too embarrassed knowing they'd most likely overheard everything. I was too humiliated. I was horrified that Dare's words had hurt so much. And I was frustratingly aware he was somewhere close behind me because my body was begging to turn around, to acknowledge the current running along my skin and the reason behind it.

But he'd made himself clear, and I couldn't handle being rejected so harshly again.

So I left.

I spent the better part of two hours wandering around, trying to find my way out of the strange neighborhoods and back to the main streets of our tiny town, Dare's words playing in my mind the entire time.

"You were supposed to be an easy fuck."

"Walk away before I drag you out . . ."

With each tormenting echo, the ache in my chest spread—grew heavy.

By the time I found a drugstore, tears filled my eyes, begging to fall. But I forced them away, refusing to show the pain from a man I should've never allowed into my heart.

After buying sunglasses and a hat, I went into the bathroom to say goodbye to Elle, then hid myself from the world as I went in search of a phone.

Chapter 19

BEACON

Dare

I dug my fingers against the unforgiving wooden doors once she was gone, and hung my head as I forced myself to stay there. All I wanted was for her to be in front of me again so I could beg her to forgive me.

My chest's movements grew more exaggerated as my breaths came rougher, faster. With a roar, I slammed my fists against the door and turned to face what was waiting for me just in time to dodge the first flying object from Libby.

"You're such an *asshole*."

The object thunked against the door just as she launched the second. I caught her shoe before letting it fall to the floor, then met her glare as I turned to leave the room.

"Demitri—"

"Not now," I ground out, not willing to get into it with my mom when she couldn't begin to understand.

I sank heavily into my old bed and let my head fall into my hands as I fought the urge to stay there long enough to give her time to leave—give her time to get so far away I wouldn't be able to find her.

But it became nearly painful when all I could see was how she'd collapsed in Libby's bathroom.

Her unconscious on this bed.

The hurt in her eyes when I told her to get out.

God, she'd even apologized. A man as savage as Johnny had attacked her—and she'd *apologized* for defending herself.

"I didn't . . . I didn't mean to. I'm sorry for hurting Johnny." She licked her lips, her eyes begging me to hear the sincerity in her words. *"I'm so—"*

I gripped at my hair, my body vibrating with the need to move. To find her.

"You may be Boss, but I'm still your mother."

I lifted my head, my eyes narrowed at where my mom stood, leaning against the doorway. *"Not* Boss," I corrected her. "Never."

She lifted a shoulder then glanced around the room. "Doesn't matter if you want to be . . . you *are.* We could've easily been pushed out when your dad died. There were other men who had the experience and the drive to take his place. But everyone looked to you."

"I was thirteen."

"Says a lot about you, if you ask me. So do the words I just heard you say to that girl. Tell me," she began as she pushed from the doorframe to come sit beside me, "what guy beats up his best friend—who's already been stabbed—over a girl, and then talks to the girl the way you did."

I ground my teeth, my jaw aching under the pressure. "I'm not doing this with you."

"I've seen you look at her at the café."

My knee started bouncing, the movement becoming faster as I fought to keep myself on the bed and in that house.

"Demitri . . ."

"She's safer away from me," I finally said, the words bursting from me like a confession. "I've kept myself from her for two years. I've never—" I bit the inside of my cheek to stop myself from saying the words I'd thought so many times before.

They felt like a sin.

Like a middle finger to *her* memory.

"I knew if I let myself have her, I'd never let her go. And if they found out about her . . . I *can't* let them find out about her."

And they would. I had no doubt about it. Because like I'd thought last night, she glowed so damn bright . . . and when we were together, it was like setting a dry forest on fire in the dead of night. Finding her, letting myself care for her, would be like a beacon to the Holloways.

"It's better this way."

"Demitri." Pain bled from her. After a moment, she stood with a sigh and turned to face me. Grabbing my shoulders, she pleaded, "Don't let what happened before stop you from loving again."

"Love isn't something people like us have the luxury of. It's used against you. It's used to slowly destroy you over years. I was ignorant enough to think I could have it, and it ruined me. I won't make that mistake again."

Chapter 20

THIS IS HOLLOWAY'S FUTURE

Lily

They'd come.

The Borellos had come, and they'd left Holloway untouched except for the guesthouse.

Not one person had a suspicion it might've been someone else. Not one person was under the delusion they'd come looking for anything or anyone but me. Not one person planned to retaliate, in fear it would provoke them to come again and again until they had what they wanted.

While the men continued to argue over what to do with me, I'd sat silently between them in the conference room, determined to force all memories of Dare from my mind.

Something I'd naively believed would've been easy.

Turns out determination is just a word if your heart isn't in it . . . and my heart was back in an alleyway, being asked "truth or dare."

My heart was in Brooks Street Café, begging a stranger to cross that invisible line.

"She can't stay in the guesthouse," Kieran said decisively, pulling my thoughts from demanding eyes and soul-freeing kisses.

" 'Course not. Not anymore," Beck added. "They went right to it."

"How they knew . . ." Mickey began, then sighed. "I'm not putting her in Soldier's Row. It's empty too often when the guys are at work. She's moving back in the house. All of you—"

"No," I said suddenly, sounding too horrified to try to explain myself.

Every man in the room stopped talking to look at me, waiting for a reason for my outburst.

I stared blankly ahead, trying to think of something to say, and finally stuttered out, "I'm not staying in this house again."

"You don't have much of a choice," my dad reminded me, that razor-sharp bite present in his words.

"I can't. Not after what happened with Aric."

Not when I won't be able to get away . . .

Although I couldn't see him, I could feel the tension radiating off Kieran from where he stood behind me.

It'd been that way ever since he'd come screeching to a halt where I'd waited outside a coffee shop downtown. He hadn't grabbed me and kissed me. He hadn't thanked God I was alive. He'd thrown open the passenger door in a silent demand to get in and had sped off as soon as I'd shut it.

But as soon as we'd crossed onto Holloway lines, he'd skidded to a stop and thrown the car into park. I'd barely settled back into my seat before he was tearing off my seatbelt and pulling me onto his lap, his arms wrapping around me like steel bands.

Minutes passed with no words spoken. They would've felt wrong in that moment as my normally calm assassin held me in his arms, tremors rolling through his body so forcefully that they felt like my own.

"You're dead, Lily," Mickey's advisor said with a frustrated laugh. "You don't have many places you can go other than this house."

"I have the guesthouse."

"No," he and Mickey said at the same time, but I noticed Conor, Beck, and Kieran were silent.

They knew how difficult it had been for me to go back into the house after Aric died—knew how rarely I'd set foot in here since—but they didn't understand my need to be able to leave the property.

They didn't know about Teagan and Brooks Street. They didn't know what missing a week with her would mean to her or to me.

And I needed those few stolen moments with—well . . . I *had* needed them before this afternoon happened.

"If the Borellos came looking, then they already know I'm alive. If they know I'm alive, they'll come back. It doesn't matter where you put me on this property, they'll find me." I stood from the chair and turned to leave, catching Mickey's glare as I did. "They won't find me in this house."

I'd only made it to the end of the table when Kieran spoke. His voice was low and even, but still rang with authority. "You're staying here—in my old room. It's the best way to protect you."

I turned to look at him, that familiar resentment building slowly inside me as I did.

The first time he'd spoken directly to me since before our lives had been turned upside down—again—and it was to give me orders.

Save Lily. Protect Lily. Hide Lily. *Cage* Lily.

It hit me so suddenly it nearly knocked me back a step.

Last night. That first kiss. Feeling like Dare had freed me but not knowing what from . . .

It was this.

All of *this*. Holloway and Kieran and his constant need to protect me in a way that suffocated me.

I'd grown up on these grounds . . . I'd spent nearly every day of my life on them. Even throughout the years I'd wanted to escape the mob, there'd been no doubt I was protected within the confines of Holloway.

But this was no longer a fortress. It was no longer a safe place. It was a prison.

Mickey was my warden and Kieran was the man who had betrayed my heart and trust to keep me there.

They'd stolen the little freedom I had. And they'd left me with nothing more than a window and some guards.

"I know how to best protect me," I said tightly, my voice wavering as everything from the last week began to overwhelm me. "That's something you should've considered a long time ago."

I left the conference room and house without looking back as I headed to the guesthouse—my refuge and cell the last four years—and came to an abrupt stop when I opened the front door.

Lamps were shattered. Chairs and couches were overturned. Curtains had been torn from the wall and were heaped on the floor. The cabinets were open in the kitchen.

And that was only what I could see of the front room.

I took a hesitant step inside, then another just as a heavy hand landed on my shoulder.

"You shouldn't go in there, Lil."

I looked back at Conor, and wished I could take away the agony that so openly played out on his face. As massive and terrifying as Beck and Conor were, they were polar opposites.

Beck had been born for this life. Conor should've never seen it. He was too sensitive to survive this cruel world, but they were all each other had. And once Mickey had gotten a look at the brothers, he'd wanted them in Holloway.

If it weren't for Kieran taking Conor under his wing, I don't think he would've made it, knowing and seeing the things he did on a daily basis.

"This is my house, Conor."

"Kieran doesn't want—"

"It isn't his decision." I twisted so I could squeeze his too-muscular forearm when I whispered, "It *was* his decision for you not to be here. Stop beating yourself up."

Conor's expression went blank as he studied me.

Kieran would've never told me he'd called Conor off, and Conor knew it. I could see him trying to figure out how I knew, but he was loyal to Kieran.

"How'd you get out, Lil?" he finally asked.

"I ran."

"But *how*?"

I searched his eyes, but found no suspicion. Worry and guilt were slowly replacing the blank look he'd been holding on to, and I knew he wanted to know what had happened last night. Wanted to know how it had all gone so wrong when he wasn't guarding the house.

But I didn't know either.

All I could give him was the truth. "Out my bathroom window. I heard them breaking things, knew none of you would do that, and I ran."

He nodded, the movement slow under his grief. "I'm so sorry, Lil."

"It would've happened one day. This couldn't last forever."

Conor's mouth twitched into a grimace, acknowledging my words. "But not last night."

"Any night would've been the wrong night." I sighed as I looked back at the destruction in the living room, then carefully stepped away from Conor. "Well, are you going to stand guard or help? Because this is my house, and this is where I'm sleeping tonight."

His only response was the loud crunching beneath his heavy steps as he quickly passed through the house to the kitchen to find the broom and trash bags.

We'd barely made a dent in the living room and kitchen when a voice like steel called out, "Leave."

I straightened from where I was picking up the shattered pieces of my French press, but didn't turn to watch Conor leave the house.

"Shit, that was quite a show you put on back there," he began, forced amusement dripping like acid from his tone. "I might've been impressed with the power and determination in your voice if you hadn't stormed out like a damn toddler throwing a tantrum. You almost sounded like the queen you're meant to be."

Determination . . . there was that word again.

I finally turned to look at Mickey, not bothering to hide my hatred for him. Let him assess it how he would. "I was done with the conversation and done listening to the five of you decide what to do with me as though I wasn't in the room. As though this isn't *my* life."

"It isn't."

His response was so immediate and brutal that it stunned me. My mouth opened but I was unable to speak.

"This is Holloway's life, Lily. This is Holloway's future. You *are* Holloway's future, and we need to protect that future however we see fit."

"Protect me?" I asked on a breath. "Is that how you see last night? *I* protected myself. If the Borellos weren't so sure I wasn't kept on this property as I have been my entire life, they wouldn't come looking for me here. They wouldn't know where to *start* looking. If I had a say in how to protect myself, last night wouldn't have happened."

"If you had a say, you would be buried next to your brothers, and Holloway would have no hope for a future."

I scoffed, and couldn't find it anywhere in me to regret the sound when Mickey's eyes burned with the need to kill anything in his path. *Me.*

"There will always be a future for Holloway, Dad. If I end up in the ground next week, there will still be a future. It's just not the one you want."

I bent to return to cleaning, but froze when his next words sounded throughout the small space.

"There is no future if O'Sullivan blood isn't at the head. You'd be smart to remember that. You'd be smart to start assuring that."

I didn't move and I didn't look at him, I just stared, unseeing, at the shattered glass beneath me.

He sighed in defeat, the sound as foreign as it was fake, because Mickey would never accept defeat. "If the Borellos know you're alive, there's no reason to continue acting like you're not. You've had a four-year vacation, and you're welcome for it. It's time you remembered your place here, Princess. So do what you always planned to. Marry Kieran and have kids. Ensure our bloodline. Try to make yourself believe you can do half as good a job as I've been doing the past twenty years, and maybe the rest of the guys will believe you can too. Maybe I'll even believe you."

He acted like he was giving me the greatest gift instead of sentencing me to a life in this prison.

For years this conversation was all I had wanted. From the day I'd turned eighteen until just before Aric had died, I'd begged Mickey to let me marry Kieran.

But it had never been the right time. Even though he knew one day it would happen, it had never benefited Mickey, so he'd brushed my pleas away. And now that the day had finally come, I wished it hadn't.

Even if I'd never known what it was like to be kissed so passionately it made my soul cry, I'd still wish this conversation hadn't happened. Wouldn't *ever* happen.

Because the man who entered my bed at night, the man who kept me at arm's length both physically and emotionally, was no longer the man I'd always sworn to love. He was no longer someone I even knew. The thought of marrying him had a panic rising deep in my gut. The need to be free of this place became more urgent.

"I'll expect your engagement as your thanks," Mickey said as he walked out of the house.

His dark warning hung in the air long after he was gone, and with it hopelessness and anger.

With one conversation, Mickey had reminded me how much control he had over my life . . . had reminded me how he could chain me to this place forever. I could feel the bars of this prison tightening like a noose around my neck, and I was helpless to stop them. Helpless to stop him.

Chapter 21

SILENT AS THE NIGHT

Dare

Johnny twitched in anticipation. After what'd happened at Holloway and with Firefly the last couple days, I'd wanted to beat him unconscious and leave him back at the house.

Which is why he was next to me.

Johnny went where I went. If I stopped bringing him, he would know why. He would know he'd fucked up in a big way. I couldn't have an unstable Johnny in my house.

Besides, I needed him with me. To remind me why I was doing this. To force me to remain calm enough for the two of us when I wanted to lash out at the person responsible for me being here.

Not just here, in the darkened office of this house.

But *here*. In this place I'd spent years slowly, painstakingly pulling the Borellos out of. The place my great-grandfather and his two brothers had first put us in when they'd moved down here from Chicago.

Gunrunning and extortion. That was how we'd survived.

No business ran in this town without giving a cut to my family, and no one had secrets we didn't know about and used to our advantage.

I'd shut down the gunrunning permanently the year my dad died, just after I'd turned fourteen. Since then, I'd been trying to legitimize the family. Most of the older members weren't happy—and most were still old school like Johnny—even after fifteen years.

But with the help of Einstein, the twins, and a reluctant Johnny, I made peace with the businesses in town where I could. Offered help when they needed it. Invested in others to keep them running. Bought out businesses from burnt-out owners who were afraid of losing money—like Brooks Street. And put an end to all extortion.

Which is why being here was so goddamn frustrating.

I glanced at my phone and blew out a slow breath as I resisted the urge to shift in my seat. "Minute," I murmured to Johnny. "Less than. Stop twitching, you look like a fucking addict."

He grunted in reply, but stopped moving. Which only made him start vibrating with the need to move.

"Jesus, Johnny," I whispered just before the door to the home office opened.

Johnny went still at the sight of the older man walking through the door, unaware of our presence. I didn't need to be able to see my friend to know he wore an animalistic smile beneath his bandana. I knew him well enough.

Something unseen clicked the door shut behind the man, casting the room in darkness once again.

"Wha—"

"Have a seat, *Judge.*"

By the time the judge flipped on the light, I was leaning forward in the chair to rest my gun on his desk so it was pointed at him.

He raised his chin in defiance but his eyes were wide with fear. "The police have been—"

"Lie."

My observation stunned him, but he didn't attempt to bullshit me again.

"I told you to have a seat. I'd say it's rude not to."

His breathing grew rougher as he looked from me to Johnny,

weighing his options. He could've easily run back out of the room, but he wouldn't make it far.

Not that he knew that.

"What do you want?"

I released my hold on the gun to sit back and gestured to the chairs on the opposite side of his desk. "If you sit, I'll tell you. This can all be over in a few minutes. We'll leave, you'll be alive. You can go back to all the illegal things you do that you think nobody knows about . . . just another Saturday night, if you ask me."

"Illegal," he said with a scoff. "I am a federal judge, I would—"

I tossed a small stack of papers across the desk, rolling my eyes beneath my hood.

His face paled and mouth opened, but no excuse left him. "Where did you get this?"

"Does it matter?"

"Where did you get this? It isn't—that's not—I don't know how—"

"Don't bother telling me that isn't your signature, I've already confirmed that it is. I also have an eye witness to you signing. And what these papers tell me is that you are a dirty son of a bitch who gets off on the thought of kidnapped girls."

"They're of legal age," he stuttered after a chunk of silence.

A shocked breath punched from my lungs.

If I didn't need you, I'd let Johnny loose on you.

"They're still stolen and sold against their will," I reminded him.

"What do you want?" His eyes were wide with panic when he looked back at me. "How much do you want? I'll give you—"

"Anything?" I asked with a wicked grin hidden beneath my bandana. "Thought you might say that. I'm sure you're good for it too because you don't want to lose your job or your reputation . . . now do you?"

He sat there gaping like a fish before he started sobbing like a child.

"Fucking hell," Johnny mumbled. "Maybe they should kidnap and sell him."

I smirked. "Here's what you're going to do if you want to keep your reputation, job, and life—in that order." I leaned forward and dropped my voice, making sure he understood every word I said. "You go along like everything's how it's supposed to be. You don't tell Mickey or anyone else about our exchange. And when the time comes, you tell the FBI everything you know about Mickey's plans for this human trafficking ring. We'll guarantee there's someone to confirm you were never a part of this."

"How foolish are you? I don't know who you are, but you can't guarantee anything except for my death if I cross Mick O'Sullivan." He snatched the papers up and waved them between us. "He already has my signature. He already has payments from me. He'll have me killed if I back out now, let alone sell him out to the FBI."

I nodded toward the corner of the room, near the doors, and huffed a laugh. "I can guarantee your death if you don't."

The judge turned slowly, his jaw falling slack as he noticed for the first time the fourth man in the room.

A man as silent as the night.

Chapter 22

COMPLICATION

Lily

I was rushed by Teagan as soon as I set foot in Brooks Street on Monday morning, nearly knocking us both to the floor.

"Oh my God, I've been going out of my mind. I didn't know if you were alive. Finn said—but I knew. Somehow I knew that if anyone could escape them, it would be you. I knew I needed to be waiting for you this morning. If they'd taken you or if you'd escaped, I had to still be waiting so you would know I hadn't given up on you," she rambled as tears streamed down her cheeks.

"I'm fine," I assured her when she paused long enough to take a breath. "I'm fine. What did Finn say? I've been home since Thursday afternoon. The guys were all informed of what happened at the meeting yesterday."

A cold, hateful look crossed her face at the news. "He came home so mad . . ."

My stare immediately fell to her neck and arms, looking for any signs that he'd hurt her recently.

"Don't. I'm fine. He just came home cussing and kicking things over before he started drinking. He passed out on the couch sometime last night." Her head shook, the movement slight as if she couldn't understand. "He got a call Wednesday night. It was late enough he didn't even bother leaving the bedroom when he called his dad to talk to him about it because he thought I was still asleep. It was about your house being trashed and you missing. He's been so quiet since. He hasn't said a word or had a call with anyone else. I was sure there would've been another call with his dad after the meeting yesterday, or Bailey would've come over. But there was nothing. When he came home so angry, I thought . . . I thought . . ." Her chin wavered and fresh tears filled her eyes.

"Let's sit and I'll tell you what happened." I rubbed her shoulder in a lame attempt to soothe her, and silently led her back to our normal booth where two coffees already waited.

I'd just helped her into her side when everything she'd said finally clicked.

"Of course Finn's angry," I whispered, a disbelieving laugh punching from my chest as I moved to sit on my side. "Of course. Now that you know I'm okay, think about it. He and Bailey have been waiting for that last big thing to happen so they could overthrow Mickey. Me being taken by a Borello would've been their perfect opportunity."

I watched as realization hit, slowly replaced by horror. Teagan's head shook quickly. "You think he set this up?"

My brows lifted in surprise. "What—no. I didn't say that, I just meant it would've been perfect. The Borellos would've handed the opportunity to Bailey and Finn on a silver platter."

And suddenly it seemed too perfect.

How the Borellos knew exactly where I was. How they knew which night to hit.

If it was even them at all.

I don't know how long I'd been staring at the table in dread before I looked at Teagan again, but she was covering her mouth as her head continued to shake, this time slowly.

"Where was he Wednesday night?"

"Home," she responded from behind her hand. "All night, and I have no reason to lie for that bastard. Finn's parents had dinner with us. He and Bailey both left the room a couple times for work calls, but—"

"That's normal," I finished for her, nodding in agreement. "It's probably just a stretch. What *isn't* is that it would've been a perfect opportunity for them, and that has to be why he was so mad yesterday."

"You're right," she said after a minute, then dropped her hands to the table. "Now tell me what happened. I've been going—"

"You ladies ready to order?"

I glanced up at the feminine voice that came from beside us, and knew I wasn't able to hide my surprise in seeing her standing there instead of Ethan. He'd been our waiter every week for the last two years.

My stomach twisted when I remembered Wednesday night, when I remembered how different he was after he'd been drinking and how Dare had been there.

And this was Dare's mom's café.

I hated thinking the way he'd acted when he drank might be the reason he wasn't here this morning. Then again, he might actually be dangerous if he'd come across a normal girl.

But that wasn't something I would know.

I'd been raised to be a pawn by a man who manipulated people, bending them to his will.

I wasn't exactly *normal*.

As soon as we'd finished ordering, Teagan said, "Right. That happened too. She came up and asked for a drink order when I first got here. Said Ethan doesn't work here anymore."

My eyes fluttered shut and I exhaled slowly. "Yeah, uh, I'm pretty sure I know why. Last week—" My words caught in my throat as that familiar, heady electricity slid over my skin.

It felt like the sweetest *Hello* after the most heart-wrenching *Goodbye*.

I opened my eyes to Teagan's frustrated glare that was slowly turning more confused, and I knew without turning around that he was coming closer.

I could feel it in the way that electric current went from a soft hum to a steady buzz.

As much as I wanted to see him, as much as I wanted to experience everything he could give me again and again, I wanted to hate him for giving me a taste of bliss before ripping it away so brutally.

"Firefly."

A shuddering breath tore from me at the ache in his tone, at having him so close, but I didn't look away from Teagan. Her shock from hearing him speak wasn't lost as she looked from him to me.

"Elle, please," he begged when I didn't respond and reached for my hand where it rested on the table. "Let me talk to you."

Teagan's eyes widened at the contact, a sneer curling on her lips.

When her eyes met mine, they said more than words could.

She felt betrayed. She was furious.

"I can explain," I mouthed to her, but she simply shook her head.

"Five minutes," Dare continued. "Plea—"

"You've said enough," I whispered, slanting him a glare and wishing more than anything I hadn't looked at him.

Because that look made me want his words and his lips and his hands despite his callous rejection.

It made me want him to try to explain away what he said.

It made me want to cry because he'd crossed that invisible barrier again.

He nodded slowly. "But not what needs to be said."

"Dare—"

"Five minutes."

I looked at him warily before glancing back at an outraged Teagan.

I knew no matter what I decided then, I was going to have to explain myself. I was going to have to tell her about last week. In detail. And while I thought I'd already known—my heart needed to know how this was going to end with Dare before I did that.

"Five minutes, and then I tell you everything," I promised Teagan.

I'd barely started sliding out of the booth before Dare was pulling me the rest of the way and hurrying us through the café and into an office.

As soon as the door was shut and locked behind us, I gritted out, "You're a bastard," at the same time he said, "I'm sorry."

Just two words, but they were filled with so much pain and exhaustion and worry.

"Yes, Elle, I'm a bastard. That and a thousand other things." He slowly moved toward me, gauging my reaction as he lifted his hands to curl them around my face. "But I am so goddamn sorry."

"Don't do this," I pleaded. "Don't confuse my heart when we both know how you feel."

His brow furrowed, those dark eyes burning and begging for me to see him the way he seemed to see me. "How I feel? Firefly . . . I'm fucking terrified."

He released me and moved away, agony lining his face as he stepped back to sit on the desk.

"Of what?" I asked when the silence became too much.

"You." He tossed the word out there like it should've been obvious. "I had someone who meant . . . she meant everything to me. And she was taken from me."

Jealousy had started unfurling in my stomach before it felt like a weight settled in its place. "Oh, Dare. I'm so sorry. What happened?"

He stared at a spot on the floor for a few seconds before lifting his shoulders. "Details aren't important. It happened a long time ago. But the thought of letting myself get close to someone else, let alone care about them, terrifies me. I've spent the past two years watching you, knowing I needed to keep my distance because you intrigued me in a way no one ever has. And then Johnny . . ." He huffed, but it sounded pained. "After he attacked you, all I could see was you dying the way she'd died, and I panicked. I couldn't let that happen. I knew you had to leave before you got hurt again. Or worse."

I released his name on a breath, unable to voice it any louder when his pain was tightening my throat with emotion. "I'm sorry. I know it doesn't help, and I know they're useless words when you've lost someone . . . but I *am* sorry."

"Like I said, it happened a long time ago. But what I did to you— what I said—I don't know how to take that back."

"Why tell me?" I asked, catching his stare. "Why not let me continue believing you wanted nothing to do with me?"

"Because all I've wanted since you walked out the door was to find you again." He slipped off the desk, his large frame so commanding and comforting as he moved toward me. "I've been counting down the damn hours until this morning because you've consumed every thought. You lit up one night . . . and I can't go back to the dark after that."

"My life is complicated," I warned as he pressed me up against the door.

His expression suddenly fell into an unreadable mask. "I've been told."

"I can't give you what you're wanting."

He gently eased his hand into my hair to cradle my head. "So, there is a boyfriend . . . and from what Libby and Einstein said, he's someone you're running from."

"No. No, it's not like that. It's so much more complicated than that."

"Libby was sure you were running from someone the other night. I can't protect you if you don't tell me what you're running from."

"I don't—I *was*, but I don't need to be protected," I said, the words coming out more harshly than I intended. "I know how to protect myself, but that doesn't change what's happening in my life."

He studied me for a few seconds before nodding. "Okay. You can't give me what I'm wanting," he murmured, tossing my words back to me. "Does that mean if it was someone else . . . if it was one of the twins?"

I relaxed against the door and him, and fought the urge to show him everything I was thinking and wanting to do. "You know that's not what I meant. You didn't have to ask."

"I'm not the one who keeps running away, Firefly," he said softly as he brushed his thumb along my cheek.

"You *forced* me away."

His mouth twitched into a frown at the reminder. "I'm afraid of what will happen to you if I keep you by my side, and there's shit happening in your life that makes you run from what you want. But we're still here," he said, his voice gruff as he bent his head closer.

"You dragged me in here."

His answering glare was almost enough to make me smile in that moment.

"You wouldn't be in here if you didn't want to be."

"I wish I'd met you in a different life," I whispered as I lifted my hand, trailing the tips of my fingers along his lips. "I've wanted something else for my life for so long, I can't remember a time where I wasn't planning to get away from North Carolina. And yet, even as those plans continued, I've hated the thought of not seeing you every week. After the street fair—" I bit down on my lip to stop the words from tumbling out, but held his stare as they begged to be freed.

After you freed me.

After you forced me to acknowledge how much a stranger had come to mean to me.

After you made me crave you in a way I've never experienced.

"But it doesn't matter what I want. I wouldn't know how to let myself have it. If I'm honest with myself—I know I can't. And if I took what I wanted, it would result in heartache for so many people, and too many lies told to you."

One of his brows lifted slowly. "Really?"

"I can't tell you what's happening, and there would come a point where you would demand to know. Don't deny that."

From the way his jaw tensed, I knew he wanted to.

I placed my hand against his chest and put the slightest pressure there. "So I think it's best for everyone if we say goodbye and I go back to my booth, and dream about a life where we might have been."

He let me push him away slowly, his face etched with frustration as he watched me reach for the knob to unlock and open the door.

"Goodbye, Dare."

I'd barely turned when he slammed the door shut and pressed my back to it again.

"Then lie to me," he begged just before his mouth fell onto mine.

One of my hands had been braced on his chest, whether to steady myself or continue pushing him away, I wasn't sure, and I no longer cared. Because my fingers were now curling into his shirt to pull him closer as I melted into his arms.

He held me tightly, like he was afraid of what would happen if he let go.

A fear I understood all too well.

With the hand that wasn't pinned between us, I brushed the tips of my fingers along his jawline and moaned into his mouth when he deepened the kiss. His tongue teased mine, coaxing more from me that I willingly gave.

More of my mind, more of my heart, more of my soul.

I knew right then he could have it all, and I would still find more to give, because nothing in my world had ever felt as right as kissing him.

"You're such a complication," I whispered against his lips, and felt him smile in response.

"You're a dream inside a living nightmare, and I'm a bastard for pulling you in."

I looked up to see him watching me, anguish filling his eyes.

"A selfless man would have let you walk away."

Everything he said was as if it was taken from my own mind. Dare had no idea just how terrified I was for him, and yet, I would fail if I tried to stay away from him.

"If I was selfless, I would've never set foot in this café. I would've never looked at you or thought of you. I would've never let you kiss me." My voice dropped to a whisper. "I wouldn't be considering impossible things that terrify me for so many reasons."

He dipped his head, brushing his mouth along my jaw, back to my ear. "Don't be afraid."

My knees weakened and my heart raced, and all I wanted was to let him continue the slow tortuous dance his lips were making down my neck.

I wanted so, so much.

But one of those terrifying reasons was Teagan, and I knew she was waiting for me—knew we'd been in the office for longer than five minutes.

"I need to get back to my friend before she comes looking for me," I managed to whisper when he lightly nipped at my neck.

Dare stilled for a second, then breathed a low, "Shit." He stepped back enough to look at me, but didn't release me. "When will I see you again?"

"I don't know. Next Monday?" I offered, making the words sound like a question that he didn't find amusing. "I don't have a phone. I don't know when I'll be anywhere or where I'll be except for here."

He stared at the door for a few seconds, then nodded grudgingly. "Okay."

"I'm sorry. I'll try to be around, but I can't promise anything," I said as I opened the door and took a step back.

"How am I supposed to find you?"

"Wait for me to light up the dark," I teased as I slipped out of the office.

"Truth or dare," he called out just as I rounded the hall to take me back into the main part of the café.

I paused, a smile pulling at my lips as I turned to face him. "Don't you know what I'll choose?"

"I can't read your mind, Firefly. I only know what you'll choose when you're afraid."

"Then *dare*."

Surprise flickered in his eyes and that carefree grin lit up his face. But his voice held a hint of hesitation and worry when he pleaded, "Give me you."

"I already have. I could deny and fight my feelings for you for the rest of my life, but I can see it was never a choice with you. But our lives . . . they aren't ready for the fallout of this."

And I hate every obstacle preventing us.

His brow pinched in confusion, but before he could question me, I turned and hurried back to a silently fuming Teagan.

Minutes passed as we watched each other. I opened my mouth at least a dozen times to tell her about Conor being sent away and running into Ethan at the street fair, but it never seemed right.

Because this had started two years ago.

And Teagan knew that.

"I hope you know what you're doing," she finally hissed when I failed to speak. "You're not just ruining your life and a lifelong relationship, you're destroying the hope of an entire *family's* future. That includes mine." Her tone was bitter and harsh, but her eyes filled with sadness. "And your ogling guy? What was his name, Darren? You've just ordered his death from a guy he'll never see coming."

Chapter 23

I'M DROWNING

Lily

I woke a couple nights later to a touch so familiar, it was as if it was my own.

It was comfort and home.

It was everything that was supposed to mean my future.

And it was full of pain.

I bit down on my lip to keep the tears at bay when they blurred my view of the large window before me, and forced each breath in through my nose and out through my mouth.

Breathe in, Lily.

Breathe out.

He pressed his forehead against the back of my head, inhaling sharply when he felt the tremor I wasn't able to suppress.

"Lily," he said softly, his voice as rough as it'd always been.

I'd always loved his voice. The gravel behind every word, whether it was seductive or filled with malice.

"Lily, don't cry."

"I'm not," I whispered, but he knew.

"Everything I do is for—"

"Me?" I asked, choking on a laugh. "Sending Conor away was for me?"

Kieran didn't tense. He didn't give any indication that he was surprised I knew. Probably because he wasn't.

"I thought you were gone," he said after a moment.

No excuses. No explanations.

That wasn't his way.

"I thought you were gone, and it would've been my fault. I would've walked through hell to bring you back to me."

Sadly . . . I wouldn't put it past Kieran to try to accomplish that task.

"Don't you understand I don't want that?" I asked, then tried to turn in his arms to face him. When he stopped my movements with his firm hold, I begged, "Let me face you."

"Lil—"

I huffed, the sound bordering on a frustrated growl, and ripped myself out of his arms to get off the bed. Once my feet touched the floor, I turned, meeting his lethal stare from where he now stood directly behind me.

That look would terrify anyone else.

But I knew the emotion hiding behind it. I knew the shock and hurt.

"I never wanted the man who would pick a fight with the devil to bring me back to life. I never wanted the man who would lock me up and treat me like a prisoner instead of loving me as his girlfriend. I never wanted Nightshade, Kieran. I wanted *you*."

He stood there, still as a statue while he waited to see if I would continue.

"If you want to beat yourself up over what happened last week, fine. I can't talk Conor out of doing it either. And according to Beck, you're still beating yourself up for what happened to Aric."

The slightest twitch in Kieran's jaw and his fingers was the only indication I'd hit home, but I didn't stop.

"But if you haven't noticed, I'm here. I'm still here, Kieran. I don't need you to tighten security on me. What I need is for you to have *been there* the last four years. I *needed* you to take me away like we planned.

I *needed* you to talk to me after I came back last week, not give me an order then disappear for nearly a *week*. I've needed you to love me and to let me love you in a way that is real—"

"You think I don't love you?" he asked suddenly, shock and rage fighting for dominance in his voice.

I stared at him with my mouth opened for a few seconds, then finally admitted, "I know you do, but I think you've forgotten *how*."

His expression fell, panic filled his eyes. "Lily, I—don't you see—?" He stopped talking as abruptly as he shut down every emotion that had managed to leak through.

A sad laugh tumbled from my lips at the sight.

"I see what you show me," I said, the words no more than a breath. "Don't forget that I know you, Kieran. I've known you my entire life. I grew up learning what emotions you hid from the world, and what your silence meant to everyone, including me. But you were always there. There wasn't a day that went by that wasn't filled with you. In the last four years, there hasn't been a day with you . . . and I've needed you the most in that time."

"Lily . . ." He blinked, flickering away the emotionless mask for a few precious moments. "I love you." He ran his hands through his shoulder-length blond hair as he took a few steps away from me, but came to a sudden halt. "Do you still love me?"

I wanted to disappear in that moment. I wanted to lie to him. I wanted the truth to be something different than it was. Because the truth was . . . "I don't know."

A look of horror crossed his face, one he didn't try to hide. Or couldn't.

"You've been gone," I tried to explain when an eternity of minutes passed in weighted silence.

He flung his arms out to the sides, his voice reverberating off the walls when he yelled, "I'm doing all of this for you."

"How can anything be for me when I don't want this, Kieran? You and I *never* wanted this. But you changed your mind and left me to slowly suffocate in this prison alone." My head dropped and a muted sob fell from my lips when I realized he still didn't understand. "You've asked me to see what you're doing, but why can't you see that I'm drowning?"

Kieran was suddenly beside me and pulling me back against his chest. The motion was as familiar as it was unwanted. "You think I can't see you? You think I'm not here to make sure you *don't*? But I saw how my mistakes destroyed you all those years ago. I fucking watched someone try to tear you away from me. If I hadn't done everything I have been doing the last four years, I would have watched them succeed. There is nowhere we could run that they wouldn't find us. The price of staying in this life is heavy, heavier than I ever imagined. But I would choose this path again and again over watching you die."

Another sob wrenched from my chest when he suddenly released me. Turning, I eyed Kieran where he now stood six feet away, his chest heaving with ragged breaths.

"And if this destroys us?"

The corners of his eyes creased before that emotionless, lethal mask of my assassin fell over his face. The only betraying movement was the ticking muscle in his jaw. With a dip of his head, he said, "I would still choose this path over watching you die."

He took a step away, but I called out to him before he could slip away into the night.

"Why won't you hold me? I, God . . ." I sighed and rubbed at my aching eyes. "I don't know how many times I've asked you this, but if you only knew how much it slowly killed me every time you refu—" I sucked in a sharp inhale when a warm, muscled body suddenly formed against mine. Long, lethal fingers curved gently around my face.

I looked up into piercing green eyes, unable to breathe, having Kieran hold me this way.

"Kieran, I . . ." My body began vibrating almost violently, and it wasn't until Kieran's chest heaved that I realized the vibrating was coming from him. "What's—?" Words failed me when I glanced into his eyes again and saw sheer panic. But that slowly faded.

And the beast rose in its place.

He pushed away from me so forcefully I stumbled back until I hit the nightstand.

Kieran didn't stop backing away, as though he was trying to force himself to leave before he could do something he knew he'd regret. But as soon as he was standing in the doorway, he gripped the frame, his wild eyes on me.

I'd never seen him so animalistic. Not even when—

A shudder tore through me at the thought.

Kieran was calm. Always. Even as Nightshade. I couldn't understand what was happening now, but I could feel the danger rolling from him as if it was a living, breathing entity in the room with us.

"Cowards," he said through clenched teeth.

"What?"

"Cowards stab people in the back. That's what my dad always said. That's how he trained me."

When he didn't elaborate, I shook my head. "I don't understand."

A look of anguish filled his face that was so unlike anything I'd ever seen from him that it stole my next breath. "*Understand.*" When I only stood there watching him, he said, "I refused to be a coward. You know how I do it, I know you do."

Of course I did. Everyone knew how he worked. "Pray Nightshade doesn't find you. He'll slit your throat . . ." I studied Kieran's expression as it started to make sense.

He nodded when he saw understanding light my face. "And I look all of them in the eyes while I do it. I can't put you in front of me, Lily. I know it's *you* when you're there. But that doesn't mean there isn't that part of me. And all it sees is the death it *needs*." He scrubbed his hands over his face, the confession hushed as if he was admitting his greatest shame.

Considering he'd kept it from me our entire lives, I wondered if it was.

"I can't put you in front of me," he repeated as all the emotion slid from his face, leaving hardened eyes.

I nodded numbly for a few seconds, watching him with new understanding that led to new pain.

Intimacy had always stood like a barrier between Kieran and me.

One he'd never tried to push past. One he'd never even tested until tonight.

And now I knew why.

He'd acknowledged his greatest strength in his job was his greatest weakness with me. He'd *accepted* it when I'd needed more . . .

"I know you. I know that beast inside you. You could've told me. And if you'd asked, I would've spent the rest of my life trying to help you overcome what Georgie engrained in you."

"Do it," he begged, the roughness of his voice betraying the lack of warmth in his eyes. "I can't do what you're asking. I can't put you in that kind of danger. But say you'll spend the rest of your life with me."

My mouth parted on an exhale as pain and confusion threatened to destroy what was left of my heart.

"Kieran . . ." I whispered, unable to continue.

"Kieran!"

I jumped when Mickey's voice rang through the house, my questioning gaze moving from Kieran to the hall behind him. All the while his intense stare never left me.

"Marry me, Lily," he said, his voice suddenly soft.

Mickey's loud steps sounded in the hall, followed by his voice. "Jesus, you have a phone for a reason, boy."

A horrifying realization hit me then. "Mickey put you up to this . . . didn't he?"

Kieran was so thrown off by my question that Mickey easily shoved his way past him and into the room.

Before Kieran could respond, a sharp laugh burst from my chest. "I've been with you for over ten years, and you only ask me to marry you once my dad *tells* you to? When he demands that we secure the future of *Holloway*?" I asked, disgust dripping from each word. "Or did the two of you come up with this together? Have Mickey prepare me for your proposal while reminding me of my *place* here, like I'm nothing more than a pawn or one of the Soldier's Row whores."

Mickey whistled and raised his hands, as if he was surrendering. "You shoulda answered your phone. Could've avoided this situation that, if you haven't noticed, is a bit on the awkward side."

But what had started out as awkward was now tense, and Mickey was too stupid to feel the change in the room.

Or he didn't care.

Kieran's expression was as impassive as ever, but his wrath clung to him like a second skin as he stared down Mickey with the intense hatred I'd always known he held for him—before he'd started working as Underboss.

Mickey twisted one of his hands that was still in the air to look at his watch, then clicked his tongue. "Time is a-ticking, Kieran. Got places to go, people to see, plans to settle, and traitors to silence. So let's head out," he said as he took a step toward the door. "You've got three minutes to be in the car."

Mickey didn't make it another two steps before Kieran was suddenly in front of him, yanking Mickey's head back with a fist full of hair and a knife to his throat.

"That girl . . . your *daughter*? She's not alive or here for you to *secure* a future," Kieran bit out in a terrifying tone. "She's here because she's mine. She's alive because she fights—"

The room swayed seeing the beast Kieran tried so hard to keep away finally unleashed, but my blood ran cold. I took a step toward the two men when I saw why Kieran had suddenly stopped talking.

"Mickey, *no!*"

"Well, hello to you too, Nightshade," Mickey said with a dark snicker as he pressed his gun harder into Kieran's stomach. His finger already tight on the trigger. "Now, I think you might be mistaken.

I don't need *you* for Holloway. If you kill me now, I guaran-damn-tee you my finger's gonna slip. Then who is Holloway left with? Lily. Only Lily. And I guess you'd just be passing her off to the next Under-boss. Which, if you think about it, is your buddy Beck."

The calm on Kieran's face slipped for a fraction of a second, but it was enough to make Mickey laugh again.

"But if you don't back the fuck off me, my finger still might slip."

Kieran continued to stare Mickey down as seconds passed at an achingly slow pace. The look so terrifying and at peace it was fascinating to see. Mesmerizing even.

In movements too quick to track, Kieran released Mickey and backed away, his knife already hidden before Mickey ever lowered his gun or his head.

Mickey's actions were so sluggish compared to Kieran's I almost wondered if Kieran *had* slit Mickey's throat before freeing him.

But then Mickey sighed. "Nothing like thinking you might lose your life to get your adrenaline pumping. Keeps you young, I guess." He winked at Kieran, then glanced at his watch as he headed for the hall. "One minute."

By the time I was facing Kieran again, it was as if nothing had happened tonight.

No fighting, no showing me his greatest secret, no threatening Mickey . . .

He just stood there, watching me carefully with that ever-present expression that hinted at nothing, yet was somehow so incredibly intense. After nearly a minute, he turned to the dresser to change his shirt then began digging around in his sock drawer.

"You weren't supposed to be in the house the night Aric died. *We* weren't," he said with his back still to me. "I'd made plans to take you somewhere since your parents were out of town. Your dad knew. Aric and Beck too." Twisting around to face me again, he shut the drawers behind him but kept his head low.

The sight made my heart pound so forcefully I knew the assassin standing before me could hear every beat.

"Your dad called that morning while we were still in bed ... remember? Told me to go on a job with Aric for him since he was gone. Once that was done, there was another call just for me. And then another. Every time I set foot on the property, he somehow knew and would send me back out. I knew he was trying to stop me from taking you."

"Take me where?" I asked when he didn't continue.

After planning to run away for so long, I knew it wouldn't have been something he would've told Mickey. Knew he wouldn't have continued to do Mickey's work if he'd been planning to get us out of Holloway.

"The last time I'd gotten back, there was another call. Before I could answer it, I heard your screams and that gunshot." Kieran finally met my confused stare, his eyes haunted as he closed the distance between us. "You would've never been in your room with them if Mickey wouldn't have been trying so goddamn hard to stop this," he whispered as he slipped a jewelry box into my hand.

My eyes burned with unshed tears. My heart that had been pounding so hard just moments ago now felt like it was in an iron-tight vise, slowly being crushed.

"Everything I do is for you, Lily," he whispered against the top of my head before pressing his mouth there.

When I opened my eyes, he was gone.

I turned, making my way to the bed. Placing the box on the nightstand, I said, "I'm sorry, but I can't marry you."

The words were just a breath to the empty room, but the freedom that came with them felt so overwhelming it was as if I'd shouted them.

"I don't belong to you anymore, Kieran. I haven't for a long time. You left me to die in this place, and that's something I will never be able to forgive."

Chapter 24

NO ID, NO DRINKS

Lily

I stared at the jewelry box as I had so often since Kieran had placed it in my hand nearly twenty-four hours before.

The ring had been his mother's.

I knew without ever having met her. I knew without opening the box or ever having seen it before. He'd told me about it so many times growing up. The one piece of her he had that he'd been saving for me.

She'd been incredible, according to Georgie. One of a kind. The kind of woman you find and never let go of.

She'd looked the darkest parts within him head-on and loved him just the same.

I wondered if she'd lived past childbirth, if Kieran would've still grown up to become an assassin, or if she would've softened the cold man who'd emerged from a violent childhood.

Then again, knowing the kind of man Georgie had been, it might've been inevitable. Although I was sure she would've still loved Kieran just the same.

Just as I had always done.

Before . . .

Everything he'd told me last night had left me confused—

disoriented with the knowledge that I was already completely gone to someone else.

After years of fighting for him to see me, years of begging for him to speak to me, and finally accepting it would never be the same—that I had lost him to my father and the mob. Suddenly he'd been there . . .

The broody boy I'd adored.

The haunting teen I'd fallen in love with.

The deadly man I'd given my heart and body to.

And he'd laid bare everything he'd hidden from me.

My soul had ached while I'd lain awake for hours, unable to sleep as I replayed every word, every touch, and every expression that had penetrated his hardened shield.

But the reminder of every sleepless night because of his coldness was never far behind. Because of his unwillingness to try. Because of what he was currently doing as though he didn't have an ethical bone in his body.

Throughout it all, and every other thought today, had been a pair of dark, knowing eyes.

And with the aches and confusion came a sudden inability to breathe when I thought about Mickey forcing me to put on that ring. What it would mean. The look on Dare's face if he ever saw it. Most importantly, how I was supposed to destroy my heart and devote my life to Kieran when my mind and heart would always scream someone else's name. *Crave* someone else.

With that thought, I jumped out of bed and ran for my closet. Once I had my bag and everything I needed out of the crawl space, I hurried into the bathroom.

I didn't let myself think about what I was doing.

I knew if I did, I would talk myself out of it.

Soon, I was sneaking out of my bathroom window and off Holloway property, and twenty minutes later, I was slipping into The Jack downtown.

I slowly made my way through the crowded place, my eyes scanning everyone as I did, looking for Libby or anyone else I might recognize from Dare's *family*. I was a few feet from the bar when I nearly thanked God out loud, because there Libby was, standing directly in front of me.

Skin-tight, torn shirt and an easy smile on her face that looked so much like her brother's as she used a liquor bottle to give a customer a mock-salute.

As soon as he turned away from the bar with shots in hand, I slid into his spot, waiting for Libby to look up.

"What can I get you, sweet—" Her eyes widened with excitement, her smile became genuine. "Elle!"

"Hey, underage. You better have ID this time."

I looked at the man I'd fought with for the phone last week, and froze as I thought of what to say and do.

"Zeke, she's cool," Libby said, hitting the guy on the shoulder. "She's with me."

Zeke dropped his unwelcoming glare to Libby. "No ID, no drinks."

"Please, like I would." She rolled her eyes, and gave me a look before addressing Zeke. "She's not underage, you dolt. She just comes from one of those communities. You know . . . . no phone, no ID, no nothing. She's experiencing everything for the first time. Staying with us while she does."

I somehow managed to keep my jaw from hitting the floor as Libby easily made up a new background story for me to what I assumed was her boss, then slowly slid my eyes to Zeke.

He was looking at me like he didn't know if he should kick me out or ask if I knew what a computer was.

"No ID, no drinks," he repeated before turning away.

Libby laughed as she watched him go, the sound low and throaty. "God, the guy is a silver fox, but he's a little too caveman for my tastes, if you know what I mean."

I didn't.

She turned to face me again. "So, what brings you to my home away from home?"

I bit my lip as a rush of excitement and fear swirled in my stomach, but couldn't stop the smile from spreading across my face. "I want to find your brother."

Her smile mirrored my own then shifted into a knowing grin. "I see. We're all still at my mom's house. He's there." Pulling her phone out of the back pocket of her dark jeans, she checked the screen for a second then put it away. "You happen to be in luck, because I'm not closing tonight, and I get off in about twenty minutes. You can follow me."

"I walked here."

Her eyebrows lifted, that grin widening. "Of course you did. Well, you can walk if you want, but it's about three miles from here, as I'm sure you remember. It'll be faster if you wait for me to drive you."

"Okay," I said, the word too soft in my nervousness.

"Go find a booth, I'll find you when I'm done. And, Elle," she called out when I started to leave, "what I said still stands. If you plan on running, make sure my brother knows."

"I don't," I replied immediately, not realizing until after she'd gone back to work the meaning of my response.

It was the first time in my life I'd ever said I planned on staying in this confining town.

And it had been instinctive.

Chapter 25

A TRAP

Dare

"It's happening soon. Sooner than we'd originally thought," he said from where he stood a few feet from Johnny and me. "And he's planning something big with it."

"Bigger than a fucking human trafficking ring? Bigger than signed contracts from twenty of the richest and most influential men in this and the surrounding states, vowing and paying to go in on bidding wars to *own* these women?"

Eyes that promised destruction locked onto me, but he didn't move or give any hint to what he might be thinking. "Something he's trying to keep from me," he said after a few tense seconds. "Something he's excited about. And that's not good. We're leaving tonight, and we'll be gone for a few days. Use that time to look for what he's planning."

I blew out a pent-up breath and scrubbed my hands over my face. "Fine. I'll—" A growl sounded in my throat when I looked back up, only to find him gone.

I got really tired of him doing that.

"I'll tell you what we need to be looking for," Johnny mumbled from beside me as he shifted his weight from foot to foot. "A trap to take us the fuck out of the picture. 'We'll be gone for a couple days.'" He scoffed. "Right. More like, 'Come on, idiots. Walk into my trap.'"

I shook my head as I turned to head back into the house. "Shut up, Johnny."

As soon as we walked into the house from the back door, I knew I'd walked into something Johnny had just imagined.

It felt like a trap.

Except my sister was at the helm of it.

"Hi," I said, wary of her too-large smile and the fact that she was sitting on the couch with my mom . . . and they weren't arguing.

"Well, hello, favorite brother of mine," she said in a saccharine voice. "Have fun working?"

Instead of responding, I let my gaze drift slowly around the large living room and over to the small part of the kitchen I could see from where I was standing.

"I told you," Johnny hissed through gritted teeth. "I *told* you. That motherfucker."

"Enough."

I could hear his teeth gnash together as he clenched his jaw tightly in order to keep from talking. Where Johnny had been anxious and shifting the entire meeting in the backyard, he was now tense and shaking as he stood still, waiting for whatever threat to reveal itself.

"Earth to dumb and dumber," Libby said with a huff. "You look like two wolves sniffing out dinner."

My hand twitched toward my gun when I heard movement off to the side, but relaxed when Maverick walked into the living room from the kitchen with sandwiches in hand and a wolfish grin on his face.

"Hey, hey. Libby tell you about your little present?"

"Hard to when they walk in and stop to pose like they're Batman and Robin," Libby muttered as she looked at her nails. "Johnny, Einstein's waiting for you in your room."

Maverick staggered to a halt in front of us, his eyes darting from Libby to Johnny.

Johnny didn't move.

After clearing his throat, Maverick turned and went to sit in the chair near the couch, dropping one of the sandwiches in front of Libby with a mumbled, "Here," as he did.

She made grabby hands at the sandwich before snatching it up. "And what did I do to deserve this? You know, besides being the only amazing one in this entire effing house." Without giving Maverick a chance to respond, Libby fixed her attention on Johnny. "If I were you, I would go before you find yourself in trouble with your girl."

"Go," I said when he made no move to leave.

As soon as he was out of the living room and headed down the hall toward the room he and Einstein shared, Libby sent me a wide smile before taking a huge bite.

Maverick wasn't eating, his head was turned just enough so he could look in the direction Johnny had just left.

"Someone tell me," I demanded.

"Maybe you should walk into the kitchen and find out for yourself."

I studied her challenging glare for another second before heading toward the kitchen, where I could hear Diggs giving directions on how to make a sandwich.

And came to an abrupt stop when I saw the girl sitting on a stool, watching Diggs with equal parts fascination and disgust as he made the biggest sandwich I'd ever seen.

Firefly.

She inhaled sharply, one of her hands reaching for the back of her neck just before she twisted on the seat to look at me.

"Dare," she breathed, her lips stretching into a smile.

I don't remember moving.

I only remember staring at her like she was a hallucination, and then the next second I was pulling her off the barstool and into my arms.

I buried my nose in her hair, breathing her in to assure myself she was there and real, and I hadn't lost my fucking mind.

"Goddamn Firefly," I whispered, then brushed my lips against her neck.

She pushed against my shoulders until I reluctantly set her down. "Is it okay that I'm here?" she asked hesitantly. "I know it's kind of late to ask now. But you can tell me to leave and I—"

I captured her mouth with my own, needing to taste her and needing her to know I didn't want her anywhere else but with me. "Where did you come from?" I asked against her lips.

"I told you I'd try to be around."

A laugh rumbled in my chest as I leaned back to look at her. "I thought you meant the next day. Or the next. Not . . . shit, *days*."

Her brows pinched, worry and exhaustion and pain filling her eyes. She tilted her head like she was going to explain then shook it instead. "I'm sorry."

"You made no promises," I reminded her.

But from the silence that settled between us, it didn't make it any easier for her than it had me.

"Dare," she began, but paused, her eyes widening and body stiffening before she slowly looked to the side.

When I looked in that direction, I found Diggs hunched over the island counter with a dopey grin as he watched us, with that massive sandwich falling apart between his hands.

"Come on." I curled my arm around her shoulders, pulling her close as I led her through the kitchen to the hall toward my room.

That constant buzz between us burned hotter, the space between us grew thick with tension. As if the energy around us already knew where this night was headed.

As soon as we were in my room I kicked the door shut and turned her around, pressing her against the hard wood—my grip tight on her hips and face buried in the crook of her neck.

"I fucking missed you," I whispered, confessing the words that had bounced through my head since she'd walked away from me at Brooks.

A stuttered breath left her, one of her hands curling against my stomach where it rested.

"Too soon?" The words were meant to be a tease, but I couldn't hide the worry in my tone from what her response would be.

Her head moved slowly from side to side, her free hand finding my jaw. Her soft fingers trailed lightly over it before she put the slightest pressure there, forcing me to lean back so she could look into my eyes.

"I think I missed you before you ever entered my days and my dreams."

Fuck, this girl . . .

I dropped my forehead against hers, pulling her body closer. "Firefly." Bending to nip at her lips, I asked, "How long do we have?"

"Don't wonder."

I met her eyes, the question in my own, and felt her shrug against me.

"It'll waste the time we have if you do. It'll make it rush by if you know."

I had a feeling any time with her would be over too soon because it ended.

"Then I won't," I promised, leaning forward to capture her mouth just as someone started banging on the door.

"Open up."

Before I had a chance to tell whichever twin was in the hall to fuck off, the door suddenly flung open.

I grabbed Elle and twisted her away when she was shoved forward, my hard glare set on my sister from where she stood flanked by the twins in the doorway. Diggs was eating out of a large bowl of popcorn with a shit-eating grin.

"Can I help you?" I asked, my teeth clenched.

"Uh, hello?" Libby scoffed and stepped forward to reach for Elle, but I pulled her deeper into my room. "Didn't you hear? We're having a sleepover."

I stared her down like she'd lost her mind. "Yeah, we have been for a while now."

"No, no. In the theater room. And it's been planned since yesterday, which means the two of you can't be the only ones who don't come."

"I just got Elle back, I'm not spending the night with all of you."

Diggs pretended to stab himself with the bowl. "Dude, we spent all day setting it up. Let us impress the nerd with our fort-making skills."

"There's food," Maverick added.

"Dude, so much food," Diggs said as he shoved more popcorn in his mouth. "Did I say there was a fort? The whole theater room is a fort."

A soft laugh sounded from the girl in my arms. "Didn't you just eat?"

Maverick huffed. "Popcorn and candy, newbie. There's always room for it."

Libby shot me a look. "I think it's so cute that you think we're giving you an option."

"Fort," Diggs said again, drawing the word out. "Fort."

Elle craned her neck to look up at me. "What's a fort?"

The twins made a sound that might've been a cry. Even Libby looked stunned.

"Aw, baby. It's okay. Diggs has got you, and he'll be real gentle with you."

A warning growl sounded in my chest when Diggs reached for Elle.

Instead of backing away, he just looked at me. "My nerd doesn't know what a fort is. Let me educate her before I cry for the childhood she never had."

"I know what a *fort* is," she said, shifting in my arms. "But I don't know about a fort you can make in a room that has to do with sleepovers and food."

Everyone gave me a look, and I knew right then I'd lost the argument.

I blew out a sigh. "All right, we'll go."

Libby snorted and gestured to something behind me with her chin. "Again, like you had an option."

I looked over my shoulder, my jaw clenching when my eyes caught on what was missing. "Where's my mattress?"

"Dude, what part of *fort* don't you understand?" Diggs asked, exasperated.

Cutting her amused gaze to where Elle was trying to silence her laughs, Libby said, "Come on, I have clothes you can change into."

I reluctantly let her go when she started following my sister, then turned to change into a pair of sleep pants.

By the time I made it into the theater room, my frustration had only grown.

I had hours or minutes or seconds with my girl . . . I didn't want to spend it with the rest of my family.

But the moment she walked in, her eyes lighting up and mouth falling open in shock and fascination as she took in the large room, my anger cooled. It was worth it to see her experience something like this.

And Diggs and Maverick had gone over the top, as usual.

Some of the couches and recliners were pushed to the walls, with a few left near the front of the room, with five mattresses scattered throughout the empty spaces behind them.

One of mine included.

Blankets and pillows were everywhere, three times the amount that were normally in the room. A table full of food sat near the door. Sheets hung from the ceiling, making it feel like we were in a giant tent, and waiting to be used for makeshift walls later on. The only openings were at the main doorway, the door leading to the bathroom, and the front of the room where the screen was.

"This is a fort?" Her question was nothing but a breath when she reached me, her hand grasping for my shirt and her eyes still taking everything in.

"This is the twins' idea of a fort. Most are smaller. Much smaller. About the size for a couple kids."

Her head shook, the action so slight I wasn't sure she knew she was doing it. When she turned to face me, a breath of a laugh blew past her lips before they pulled into a wide, unrestrained smile.

And everything stopped.

My heart.

Time.

The whole goddamn world.

The second it happened, I knew deep in my gut I'd been waiting my entire life to see that smile.

Elle was beautiful . . . she had always been beautiful. But the smile she'd offered everyone since the first day I'd seen her held so much sadness and pain. Like she didn't know how to truly smile anymore.

This?

It was like a punch straight to my heart, because I knew it was real and it made this beautiful girl fucking breathtaking.

I wanted to wrap her in my arms and never let go.

I wanted to kiss that mesmerizing mouth.

I wanted to pull her away from here so I could have her to myself.

But I was afraid to move . . . afraid to do anything that would take that smile from her.

"Oh, oh!" Diggs came crashing into us, pulling Elle away and waving his free arm in the air, like he was showing off the room to her. "What do you think, nerd?"

"This is amazing," she said, her eyes searching me out . . . that smile never fading.

"Damn straight it is. Get you some food." He gave me a victorious look as he released her and walked back to the door. "And you were gonna skip this."

I wanted to hug him and thank him for forcing us all into this, but my attention caught on Johnny where he stood near the door with Einstein, his wide, crazed eyes locked on Elle.

I grabbed for her, pulling her close and slanting a warning glare Johnny's way when Diggs called out, "And it's official. Locked in, fuckers."

The brief moment of wanting to hug him vanished when I watched him yank on the door a few times, then walk away with a satisfied smirk.

"What does he mean?" Elle asked when I bit out a curse, a slight tremble in her voice.

"It means he just locked us all in here for the next five hours."

It meant he just locked Elle in here with my psychotic best friend.

And now that her smile had vanished and her chest was moving too quickly with her rough breaths, I couldn't get her out of here at all.

"No . . . No, I can't—"

I pulled her close, pressing my lips to her ear and trying to calm her. "It's just the twins' way of making everyone stay. It's not just a theater room, it's a safe room. There's a lock on the door, and when it's activated it won't unlock for five hours. Johnny won't come near you."

She shook her head, her tongue darting out to wet her lips as she pushed away enough to look at me. "No, you don't understand. I can't be here that long."

My stomach dropped, knowing I wouldn't have even had five hours with her.

And that's when I understood why she didn't want me to know how long we had.

I would've made every minute count if I hadn't known.

I would've dreaded every minute that passed if I had.

"I'm sorry, I can't open that door. There isn't a way."

Her chest heaved, panic covering her face.

"Fuck, Elle, I'm sorry."

She shrugged, the action a quick jerk of her shoulders. "We can't change it."

"Nerd," Diggs called out from the food table. "What are you doing standing over there? Get some food and find a couch. Movie's starting in five."

Elle watched Diggs for a few seconds before looking back at me. The panic slipped from her expression, leaving resolve in its place. And with a steeling breath, she offered me a smile.

A pained smile.

Fuck.

Chapter 26

DON'T EVER LEAVE

Dare

"Boo," Libby yelled from her spot at the front row of couches a couple hours later, drawing out the word and making Elle jump.

I pulled her back against my chest when Maverick mimicked her tone, firing back, "Shut up."

"I vote something else," she continued. "Anything else."

"We already played your vote," Diggs said. "Now it's ours."

Elle turned her head so she could whisper, "What's happening?"

"Libby hates shoot-'em-up movies." I nipped at her bottom lip, my hands tightening on her thighs when she relaxed against me and sighed.

God, this girl.

It hadn't been long into the first movie before her worries about being in the room had faded.

Guess I could thank Diggs for that too since he'd come back to talk to her every ten minutes. Getting closer and closer until Elle had gone from sitting beside me to being between my legs with my arms tight around her.

Sometime near the end, hands had started searching, and I'd pulled her onto my lap, her mouth parting for me when I'd begged entrance.

It'd been like high school all over again, and I was pretty damn sure I was having the best night of my life.

She pressed a gentle kiss to my lips, turning when gunfire sounded through the speakers, filling the room. Her chest moved with her muted laugh. "Killed two guys in the first five seconds. Very telling. Very different from Libby's vote."

Also extremely loud.

And I knew from experience it would put Libby to sleep and hold the guys' attention. Which meant Diggs would stop wandering back here.

I went back to trailing my fingers up and down Elle's thighs, every few passes going higher than the last now that I knew we'd be left alone—every few passes barely catching the hitch in her breathing when I did.

She gripped the edge of the blanket that covered us tighter, her teeth sinking into her bottom lip when my fingers brushed the inside of her thighs. And then again. But her eyes never once left the screen.

On the next pass up her legs, she shifted, spreading them wider for me in a silent plea and the greatest tease. Because that movement had caused her to rock against me, and it was torture not to respond the way I wanted to.

I slid my hand higher into her shorts and was teasing the edge of her underwear when she did it again—that slight rocking that made my need for her grow. That made me forget where we were. That made me forget everything else except for her.

She glanced over her shoulder, her heated eyes locking with mine when I moved my hands away to grab her hips.

Hooking my fingers in the band of her shorts, I started dragging them and her underwear down.

"Dare . . ." She gripped at my hands through the blanket that covered her, her voice hesitant, unsure.

I nipped at her jaw. "I won't let anyone see you, Firefly."

Holding my stare, she released my hands and lifted her hips to let me slip the fabric off her. A groan sounded in my chest when she sat on my growing erection, rocking her ass harder against it and letting a whimper escape her parted lips.

I gripped her hips, pressing her harder against me for a few seconds before I moved my hands to spread her legs.

"You okay?"

She nodded, her breaths growing rougher.

"Tell me."

"I'm okay," she whispered, a soft cry sliding up her throat when I trailed my fingers along her sex. "Oh God."

Her head dropped back to my shoulder when I pressed a finger inside her, her hands gripped my hips when I pushed in another.

"Still okay?" I asked, my voice gruff with the need to sink into this girl.

"Yes."

True.

I held my other hand to her stomach, keeping her from arching too far away and keeping her ass pressed firmly against me as she rode my fingers. A shiver tore through her when my thumb found her clit, her whimpers and moans getting lost in the yelling and gunfire from the movie.

"Stop." Her voice was a throaty mixture of pleasure and need. "Stop, I'm going—oh, God. I'm going . . ."

A smirk tugged at my lips when I whispered, "I dare you."

She reached up with one hand to grip at my hair, her body tensing and trembling.

I quickly released my hold on her to cover her mouth when a shocked cry burst from her chest, pride surging through me as I pushed her through the tremors rolling through her body.

I kissed her cheek and lowered my hand when she relaxed against me, my eyes darting from couches to chairs to make sure no one's attention had left the screen.

She loosened her tight hold on my hair and pleaded, "Let me face you."

I helped her turn so she was straddling me, making sure the blanket still covered her, and fought back a groan when she pressed her mouth to mine, reaching for where I was straining for her.

I gripped her forearms to stop her, placing another quick, hard kiss on her lips when hurt and confusion flashed across her face.

Bending to grab her discarded clothes, I handed them to her. "Hold these and hold on to me."

That was the only warning I gave her before I stood from the couch with her in my arms and turned toward the mattresses.

I needed to thank Diggs or Maverick. Whoever had put mine in the farthest corner, away from the table and couches and doors.

I pressed my mouth to Elle's as I knelt to lower her onto it. "Wait here."

I pulled the ties that kept the sheets secured to the posts throughout the room, spreading them out to create our makeshift room, then turned to face Elle.

She was propped up on her elbows in the middle of the mattress, her eyes wide and teeth sinking into that full bottom lip as she watched me.

"Tell me what you want," I begged from where I stood. "Tell me you want to talk and we will. Tell me you want to sleep and we will. Tell me to go share a mattress with Maverick or Diggs . . . and I fucking will."

Her head fell back, a gorgeous, husky laugh bursting from her.

When she looked at me again, she lifted one of her hands toward me in offering. Once our fingers were touching, she gently pulled me onto the mattress and rose to her knees.

"I want you," she whispered, a shy smile playing at her lips as she reached for the hem of her shirt. "I want to shut out everyone and imagine a world where I never have to leave."

"This is that world, Elle."

I took the shirt from her fingers and lifted it off her, letting it fall to the floor as my eyes fell over her mostly bare body.

Trailing my fingers over the swell of her breasts, I said, "You're beautiful."

Leaning forward, I pulled one of her nipples into my mouth, my blood heating when she moaned and arched, offering more of herself to me.

I unwrapped the blanket from her hips as I lowered her back onto the mattress and hovered over her for long moments as I took in the perfection now underneath me.

Meeting her gaze, I whispered, "Fucking beautiful."

With one last kiss to her lips, I bent to suck her nipple into my mouth again, rolling my tongue around the hardened bud before moving to do the same to the other. She sucked in a sharp breath and reached for me when I bit down on the underside of her breast, but I was already moving down her stomach, leaving a trail of slow, open-mouthed kisses as I went.

"Dare." My name was a warning and a plea as I moved lower, her heavy-lidded eyes widening as she watched me.

I spread her legs, keeping my eyes locked on hers as I lowered myself, nipping at her thigh until I was hovering just above where she was ready for me.

I leaned forward to taste her, teasing her with the tip of my tongue and nearly losing my mind when I did.

She twisted on the mattress, her hands fisting in the blanket as my name fell from her lips.

I wanted to consume her.

I wanted to worship her.

I wanted to hear her whimper like that for the rest of my life.

"Please," she said on a breath when I gave her another teasing lick. "Oh God, please."

I shifted away just enough to press a finger inside her and then another. My blood heating and pounding when I finally covered her with my mouth, devouring her the way I'd been keeping myself from.

"That's it, Firefly," I growled when she tightened around my fingers, a shudder tearing through her as I spoke.

Her hands gripped at my hair, her pleas nearly silent as she writhed, trying to hold on. She cried out when I nipped her clit then flattened my tongue against her, riding out her orgasm as she shook mercilessly against me.

Those hooded eyes locked on me when I moved up her body, her mouth parted in ecstasy as she grabbed for me, trying to pull me closer and frantically tearing at my shirt as I pulled down my pants. Her legs wrapped around my hips when I positioned myself between her thighs. Her eyes fluttered shut when I pushed inside her, a whisper of a moan leaving her lips when I began moving.

Each roll of my hips brought me closer to the end when I'd just started.

It'd been too long.

And it'd never been her.

"Look at me," I demanded.

And she did. Her eyes lit up as if I'd just offered her the world with those three words, and God if I didn't want to after all this time waiting for her.

I bent, claiming her mouth the way I wanted to claim her. The kiss was rough, our lips and tongues fighting the way it felt like I was fighting to keep her.

Her fingers tightened on my back, her nails digging in and urging me faster.

Urging me to keep going.

My head fucking spun as the need to make this girl mine nearly consumed me.

But her fears and the darkness that crept back in when she disappeared had me pulling out at the last second, gripping myself in my fist and pumping my release onto her belly.

Her eyes were wide with fascination, her chest moving with her exaggerated breaths as she watched.

One of her hands slid from my back, her teeth sinking into her lip when she hesitantly slid the tips of two of her fingers through the mess on her stomach.

And, fuck if that didn't make me hard again.

"I'm sorry. I don't have protection, but I'll get some," I said, my words pushing through my rough breaths as I grabbed my shirt to clean her stomach and fingers. "I swear I'm clean. I just wasn't expecting you."

"I know . . . I know. I trust you."

I pressed my mouth to hers and whispered, "Where did you come from?" The need that swirled deep in my gut was lighting her eyes when I pulled away. "Truth or dare."

A coy smiled tugged at her lips. "Dare."

"Don't ever leave."

Chapter 27

LIKE FIRE

Lily

I blinked, trying to force my heavy eyelids to open.

The room was quiet, void of any sound other than my rapidly pounding heart and Dare's soft breathing beside me. So unlike the loud movie we'd fallen asleep to.

And I felt like I'd slept for hours.

The panic of not knowing the time—of knowing I'd fallen asleep—rushed through me quickly. Consuming and choking me.

I maneuvered out of Dare's hold and off the mattress, trying not to wake him but unable to ease my incessant need to hurry. Even still, I paused when my feet touched the cool, hardwood floor, my weight shifting from foot to foot as that electricity that thrummed between us called to me, pulling me back in the direction of Dare and the warmth and comfort he promised.

But the new day promised things too.

Even if Kieran hadn't come back last night, Beck might be home by now. Depending on the time, he could be awake soon and notice my absence.

My face pinched, an apology on my lips when I heard the mattress shift behind me.

I twisted to see Dare now on his stomach, still asleep . . .

I couldn't breathe.

That panic and fear from what seemed so long ago? It was nothing. Nothing compared to the horror rushing through me like gasoline.

One breath would light a match. One step and I would go up in flames.

Every nightmare I'd ever had was now just feet away. A reality. And it was on the man who had somehow captured my heart.

Five lines—four horizontal, one vertical. One circle.

The Borello symbol.

Not just somewhere small on his body as I'd seen that one night so many years before, but covering the entire length of Dare's toned back.

A steel fist gripped my heart, crushing it slowly as I stared, silently begging for the image in front of me to disappear.

Men who use the dark to their advantage.

Lines and circles.

Blood staining my carpet.

A stuttered breath that sounded like a cry wrenched from me, and I slapped a shaking hand over my mouth in an attempt to mute it. My world was spiraling into confusion and betrayals and unknowns. *How? How is this happening?*

Tears slipped down my cheeks as I hurried to grab the clothes Libby lent me, sneaking out of the unlocked room once dressed.

My throat ached from holding back my sobs, but I needed to get out of this house. I needed to get away from these people who were tied to the family that had caused me so much pain.

That wanted me dead.

But even as I tried to force myself to keep walking—to grab my bag and run—I found myself slowing . . . found myself stopping and slumping against a wall until I was sliding down it. I buried my head in my hands as silent sobs wracked my body.

I didn't know how to handle what I'd just seen, but I couldn't forget the past week. The last two years.

I needed to leave. I needed to get far from this place. I knew that. But I couldn't cage my heart now that it'd been freed.

I couldn't run from him because of who he was, when I'd been running to get away from myself for so long. A fact Dare had accepted without explanations.

"Then lie to me."

I shakily stood, rubbing my hands across my face in a vain attempt to brush away the relentless tears.

"Decision made?" a feminine voice called out.

I jerked back against the wall, my hand flying to my chest to calm my racing heart. "God, Einstein."

She searched my face for a few seconds, then nodded toward the living room before walking past me to head that way. Never once checking to make sure I was following her.

"I'm surprised it took you so long. Gotta say, I'm a little disappointed," she said matter-of-factly, then clicked her tongue.

"I sat down within seconds—"

"Not what I meant."

I swiped at my cheeks again to brush away any lingering wetness, huffing when I said, "Then, as always, I'm not following you."

"Not many people do, Lily O'Sullivan."

My head snapped up, eyes widening when my name left her mouth. I quickly looked around us to see if anyone was within hearing distance, but it was just us.

I tried to calm down. I tried to tell myself to channel the Lily that sat in on meetings. Blank stare, no reaction, impenetrable wall.

But I couldn't stop.

I had already been too blindsided by Dare's tattoo to respond rationally now.

"I—what did you—I don't under—"

"Relax, no one else knows," she said in a soothing tone I would've never expected from the wild-eyed girl in front of me.

I couldn't relax. She knew my name and her boyfriend's best friend was a member of the Borellos.

"If it helps you at all," she went on when her keen eyes caught my rising panic, "I've known this whole time. I told you, there's just something about your mouth."

"I don't . . . I don't understand."

"You're Lily O'Sullivan. I know who you are. Earth to the not-so-dead princess." She rolled her eyes and settled back into the chair.

"What do you mean by *whole time*, and . . . and how do you know me?" My chest hitched with my too-fast breaths, and I fought to calm myself. "Why would you let me say I'm someone else? Who are you?"

She drummed her fingers quickly on the arms of the chair as she waited for me to finish demanding answers, and sighed once she was sure I was done. "Well, I guess who I am depends on the decision you just made in the hall."

I glanced at the empty hall instinctively, then back to her. "What decision?"

Einstein's eyes rolled again, like she was frustrated with having to spell out things that should be simple. "I thought a mob princess would've put things together faster than you did, but I have my own theory for why you didn't. I figured we'd never see you again because you would've figured it out. When you showed up last night and proved me wrong, I knew a day would come when you looked like you were a step away from a panic attack because you learned something about the man you were falling for. Today happened to be that morning. But since you didn't leave, I can only assume you made a decision. Unfortunately, there are a lot of decisions you could've made. And I'm waiting to hear yours."

"You're one of them," I whispered, studying every movement she made as I did.

But she simply sat there, waiting for my answer without seeming to care that I knew.

Then again, if she was a member of the Borellos, she'd known about me and hadn't said a word . . .

"Decision?" she prompted after nearly a minute had passed.

I loosed a weighted breath, lifting my hands helplessly before letting them fall. "How do I walk away from what we have? How do I pretend he didn't completely change my life?"

"How indeed?" she asked with a raised brow.

"Look, I know how this ends," I whispered harshly, leaning in toward her so my voice wouldn't carry. "I knew when I couldn't force myself to leave. I knew before you said my name. One day he'll realize who I am. One day one of you—another one of you—will realize who I am. If I'm not killed immediately, then I'll be turned over to Demitri Borello so he can do it. But I'd rather spend my time until that day comes loving Dare, than never experiencing another moment with him."

Einstein's lips twitched into a smile. "So that's it then?"

"Yeah," I said on a breath as I sat back. "That's it."

We sat in uncomfortable silence before she said, "I finally put it together after you stabbed Johnny and everyone was waiting for you to wake up. I was putting your clothes in your purse and found your contacts in there. I wondered what you would look like without your glasses on . . . then I realized they were colored contacts. It didn't take long after that."

"So, you've known for a week and haven't said anything. Why?"

"Two reasons." She raised her hand so it was just barely hovering over the arm of the chair and lifted a finger, indicating *one*. "If you were really running from a man, then I knew exactly who you were running from, and I didn't blame you for doing it. You know who I'm dating, but I refuse to be in the same room as the man *you're* dating because he terrifies me in a way nothing ever has or will."

I started when I realized she meant Kieran. If only she knew how twisted her confession sounded to me. Or that I'd felt—and still feel—so terrified of Johnny and knew I never had to fear Kieran.

"I wanted to make sure you had a place to go." She lifted a second finger, indicating *two*. "And I was fairly sure *this* heart-to-heart would happen eventually. I wanted to make sure when it did that we understood each other. If I could keep you a secret to *this* house, then anything you found out about us didn't need to be relayed to *your* house."

"Why would I say anything to my dad about Dare or his friends?"

That hint of a smile widened. "Still don't get it, do you? I really thought you'd be smarter." When I stared at her blankly, she said, "Think about all of us, *Elle*. Who do you think we all are? Who am I?"

"Einstein."

"And what do I do?" she prompted, dragging the last word out.

"You frustrate me," I responded immediately, but as soon as I said it, I remembered her words from last week when I'd woken up to find her fixated on my mouth.

"I have a thing for locks and codes and puzzles."

"You're a hacker," I mumbled, my tone numb.

The smile that lit up her face was feral. "Johnny, well . . . Johnny's just Johnny. And the twins aren't just hanging around because they're hot. One's a tracker, the other is a sniper. Combined? They're basically our version of your boyfriend. Well, they're not silent and invisible . . . but not everyone can be like Nightshade, and at least the twins have souls."

I was too stunned to defend Kieran. Not that Einstein gave me a chance to speak anyway.

"Libby *is* actually Dare's sister. But, as you can tell, she doesn't really love being part of us. She sort of hates that she's a—"

"Borello." Horror laced my tone and all the blood quickly drained from my head. *"Elizabeth Borello. Oh God."* I shot off the couch and stumbled blindly away from it.

Libby is Elizabeth fucking Borello. That means . . .

"No. No, you're just—no."

"You made your decision," Einstein reminded me calmly.

But that was before I'd known.

The large room seemed to close in on me, a high-pitched ringing filled my ears.

"I didn't—I didn't *know*!"

Knowing he was a member of the Borello Gang was one thing. It was horrifying, but I knew I could still get past it.

Knowing he was an actual Borello? Knowing he was *Demitri* Borello, the man responsible for so many Holloway deaths? The man whose father had been responsible for even more of our spilled blood?

"Well, everybody is going to know who *you* are if you don't calm down."

I reached for the couch, but still roughly fell onto it when it felt like the world was ripped out from under me.

I'd given him my soul, and he wanted to destroy my heart. *Destroy me.*

"He wants to kill me." My voice was nearly inaudible even to my own ears.

Einstein was silent so long that I finally looked at her, but her mouth was set in a grim line.

"He's going to kill me, isn't he?" I asked, looking for confirmation and praying for a denial. "Oh God. Was it him? Was it him last week in my—" Words failed me when Einstein's eyes flashed to mine only to quickly dart away.

"We were tipped off," she finally admitted.

A sharp exhale burst from my chest, and suddenly I was off the couch again. I don't remember moving. I only knew I had been sitting, trying to stop the room from spinning, and suddenly I was across the room and headed for the front door.

Einstein slammed her weight into me, sending us both into the door and making it so I could no longer get away. When she spoke, every word was sharp and edged with frustration. "I've kept your secret, so you're going to hear me out. Someone sent a recent picture, trying to prove you were alive—which we just found out days before," she added quickly when a pained laugh tumbled from my lips. "But I couldn't use it, there was nothing identifying, and it was too far away. I told you last week, you're safest here. I meant that. The most recent picture we have of you is from twelve years ago. It looks nothing like you, except—"

"My mouth," I finished for her. I whirled around when she pushed off me. "That doesn't change who he is. That doesn't change who I am. It doesn't change that his family killed both of my brothers and tried to take me, or that he just destroyed my house looking for me. All my feelings aside, the man I just gave myself to wants to kill me." I gritted my teeth, hating that my voice was shaking. "I can't—"

"And for good reason," Einstein mumbled, then turned to walk toward the couches again.

I stood there, stunned and unable to move as I watched her sit on the arm of the closest chair so she was facing me again.

"If you were Elle and he was Dare, would you leave right now?"

A sigh punched from my chest, and I sagged against the door. "No," I finally whispered.

"If you were you, and he was just a member?"

"You already know what decision I made earlier, why are you asking?"

Without responding to my question, she continued on, "If he were to come out here right now, knowing what you know about him, knowing who he is. Would you run away, or would you stay?"

I opened my mouth to tell her she'd just prevented me from leaving, but hesitated.

Every moment over the last two years flashed through my mind. Every look. Every note. Every kiss and every touch over the last week. Every word marked on my heart.

"I would stay until it ends."

And just as I'd told Einstein earlier when I thought he was *only* Dare, member of the Borello Gang, I knew how this would end.

We were like fire, but fire never lasts. And when it's over, devastation is left in its wake.

I swallowed past the agony tightening my throat, and said, "I still have to leave now. I have to get back before someone realizes I'm gone."

"Makes sense," she mumbled. "I'll take you."

"That's not—"

"I told you, I wish my sister would've accepted our help. I know why you have to be there, and I know why you don't want to be. Let me help you because I'm the only one who can."

I wavered, thankful and wary and worried for this girl all at once. "You can't go near the property line."

"I'm crazy . . . but I *don't* have a death wish."

For the first time that morning, the corners of my mouth twitched into a smile. "If you think Johnny and Dare won't find out, then I appreciate it."

But Einstein was already walking . . . again, without looking back to see if I would follow her.

As we hurried down the driveway, she slowed and blew out a steadying breath, her eyes fixed on the ground for a moment before she met my gaze. "Do you even know why?"

I lifted a brow. "Why I would stay?"

"Dare doesn't have solid proof you're alive. He's just been told— well, and I guess your house told him all he needed to know. But do you know why he would want to kill you if he knew you *were*?"

"Because that's what you do. That's what our families do. That's what this fucked-up world we live in thinks is necessary. They steal and retaliate. Kill and retaliate. It's endless."

Surprise flickered across her face but was quickly replaced by grief. "You really don't know, do you?"

I bunched my shoulders up in a shrug and relaxed them with a frustrated sigh. "What? Is it because Kieran stopped them from taking me four years ago?"

"No." She tilted her head and looked at me carefully, like she knew she was about to turn my world on its side again. "Mickey murdered Dare's fiancée."

Chapter 28

TOO LATE

Lily

I sat on my window seat, head pressed to the glass as I replayed everything I'd learned that morning.

"Mickey . . ." Einstein said uncertainly as she drove me back toward the Holloway property. *"He snuck into Dare's apartment in the middle of the night about two months after your funeral. Dare woke up to his fiancée, Gia, being torn out of their bed. Your dad didn't make a big production out of it, just said, 'This is for Lily' and shot Gia in the head."* She glanced at me a couple times before focusing on the road again. *"That's why Dare wants to kill you. Not because you're an O'Sullivan. Not because they didn't get you four years ago. It's because his fiancée died as retaliation for your death that never happened."*

It all seemed unreal.

Einstein had told me I was never supposed to be taken the night Aric died. The man who killed Aric was Johnny's cousin, and he wasn't supposed to have even touched me or woken me.

She hadn't said a word about why they'd been there or Aric's death, but all I kept thinking was if that man hadn't touched me, I wouldn't have screamed. Aric wouldn't have come running. That man wouldn't have shot Aric and wouldn't have been killed by Kieran. Dare wouldn't be planning my death, and his fiancée would be alive. And Kieran and I would be somewhere far away.

We'd be living such a different life.

I would've never met Dare.

I couldn't help wonder if things had gone differently, if Kieran and I had left as planned, if I would've ever known I was missing something amazing in my life. If Dare would've been happy with his fiancée—or, I guess *wife* now—or if he too would've felt empty. Or if we were only so perfect for each other now because of the death and grief that had led us to this point.

So many what-ifs.

"Why are we mad at that window?"

I jerked back, startled by Beck's voice, and twisted to look at him from where he towered above me. "What?"

"Just wondering why we're mad at the window. I think I might've missed that meeting, and if I'm gonna be mad at some fucking glass, I oughtta know why."

The corner of my mouth curved up but quickly fell. "I'm not mad at the glass, you hulk."

"Sure looked like it." He settled himself on the other side of the seat, his questioning stare fixated on me. "So?"

"So what?" I mumbled, trying to seem interested in the grass so he wouldn't continue asking questions.

"*So*, I'm about to leave for work and haven't seen you because you're keeping yourself locked in here. I had to make my own coffee, and it was probably the worst thing I've ever tasted in my life. I don't have your dad or Kieran breathing down my neck, so that means *I* can breathe. And you're fucking mad at motherfucking glass. So . . . tell me what's wrong."

I fell for a stranger.

Somehow, somewhere along the line, I think I fell in love with him. He's my greatest enemy, and I've never felt safer than I did in his arms last night. And even after I learned who he was, I knew there was nowhere else I wanted to be.

Tell me I'm insane.

I glanced at my best friend and offered him a weary smile. "Kieran proposed a couple nights ago. Sort of."

Beck's eyes widened in surprise and excitement as they dropped to look at my left hand, and the smile that had quickly covered his face fell when he found it bare. "Oh, well. Eh. You said *sort of*?"

"We were fighting—"

Beck snorted. "Right."

"Really," I pressed. "Actually fighting. Yelling at each other. I think you saw the beginnings of it the afternoon he left for Texas."

Beck continued to give me a disbelieving look, so I went back to looking out the window as I told him about what had happened with Kieran that night. I understood his doubt. Kieran didn't know how to argue, he didn't know how to have fights like a normal couple. He was too calm and unmoved by anything for that to happen.

That didn't mean there weren't times when we weren't angry at each other. It was just handled differently because *Kieran* was different. He always would be.

Even if I hadn't met Dare. Even if I hadn't started questioning my love for Kieran. I would've known something drastic had shifted between us as soon as the real fights began.

"Fucking Mickey," Beck grumbled once I was finished.

You have no idea.

My heart ached for Dare as I thought about how terrible it must've been for him. I knew the pain of watching your enemies kill your loved ones. But to be woken up in the middle of the night by your greatest enemy killing your fiancée? I couldn't imagine.

"Yeah . . . yeah." Something Beck had said earlier finally clicked, and I glanced at the early afternoon sky. "Wait, what time is it?"

"About three."

"You said you were leaving for work soon. You don't go in until late."

He shrugged, his playful expression suddenly hidden behind barely concealed frustration. "With Kieran and your dad out of town for a few days, Kieran wants me to do a couple things for him today and tomorrow before my normal shit. I probably won't be around until after the meeting on Sunday, but Conor will be outside."

I stared at him for a few seconds, and saw when he understood.

"You didn't know he was gone, did you?"

"No."

He heaved himself forward and pulled me into a bear hug. "I'm sorry, Lil. Just don't give up on him, okay?"

I didn't respond. There was no point telling Beck that it was already too late.

Chapter 29

BEFORE THE LIGHT FADES

Dare

"If I say the bitch is alive, then she's alive." The man's natural cockiness gave way to frustration at being asked again. But he wasn't able to hide his nervousness. His pulse was visible in his throat from where I was standing.

I grabbed Einstein's tablet from off the desk, then walked calmly to where the man sat, guarded by Johnny. I pretended to look at the picture I could recreate in my sleep for a few moments then turned the tablet so the screen was facing him.

"What exactly did you expect us to do with that? You said you had a picture proving she was alive. This is just a shitty attempt at Photoshop."

He gestured to it, his anger growing. "That's her. Ask any of the guys, they'll all agree."

"They'll agree it's a girl with blonde hair."

"It's the girl I have to put up with on a daily basis," he said with an edgy laugh as he grabbed a pack of cigarettes out of his pocket.

Despite how nervous he'd been ever since I'd had Johnny pick him up and bring him here, that was the first outright lie I'd caught.

"Lie," I said on a low growl.

His eyes darted to mine as he placed a cigarette between his lips. "She's in that house every day, all day unless she's in a meeting with us. She's at that window most of the time."

"And yet, she wasn't there."

"Not my fault you idiots don't know how to play fetch."

Johnny twitched from behind the man, wanting to inflict pain I knew he'd been dreaming of. But this guy was only running his mouth because he was trying to seem like more than he was.

"Or maybe she wasn't there at all," I said, hinting he'd led us on a wild goose chase. "Maybe there was supposed to be a trap you forgot to set. Do you want to know what I do to people who set me up?"

For the first time since he'd been thrown in here, his pupils dilated and brow started to sweat.

"Truth or dare," I continued when he didn't speak.

"Uh, I . . . I-I—"

"Truth," I answered for him. "Did you set us up?"

"No, n-no. I'll h-hand deliver her to y-you," he said, stuttering over himself. "I'll do it personally."

If I wanted her brought to my feet, I'd send the twins to hunt her down.

"I don't want her delivered to me," I said with a sneer, then bent so I was face to face with him. "I want to rip her away from the walls she's been hiding behind. I want to watch fear fill her eyes before the light fades from them. Now get back to the hole you crawled out of before you piss yourself in my chair. Next time you see her, call me."

I watched as he scrambled to leave, then met Johnny's shocked glare.

"You let him go?" he asked, disgusted.

"He has access to what I need," I replied with a weighted breath as I tossed the tablet back on the desk.

Staring at the now darkened screen, Gia's face flashed through my mind and was immediately replaced with ice-blue eyes as cruel as the devil.

"This is for Lily."

If Gia died as retribution for the princess, then that princess needed to die.

Chapter 30

WITHOUT LOVE

Lily

I'd known as soon as I'd woken this morning I wanted to get away. It was like Beck had said the day before—Kieran and Mickey were gone. They weren't breathing down our necks . . . and I knew Beck would be gone doing errands for Kieran.

With Kieran's proposal, I'd known I wouldn't be able to handle staying on Holloway with nothing to do but stare out a window. I needed to have a day where that suffocating weight wasn't pressing down around me—one where I wasn't worried about getting back before someone noticed I was gone.

After finding out why I was being hunted by the Borellos and that I was the reason Dare's fiancée had been murdered, it felt impossible to face him.

But I didn't know how to stay away from him.

So it didn't surprise me when I found myself walking into Brooks Street Café.

I didn't look around to see if he was there, I didn't need to. My body wasn't thrumming with excitement as if it knew the person I had been made for was close by. I kept my head down as I sank into a booth, and tried to wrap my head around my life, as I had been for so long.

I wondered if it was even possible.

I'd wondered a lot of things lately . . .

I tensed when someone suddenly slid into the booth across from me, then loosed a slow, calming breath when I recognized the older woman.

Dare and Libby's mom.

My dad killed your husband. Do you even know? What would you say if you did? The ache in my head was nearly as real as the one twisting my stomach.

When tense seconds passed in silence, I ignored the tightening in my throat and managed to say, "Hi, Mrs.—"

"Sofia. Please, just Sofia."

"Sofia."

"I called Demitri, he knows you're here."

My eyes widened, and I sucked in a sharp breath at his name—*that* name—being said so casually.

His mom dropped her head into her hand and stifled a laugh. "I'm sorry. *Dare.* Those kids and their nicknames." With a roll of her eyes, she murmured, "Maybe one day I'll catch up with them."

I forced a twitch of a smile. "I would've never known that was his name." When she lifted her brows in surprise, I explained, "My friend thought he said Darren. I thought maybe that was his real name, and Dare was just a shortened version."

And what I wouldn't give for that to be true.

She laughed softly, her tired eyes studying me curiously for a moment. "Every time I see you, I think you look so familiar."

Because I look like my mom like this, I thought to myself.

With these colored contacts, if I lost the glasses, I looked exactly like she had at my age. And rival families tend to know everything about each other . . . unless the kids are kept sheltered from the world, as I had been.

"Dare thought the same thing," I admitted, only because I didn't want to seem rude by keeping silent.

"It's strange, almost like déjà vu." She quickly shook her head, then glanced at the delicate watch on her wrist. "Well, I suspect they'll be here soon, but I wanted to catch you before they arrived."

I sat silently as she played with a gold wedding band hanging from a chain around her neck, trying not to worry over why she wanted to see me—trying not to apologize for everything my dad had done and demand to know why their family had delivered their share of heartache.

"You make Dem—Dare . . . *Dare* happier than he's been in a long time. I don't know if you know that, or if you'll ever know." She eyed me, suddenly wary, then whispered, "But I need to know why you're here."

"What?" I asked, stammering over the word when she caught me off guard at the direction of her question.

"You come and go, there's no way to get in touch with you. I know because they talk, and we're all in the same place for the time being. Well, Libby talks," she added quickly. "And it worries me for my son when he's already suffered so much. I want him to be happy, and I want him to have things he thinks he can't . . . but I see what he won't because he's too caught up in you."

I stared at her blankly, waiting for her to acknowledge who I was.

"He's found the first girl to make him feel again, but I would rather him hurt for a while longer than be played by you until you decide you're done with him and disappear."

When I realized she wasn't going to continue—that she was finished with her rant—I let the blank mask lift from my face.

Disappearing was something I'd been planning forever, but it wasn't something a Borello would know. Hell, Beck didn't even know.

I thought back through everything she'd said about me, thinking about it through her eyes, a mother looking out for her son whose fiancée had been taken too soon, slowly nodding as I did. "I understand."

My stare fell to the table as I opened my mouth to speak again.

Every explanation to all of her worries was on the tip of my tongue, but somehow felt wrong.

"I could try to reassure you, but they would only be reassurances from a girl you don't know, and a girl who is already worrying you. They wouldn't mean much." I met her steady gaze. "However, he saved me, and I think—given time—I might save him from what's haunting him."

"You know," she assumed, her voice low.

I dipped my head in confirmation. "But he wasn't the one to tell me."

I wanted to tell her I was sorry for her loss, because clearly it would've been her loss as well, but I didn't know how when the reason for it was sitting directly in front of her.

Instead, I found myself saying, "The thing is . . . we're not meant to be. And yet, I'm positive I was made for your son, and he was made for me. I fell in love with him knowing the universe would do anything to prevent it. And it's an irreversible, world-changing kind of love."

Sofia studied me for a long while before asking, "And my son knows you feel this way?"

"No," I answered honestly. "Because like you said . . . I come and go. But I have no intention of playing him and then leaving him."

"I wasn't expecting anything that honest, and I don't think I'll get anything better than those answers." She cast me a little grin. "I should probably get back to work before Demitri comes in and catches me grilling you."

"Sofia," I called out when she slid out of the booth and turned to leave. "Do you think it's possible to love someone after a tragedy?"

"You want to know if my son loves you?"

I shook my head, because of all the reasons I'd asked that question, that hadn't been one of them.

I wanted to know if *she* thought love was possible after all she'd been through since she'd never married again.

I wanted to know if love was possible for Kieran after everything he'd seen—after losing his best friend. After losing me.

I wanted to know if love was possible for Dare when his heart was so full of hatred and his mind so set on revenge.

I wanted to know if it was wrong of me to love after having witnessed both of my brothers killed in front of me.

I wanted to know from the mother in front of me, because mine had never recovered after the loss of my brothers.

She stepped forward with a soft smile playing on her lips, and bent to rest her arms on the table, her face close to mine. "There are tragedies all around us, Elle. Every minute, every hour, every day. Without love, there would be no reason to stand back up and fight. Without love, there would be no reason to live."

With a gentle squeeze of my hand, she pushed away from the table and left me alone with my thoughts. Left me alone with hope.

Chapter 31

GHOST

Dare

I stared down my mom as she walked away from Elle, and was met with a challenging glare offset by her warm smile. But instead of stopping or saying a word, she just gestured to Elle with her eyes and continued to the back.

Palming the scrap of paper, I kept my pace steady as I walked toward the girl I'd been aching to see, and slid the paper onto the table in front of her as I passed by to sit across from her.

The soft inhale that came from where she sat was enough for me. The unknown . . . it was worth it.

God, what was she doing to me?

"Can I read it?" she asked softly, mischievously as she eyed me with a raised brow.

I nodded toward the note, silently urging her to.

She bit her lip, her eyes lighting up as she unfolded the paper, her mouth breaking into an unrestrained smile when she read the words.

God, you're beautiful.

"Charmer," she whispered, her attention fixing on me. "What made you start writing the notes?"

I leaned forward to take the paper from her fingers. Setting it to the side, I gripped her hands in mine. "I had to say something to you. Whenever I saw you, I wondered what could be so bad about your life that even your smiles looked sad. But at that point I still couldn't bring myself to come near you. And then I noticed there would be days where you would write in a notebook. Just for a minute or two. But your friend would spend the whole hour reading whatever you'd written, and you always had this look like you were in denial and waiting for your life to change. And then I *had* to know. So I wrote to you."

"I kept them all," she admitted shyly.

My eyebrows lift in surprise. "Yeah? Is that what your friend spent hours on?"

"No." She huffed, but the amusement was suddenly gone from her face. "No, she, uh . . . she has a thing with trying to understand dreams and nightmares. I would write down my nightmares, and she'd try to figure them out."

"Just your nightmares?" I asked. "Do you have a lot?"

"Only one. It's recurring."

I could tell from the tense way she held herself she didn't want to explain, so I didn't push her. I wouldn't want to relive my nightmare over and over again.

Unable to avoid it any longer, I lowered my voice and asked, "Why were you gone?"

Her expression fell, panic and pain so intense flashed across her eyes before she was able to drop her head to stare at her lap. "I'm sorry. I—" A pained sigh ripped from her, her jaw clenching in response.

I slipped out of my side and into hers, wrapping my arm around her tensed shoulders and pulling her close. "Elle, hey . . . what happened?"

"You knew I would have to come and go."

"Yeah, but I thought you'd say bye."

Her face pinched and mouth opened to respond, but nothing came out.

Pressing my knuckles under her chin, I lifted her head until she was looking at me again. I pushed the glasses back up her nose, the corners of my mouth tilting up in response to her amused huff. "Elle, what happened?"

"I panicked," she said with a shrug. "You knew I couldn't stay as long as I had to. I should've been gone as soon as those doors unlocked, but I fell asleep. As soon as I woke up, I panicked."

My chest rose and fell roughly once when I picked up on the catches on some of her words.

She was telling me the truth.

Kind of.

There was something she was keeping from me.

But she'd warned me this was what she was going to do, and I'd begged her to lie to me just so I could keep her in my life.

And I was a bastard for being frustrated with it, because there were about a dozen things I was keeping from *her*.

"If I pushed you too fast that night—"

"No. No," she said adamantly. "I needed to get home. I was already so late. That night . . . God, Dare, I can't explain—"

A body slammed into me just as a voice cried out, "Oh, *oh*!" from behind me.

I glared over my shoulder at Diggs as he pushed Elle and me farther into the booth, but quickly forgot about him when I found his brother sliding into the other side. "Hey, hey, newbie."

"Leave," I demanded on a low growl just as Libby walked around the corner of the booth and pulled Diggs out from behind me.

"My seat," she said with a roll of her eyes before looking at us. "The second you left, they decided they were coming too. Clearly we couldn't let them come alone."

Before I could ask what she meant by *we*, Johnny and Einstein came into view. He was leading her with his hands on her shoulders while she tapped relentlessly into her phone, whispering to herself the entire time.

The dark look I sent him when they slid in next to Maverick didn't faze Johnny. And I knew no matter what I said, he had no plans to leave. Despite the warning to stay away from her, he still didn't trust Elle.

Johnny had nearly lost his mind the other morning because she'd stayed over. Upending the couch was all he'd gotten away with before I'd put an end to it.

But his rage had only amplified when he'd realized how much she was growing on everyone else. Not that I'd expected anything less.

Anyone who could stand up to an unhinged Johnny would have my family's respect. Anyone who could make me this happy after Gia would automatically be welcomed by all of them—Johnny not included.

That said, I didn't want the little time I had with Elle to be shared with my family.

Once Libby was next to me and Diggs had pulled up a chair at the edge of the booth, I took my time to catch all of their gazes—except Einstein's, who was still working on something. "Is this necessary?"

"Food is always necessary." Diggs seemed confused that I didn't know this.

How he didn't realize he wasn't wanted here confused me.

"Food," Maverick agreed, then started slamming his fists on the table. "*Food.*"

"We're starving," Diggs added, leaning across the table and stretching his hands toward me. "You starve us." The look on my face must have finally registered with him, because he grabbed a sugar packet and sat back. "Actually, I just came for the sugar."

I turned to Elle and dipped my head closer to hers. "Let's get out of here."

"They want to hang out with you."

When I leaned away, she was looking at everyone with wide eyes, like she was seeing them for the first time. There was a hint of fascination behind the look, but with how close she was to my body, it was impossible to miss the tremors now rolling through her.

"I see them every day. I never know when I'm going to see you."

She turned to look at me then, a ghost of a smile on her lips. "You're seeing me now."

Libby smacked my arm, then pushed against my chest, trying to press me back against the booth. "I've dealt with you for the past twenty-nine years. Let me sit next to Elle."

I never once took my eyes off Elle, silently pleading with her to let me take her from here . . . anywhere where we could be alone.

Yes, she was here. I could see her and touch her, breathe her in and hold her. But that didn't change anything.

She could disappear at any second. And I would be left wandering around . . . searching and waiting for her to reappear.

If she reappeared.

She didn't understand the fear that came with being near her and knowing I'd have to let her go.

Before I could remind her of any of those things, she leaned forward, passing her lips along my jaw before she whispered in my ear, "They're your friends. They're your family. If a stranger comes in to something that is as close as what all of you have, and pulls you away from them, resentment is going to build. Trust me."

There was an ache in her words that I felt in my stomach, as if she was talking from experience.

With a reluctant sigh, I lowered my arm to wrap it around her waist and pulled her onto my lap so we could switch positions.

Before I could slide her to my other side and hand her off to Libby's twenty questions, she gently grabbed my face in her hands and pressed her forehead to mine. "That night? It meant *everything.*"

True.

I placed a quick kiss on her lips. "Let Libby talk at you before I decide to take you away from here and keep you to myself."

Her head tilted back and a soft laugh sounded in her throat, and fuck me if that wasn't the sweetest thing I'd ever heard.

I wanted to keep her where she was. I wanted to drive my hands into her hair to pull her back to me so I could capture that mouth. I wanted to beg her to laugh again.

I wanted to make her smile . . .

It wasn't until she was sliding off me to sit next to Libby that I realized I was studying the girl who had somehow become my world. Watching every movement and shift of her body like a man transfixed. Not to look for cues, as I so often did, but because I was mesmerized by everything she did.

"Hey, nerd," Diggs said as he finished dumping sugar into a pile on the table. "Pay you ten bucks to eat this."

Libby smacked him on the back of the head. "What are you, *five*? Don't be an idiot."

Elle leaned into my side as she laughed again. That same low, husky sound that was almost too hard to hear.

I wanted to capture the sound so I could play it again and again.

Grabbing for my phone when it vibrated, the smile immediately dropped from my face when I read the text from Johnny.

She's gonna make you forget. Thought you swore you never would.

Pain and hatred burned through me when I looked up at my best friend. But instead of releasing Elle like I knew he'd expected me to, I tightened my arm around her waist as I dropped my phone on the table, and demanded everyone else do the same.

"We haven't even ordered yet," Einstein cried out from where she was trying to disappear between Maverick and Johnny.

"I don't care," I growled, my voice still rough from the emotions coursing through me.

Elle stilled when Johnny asked, "Still no phone?"

She looked his way when she realized he was talking to her, her head shaking subtly. "No."

"How convenient."

"I don't have a computer either. Or a car." She lifted a shoulder in a brief shrug. "You should try it sometime. Convenient is the last thing you'd call it."

"Are you Amish?" Libby suddenly asked. As soon as Elle started to shake her head, Libby was firing off another question. "Technologically challenged? Because Einstein could help you with that."

"I think I can figure—"

Libby gasped and slapped her hand on the table. "Or maybe you were in a coma for a bunch of years, and when you woke up you didn't know how to drive or use phones."

"Jesus Christ, Libby," I groaned. "This isn't a soap opera."

"It could be," she shot back.

"I just don't have those things," Elle interjected.

"Are you poor?"

"Fuck, Libby. Shut up."

She leaned around Elle to send me a glare that would make lesser men fall to their knees and beg her forgiveness so she wouldn't murder them.

Unfortunately for my sister, I'd grown up with her so I knew which one of us was more lethal. That look did nothing to scare me. It only proved there would always be a part of her that couldn't deny what we were.

We both hated the world our family had been involved in for generations, but while I'd been trying to change it from the inside since I'd been forced to take our dad's place, Libby had pretended to shun it.

Not that that made a difference. If I needed her to have my back, she would. And when it was done, she would hate me for it.

We both would.

She sat back with a huff when I didn't wither under her stare, then turned her attention on Elle again. "You know, if you're poor—"

"Libby," I said in warning.

"Hell, my little trippy hippy is just all about world peace, aren't you, baby?" Diggs asked. "Don't hurt the environment. Hug trees and all that. I'll let you hug my—" His gaze slid my way when a growl sounded in my chest, then he dropped his head to stare at his sugar pile. "I mean, I bet Dare will let you hug his tree."

"Food," Maverick suddenly shouted, pointing at a waitress who was walking our way. "For the love of God, we need food at this table before everyone starts killing each other."

I cut my eyes to Johnny. His were narrowed into slits as he studied the girl in my arms.

Johnny pinning Elle up against the wall, blood dripping down their arms flashed through my mind, quickly followed by the vision of *her* lifeless in my arms, both of us covered in her blood.

I shook my head trying to force the images away, trying to separate them, then looked down at Elle as she listened to Libby.

We didn't need food.

I needed to take Elle someplace where nothing in my world could ever find her. Including Johnny.

Breakfast passed without incident.

If you don't count Diggs throwing a sugar packet in Einstein's eye when she tried to snatch her phone mid-meal and Johnny trying to stab him with a butter knife in turn as an incident. Which I don't.

Though I would've bet money the girl tucked into my side would have.

But Elle hadn't so much as flinched as she'd watched the entire thing unfold in front of her before I could force Johnny to sit down and drop the knife. Granted, it had been over in less than five seconds, but there hadn't been a single reaction before she'd turned back to Libby to continue their conversation.

And it was eating at me still, long after.

Considering Johnny had been attacking *her* just over a week ago, there should have been some reaction. Some hint of fear, at the very least. But there was nothing.

The guys and Einstein abruptly stopped talking, catching my attention. Their gazes were fixated on the table except Einstein's. Hers was wide and unyielding as she stared at the girl next to me. I turned my head, slowly following their line of sight until I found what had halted their conversation.

Elle, absentmindedly drawing our symbol in the middle of Diggs's sugar pile while listening to Libby.

Elle noticed our silence before Libby, her eyes dragging from my sister to meet mine. Her brow pinched and she started to sit up as she looked around the table where everyone was now staring at her. "What—?"

I gripped her hand gently to lift it from the table, my eyes never leaving hers as she looked down at the sugar.

It took less than a second.

Her breath hitched and pulse quickened beneath my fingertips. Her eyelids fluttered and she swayed toward me, and for a second, I thought she was going to faint.

But just before she hit me, she stopped herself. After another second, she slowly let herself lean against me for support.

"What?" she finally asked, her voice lacking any of the warmth I was used to from her.

"Uh, just watched you trace that without a second thought, newbie," Maverick said.

"And? It's some lines and a circle."

Johnny slapped his hand against the sugar pile, sending most of it flying and the symbol into distorted chaos. "You know what that is?" he asked, his tone all growl and pure challenge.

"I know it's on Dare's back."

I bit back a curse as soon as the words left her mouth.

Of course she knew that. I should've known she would see it, but I hadn't been thinking. If I had been able to think around her, I would've been more careful. Gia hadn't seen it, hadn't known, for years. One night with Elle and I'd apparently lost my fucking mind.

Johnny's hardened gaze flicked to me before going back to Elle. "I asked if you knew what it was."

I didn't miss the way Elle flinched each time he spoke, but if I hadn't been wanting to know the answers to his questions too, I would've kissed her when she lifted her chin slightly in response. "To be honest, I think most of Wake Forest does even if they won't admit it."

"You wanna see mine?" Diggs asked as he stood, his hands already going to his belt as the tension quickly eased from the table.

"No," everyone said quickly, shutting him down.

"Dare showed his," he protested. "It's only fair."

Leaning in to Elle's ear, I whispered, "Don't ever agree to see theirs. Trust me."

"Gross," she mumbled.

"Does it scare you?" Maverick asked. "Knowing about us?"

"I don't know. You guys have never seemed scary to me." But even as she spoke, her eyes flashed to Johnny.

"You want us to change that?" Maverick continued, his tone a mixture of a challenge and a tease.

I shoved my foot into his leg before he could taunt Elle anymore, then pressed my lips to her ear again. "That's what you're keeping from me. That's why you panicked and left. You saw my back."

She turned to look at me, her nose pressed to mine. "I left because I should've been home long before the doors unlocked. I panicked because I fell asleep." Her worried eyes searched mine for a few seconds before she finally admitted, "My panic increased when I saw your tattoo before I decided it didn't matter."

"Libby." Her name was a rumble from deep within my chest, it was also a command.

Without asking or saying a word, she slid out of the booth, and I gently nudged Elle to follow.

"Let's go." As soon as we were out, I grabbed my sister's arm and pulled her close. "Keep Johnny away from me."

Elle started heading toward the front, but I gripped her hand in mine and hurried her to the back door to the secluded parking lot reserved for family. As soon as I had her outside, I led her to my car then released her.

Raking my hands over my head, I pulled at my hair as I walked away from her, releasing a pent-up breath when I turned to face her again.

She was leaning against the hood of my car, looking more contradicting than I'd ever seen anyone. Her shoulders were hunched and acceptance swam in her eyes, making her seem so vulnerable. But there was a fierceness in the set of her eyebrows and her jaw was locked tight like she was prepared for a fight.

"You decided it didn't matter."

She crossed her arms under her chest, dipping her head in a nod as she did.

"If you know what that symbol means, then you know who I am. You know *what* I am. How can you decide that doesn't matter?"

"Because I can't imagine walking away from this, and you aren't the only one with secrets. You know I have secrets, you *told* me to lie to you."

"That isn't the same as deciding what I am doesn't matter."

"Why isn't—?"

"I'm why," I yelled, my voice echoing between buildings. I rubbed a hand against my aching chest and looked at her uncertainly. "The girl who died, the one I told you about, *I'm* why she died. Who I am. *What* I am. *That* is why she was killed. Do you see why it *should* matter? Do you see why I pushed you away? Why I want to keep you safely by my side—hide you—so no one can hurt you?"

Instead of fear or remorse, or any normal reaction I'd expect from her, she just stared at me with pained eyes. "Knowing who you are can't keep me from you. I'll even face your hurt and try to help heal it," she vowed as she pushed away from the car and took a step forward, leaving a couple feet between us. "But you won't ever find me again if you try to hide me. And I can't compete against a ghost. I can't be someone you use in place of her to try to correct the past."

I stepped closer to pull her into my arms and lowered my chin so I could look into her eyes. "You're not competing. I'm not trying to correct anything because I know I can't. I'm just terrified of watching the same thing happen."

"I have fears too," she said simply, not bothering to expand or explain.

"Tell me one of your fears, Elle . . . I dare you."

"I'm afraid of what happens when the lying stops." Her eyes slipped closed as soon as the confession passed her lips, as though she was afraid to see my reaction to her truth.

"That's when I keep you."

A tremor rolled through her body and a shuddering breath forced from her lungs. If I hadn't been watching her so closely, I might've missed the flash of pain when she opened her eyes again.

"If only it were that simple."

"It is," I assured her. "Whatever's happening in your life, it's not something that can scare me away."

"But you expect your life to scare me away?"

I didn't know anyone who wouldn't be intimidated and terrified of my world. *Especially Johnny. She* should *be fucking terrified of him.*

"Yes. Elle," I said when she started turning from my arms.

"My life would *ruin* you," she said, her jaw clenched. She placed her hand on my chest, her eyes pleading. "Don't you feel it? We're fighting against something unstoppable. We're not supposed to be together."

My expression darkened, but my hold on her tightened. "Is that right?"

"You and I together? We're devastation."

"Since when?" I demanded, my voice rough. I stepped forward, leading her back until she was pressed against my car again. Lifting one of my hands to secure it in her hair, I pulled her as close as we could get in that moment. "Because the other night—*fuck*, every minute since I first kissed you—I could've sworn we were the best goddamn thing I would ever have in my life. And before that first day you walked into Brooks Street, I was positive I would *never* have *good* in my life again."

"You don't understand." A sound like a pained cry ripped from her throat, her chin wavering as she placed her fingers over my lips to prevent me from arguing. "And I wish there was a way you never would," she whispered after a few moments. "God is playing a cruel trick by letting me fall in love with you when I can't—"

I slammed my mouth down onto hers, swallowing her gasp of surprise. "Don't finish that thought," I begged, nipping at her lips before devouring them again.

I leaned her back against the hood of my car, following her down, and groaning into her mouth when she locked her legs around my waist. Her hands slid through my hair, gripping and pulling as I made a trail of open-mouthed kisses and teasing bites across her jaw and down her neck.

"Tell me."

Her throat vibrated against my lips with her laugh. "The one thing of everything I said that you heard—"

"Tell me," I repeated.

She lifted her head off the hood, pulling at my hair so she could look into my eyes. "I love you."

True.

And it made me want to beg her to say it every day for the rest of our lives.

Because I was pretty damn sure I fell in love with this girl the first time she looked at me. But I was terrified that the moment I voiced those words, someone would rip her from my arms.

"I was made to love you. I just found you in the wrong life."

"Only one life, Elle," I murmured, shaking my head. I dipped my chin to place a series of soft kisses across her chest then met her stare again. "I think I found you at just the right time. Your life . . . whatever it is, we can handle it."

Her mouth opened, the protest clear in her eyes.

"Truth or dare," I said before she could speak.

Her eyes were cautious as she searched my face. "Dare."

"Lie to me . . . ruin me. Just let yourself love me."

She nodded without hesitation. "I told you, it's cruel. Because I'll love you wholeheartedly until the very end."

There was pain behind her words. And for the first time, a hint of unease crept down my spine as her fears became mine. And I wondered what *was* waiting for us when the lying stopped—what was waiting for us at the very end.

Chapter 32

WHO I AM

Lily

"What's this?" I asked that afternoon, trailing the tips of my fingers across a tattoo on Dare's bicep.

It was four horizontal lines, just like the ones on his back. But the rest of the symbol was missing.

He pushed up so he was hovering over me and glanced down at it for a few seconds. "It's who I am," he finally said.

Something flashed in his eyes, like the tattoo held a physical weight over him, before he was able to push it away.

"It bothers you?"

He cocked his head to the side, a smile tugging at his mouth as he looked down at me. "A little. But it's something I have to do for now."

"If only we could just do what we actually wanted to . . ." I leaned up to brush my lips across the tattoo and whispered, "I would take this weight off you."

"I would keep you with me," he countered.

"You say that, but you might get bored if I actually stayed."

He lifted a brow. "I doubt that."

Leaning back so he was on his knees, his hungry eyes fell to where I was already bare from the last time. His thumbs went to my wet skin, spreading my lips and teasing my clit as he slid down to my entrance.

"If this is boring, I can stop . . ."

"Oh God." The words were said under my breath when he slid two fingers inside, his thumb moving back up to my clit.

Pumping his fingers slowly, he pulled them out and trailed them down the line of my bottom. A carnal grin crossed his face when I twisted against the bed, whimpering at the touch.

I reached back, my hands fumbling with the nightstand drawer, searching for the protection he'd bought as he made that same pass again and again.

Each time I wanted to shy away from it.

Each time I wanted to ask for more.

Each time I nearly came undone.

As soon as I had one of the foil packets in hand, I struggled to open it when all my body wanted to do was succumb to his touch.

One hand tortured my clit with teasing touches, the other sought my entrance again, his fingers pushing in roughly a few times before they were trailing back again.

Heat swirled deep in my belly. My body ached with the need for him to keep going, for him to put me out of my misery.

I reached for him, savoring the husky groan that sounded in his chest when I had his long, thick length in my grasp, my head dropping back when he teased me with the faintest pressure once again.

"*Please.*"

"Fuck, where'd you come from?" he asked, his voice a gruff rumble.

He released me long enough to roll the condom on, only seconds passing from when his hands left me to when he was pushing into me, a cry tumbling from my lips as he pushed me over the edge.

Wrapping his arms around my back, he lifted me so I was seated on his lap—facing him—then brought me down on his thick length again and again . . . then harder still until I was biting down on his shoulder to silence my screams.

One of his hands lowered, his fingers sliding along the crease of my bottom in silent reminder of the torture he'd just been putting me through. And when he pressed one of his fingers there, pushing in slightly, I fell apart in his hands, sending him into his own release.

My world spiraled into nothing but darkness broken up by the light we created together as waves of pleasure ripped through me unlike anything I've ever known.

Beautiful and sensual. Passionate and heartbreaking.

That's what it had been.

That's what we were.

I pressed a kiss to where I'd bitten down on his shoulder, trying to cling to this moment as long as possible.

I jerked against him when loud pounding sounded on his door.

"*Dare*," Johnny called out, his voice laced with frustration.

"I'm gonna kill him."

"It's the third time he's tried to get you to leave. I think you should go before he comes charging in here," I murmured, squeezing him tighter before reluctantly sliding off him. I tried to smile, but the possibility of Johnny doing exactly that was too real. "I need to go anyway."

"We need to check in with someone, but it'll only take ten minutes. Fifteen tops. Be here when I get back."

I squinted my eyes at him, but kept my tone teasing. "That sounds sketchy and very mob-like."

Dare's chest moved with the force of his laugh, his eyes bright with amusement. "Check in with a *business partner*. Johnny's only coming with me because I don't trust him anywhere but by my side."

I didn't trust Johnny at all.

His fingers trailed over my waist and down my thigh, his touch and stare begging. "Stay," he breathed, the plea enough to make my heart race and my will crumble.

I bit at my lip, trying to remember why I needed to go. "Okay."

"Yeah?" Surprise lit his eyes, that carefree smile spreading across his face.

"Yeah." A laugh bubbled free when he wrapped me in his arms, pulling me close to kiss me. "But only for a few more hours. If I don't go soon, I don't know when I'll ever be able to get back to you."

Even with Kieran gone, it felt like tempting fate.

That smile of his froze. Worry and something like anger swirled in his eyes. "Then I'm not going. I'm not wasting the time I have with you."

"Go." When his jaw hardened, I laughed and pushed against his chest. "Go. We've already spent hours locked in here. My body needs to rest. I need to shower."

One of his dark brows rose, a mischievous grin suddenly playing on his lips. "Oh, then I really think I should stay."

"No, you need to go. You have to check in with that *business partner*."

His only response was a slow shake of his head as he shifted us to lay me on the bed.

I tilted my head back, my laugh pouring free as he dipped his head to place teasing kisses on my neck.

"Dare, my body is so worn out," I whined, my protest weak and forgotten by the time his lips reached the swell of my breasts.

I arched, silently begging—and immediately sagged back against the bed, bursting into laughter when my stomach's growl filled the room.

Dare's shoulders shook with his silent laugh. His dark eyes were dancing when he lifted his head to look at me. "Jesus." Bending to press his lips to my stomach, he mumbled, "Point taken. I'll bring back food."

I watched as he stood from the bed and went to his bathroom to clean up, my smile still uncontained by the time he was walking toward me again, jeans on and pulling a shirt over his head.

He slowed, his expression unreadable as he searched my face. "That smile," he whispered as he bent to kiss me. "Been waiting my entire life for something to make me feel the way that smile does."

My heart ached, crying out in pain from being torn in two over this man.

Because I knew he was sincere. And I knew one day those words, the raw emotion in them, they would all be gone. Replaced by hatred.

"Don't go," he pleaded, an edge of worry to his voice.

"I'll be here," I promised.

Until the very end.

Chapter 33

DEVIL ON HIS SHOULDER

Lily

The knob suddenly twisted, the door moving with the weight of whoever was on the other side. My heart stopped before taking off as I scrambled to fold the towel over my naked body.

I didn't call out to see who it was, because I knew it shouldn't have been Dare. But whoever it was wasn't leaving. Something scratched at the knob a second before it gave a little wiggle.

Images of the last time I was in a bathroom with a member of the Borello *family* flashed through my mind, making it feel like my blood had turned to ice.

I rushed to put on my glasses just as the lock on the door clicked, my heart rate so fast that it felt like my heart would tear from my chest at any moment.

By the time it opened, I had Kieran's knife in hand and open.

A strained huff burst from me when Einstein peeked her head in.

"God, Einstein." Closing the knife, I tossed it into my bag. "What's so important that you couldn't wait until I was done? Or couldn't ask me to open the door?" When she didn't respond, I glanced up to find her staring at me with a look of frustration. "Einstein?"

She jerked her head for me to follow her out of the bathroom, not bothering to see if I did.

Typical.

I made sure my stuff was in my bag, then shrugged into Dare's shirt again before following her into his bedroom where she was pacing. Once she saw me standing there, she shoved a small stack of papers at me without a word.

"What is this?" I asked, somehow already knowing she wouldn't respond.

I stilled when I saw a picture of me on the first page. Except it wasn't *me*, it was Elle. And it was her driver's license.

"Einstein, what . . . why'd you do this?"

Elle Landry from Springfield, Missouri.

She'd even changed the way I'd been styling my hair in the picture. Given me different glasses and made me look younger.

The next page was a copy of a Social Security card. Then a birth certificate.

The next page was a—"Oh my God."

I rushed through the rest of the pages. High school records. College records—before she'd dropped out. Police and missing person reports.

"Einstein, what is this? Did you do this?" I demanded. "You made me into a person. A person who is *married* to an abusive man and a runaway. What the hell were you thinking?"

She stared at me a few seconds longer before gritting out, "Dare's worried about you. He thinks you're in *real* danger, and he knows you won't tell him. The day I drove you back to that *place* and he woke up to find you were gone, he nearly lost it trying to figure out what could have that kind of pull on you—could put that kind of fear in you. He told me to find out who you were. I've never not found someone before."

I watched her, the normally wild-eyed, hyped-up girl who was now seething, and asked, "Why did you bother?"

One of her brows ticked up. "Do you want to die?"

"Of course not. But have you ever lied to him before?" When she didn't respond, I said, "And you're already keeping what you know about me from him. If it makes you this mad, I don't know why you bothered. You don't owe me anything, you don't even know me. And if you've forgotten . . . he's going to find out eventually."

"I'm doing this because I want him happy. We all want him happy as long as possible. And for some fucked-up reason, the Holloway Princess makes him happy. I like you, but I hate you for being the reason I'm lying to my family for the first time in my life. Do you know what it's like lying to Johnny? Or *trying* to lie to Dare?"

"You think I don't want him happy?" I asked, my throat tightening as I fought back tears. "You think it doesn't shatter me knowing *I* am who he hates? *I* am what has caused him so much pain, and will cause him more in the future? I want him as long as possible, but I've been trying to prepare him for what's coming because it's inevitable. I've been giving him as many truths as I can and letting him make of it what he will. But tricking him like this? It's going to cause unnecessary hurt."

Gripping the pages in my hands, I tore them in half, ignoring the horror in Einstein's eyes.

"I already wiped the files so Johnny wouldn't find them," she whispered.

"Good. Destroy these too. Burn them . . . I don't care. Just don't tell Dare I'm someone I'm not. He may not realize who I am yet, but I haven't told him I'm someone else entirely, and I don't plan to."

"Yeah. Okay, *Elle*," she said my name with a scoff as she took the torn pages from my hands.

"My friend only used my initials when I first started sneaking out. '*L*' stuck as an actual name. Considering nearly all of you go by nicknames, I don't think you have room to speak."

She nodded after a few seconds. "Fair enough." With a sigh, she dropped her hands so the torn pages hit her legs, and looked up at me. "I was giving you time with him. Doesn't mean it didn't make me hate you."

"I know. Stall him," I said weakly, and attempted a laugh. "After all, you're looking for a girl who died four years ago who never had ID."

"I can't. He knows I don't know how."

I nodded in acknowledgment. "Maybe just warn me before it happens. I'd like one last night with him."

Einstein studied me for a minute in a way only she could, those wild eyes searching for something hidden. "You know, I think it's unfortunate. What's going to happen," she added on as an afterthought. "No one else would've thought twice about using the fake life. I don't think I'll ever meet someone else who's as straightforward in her deceit as you are. It's a shame."

I didn't need her to explain.

I knew what was a shame.

"What's sad is I'm not enough to ease his need for revenge."

"You might've been. I know you're perfect for him. I think the two of you are what your families need to stop spilling blood. But Dare has a devil on his shoulder who's always whispering in his ear, reminding him of his promises and his hatred. And his devil won't let Dare stop thirsting for blood."

"You mean Johnny, don't you?" I asked when Einstein turned to leave.

She looked back at me, a sad smile playing on her lips. "Who else?"

"Can't you see that he's poison?" I asked, the question tumbling from my mouth before I could stop myself. "How can you look away from the kind of man he is?"

"Poison, huh? Interesting description. Do you need to be reminded whose bed you've been sharing for years?"

My mouth opened, a defense for Kieran on the tip of my tongue before I stopped. Because Kieran wasn't the boy who hated what he'd been made in to anymore. He hadn't for a long time. "I don't turn a blind eye to what he does. I think the fact that I'm standing here says as much."

"Just because you see him for what he is doesn't mean there isn't a part of you that hopes you can fix him." From the way she seemed to stare through me, I had a feeling she wasn't *just* talking about Kieran and me. "Everyone's a puzzle," she said suddenly. "He's just missing a piece, but I'll find it. I always do."

"But, Einstein—"

"You can't help who you love." Her words were as much an explanation as they were a reminder. Before I could respond, her eyebrows lifted and head tilted. "Did you hear that? I think . . . I think my operating system just crashed. My motherboard might be fried. I can't search for you the way I need to. Funny how that happens."

I blew out a weighted breath and sent her a grateful smile. "Thank you, Einstein."

I watched her slip out of the room and started to turn to get dressed when I heard Dare's deep timbre from somewhere in the house.

Following my rumbling stomach down the hall toward the kitchen, my brow pinched when I found the kitchen full of takeout food, but void of people.

I peeked in one of the bags as I rounded the counter to continue following Dare's voice into the living room, but turned right back around to get a drink instead when I heard Johnny's distinct sneer.

"Maybe if you paid more attention to your own house, we wouldn't have to do your job for you."

"Enough," Dare growled.

I slowed as I pulled a glass down from one of the cupboards to fill with water, wondering who they were talking to and knowing I probably shouldn't be hearing this.

But even as my mind yelled at me to slowly and quietly retreat back to Dare's room, I couldn't stop listening as Dare continued.

"He's got plans to take her within the next two weeks. No set date."

"Jesus fuck . . . all right."

My head snapped up and I nearly choked on my next breath when I heard the familiar curse.

No. No, no, no. That's not him. Please, God, be anyone but him.

"He's either trying to shut some people up, or start a war with that. We knew he was planning something, just had no idea it would be something like that."

"You know her then?" Dare asked.

"Yeah. Yeah, I do." There was a rough sigh before he continued, "There were two more visits. Were you able to get them taken care of?"

"Everyone's accounted for," Dare said smoothly, like he wasn't talking to an enemy. "The last two needed a little convincing. Think they're still worried they'll be killed if they go against Mickey. Might be worth another visit when he gets back into town."

I staggered toward the counter, my free hand shooting out to grab it in order to keep myself standing.

What am I hearing? What the hell am I hearing?

"Solo or all?"

"I don't mind—"

"There's no point for us to go back," Dare answered, cutting Johnny off.

"All right. I'll let Kieran know. He can take care of them when he gets . . ."

I didn't hear the rest of what he said.

I didn't hear anything at all past the roaring in my ears.

Kieran.

Kieran.

Kieran.

Kieran's working with . . . Beck and Kieran are working with . . . Jesus Christ.

The edges of my vision went black and the room felt like it was spinning around me.

The next thing I knew Dare was in front of me, grasping my cheeks and forcing me to look into his calming eyes as he spoke to me.

"Elle? Elle, baby, look at me. Are you okay? No, don't try to move, there's glass everywhere." He was trying to sound soothing, but there was an underlying hint of panic to his words.

And I couldn't understand what he was saying, because my best friend was standing right behind him.

It felt like I was in a never-ending nightmare that just continued to get worse. No matter how hard I tried to tear myself from it, I kept getting sucked in.

"There's what?" I asked, my voice heavy and slow. I tried to look down but Dare stopped the movement.

"I'm gonna get you out of here, okay? Stop trying to walk."

I didn't want to walk. I wanted to run.

Needed to run.

Because Dare had shifted to give Johnny an order, and now Beck and I had a clear view of each other.

It only took seconds for his expression to fall as he stared at me, his curiosity giving way to denial and confusion. His chest heaved with a ragged breath before rage and accusation burned in his eyes.

I'd never seen him so terrifying.

He turned his back on us just before Dare grabbed me in his arms and looked over his shoulder to snap at Beck, "We're done here."

Chapter 34

UNTIL THE VERY END

Dare

I was losing my fucking mind.

To put it mildly.

In the hour since I'd found Elle standing in a sea of glass, she'd barely said a word. She'd let me set her on my bathroom counter and pull the slivers of glass from her feet and legs with a face of stone.

Libby had freaked out for her.

Johnny had come storming into the bathroom, demanding to know why she'd been in the kitchen and what she'd heard before I'd been able to shove him out. But Elle hadn't so much as flinched or looked at him.

She hadn't touched the food I'd given her.

And when I'd put her in my bed, she'd tried to stand, saying she had to leave.

But that was it.

She hadn't fought when I'd told her to rest instead. She'd just lain down and had been staring blankly ahead ever since.

"Let me try talking to her alone," Libby offered from where she sat on the end of my bed.

"Because that went so great last time," Einstein said with a snort from where she stood, leaning against the wall next to Johnny. As always, her face was buried in her phone. "You took one look at her feet and started screaming. Since when are you afraid of blood?"

"I'm not leaving her alone with you," I said before Libby could snap back. "She was fine. I leave and this happens. I need to know what happened to her while I was gone."

My accusing stare darted to my sister.

"I was getting my nails done," Libby shot back, annoyed that I would blame her for having anything to do with this.

"I was in the middle of a computer crisis, still—"

"Or maybe," Johnny said, cutting off Einstein, "it's like I said. She was listening when she shouldn't have been. Maybe she heard something she shouldn't have."

"*She* is right here," Elle mumbled.

I turned to look at her. Eyes and face still blank.

"Newbie," Maverick shouted, running into the room just before Diggs barreled in behind him. "Nerd. Dude, what happened?"

"Out," I said through clenched teeth. "Everyone out."

"We just got here," Diggs complained, but immediately put his hands up in surrender as he stepped back. "But we're leaving."

Johnny slanted a glare at Elle as he stepped toward the door, then gave me a look as he slipped out.

I knew what it meant . . . I knew what he wanted.

He wanted to interrogate her.

He was fucking insane if he thought I'd let him near her.

Biting back a groan, I rubbed my hands over my face and turned back to Elle just as she pulled herself into a sitting position.

I studied every movement, looking for any indication she was going to faint like I'd been waiting for all hour, but there was nothing.

"Elle . . ."

"I'm sorry," she said immediately, the emotion finally back in her tone even if there was no life in her eyes.

"Sorry? Why are you sorry? I just want to know what happened and what I can do to help you."

She blinked before meeting my gaze, the action slow, like it was taking all her strength. "I don't know what happened," she said honestly. "I was standing there about to get water. I could hear you talking in the other room, and then everything went dark and it was so loud. Then suddenly you were there."

True.

Every word.

"Has this ever happened before?"

Her head tilted as though she was about to start shaking it, but then she paused. "Yes," she whispered. "A long time ago." She swallowed, then dropped her head like she was ashamed. "But I passed out for nearly an hour that time."

"Jesus, Elle."

The corners of her mouth curved up before falling, the first sign of life on her beautiful face. "Progress, I guess."

Pressing my knuckles under her chin, I lifted her head to look into her eyes. "Not funny," I told her as I pushed up her slipping glasses.

She swatted at my hand, another hint of a grin flashing across her face. "No, it's not." She dragged her fingers through her long hair as she sucked in a deep breath, then released it. "Dare, I have to go."

"Are you kidding? You just—I don't even know how to describe what happened to you. You've been a zombie for the last hour. I'm not letting you go."

"I need to go before this gets worse. And I promise you it is going to get worse."

"Then stay," I urged. "Let me take care of you."

"Remember what I said?" she asked, her voice calm and eyes filled with sadness. "If I don't go soon, I don't know when I'll ever be able to get back to you." She slid her hands into my hair, then let her fingers slowly drag down until they were intertwined around the back of my neck. "Let me go so I can come back to you."

"Do you have any idea how frustrating you are?" I asked as I gripped her waist, pulling her closer to me. "If you never left, you wouldn't have to worry about when you'd be able to come back. I wouldn't have to wander through the dark, waiting for you to light up the night. You'd already be here."

She sat up, crushing her mouth to mine. "Until the very end."

Before I could try to stop her, she was slipping out of my arms and off the bed.

"Let me do what has to be done, Dare," she begged when I started to follow her. "I would've stayed that first night if things were different. I hate that they're not. I hate that I can't change them. And I hate that I put you in a position where you only know so much. But let what you do know be enough, because that's all I can give you."

Once she was in her own clothes and had her purse slung over her shoulder, she took a step toward the door, but stopped, rocking back on her heels.

Turning toward where I stood with my arms crossed over my chest so I wouldn't reach for her and keep her with me, she walked up to me and leaned up on her toes to whisper in my ear, "It shreds my soul walking away from you."

I love you. Stay.

The words were there, begging to be freed, but the fear of what would happen to her kept them choked back like a rock in my throat.

I watched her go, my jaw ticking and muscles twitching as she did.

She got a foot from the door before I ate up the distance and grabbed her, turning and pressing her against the wall to claim her mouth one last time.

Her body immediately relaxed beneath mine, her hands gripping at my shirt to pull me closer. I teased the seam of her lips, begging entrance and groaning when she opened for me.

My fingers curled against the wall, wanting to grab her and pull her back to the bed, but knowing I couldn't keep her there forever.

A whimper scraped up her throat when I nipped at her lip, and I knew I was seconds from forgetting what she needed.

"Five seconds before I remind you why you shouldn't go," I warned, leaning back just enough to give her space to get away.

Her chest moved roughly with her heavy breaths as she looked up at me with indecision in her eyes. But just before I grabbed her and hauled her back to bed, she kissed the tattoo on my bicep, then ducked from under my arm to slip out of the room.

Chapter 35

SAY GOODBYE

Lily

I'd made it three houses away when a familiar car rolled to a stop next to me.

I wanted to hit and scream at him.

I wanted to run far from him and his accusing stare.

Knowing he would continue to follow me and needing the relief from my stinging feet, I jerked open his car door and slid inside to face a seething Beck.

"Drive," I demanded as I slammed the door behind me.

"Tell me—"

"Drive so they don't see us!"

"What?" he shouted. "Worried about your *boyfriend* seeing you with me? You and I are a team, Lil. I'm your best fucking friend. We're on the same goddamn side, if you've forgotten."

"If *I've* forgotten? Beck! You were just in a meeting with the enemy, and I want to know why and how long this has been going on." Smacking my hand against the dashboard, I yelled, "*Drive.*"

He thankfully pulled away from the curb, but hadn't let more than a few seconds pass before turning on me. "You wanna explain what the fuck I walked in on?"

"*Me?*" I shouted. "What the hell did I just hear? You and Kieran are—"

"No. *Fuck no*, Lil. Not only—" He let loose an inhuman growl, ripping a hand through his hair. "Not only did I just catch you in your little getup," he said, gesturing to me. "You were looking like this *off* property. At a Borello's house. But not just *any* Borello's house. The *main* Borello house. In nothing but *Demitri Fuckin' Borello's* goddamn shirt. And he called you *baby*. Now considering the facts that you're supposed to be all cozy at home and engaged to my other best friend, you better start explaining."

I was seeing red. Yet at the same time, I felt like I did the first time my mom walked in to find Keiran in my room when we were teenagers.

"After *everything* I've found out recently—"

"You first," he bellowed, his voice thundering in the small space.

Instead of shrinking into the seat, I turned, putting my back against the door so I could face him. "I don't know what you expect. I've been *trapped* on Holloway my entire life. I got why. I did. But after Aric's death, that place suddenly became a prison and I was treated like a prisoner. I was being suffocated by all of you. I got in trouble if I went to the main house without getting permission, Beck."

"It was to protect you," he roared in response, the car jerking with his rage.

"Fuck protecting me. I can protect myself. If only Kieran would understand that. If only Kieran were ever around. But he isn't. He hasn't been for four years. He didn't just take Aric's place, Beck, he *left* me. He broke our promises. He's been destroying our relationship and my heart a little bit at a time while I scrambled to put it back together each time he left. And I'm so tired of trying to keep us together when he doesn't care."

"You think he doesn't care? You think he isn't doing all of this bullshit for you?"

"Oh my God," I said with a frustrated laugh. "Stop with that.

None of this is for me. That is the biggest punch to the gut to say any of his work is for me. And then to find out that you're also working with the Borellos? The people you've been working so hard to hide me from?"

"Clearly we've been doing a hell of a job seeing as you're fucking the deadliest one."

Air burst from my chest, my shoulders sagging in response.

He suddenly jerked the car to the right and hit the brakes, slamming his hands against the steering wheel once we were stopped. After a few ragged breaths, he turned to look at me. "How long has this been going on?"

I leaned my head against the seat, suddenly weary. "There's not one real answer to that."

With a steadying breath, I told Beck about Teagan finding me. About our Mondays at Brooks Street Café and Dare's notes. About the street fair and everything after, skipping the intimate details.

When I was done, he was leaning back in his seat. One arm folded over his chest, the other draped over his head. Instead of the intense glare he'd been sporting earlier, his expression was wavering somewhere between worry and anger. "Jesus fuck, Lil. I . . . shit, I don't even know where to begin."

I scoffed. "How about when you started working with the Borellos?"

"I can't. It's not my story to tell." He lowered the arm from his head and looked at me helplessly. "I've been telling you—*Kieran's* been telling you—everything he has been doing for the last four years has been for you. You just wouldn't listen because you were too upset."

"Upset? Beck. He left—"

"I know, Lil. I know. But it's Kieran. He doesn't even know that shaking hands is the right way to say hello. Or that it's polite to say *thank you* or *you're welcome*, or *goodbye* when you walk away from a conversation. Kieran's focus is you, and he was trained to put his all into his job. And he's doing this job for you. So, in his mind, he's doing the right thing. The Borellos . . . again, it's not my story. But, Teagan . . . Lil, I gotta tell you."

"Tell me what?" I insisted when he didn't continue.

"Jesus fuck, where do I begin?"

I cringed at the curse. I knew I'd never be able to hear it and think of Beck in the same light again.

"I don't know what to say, because like I said, it's not my story to tell. But, Mickey . . . he's up to something bad. You heard about the contacts we have in Texas."

"The human trafficking."

"Right," Beck said with a sigh. "Mickey has had that contact for years, longer than any of us realized. I mean, this all began right around the time that Aiden died and Mickey took out Dare's dad."

I didn't know how to be shocked that Mickey had been working with a guy who dealt in human trafficking for over sixteen years. After what I'd heard from Beck this afternoon, I wasn't sure I could be shocked anymore.

"This contact, William, the reason he and Mickey are so close— the reason Mickey wouldn't let Kieran kill him when he went radio silent for that week—is because William's been helping Mickey out for years. Mickey's building his own ring and he's forming it here. It's going to be exactly the same. Bringing the girls here in shipments. Men buying them. He already has a list of men who have been campaigning for this with him. And he's getting close to starting it."

I was wrong.

"Oh God."

"Kieran knew he was hiding something from him and knew it had something to do with the ring starting up. Your *boyfriend*," he said with a sneer, "was able to find out what that secret was." He looked at me for a few seconds, his anger slowly growing. "I still can't believe you'd fucking do this, Lil! I just keep seeing you standing there in that kitchen. How could you do this to Kieran?"

"Beck," I snapped. "What did Dare find out?"

He let out an animalistic growl, dragging his hands over his head. "Mickey's trying to start a fucking war within Holloway. He's trying to get Finn and Bailey to do something so he can take them out."

"That's been coming for a long time," I murmured, not understanding.

"He's gonna have Teagan kidnapped and sold in the first batch of girls," he explained, stunning me into silence.

"I have . . . I have to warn . . ." My stomach rolled. "I'm gonna be sick," I whispered, fumbling with my seatbelt then turning to claw at the door handle.

I tumbled out of the car and onto the grassy side of the road just as my stomach lurched, desperately trying to find anything to get rid of.

"It's happening sometime in the next two weeks," Beck said once my stomach finally settled.

I looked over to see him leaning against the car.

"I have to warn her. We have to save her, Beck."

I didn't realize I was crying until I could no longer see him.

"She can't go from what Finn's been doing to her to what Mickey has planned."

"I know," Beck said as he placed a hand on my back to lead me into the car again, his voice gentle. "We'll stop it. I promise."

"Thank you."

"Lil . . . do you have any idea what you're doing?" he asked once he was on his side again. "Do you have any idea who *Dare* is?"

"Yes, I know. I know who he is and who everyone in that house is. I didn't at first, but by the time I did, I was so gone it didn't matter."

Beck was quiet for so long I didn't think he was going to talk anymore. "He wants to kill you."

"I know. Einstein told me about Gia—about what Mickey did."

"What happens when he finds out who you are?"

"He'll either find me on Holloway, or find out who I am while I'm with him. What's the difference, Beck? He kills me either way."

"The difference is we can't lose you, and you've accepted it's going to happen," he gritted out. "You've been my best friend my entire life. You've been Kieran's . . . you've been his everything. We're not going to let you die."

"You can't stop it because I don't want to live without him."

"That's bullshit. He wants to fucking kill you."

"That girl you used to love, the one you said you'd do anything to be out on the streets every night just to be able to check on her . . . what if she was your undoing, Beck? What if you knew she was *going* to be? Would you still be there every night to check on her until that time came?"

Beck studied me, and I knew he wanted to say *no* for the sake of the true argument here.

When he didn't respond, I nodded, because it was answer enough.

It also made me think maybe Beck was still more in love with her than he let himself believe.

"It's not so different," I whispered. "I just want time with him, and what kills me is that I have so little of it. We're so close to the moment when he finds out, I can feel it in every second that passes. It's like there's an ache I can't explain, growing inside me because my soul knows what's coming."

"Have you thought about what this is going to do to Kieran?" he asked after a minute had passed.

"For nearly two years," I said with a pained huff.

Beck sighed, then stared straight ahead, not bothering to start driving again.

For the longest time, we didn't speak. There was nothing more I could offer him, I'd already told him everything.

"Kieran and Mickey are supposed to be back in time for the meeting tomorrow," he mumbled, turning his head to notice me nodding. "What happens when I take you back to Holloway?"

"You tell me." I lifted a shoulder in a weak shrug. "Am I going to be handcuffed to Conor?"

"I can't tell him what happened. I mean, what happens when I sneak you back into the guesthouse, and then go back to work? Do you sneak right back out to meet him because you know Kieran and I won't be back tonight?"

Guilt swam in my stomach, but I decided to be honest with him. "Yeah."

With his jaw clenched, he gave a firm nod then reached for his seatbelt. I'd barely grabbed mine when he flipped the car around to go back the way we'd come. "I know I can't stop you without risking you telling my brother what you know, but I can stop you from walking all over this town."

"Conor doesn't know you're—"

"Keep him out of it," he snarled. "I've been trying to keep him as far away from the bad shit on Holloway as possible."

"Okay," I whispered, and pressed my hands to my weak stomach.

The excitement of seeing Dare mixed with the guilt of what I was doing, and what I was now pulling Beck into. But Beck? He understood love. And I hoped he would eventually forgive my choices.

"I'm picking you up on my way home from the streets. If you're not in my car by four, I'm storming into that house and dragging you out. If Kieran finds out—"

"He won't know about you," I said on a rush. "I promise he won't know."

Beck looked over at me, pain etched on his face. "Lil, we've been working together . . . but something's about to give. Be careful, and for fuck's sake, figure out a way to say goodbye to him for the last time. They broke in and tore apart the house, looking for you."

"I know."

"No, you don't," he said roughly. "We didn't mention to them about the destruction in the house. We didn't mention the break-in. But Kieran picked up elevated anger from Johnny, and I could see it in the way Dare was looking at me. You were told *why* Dare wanted you dead, but do you not get that we've been working together for years, and Dare's just realized that *we've* been lying to him about you this whole time?"

No. I hadn't picked up on that.

"Dare's taking his time. He wants us to know he's coming. And he's doing it to get back at all of us. There's more that you don't know, but Kieran has to be the one to tell you."

I looked at him warily then sank deeper into the seat.

So many lies, so much withheld. And still I knew I wouldn't have done any of this differently.

Because with Kieran, I'd felt shut out, locked away from people he trusted over me. I'd felt alone and shattered.

And Dare had put me back together.

The only shock after learning who Dare truly was had been realizing how utterly wrong I'd pegged him and his family all these years—Johnny excluded.

His need to avenge Gia obliterated a part of my soul. But I knew if the roles were reversed—if someone had taken Dare from me— seeking revenge for his death would be the last thing I did before I left the mob forever.

Beck rolled to a stop a handful of houses away, his knuckle-white grip unforgiving on the steering wheel. When I opened the door, he repeated, "Find a way to say goodbye, Lil."

I wasn't ready.

I was sure the moment would come when he had a gun to my head, and I still wouldn't be ready.

Chapter 36

DEEPER THAN BLOOD

Dare

I paused, my pencil hovering over the records book in front of me. An ominous silence filled the house, leaving the office tight with tension.

Without lifting my head, I looked at the twins from where they were sprawled out on a couple of the chairs and noticed that Maverick had stopped tossing the baseball in the air and Diggs was straightening in his seat.

I slowly leaned over, my hand going to the middle drawer of the desk I was sitting at.

"Where's Johnny?" My question was hushed, but still sounded like an ear-splitting scream in the weighted silence.

Neither of the twins responded with anything more than a slight shake of their heads as I eased the drawer open and grabbed my gun.

I didn't have time to continue worrying over why he'd never come back. I was thanking God that Elle was gone.

Because this was what we'd been waiting for.

Why we were all here.

I held the twins' stares as they reached for where they'd stashed their guns, my ear trained to whatever was happening outside the room we were in.

I blew steady breaths out, slowing my heart rate and clearing my mind until I was someone I hated.

"Get the girls," I said on another breath out. "We bury no one."

Diggs stood without making a sound and pulled a black bandana from his back pocket, his brother quickly following.

Once the lower half of their faces were covered, I reached for my own bandana, my heart stopping when I heard one of the girls yell.

Instead of rushing into action, the sound made all of us pause.

Because it wasn't the kind of scream I'd been expecting and praying I wouldn't hear.

Maverick took an uncertain step forward, his furrowed brow and confused eyes all I could see as he looked between Diggs and me.

"What are you doing?" she yelled again. "Johnny, *stop*!"

The lethal calm I'd just achieved was nowhere to be found. Panic and white-hot rage pounded through my veins as I reacted, shoving the heavy wooden desk out of my way as I stood.

Johnny's name tore from my chest as I ran out of the office, sliding into the hallway wall when I rounded the corner too fast.

The silence that had seemed so threatening had been a clear warning.

But I'd read it wrong.

I should've known when Johnny hadn't come back and hadn't alerted anyone. I should've fucking known.

"Oh my God, Johnny . . . Johnny, *stop*!"

I skidded to turn back toward the kitchen when I realized that's where the yells were coming from, and barreled into the twins. "Move, move, move—"

A scream ripped through the house, slowing my movements and stopping my heart before I could find the ability to move across the living-room floor that now felt like quicksand.

Seconds felt like hours.

And when the kitchen finally came into view, the moment it took for me to hurl myself into the chaos felt like an eternity in hell.

Einstein was gripping one of Johnny's arms and his shirt, pleading with him to stop, but darted away when she turned and saw us coming.

And Johnny . . . he had Elle bent over the island counter, his body covering hers. He had one of her bloodied arms extended, a large knife resting in his other hand as he sneered in her ear.

Grabbing Johnny's head and the hand holding the knife, I wrenched him backward, away from Elle, then turned to slam his head against the opposite counter near the sink.

The knife dropped with a clatter against the floor, and I released his hand to wrap my arm around his neck. He shoved away from the counter, ramming my back into the island in an attempt to dislodge me. His fingers dug into my forearm, but I didn't release him.

"Ask her," he choked out. "Ask her."

"I'll fucking kill you," I seethed as I tightened my hold around his throat.

"Ask why she left. Who she was with." Johnny roared as he slammed my back into the island once again, then spat, "Fucking *Holloway*."

The name caught me so off guard that my hold on Johnny slipped enough that he was able to break free.

He planted a hand near the sink, sucking in air. "I knew not to trust her. She's a fucking rat."

"He was *waiting* for me," Elle bit out as Einstein tried to pull her toward the kitchen table. "He wanted to know how long I've been with Dare."

I shot forward when Johnny took a menacing step toward the girls, and demanded, "Who was waiting?"

The crazed look in Johnny's eyes as they focused on Elle promised everything I'd been trying to keep locked up our entire lives. "Went to take a piss, looked out the window and *Beck* goes driving past. Not twenty seconds later, this fucking whore comes walking up. You god-damn dirty—"

I threw a punch into his curled mouth, using all my weight as momentum, advancing on him when he swayed back. "I told you not to touch her. I told you not to go near her. Leave before I change my mind on letting you live."

I looked at where Einstein was holding towels against Elle's arm, and stepped in their direction.

"I knew something wasn't right when that glass shattered," Johnny taunted. "Bet it was because she knew exactly who—"

"Fucking *leave*."

He stepped close, his eyes narrowed and face covered in blood. "You know there's something not right about her. Ask her and see how she responds."

Looking at the twins, I gestured to Johnny. "Get him out of the house."

"Babe, let's go," Johnny called out as Diggs forced him out of the kitchen, but Einstein wouldn't look at him. "*Babe.*"

I looked over my shoulder and knew from the pain and promise of death in his eyes I could never let Johnny near Elle again.

Einstein mattered most in Johnny's world, and she'd just chosen Elle over him.

We both had.

"I've got this," I murmured to Einstein once I heard the front door shut. "Where's Libby?"

Einstein didn't meet my gaze when she replied, "Work."

"Go there, stay until she's off. I don't want any of you alone right now."

She walked away without another word, Maverick trailing close behind her.

I didn't ask if she was okay, because I knew she wasn't. And Einstein didn't like others knowing her heart was made of anything less than stone—just like Johnny's.

With a sigh, I finally looked at the girl next to me. "I have about a hundred things I want to say and ask and do. Including kissing you and demanding to know why the hell you didn't scream for me the second you saw him coming toward you. But those can wait." Opening up the towels, I looked at the cut running up her forearm, my blood boiling when I saw it. "Right now, we need to get this taken care of. Can you walk or do you think you're going to faint?"

"I can walk."

"Let's go." Wrapping my arm around her, I led her through the house to my mom's room.

Knocking on the door, I waited for her to answer.

From the grim look on her face, she'd heard the screams and had been waiting for this visit. When she saw Elle tucked into my side her eyes fluttered shut, and she muttered a curse with Johnny's name attached to it.

"Come here, you poor girl. Let me see what happened and what we can do for you." When I started to follow them in, Mom released Elle and whirled on me. Shoving her hand into my chest, she pushed me out of the room. "Johnny is going to be the death of you in every sense of the word, Demitri. Don't let him lead you and everyone else to your deaths because you feel responsible for him—because you feel like you owe him."

"Mom . . . he's—"

"I understand family that runs deeper than blood," she ground out. "I understand loyalty. You're a fool if you think he does too." With another hard shove to my chest, she jerked her chin. "Get this girl something for the pain. Get her food. And for God's sake, think about what you're putting this family and this girl through by letting him control your mind."

I stared at the door in shock and denial for long minutes before turning to go back into the kitchen where Elle's blood still lingered all over the island and floor.

Searching the takeout drawer for a menu, I called in for food, then started cleaning once I found a bottle of aspirin. The entire time my mom's words replayed in my mind.

But none of it made sense.

If anyone was controlling the other—it was me controlling Johnny.

I'd been the one reeling him in our entire lives. I'd been the one calming him.

But for the first time, I didn't know how to quiet his savage side. And it fucking terrified me.

Chapter 37

AFTER

Lily

"You're a brave girl," Sofia said, her voice sad as she bandaged my arm. "I'm sorry we couldn't take you to a hospital to do this."

I watched as the last of the perfectly neat stitches disappeared under the wrappings and nodded. "I understand."

I understood more than I could say.

Hospitals were a last resort to prevent death.

Police were only involved if they happened to show.

Mob life.

I handed the bottle of vodka back to her, meeting her gaze at her huff.

"You were supposed to drink it to help ease the pain. Not hold it for me." Standing, she took her large kit and vodka back to the chest she'd grabbed them from earlier and put them back with a practiced ease.

I wondered for a brief moment how often she'd had to use that kit, then I realized I'd rather not know.

"Thank you," I said as I stood. "I'm sorry you had to—"

"Don't apologize to me. Just promise me one thing." She waited until I nodded to continue. "If my son doesn't find a way to keep you from Johnny, keep yourself away from this house."

"Of course," I murmured immediately, trying to hide my panic at where I would see Dare. I didn't want to spend the rest of the time I had with him at Brooks Street or at The Jack.

I wanted some sense of normalcy and privacy while I could still pretend the fast-approaching end would never come.

I accepted a kiss on the cheek from her before slipping out of her door, then wandered down the halls until I found my way to the living room, rocking back on my heels when I found Dare in there, sitting on a couch with his head in his hands.

His hands fell, and he looked up as soon as I stepped into the room, his expression tortured.

"Come here."

I walked slowly to him, stopping just in front of his legs. My teeth sank into my bottom lip when he leaned forward to run his hands up the back of my thighs, pulling me forward until I was crawling onto his lap, straddling him.

He leaned over, grabbing a glass of water and two pills from the end table before handing them to me. "For the pain," he mumbled. Once he had the glass on the table, he sat up, his gaze falling over my body again and again. "How are you feeling?"

I lifted a shoulder. "I've had better days."

"Why didn't you scream, Elle?"

Because he came up behind me so suddenly I hadn't even known he was there before he had me bent over the counter, my face smashed into the granite and his harsh words in my ear.

Because he'd had a knife inches from my face.

Because I didn't want to die.

"Scream, and I'll slit your throat. Lie, and I'll gut you, you fucking rat."

When he'd forced my arm onto the counter and dug the blade into it, it had been the first time I'd allowed myself to make a sound.

"That's called payback, you Holloway whore."

"I did when I could," I finally said.

Dare pressed his head into my stomach, his back shuddering with his rough exhale. "I'm sorry. I'm so goddamn sorry." His hand lifted to lightly trace the bandage, then dropped to grip my fingers. "I should've known something was wrong when he didn't return, but I wasn't expecting you back yet."

"I told you I needed to leave so I could come back to you." I tried to make my tone light and slightly teasing, but his back tensed and fingers tightened on mine in response. "Johnny's actions aren't your fault," I murmured, pressing a kiss to his head. Running my free hand through his hair, I tugged so he would meet my gaze and tried to smile. But it felt forced.

I could see it, he was thinking about what Johnny had said to him . . . what he'd heard me admit.

"If you want to ask, then do it."

"I don't," he said automatically. "I heard what you said."

"But you're wondering, and that wonder is going to turn into doubt. Just ask me what's on your mind."

"What's on my mind is that everything I've been terrified would happen began this afternoon. That guy you saw? He was the business partner I told you about—the one I was supposed to meet. But he didn't show, and I couldn't get hold of him. When we got back to the house, he was here waiting. And I about lost my fucking mind because I had to act like there wasn't someone in the house I didn't want him to see—I had to act like I wasn't terrified of him seeing you and real-izing what you meant to me. And then the glass . . ."

"I'm sorry." The apology left me automatically, effortlessly.

"Don't be."

But I was. Even though in that moment my world had felt like it was falling down around me, dying the way his fiancée had was Dare's greatest fear. And I'd put him in a position where he'd revealed everything he'd wanted to protect and conceal.

"But when he left earlier, he should've never come back. The fact that he did . . ." Dare blew out a harsh breath, his eyes narrowing into slits. "Him being there, waiting for you when you came back and asking about us . . . it's like starting a game. Only our games don't end until there's a body count and so much blood spilled you can't seem to ever get clean again."

The drop in his tone sent a chill up my spine.

His eyes scanned my face, searching for long seconds before he finally asked, "Have you ever heard of Holloway?"

I knew as soon as the question passed his lips why he was staring at me so intently.

He was waiting for my response.

And *there* was that doubt.

At the slightest dip of my chin, it was as if Dare's expression had turned to stone. "Johnny demanded to know what my role was with them about a dozen times in the kitchen."

His eyes slid closed, his hands releasing me to run through his hair as a harsh breath left him. "I'll kill him," he muttered so softly, I was sure the promise wasn't meant for me to hear.

Bringing my injured arm to his lips, he passed a feather-soft kiss across the bandage and dropped his hands to my hips, pulling me closer as he leaned back against the cushions.

"Doesn't surprise me that you haven't," he began. "Holloway is a gang that came to the city a generation after we did. At that point, we'd already taken over the city and were territorial."

"Shocking," I murmured, offering him a wry grin.

He pinched my side in return. "They bought a huge chunk of land, and for the most part didn't leave it. If a Holloway was in town, it was immediate bloodshed."

I knew all this. I'd grown up hearing it.

But it was captivating hearing it from the enemy, to see how much it seemed to weigh on him when I would've expected something so different.

"In the last decade there's been a shift," he said, his brows furrowing. "For the most part, members of Holloway are still on their plot of land, hiding out. If they leave, they lie real low. But now they're

into bigger, worse things than ever. And we're pulling out of everything we've ever done, trying to dissolve it all."

"You are?" The words were out before I could attempt to stop
myself, my tone dripping with relief.

A huff punched from Dare's chest. "You think I *want* this? The
mafia has controlled and stolen my entire life. I've worked endlessly
for years to get this family on a different path. But there are old-
school members like Johnny who fight that." He attempted a laugh
then sighed. "And then there are setbacks."

"Like what?" I asked, fascinated to know this information that
was widely unknown among Holloway. Or, at least, kept hidden from
most of us.

"Like today. That guy who talked to you, he was a Holloway. And
a Holloway . . . a Holloway killed Gia."

Hearing her name from his lips for the first time left a hollow feeling in my chest. It was so much more than being reminded of the love
I'd involuntarily stolen from him. It was as if her name alone breathed
life into the vengeance that simmered in his veins.

"Now they know about you." One of his hands gently wrapped
around the back of my neck to pull me closer. His lip curled. "We've
been waiting for them. We knew they were going to come for us
eventually. But I didn't think *he* would wait for you outside."

I knew I wasn't able to hide my confusion, because his frustrated
admission was so opposite of what I knew—what the men who'd
been hiding me for years had been telling me and each other.

I twisted my body to slide onto the couch next to him, curling
against his chest and leaving my legs draped over his lap in a weak
attempt to hide my emotions. "Why are they coming for you?" I
asked, my voice a breath as I tried to prepare myself for whatever he
might say.

I couldn't handle any more surprises.

For a long time, he didn't respond. When he did, the reply was
hesitant. "There was a setback. We messed up. Revealed ourselves

and our plan too soon. And I know there's no way they're going to let it go. They'll try to prevent it, and the way to prevent it is to take us out first."

It didn't take long to understand what he was vaguely describing. The break-in.

He thought they were coming for them because of the break-in, and Beck and Kieran were so sure that Dare was using it as an aggressive move to keep us scared until they attacked again.

And suddenly everything began falling into place.

"Is that why you're all in this house together?"

"Of course." He tipped my head back to look into my eyes. "The best time to attack is when we're at our weakest. We're weakest when we're alone. So, for now, none of my family is alone."

"Libby's been at work," I reminded him.

"The bouncers are members."

I wanted to be surprised, but I wasn't. "And you? You're always alone."

"There's only one way to hurt me, and now they know that way exists." He dipped his head to pass a kiss across my lips, lingering when he said, "Now you know why it feels like I'm dying every time you force me to watch you leave."

"I'm sorry."

Wonder filled his eyes as they searched my own. The corner of his mouth twitched into a grin as he whispered, "Goddamn firefly."

His mouth fell onto mine in a soft, but breathtaking kiss, his tongue tracing my lips before teasing my own just as the doorbell rang.

A growl sounded in his chest and his forehead fell to mine. "That's probably dinner." Sliding my legs off his lap, he stood from the couch and pulled me up with him. "I'll meet you in my room with the food."

"Something wrong with the kitchen?" I asked wryly as I walked away, a low laugh sounding in my throat at his answering glare.

But as soon as I was in the hall heading toward his room, my smile slipped.

There were similarities—*so* many similarities.

I'd known the Borello family had lived freely while we'd remained out of sight. Staying on the property or slipping from shadow to shadow throughout town.

It was why my brothers and I had been homeschooled. It was why most of the Holloway men chose to live in Soldier's Row, keeping their families in Raleigh. Keeping them a secret from our dark world.

It was why I'd been mostly kept from the outside world long before my faked death.

But even with all their freedom, the Borellos were still hiding.

Dare was hiding them.

Even if there was a way to stop what was coming—if there was a way for us to be together—it would still be a life of fear and protection and being kept from enemies.

And yet, even at that realization, I knew I would gladly live that life if it meant a life with Demitri Borello.

Because living without the man who could touch my soul—the man who had silently put my destroyed heart back together—would be a slow, agonizing death. More painful than anything Johnny could do to me physically, or Kieran and Mickey could inflict on me emotionally.

That familiar energy slid over my skin a second before his deep voice rumbled, "What is it?"

I turned to find him watching me intently, a bag of food in hand.

"What is it that sometimes makes you look like you're being tortured by something worse than Johnny?"

"What I want and what I would give up to have it," I said honestly. Lifting a shoulder in the barest hint of a shrug, I let a sad laugh tumble from my lips. "And what I can't change."

He stepped into the room, setting the food on his dresser so he could pull me into his arms. His eyebrows drew together, his dark eyes begging to understand.

"Will I ever know?" As patient as he'd been, I could hear the wariness in his tone. I knew he couldn't handle the half-truths for much longer.

Then again . . . we didn't have long left.

"One day," I answered with a forced grin as I slipped from his hold. "One day soon you'll know it all."

I grabbed the bag of food off the dresser and slid my hand down his arm to intertwine our fingers, pulling him toward the couch.

Tilting my head back to look at him, I said, "But tonight, I just want you and me. I don't want to worry about what's happening in our lives. I want to eat . . ."

"Thai," he answered with a smirk that was quickly widening into one of his blinding smiles.

I scrunched up my face and teased, "Italians eat Thai?"

He twisted our joined hands around my back and pulled me close, his fingers digging playfully into my side as he buried his face into my hair. "I'll show you what I want to eat." The huskiness of his tone sent a shock straight to my core.

My head dropped back and my eyes fluttered shut when he ran his fingers between my legs, a plea for him to continue on the tip of my tongue before the bag of food was suddenly snatched from my hand, and he pushed me backward onto the couch.

When he followed me down, I slid my fingers into his hair and placed a teasing kiss on his lips. "I want to have tonight to know this is real."

To remember it was.

He looked at me as if he knew what I wasn't saying—as if he could suddenly feel the weight of what was coming for us—and he couldn't fathom why a time would ever come when we weren't together anymore.

The lighthearted moment we'd been in shifted into something else entirely.

Something profound and devastating.

"Real?" he asked, his voice pure gravel. "Elle, you made me

breathe again. You made me aware I was alive. Nothing's more real than that. I love you."

My heart swelled and my soul cried out.

My throat tightened and my eyes burned.

Those words were my greatest pleasure and my greatest pain.

I would never forget the way they sounded coming from Dare's lips, but I'd known the second they had that this was the moment I'd been dreading. This was the goodbye.

"I love you. Until the very end."

"After, Elle," he whispered. "*After.*"

Movements slowed. Kisses deepened. The world apart from us was completely forgotten as Dare lifted himself off me, his hands trailing up my stomach, taking my shirt as he went.

He angled down, his mouth covering my lace-covered breast as he wrapped his arms underneath me and shifted to stand.

I tightened my legs around his hips, my head falling back when his teeth raked against my hardened nipple.

Fisting a hand in my hair, he forced my head up in time for his mouth to fall onto my own, his tongue begging for entrance as my back hit the comforter.

I grabbed for his shirt, my movements slow as I dragged it up his body and over his head, letting it fall to the floor when his mouth moved across my jaw and down my throat.

My bra and jeans were soon added to the clothing on the floor, but when I reached for the button on his jeans, he gripped my wrists and gently placed my hands over my head.

Warmth pooled low in my stomach when he nipped the sensitive spot behind my ear and breathed a gravelly, "Patience."

With a light squeeze to my wrists, he lightly trailed his fingers down my arms and over my waist, stopping to knead my breasts.

Each touch was unhurried and alternated between achingly tender and blissfully rough. And with each touch, I nearly went out of my mind with need.

Need to be able to touch him. Need for more. Need for this for the rest of my life.

His tongue teased and fingers tormented. His teeth grazed and his mouth brushed.

Everywhere he touched, that connection we'd always shared magnified in a way I couldn't define . . . in a way I never wanted to end.

By the time he lowered himself between my thighs, his breath washing over where I was aching for him, I was already panting and writhing against the bed. My core was wound so tight I was sure I would fall over the edge the second he touched me.

"Jesus, Elle, look at you." Desire and awe filled his tone as he ran his finger along my entrance, a shudder surging through me at the contact. "Fucking perfect." The rough way the words fell from his lips had me looking down, my blood heating at the predatory way he was watching me.

He dipped a finger inside me, the action tentative . . . a tease.

My thighs clenched and a whimper sounded in the back of my throat when he angled his face so his mouth brushed against me. And with a carnal smirk, he growled, "Come."

I cried out, my head falling back when he slanted his mouth over my clit, sucking and raking his teeth over the knot of sensitive flesh.

I shattered, my body bowing off the bed when he added a second finger, pushing hard and deep. Curling them and hitting that spot inside me that heightened my orgasm and stole my breath.

Unable to resist any longer, I reached for him, sliding my fingers into his hair and holding tight as he lapped at me, drawing out the pleasure that continued to rock through me.

I sucked in a sharp breath when he placed another teasing bite to my too sensitive clit, trying to twist away and close my legs even when his broad shoulders prevented the movements.

A low laugh rumbled in his chest and his dark eyes flashed up to meet mine. With another graze of his teeth along my thigh, he removed his fingers, sliding them down, down, down until my body arched and a plea tumbled from my lips.

"Fuck," he groaned, teasing me for another second before he removed his hand and gripped my wrists to place my hands flat on the bed again.

He stood from the bed, his eyes swirling with need as he removed his pants and boxer briefs. The heat in my belly intensified when he fisted his length in his hand, pumping slowly as he knelt on the bed between my thighs.

"Say it, Elle," he begged. "Give me *after*."

Before meeting Dare, I was sure when I died, that would be the end.

In reality, I had died, until I found him two years ago in the café. His unconcealed strength, dark yet light force, unforgiving resolve shown through his notes and self-control . . . somehow, even in our silence we'd become *us*. Our souls had known each other, even in our wordlessness.

As a result, even death couldn't extinguish what we had.

The connection that hummed between us proved that.

We would always find each other. We would always be together.

So I would love him until the end of this life . . . and then I would love him long after, wherever death took us.

"I'll be yours forever."

A stuttered breath ripped from my lungs when he pushed into me. He grasped my hips to hold me still while he pulled out with agonizing slowness, his length trailing over me before he slid back in, inch by inch.

He bent to hover over me, his tongue flicking and flattening against my nipple as his forearms came to rest on either side of my head. And then he moved. His hips rolling to fill me again and again while his whispered words filled my head.

I was his.

He was never letting me go.

Forever. Forever. Forever.

It was the sweetest bliss and purest torture.

I clung to his back, holding tight when he found his release deep inside me.

His mouth brushed along my shoulder when a little aftershock passed through my body and into his. "I don't know where you came from, Firefly, but, God, don't ever leave." His pleading eyes met mine when he breathed, "I love you."

After. Please . . . love me after.

Chapter 38

LINGER

Lily

Dare and I spent the night wrapped up in each other, eating Thai and laughing over stories of what it was like growing up with his generation of Borello members. We'd spent hours kissing and touching, learning what drove the other crazy.

All the while I knew it wouldn't matter come morning.

And when he'd finally fallen asleep, I allowed myself a few minutes in his arms before I'd slipped out of bed to dress, fighting back tears the entire time.

For the first time, I let myself linger.

I told myself we could figure things out. I told myself he would get past his need for revenge if he knew *who* Lily O'Sullivan was. But I knew I was only kidding myself.

So Beck had found me waiting outside the house he'd dropped me off at the night before, thinking over my time with Dare and trying to commit it to memory.

He took one look at me when I slipped into the passenger seat and let loose a sigh, squeezing my hand in a wordless apology.

He knew.

I bit down on my cheek, forcing myself not to cry in front of Beck. He wouldn't understand my tears—would most likely be insulted by them. I had to be thankful he'd given me one last night with the enemy who had become my everything.

"Jesus fuck, Lil. What happened?" he shouted when he saw my other arm.

I instinctively tried to cover my bandaged arm and gave him a cautious look. "Um . . . Johnny stabbed me. He's not there, Dare sent him away," I added quickly when I saw a look of pure rage settle in Beck's eyes.

"I'll fucking kill that psycho."

"Yeah, well you might need to get in line. He did it because he saw you drive off not long before I walked up to the house last night, and he's been suspicious about me from the first night he met me," I explained. "And I think he just wanted to pay me back."

"For what?"

I lifted my arm.

Beck looked at me blankly for a few seconds, and then his face morphed into shock. "No shit, Lil. You stabbed *Johnny*?"

"He came after me when his paranoia was at an all-time high about a week and a half ago," I said, and tried to ward off the chill from the memory. "But I keep one of Kieran's knives in my bag . . ."

He fought back a grin before putting the car in drive and taking off. "I don't know if I should smack you or high-five you or lock you up for the rest of your goddamn life. But, Jesus, I'm fucking proud of you."

"Yeah, well—"

"That's not something you're gonna be able to hide from Kieran."

My stomach clenched, and I sucked in a swift breath. I hadn't even thought about Kieran seeing my arm, but now that Beck mentioned it, I wondered why it mattered.

He was going to find out everything anyway. One way or another.

"You're wrong, you know," I mumbled to Beck when we were nearly home. "About Dare."

He huffed, the sound tired and frustrated. "Oh yeah?"

I turned my head where it was resting against the window to look at him. "We all know eventually they're coming back for me, but they're not doing it to get back at you for lying to them. They're not biding their time to scare us with what they're planning. *They're* scared."

From Beck's furrowed brow, I knew he wasn't sure what to do with what I was suggesting.

"He's worried because they messed up by destroying the house. He's waiting for the day that Holloway comes after them to *prevent* them from coming for me." When Beck's eyebrows shot up, I warned, "I'll never forgive you if that's what you do."

"I'm not who you have to worry about. When Kieran finds out, he's gonna go on a hunt."

"Beck." His name sounded strangled coming from me. "Beck, you can't let him. *Please* don't let him."

"Lil, the guy wants to kill you. Who cares if Kieran stops—"

"Beck, *please*."

"Lily," he barked. "Do you realize how fucked this whole situation is? You fell into it with a Borello. *The* Borello. You turned your back on us and—"

"Don't talk to me about turning backs. Don't you dare."

"You've been sleeping with a Borello. You've been hanging with Borellos. You got stabbed by a motherfucking Borello and acted like it was just something that happens. And look at you. For someone who gets so pissed about being kept hidden in the guesthouse, you're *hiding* yourself." He let out a sound of frustration and flung his hand out. "Take that shit off."

I ground my teeth, but didn't respond as I put the glasses away and took out the contacts, then threw my hair into a bun on top of my head.

"You're going to the meeting with us this afternoon. You're not leaving my sight after this. I don't care what he said to you or how in love with him you think you are. They're still coming for you, and I'm not leaving you unprotected for anything."

Anger burned so deep, but I forced myself to breathe as I searched my bag for the makeup remover. I knew I couldn't respond to him without lashing out.

Even with Dare's need to keep his family protected, he'd still known he couldn't keep me locked up. He'd heard me when I'd told him that if he'd tried, he would never see me again, and he'd respected it.

"Now you know why it feels like I'm dying every time you force me to watch you leave."

My hands slowed and my body stilled as more of the conversation from last night played through my mind, something about his words triggering a thought. It felt like a word I'd been trying to think of was on the tip of my tongue, and I was reaching . . .

"The best time to attack is when we're at our weakest. We're weakest when we're alone. So, for now, none of my family is alone."

"We're at our weakest when we're alone," I whispered, catching Beck's attention.

"What?"

"The meeting. The meeting, Beck, oh my God!" I gripped his arm, accidentally jerking the car. "We're weakest when we're alone. It's the meeting, Beck."

"Jesus fuck, Lil. Calm down, what are you talking about?"

"Don't you see? Teagan's being taken during a meeting," I nearly yelled, still gripping and shaking his arm, trying to make him understand. "Every Holloway member has to attend, so no one will be with her to protect her. It has to be during a meeting."

"Shit," he whispered, a frantic look suddenly taking over his face. "But I—we don't know which meeting—"

"It doesn't matter, you idiot. Let's get her before they even have a chance."

He shot me a look, then gestured to the clock on his dashboard. "It's just after four in the morning. I can't just barge into their house and take her. Finn would lose his shit and it would ruin everything.

I'll—Christ, I don't know. I'll figure it out. We'll get her though. I told you we'd stop it from happening, and we will."

"Let me call her, I'll tell her what's happening. She's planning on running from here anyway, I'll just have her make it look like she left Finn. We can figure out somewhere to hide her until she can leave."

"You're supposed to be dead," he said harshly. "Even though Finn knows you're alive, he knows you can't have contact with the outside world at all—and that includes Teagan. If he answers the phone and it's you on the other end of the line, we're gonna have bigger problems than me barging in there to keep her safe from a kidnapping. Let me get us back to Holloway, and I'll handle this."

I settled back into my seat and pressed my head against the window. "Holloway's the problem," I breathed, too low for him to hear.

When we pulled onto the property, I reached into my bag, trailing my fingers along the hard edge of the folded paper over and over again before clearing my throat.

"Dare's going to be at Brooks Street Monday morning," I began, sliding out the note as I spoke.

The paper quivered in my hand as I stared at it, wavering in my decision.

I wanted one more day with him.

One more hour.

One more minute.

This letter confirmed I'd already spent those, and they'd gone too fast.

With a trembling breath out, I opened the center console just enough to drop the letter inside. "He'll expect me to be there. Promise me you'll get that letter to him."

Beck stared at the console for a few more seconds before looking at me from under his lashes. "You sure about that?"

"It's the only way I can truly say goodbye."

"Then I'll make it happen."

I offered him a weak smile, then opened the door and set foot onto Holloway Estate. A heavy weight settled in my gut as I looked around the place I'd grown up in, knowing that this was the last time I would ever walk *on*to the property, and that the chance of leaving it again— *alive*—was slim.

Chapter 39

GONE

Dare

I knew when I woke she was gone.

The bed felt empty and cold, and that heady electricity that clung to my skin when she was near was gone.

Even still, I pushed up from the bed to look around and quickly slid off the side, hurrying into my bathroom in search of the girl I couldn't seem to get a grasp on.

My hands dug into the doorframe of the bathroom, my stomach sinking when I found it empty. Pushing away, I turned to search the rest of the house but slowed when I found a paper and pen resting on top of my dresser.

Dread filled my veins like poison as I reached for it.

Something in the way she'd looked at me the night before.

Something in the way she'd clung to me . . .

It made her absence and this note all the more foreboding now.

Gritting my teeth, I blew a sharp breath out through my nose and looked down. An amused huff left me when I read her words the first time . . . a ghost of a smile pulled at my lips the second.

Gladly, Firefly . . . Gladly.

~~Truth or~~ Dare
Love me forever.

Chapter 40

BURIED ALIVE

Lily

I shot from my chair and hurried to leave the room as soon as the meeting ended that afternoon.

I didn't care about keeping up my usual indifferent expression, I *couldn't* care. Because Mickey had been waiting in the conference room before anyone else had entered, but Kieran wasn't with him and hadn't been by the guesthouse once that morning.

He also never showed up during the meeting.

Considering what Beck now knew about Dare and me, I'd been terrified about where Kieran might have been throughout the meeting—what he might be doing or who he might be confronting.

Killing.

"Princess," Mickey called out, his voice full and authoritative, but still somehow holding a deceptive edge of fatherly love.

Bullshit.

I kept walking.

"Lily, wait a second."

A few of the members cast wary glances my way when I didn't stop, but no one said a word.

It wasn't until I was out of the room that I was yanked back to come face to face with the blue-eyed devil himself.

"When I tell you to wait, you better damn well do as I say." Despite the venom-coated warning, his smile was blinding, and his eyes held false warmth.

I hated him.

I hated everything about him and hated that I shared his blood.

"Where's Kieran?"

Mickey sucked a settling breath in and held it for a few seconds before allowing himself to respond to me. "I would suspect he's sleeping for the first time in a few days. As his future wife, it would've been nice of you to have been there to help him relax."

I jerked back in disgust, but Mickey only tightened his grip on my arm and pulled me closer to hiss in my ear.

"And when I say *future wife*, I already know how your little argument ended. Don't be stupid, Lily. Don't make a mistake that you *really* shouldn't make, if you know what I mean."

I opened my mouth to argue, but nothing came out.

There was no reason to fight with Mickey over this. I almost wasn't sure if there was any fight left in me regarding my relationships.

I felt beaten down and exhausted.

"Now, the reason I wanted to talk to you before you interrupted me—something else you should really think twice about before doing again," he said with a subtle narrowing of his eyes. "You're moving back into the house. It's been decided."

"No, I'm—"

"It's not up for discussion," he bit out. "I let you play house back there for longer than I should have, and now that place has been compromised. If you try to spend another night there, I'll drag you back here myself by your hair. Understand?"

He didn't wait for me to respond, he just let out a loud laugh and grabbed the back of my head to press a kiss to my forehead.

"Knew you would, Princess," he called out over his shoulder as he walked away.

I turned slowly to find my way out, and bit the inside of my cheeks to hide my embarrassment when I saw other Holloway members pouring out of the room. Beck stood a few feet away with his arms crossed over his chest as he leaned against the wall, not seeming to notice the other guys surrounding us.

From the warring looks of frustration and indecision on his face, he hadn't known what Mickey would say, but he didn't disagree.

"It's not the worst idea, Lil," he mumbled when he finally fell into step beside me once we were outside.

"What? Marrying Kieran or moving back into the house?"

"Both."

"Did Kieran say anything to you?" I asked, slanting a glare his way. "He should've been in the meeting. I've never known him to choose sleep over work—even a meeting."

But Beck simply shrugged. "They were gone a long time, Lil. You know he never sleeps on a job. Maybe it's catching up with him. It was bound to after all this time, ya know? He can't do this forever."

Or maybe Beck was lying since he was rambling.

Even with all the lies that had come to light in the last weeks, I trusted Beck wholeheartedly. There were things he hadn't been able to know at the time because of his loyalty to Kieran, and for the same reason, I knew there were things he hadn't been able to tell me.

But while I knew Beck would never lie to me if given a choice . . . Mickey and Kieran had the power to take that choice away.

I stopped walking, a sigh bursting from me. "Beck, I can't do this. I've been repeatedly hit by news that was too much to handle. I feel like as soon as I start to get the slightest grip on what I've learned, I get knocked back down by something else. It's getting hard to breathe from more than the walls that close in on me here," I said, gesturing to the guesthouse that was now only dozens of feet from us. "I know you're lying. Just tell me so I'm not ambushed as soon as I walk into that house."

With a firm nod, he placed a hand on my back and turned me toward the guesthouse, forcing me to continue walking. "He got back when you were in the shower. I told him what Dare found out about Teagan, and what you figured out about the meeting—but made it sound like it was something I'd come up with. He left immediately and was going to sit on Finn and Teagan's house until Finn left. He's gonna get her set up in a hotel, paid with cash, until she can get out of here."

The relief I felt was so profound I felt dizzy. I hated knowing I would never see Teagan again, but I would take never seeing her over her being kidnapped and sold. Covering my mouth when I choked on a sob, I stepped onto the porch and whispered, "Thank you, Beck."

"Don't mention it, Lil."

As soon as we stepped into the house, we both froze.

"This isn't a hotel," Beck mumbled, then hurried to shut the door and started closing all the blinds so no one would see Teagan.

"What are you doing here?" My throat was so tight my question sounded strained. "I thought they were going to hide you . . ." I stopped rushing toward her and looked around when I noticed the hard look on her face and the terrifying charge filling the house and pressing down on me.

"Tell me."

I jumped and sucked in a gasp when his voice came from the hall.

Without making a sound, he appeared at the entrance, his face tortured. "Tell me," he repeated.

"Tell you what?"

"Tell me what she said isn't fucking true, Lily," he roared.

I shakily looked over my shoulder at Teagan, her face pinched with an apology, but the same betrayal and fury burned deep in her eyes.

"What did you do?" I asked, the question no more than a breath.

She lifted her chin high and clenched her jaw. "He needed to know."

"He would've found out anyway, Teagan, but he shouldn't have found out from *you!*"

I jumped, staggering back when a crash sounded from in front of me, and found one of the new replacement lamps shattered on the floor by the wall.

Kieran was gripping his hair, his chest moving roughly as he tried to calm himself. "There should've been nothing for me to find out."

"Kieran, I—"

"There should've been nothing for me to find out!"

"I know, I'm sorry. I'm so sorry. I didn't mean for this to happen, I—"

"He's a goddamn Borello, Lily," he yelled, like that fact had possibly been lost on me until that very second. "He's the guy who wants to end your life."

"I know—"

"You've been saying 'what about us,' and this is what you've been doing?" He swung his arm, slapping a vase off the end table. "Fucking *what about us?*"

"You left me," I screamed. "You broke my heart and your promises, and left me here. There was no *us* left."

Kieran looked dumbfounded. "Everything I've been doing has been—"

"Oh my God, don't," I pleaded. "Don't say that again. Not one thing has been for me. I told you, Kieran, I've *been* telling you I've been here needing you and begging you to see me, and you were never here. You left me for Mickey. You've been doing things that are completely unforgivable. And I know that you've been working with—"

"Ah-ah," Beck cut in loudly. "Don't."

The look on Kieran's face as his gaze darted from me to Beck was truly frightening.

"Take Teagan somewhere safe," Kieran growled. "She has everything she needs."

"I don't think it's a good idea for me to leave you two—"

"Go."

Beck ground his jaw, and after a few seconds finally nodded.

Once he and Teagan were gone from the house, Kieran looked at me.

The rage and anger were gone and replaced by a hurt so deep that I wanted to fall into his arms and cry.

"Why?" he asked after minutes spent in agonizing silence.

"Kieran, I never planned to even speak to him. And I think it all happened without ever saying a word to him or knowing his name."

"What all happen—?" He grit his teeth, the muscles in his jaw working under the pressure.

A sob burst free at the agony that crossed his face. "I'm sorry."

"Lily, how? We had plans—we'd planned *our* future."

I leaned against the wall and shakily sank to the floor, cradling my head in my hands. I don't think Kieran would ever understand, no matter how many times I told him.

It was like Beck said.

I was Kieran's priority, and he'd been trained to put his all into his job. And, according to Kieran and Beck, he'd been doing this job for me. So he'd never done anything wrong.

"I wanted that future. I wanted those plans. I've been begging you to make them happen. After so many years of being brushed aside, I realized I was the only one who wanted it. I realized I was the only one who wanted *us* to work."

"Brush you aside? Lily, I've been working my ass off for—"

"God, Kieran!" I dropped my hands and lifted my head to look at him. "Instead of telling me you're doing all this for me, why don't you explain it to me?" I gripped my stomach and said, "Do you know how disgusting it feels for you to tell me you're involved in the middle of a human trafficking ring *for me*? That you're helping Mickey *start* one *for me*? Or the very men you've been protecting and hiding me from for years, you've been *working with . . . for me*?"

His face fell. "Who told you that?"

"It doesn't matter. Whenever you say these things, it makes me sick. It feels like you're punching me in the stomach. You were trained to be a murderer, Kieran. That's a truly horrifying thought, but it's something I came to terms with so long ago because I know who you really are. I know you hated that side of you and hated your dad for making you into this. And because I *knew* you wanted to escape it. But the way you've embraced this life—"

"I fucking hate this life," he ground out as he slowly closed the distance between us. Once he was in front of me, he dropped to a crouch and caged me in with his hands pressed to the wall. "I hate your dad. Aric found out what Mickey was doing with this human trafficking ring a long time ago, and started digging deeper to try to put an end to it before it could get too far along. I only did the minimum because I was about to get us out of here. We kept hitting roadblocks because your dad knew every move we made, so I reached out to someone I knew Mickey would never suspect."

I sucked in a sharp breath when it hit me. "Dare."

That anger slowly started creeping back in the moment I said his name. Kieran's breaths grew rougher, his green eyes became harder, but even with me sitting here in front of him, the beast inside him stayed locked up.

"Right. *Dare*. He didn't want to pass up on an opportunity to take down the guy who killed his dad . . . and then Aric died and Mickey killed Dare's fiancée." Kieran searched my face to see if he was telling me anything new, and continued when I didn't react. "Mickey got more involved, and so did we. We knew he didn't have to only be shut down, he needed to be put in the ground. But with how far into the process he already was, it wasn't as simple as killing him. We needed to destroy his business, Holloway, and stop the ring from happening, which takes time. Longer because he wants me by his side for every single thing. He didn't like that Aric was pulling away and had members looking into *why* he was. He expects me to be like my dad."

I nodded, remembering how Mickey was never seen without Georgie. He wasn't just Mickey's advisor, he was Mickey's bodyguard and best friend.

"Most of my week is spent working for Mickey, which only leaves me a few hours to work on taking him down because Beck has to continue selling, and I can only rely on Dare so much. And not only has there been a damn clock ticking over my head to get this done before Mickey can make things happen, I've been working longer hours and days to get it done faster so I can get us the hell out of here. But this was something Aric and I started before he died, and I know it's important to you. I know you hate Mickey and Holloway as much as I do, and I know you want to see it destroyed. I've been destroying it, Lily. It just takes time. And now that I'm days or weeks from being done, I find out you're . . . fuck, I find out I've lost you because of it?"

I wished I could tell him he was wrong. "Why didn't you just tell me what you were doing? Why did you shut me out?"

Again, that baffled look.

He had no idea he had.

He rocked back to sit, and drove his hands through his hair again and again. "What was I going to tell you, Lily? I've never told you about a job. You made me swear when we were younger I would never tell you."

"I meant killing. I didn't want to know about what you did as Nightshade."

He shrugged. "There's no difference."

"Things might've been different if you'd told me why we weren't running away. We might still be happy if you'd just told me what you were doing."

"We can be happy," he said sincerely. "I can make you happy, Lily." When I began shaking my head, he reached for me. "We'll leave. Today, tomorrow, whenever you want."

"Kieran, the part of me that loved you is so shattered, there's no—"

He sat forward, crushing his mouth to mine in a kiss that I'd spent a decade begging for.

"I'll spend the rest of my life putting every piece back together," he said against my trembling lips, his hands cradling my cheeks. "I know you're hurt."

"I can't." I gripped his hands and pulled them off my face, my eyes blurring with tears when I did.

His hands slid back up my arms, the movements sluggish. "Lily, don't do . . . what the hell is that?"

Before I could stop him, he grabbed for the bottom of the long sleeve on my top and pulled it up, his body going unnaturally still when he saw the bandage.

"Um, I . . ." I swallowed through the lump in my throat and forced myself to tell him the truth. "Johnny got—*Kieran*," I shouted when he suddenly pushed away from me and took off for the bedroom.

I scrambled to stand and hurried to follow him. By the time I made it in there, his expression was blank and his eyes were the kind of lifeless, too horrifying to look into, and he was arming himself with knives.

"Kieran, please," I begged as I gripped his arms. "Don't go over there—Johnny isn't even there anymore."

He didn't have to tell me what he planned to do, it was written all over his stone-like face.

"Move."

"No, I know what you'll do if you go there. I know what will happen if you find Dare instead of Johnny. I can't let you go."

The moment Dare's name slipped from my lips, I regretted it. That beast that had stayed subdued throughout our confessions flickered to life. Kieran's chest expanded and contracted with his breaths, each rougher than the last.

My hands began shaking, and if I was smart, I would've turned and ran.

But I held on.

Kieran gripped my waist and rushed me backward until I was pressed against the wall. Despite how fast we'd moved, I landed against it softly—like Kieran was still fighting against the beast to try to keep me safe.

"Kieran, you can't go. I can't let you."

But with each second that passed, more of Kieran disappeared until all that stood in front of me was Nightshade.

I'd never been more afraid or destroyed in my life.

"I hate what he did to you," I whispered.

Keeping my grip on him, I slid my hands down his arms until they were gripping his hands. With one last look at those disturbing eyes, I slowly turned my body so my chest was pressed to the wall and my back was facing him, and I pulled him against me.

And I waited.

"Lily." His arms curled around my torso, pulling me tighter into his familiar embrace. A shuddering breath tore through him as his head dropped onto mine. "I would never hurt you."

"I know."

"Look at me," he begged, his voice rough.

A plea I'd waited for my entire life. A plea that was years too late.

When I glanced over my shoulder, he forced me to turn so we were face to face. His grip on me tightened and his jaw clenched, but he remained unwavering.

"I felt like I was buried alive the day they lowered those two caskets in the ground, and ever since I've been trying to dig myself out," he confessed. "But no matter what I do I bury myself deeper instead. You think I don't see that you're drowning, Lily? My mistakes are why you are. I just didn't know *I* was drowning you when I've been spending every day of the last four years trying to fix what I ruined."

He'd said something similar the night he asked me to marry him, only now it finally made sense.

Kieran was destroying the world and man I hated so much. He was getting his revenge on Mickey for being the catalyst that ultimately led to Aric's death.

So much made sense . . . *now*. If only he had told me long before tonight.

I stilled when I noticed my body was trembling, and I slowly let my gaze travel from his arms to his fast-moving chest to his tensed jaw.

When I met his eyes, I forced myself to hold his stare and placed my hands against his chest, putting the slightest pressure there.

He released me immediately, taking a few steps away as he shoved his hands into his hair, locking his fingers behind his head.

It was then I considered how Kieran always thought through every move, and that the times he'd placed himself in front of me today were intentional. He was trying to prove he could give me what I'd been asking for. Even in his anger, even in his hurt, he was trying to prove himself.

And it was wearing on him in a way I'd never seen before.

Rubbing my hands over my face, I blew out a strained breath and looked back at the man in front of me. "I wish you would have told—" The rest of the words caught in my throat when I caught a glimpse of one of Kieran's tattoos. It was small and irrelevant, placed on his bicep among a variety of others.

But it was in the exact spot as Dare's, only Kieran's was a solitary vertical line.

It was something he'd had for years, longer than I could remember, and one I'd always dismissed.

I moved toward him without realizing it, without remembering he needed space, and traced a shaking finger over the tattoo. "What is that?"

He sighed, a look of frustration settling on his face as he dropped his arms to fold them over his chest. "It's me."

"I don't understand," I said when he didn't elaborate.

"Aric had a circle," he said after a few moments. "When he died, Beck got the circle."

Lines and circles.

Oh my God.

I knew what he was going to say before he continued, but it didn't make it any less difficult hearing it.

"Dare has the four horizontal lines."

"You've worked together for so long, have kept me afraid of them, and this entire time you, Aric, and Beck had pieces that made up the Borello's symbol tattooed on you?"

"It was how we communicated so Mickey wouldn't know. It's who we are."

I jerked back, my eyes widening with shock and disbelief. "You're a *Borello*? When—"

"No," he said quickly. "The Borello family was originally part of another gang way up north. There was a rebellion within the gang. Three families were involved and they used symbols to communicate. The Borello brothers were the only ones who made it out alive."

"You're rebels," I whispered, stunned. I nodded absentmindedly, then shook my head. "I just—I can't wrap my head around this. I thought you were going to kill Bailey for saying something stupid to me, so I can't understand why you of all people would continue to work with Dare when you know he wants to kill me. I can't understand why you would continue working with him when members of his family snuck into my room, killed Aric, and tried to take me."

One of Kieran's eyebrows ticked up. "He didn't tell you?"

"Tell me what?"

"Johnny's cousin killed Aric. Dare and Johnny were the other two in your room that night."

"One of the other rooms?" a harsh, masculine voice asked from across my room, the hushed whisper floating over to me on the breeze.

"No," another deep voice responded. "He said it was in here somewhere."

Oh God. I'd woken to a steady thrum dancing along my skin.

It suddenly felt difficult to pull in air.

"You knew?" I asked through the tightness in my chest and throat. "You knew and you still—he was working with both of you and he—"

"You weren't supposed to be there," Kieran reminded me as he gently led me to sit on the bed. "Johnny's cousin wasn't supposed to be there, and he got trigger happy. Dare and Johnny were supposed to be in and out, but they couldn't find what they were looking for because you were in the room and they couldn't use lights."

My head snapped up. "What were they looking for?"

"Aric's notes. Everything we'd been gathering on Mickey. Whenever he finished with them he stashed them in your room because Mickey had guys checking on him."

"In the baseboard," I whispered.

Kieran's head cocked to the side, his eyes narrowing in confusion. "How'd—"

"I searched my room, trying to find why they were there. I found the baseboard, but it was empty."

"I got them out after everything happened. We've added on over the years, but Dare keeps them so Mickey can't find them."

The piece of the nightmare that had been haunting me . . . all this time, Dare had been holding it.

Despite Kieran's insistence it was his fault for not being there sooner, or that it was Mickey's for keeping him away, I'd blamed and hated the Borellos for Aric's death for four years.

It was odd knowing the person I had hated was now the man I loved.

It was saddening.

And yet, I still wanted his arms around me to make this go away.

"You ask how I can work with him after what's happened. How can you want to be with someone who wants to kill you, Lily?" Kieran asked, his blank expression unable to hide the pain in his eyes.

We don't choose who we love.

Einstein had told me that, and it couldn't have been more true.

"Probably for the same reason I was able to look past what you are," I whispered, meeting his eyes.

A minute passed in unbearable silence before he asked, "I did this, didn't I?"

"It just happened, Kieran. Stop blaming yourself for everything that happens. Try to continue on with life instead of trying to fix what happened, or soon your life will be so consumed with revenge you won't realize when it's gone."

"It is, Lily."

It would've hurt less if he'd yelled at me. But the whispered words were full of so much pain and sorrow it felt like I would drown in them.

"Don't you get it?" he asked. "My life *is* gone."

Kieran understood. Knew he'd lost me . . . knew he'd lost us.

I dropped my head and covered my mouth, trying to mute my sob when he turned to leave the room. I didn't notice when he stopped, only heard his broken sigh from the far side of the room seconds later.

"I'll love you until the world stops turning, Lily O'Sullivan."

Even the house seemed to mourn with me once he was gone.

For what we'd had.

For what I'd done.

For every lie and betrayal, and for the life we would never have . . . my heart broke open and tears rolled, fat and heavy down my cheeks.

Chapter 41

RETALIATION AT ITS FINEST

Dare

I glanced at my ringing phone, my body locking up when I saw who was calling.

For what felt like minutes, I stared at the name on my screen before finally answering the call and slowly bringing the phone to my ear.

"Yeah?"

"She's here," the guy whispered. "She was at the meeting and everything."

Fucking rat. What he wouldn't do to stir up chaos, seeing as I wasn't paying him for his information.

Then again, the kind of chaos he wanted to start was exactly what I'd been waiting for.

"You get me a visual confirmation?"

He barked out a laugh. "Right. Let me put myself in front of Nightshade while I'm at it. Idiot."

I gritted my teeth and was about to tell him to not bother calling back until he had a picture or video of the girl in question when he continued talking, his voice dropping even lower.

"But I've got news . . . Mickey stopped her from leaving after the meeting. Told her she can't be staying in that damn shack on the back of the property anymore, and said she has until tonight to move back into the house. And get this, her and Nightshade are gettin' married."

The anger that pounded through my veins made it hard to remember why I couldn't leave right then. Made it hard to remember why I couldn't kill Kieran for lying to me for all these years when he'd pulled me back into a world I'd worked so hard to leave.

"Is that right, Finn?" I finally asked. "I'll have to go congratulate them."

Fiancée for fiancée.

Retaliation at its finest.

Chapter 42

BREAKING POINT

Lily

I was in that place where sleep begins to reach out for you when an arm curled around my waist, pulling me back into a hard, muscled chest.

Even in the near-dreamlike state I was in, I couldn't fool my mind into believing it was someone it wasn't.

The muscles weren't broad and comforting, they were lean and built for stealth.

A hum of electricity wasn't rolling along my arms and burning where he was touching me, but the air felt thick with his presence, and I would know that presence as if it were my own shadow.

My eyes slowly opened to the old room, the moonlight shining brightly through the floor-to-ceiling windows. A rush of nostalgia hit me like a wave waking to *this* room in *his* arms.

"I remember the first time I came home from a job and found you in my bed," he whispered against my shoulder.

Despite the heaviness of the day, a soft laugh sounded in my chest.

"I stood at the foot of the bed trying to memorize how perfect you looked. I knew I wanted to come home to you waiting for me every night. I'd known it my whole life." He dipped his head, running his nose along my shoulder and down my back before pausing. "And then I woke you."

"And I punched you."

"You fucking punched me." His chest moved with his silent laugh, his lips grazing along the skin bared by my tank. "I was so shocked I just watched you climb off my bed and walk out of this room."

"I told you not to do that job for Mickey," I whispered. "I *told* you, and you went anyway. I wanted you to know that I was mad."

"I had an idea." The slightest hint of amusement coated his words before we fell into silence. After a few moments, he pleaded, "Tell me this isn't happening, Lily."

I gripped the hand that was clutching my waist, emotion tightening my throat. "I'm so sorry."

"What do I have to do? How do we go back?"

"I don't think we can," I whispered, pain etched into every word.

"Give me a chance to fix this. You can't just stop loving me after a lifetime of—"

"I didn't. I don't know how to stop loving you," I admitted. "But there is irreparable damage made to the love that we have, and there isn't a way to fix that."

I started to twist in his arms but stopped before he could instinctively attempt to halt the movement. I knew he would try to let me face him, and I knew it wouldn't last. And even though I wanted desperately to look into his eyes while we had this conversation, it was easier this way . . .

It felt right.

This was how Kieran and I had always done things, and it should end the same.

"You're the most loyal man I know, Kieran," I said, settling back into his arms and gripping his hand. "I think that's why it was so earth-shattering when it seemed like you were a completely different person after Aric's death. But while you were doing things for the right reasons, I was left in the dark. Wondering when you were going to come back and stop breaking my heart. And four years of broken-ness and that kind of isolation is . . . it's too long. It's damaging. I knew I'd lost you long ago, but I refused to accept it because there was a part of me holding out hope you hadn't really turned into *him*. And then I found out about Texas, and that was the breaking point for me . . ."

His arm constricted around me, as if his hold on me now could prevent what had happened all those weeks ago.

"But I promise you, I never meant to break your heart too. It just . . . it just happened. I fought it, but . . ."

How do you continue fighting that kind of pull?

How do you continue fighting the kind of love you only find once in a lifetime?

"Beck told me," he said gruffly. "He told me everything you told him. So I know you ended it with Dare."

My heart contracted, the pain so sudden that I gasped.

Kieran rolled me so I was mostly on top of him, my face an inch from his. "Give us another chance. We'll leave. We'll disappear."

"We can't. You've told me countless times we can't."

"There's no reason to stay here. Beck can finish the job. I'll find a way to keep you safe. Let me remind you how we can be."

I tilted my head, my face pinching in pain. "Kieran—"

"He wants to kill you," he ground out. "Why would you want to stay . . ." His brow furrowed for a few seconds before his face slowly slipped into an emotionless mask. "You think you can change his mind."

I swallowed past the dryness in my throat and looked away from the horror filling his eyes.

"Lily, he won't give you the chance."

"You don't know—"

"Lily," he bit out, grabbing my face to make me look at him. "He won't give you the chance. What were you planning? To wait for him to come for you and try to explain before he could shoot you?"

When I only stared at him with a helpless expression, he cursed. "Jesus." He leaned up to press his mouth to my forehead, leaving his lips there when he whispered, "I'll end his life before he can try to take yours."

"Kieran, please don—" I tensed when his phone rang, and slowly looked at his frustrated expression.

For a few seconds he didn't move, but with a sneer he pushed away from me and grabbed his phone out of his pocket.

Other than his answering growl, he spoke too low for me to follow the conversation. From the way his head suddenly snapped around to face me, I knew whatever was happening wasn't good.

"That was Mickey," he explained when he slipped the phone into his pocket. When I only continued to stare at him, he roughed a hand into his long hair and let loose a heavy breath. "Lily, I have to—"

"Right." A frustrated laugh bubbled past my lips.

"Lily, I swear to you we'll leave. Say the word, and we're gone. But everything we've been working for since before Aric died is happening *now*. Finn knows Teagan's gone and is losing his mind. *Mickey* knows Teagan is gone and is about to go hunting because he thinks Finn is hiding her. This is where they all start slipping up and taking each other out, and I need to make sure Mickey's plans go down with them."

"Then go," I whispered.

I couldn't understand why I sounded disappointed. There was nothing keeping Kieran here with me other than Kieran. As much as I'd tried over the years—maybe that was it.

Maybe I'd waited and hoped for so long that a part of me would always hope for Kieran to prove me wrong even though I'd finally accepted reality.

I wasn't sure it was fair to him . . . then again, nothing about these last years was fair to either of us.

"Say the word and we're gone," he repeated, catching my stare to let me know he meant it.

"You need to go," I said, curling my arms around my waist. "This is what you've been waiting for. I shouldn't be the reason you miss it."

If he hadn't been so close, I might've missed the hurt that flashed through his eyes.

Without a word, he turned and moved quickly throughout the room, changing and arming himself with knives and blades. He headed for the bedroom door after slipping the last one into his boot, but stopped before he could get there.

After standing there for a few seconds, he abruptly turned and stalked back to the bed to pull me into his arms.

One of his hands curled around my neck and his eyes searched mine, the struggle to stay or leave evident.

But the time for staying had long past.

"Go," I said gently, trying to let him know it was okay.

His brow pinched and his mouth formed a hard line, and for just a second, he gripped me tighter. "You could break my heart for the rest of our lives and I would still love you."

He tugged me forward to press his lips to my forehead, and when he pulled away, the familiar war with the beast raged in his eyes. His hand trembled against me as he forced himself away, his expression hardening with each step back.

His gaze darted over my body, lingering on my bare legs and arms one last time before he was gone.

The familiar ache from Kieran leaving bloomed in my chest, but for the first time it was muted, as if I was experiencing it from far away. For the first time, I didn't resent him for going.

Incredible, the strength you didn't know you had when you learn to let something go.

I wandered to the large windows to look across the grounds a few minutes later, my gaze finding its way over to the mostly darkened guesthouse.

A jail in its own right. A refuge when compared to the prison I was standing in. And the home I wished I could be slipping out of to say goodbye one last time . . . only to find a reason to say goodbye again tomorrow and the next day.

My attention snapped from daydreams, and my body stilled when the electricity suddenly cut off, silencing all the white noise surrounding me.

I looked over my shoulder as the fan slowed to a stop, then glanced back out the windows to see that the guesthouse's porch light was still on and Soldier's Row was lit up.

Breathe in. Breathe out.

I turned fully to face the empty room, my heart thundering in my chest as I waited for something to happen.

The power to kick back on.

Someone to come rushing in here.

Breathe in. Breathe out.

Fear was pounding through my veins, but I somehow knew the man my heart longed for was somewhere on the property, and it was all I could do to stand there and not go looking for him. But Kieran's words kept me silent and still.

"Lily, he won't give you the chance."

I told myself repeatedly that Dare would . . . he had to. But the truth was, I couldn't be sure.

It had taken Einstein physically stopping me when I'd tried to leave out of fear when I'd found out who Dare was. And Dare was acting on hatred tonight.

Both consuming. Both nearly impossible to ease.

Nearly.

The bedroom door suddenly flung open, Conor charging in before I had the chance to move. He halted when he saw me, his expression fierce.

"Where's Kieran?"

"He left five . . . eight minutes ago. Mickey called—"

"Fuck," he hissed, pulling his phone from his pocket and tapping on it before putting it to his ear. He let out a growl of frustration as he started tapping on it again.

"Come on, Lil," he whispered as he hurried forward to snatch my hand, tugging me across the room, away from the windows.

"What are you doing?"

"I already called Beck and told him what's happening," Conor said when we stopped at Kieran's old set of dressers, which had been empty until this afternoon when we moved back into the house. "Kieran's phone is off. If this is what I think it is . . ." He let the possibility hang between us, dark and heavy and threatening.

Yet I still couldn't help but look toward the door in hopes that tonight could go a different way.

I jerked, my attention pulling from the door back to Conor when a piece of clothing hit me.

"Kieran said if they come for you, they're not going to surround the place. They're going to come right in and try to take you." He opened another drawer and started to shut it, but grabbed a dark shirt out of it and threw it at me as well. With a hard jerk of his head in the direction of the windows, he explained, "So we're going off the balcony."

The blood immediately drained from my head.

"We're on the second floor."

Frustrated that I wasn't moving, he took the clothes from my hands and forced the shirt over my head. "It's taken care of."

I finished pulling my arms through the lightweight, long-sleeved shirt, the irony not lost on me when I fixed the hood so it rested on my head.

I looked like my own nightmare.

Hooded figures that use the dark to their advantage.

Lines and circles . . .

"Hurry," he murmured, flinging the pants at me before heading toward the closet. "I'll get your shoes."

A menacing weight settled over me less than a second before a muffled sound came from behind me.

Ice-cold fingers gripped at my spine, forcing a shallow breath from me as I slowly turned to look over my shoulder.

The air fled from my lungs in a cry when I saw what was happening behind me, highlighted by the haunting light of the moon, my chest seizing and my mind conjuring up unforgiving images from so many years ago.

Conor thrashed, punching and elbowing at the man on his back and trying to knock him off. But the man held strong, tightening his chokehold on Conor so that even in the muted light flooding the room, I could see the horrible shade Conor's face was turning.

And I knew without a doubt exactly which man could withstand what Conor was trying to do, just as I knew he could take being stabbed and continue to fight.

"Run," Conor choked out.

I dropped the pants and ran for the nightstand where Kieran used to keep extra knives, but there was nothing there.

My head snapped up at the sound of Conor slamming the man against the wall, but when my eyes caught Conor's, he flung his hands in front of him and mouthed, "Run."

I looked at the drawer one last time, then glanced at Conor helplessly.

His eyes were wide and panicked, and his mouth was wide and gaping, but he was still managing to mouth, "Run."

I started backward, an apology on my lips, when Conor's eyes rolled back and his jaw went slack.

No. No, not Conor. Not Conor too.

The sight made me falter, but I forced myself to keep going—forced myself to turn and hurry toward the windows. I wrenched them open and ran onto the balcony, my attention catching on the knotted rope that lay coiled and already attached to the railing.

I didn't know how to rappel, but it didn't matter in that moment.

I would've rather flung myself off the second floor than let the man in the room catch up to me.

I bent for the thick rope but was hauled back against a hard chest, a scream tearing from my lungs before he could clamp his hand over my mouth.

"Hello, *Princess*," Johnny sneered.

Chapter 43

SHE WAS NEVER YOURS

Lily

"I have someone who's excited to meet you," Johnny mocked once he'd forced me back through the bedroom and out into the hall, dragging me when I let my body become a dead weight.

"I can assure you he won't be *meeting* me," I hissed, jamming my elbow into his stomach.

He only laughed.

It didn't matter that I'd been aching to find Dare earlier. I *knew* Johnny and I doubted he would take me to Dare now if he realized I was Elle. Then again, I was under no delusion he wouldn't kill me himself anyway.

He was the reason behind Dare's continued need for vengeance. It was like Einstein had said: Dare had a devil on his shoulder. And that devil had me in his grasp.

My mind raced as I considered what I could do, but his large body and the way he was dragging me as if I weighed nothing was paralyzing me.

"This world will be a better place when your heart sto—"

I shoved my feet against the floor and smashed my head into his face as hard as I could, staggering forward into a run, blinking away the black spots in my vision when he released me.

"Shit," I cried as I tried to shake away the pain shooting through my skull. Screams for help tore from my lungs when Johnny's large arms wrapped around me from behind, lifting me into the air to haul me backward again.

But my screams were futile.

The only people left breathing in this house wanted me dead. The men who lingered on the property wouldn't be able to hear my screams from Soldier's Row.

"Shut the fuck up!" he bit out, pressing his hand over my mouth.

My body went cold, my mind flashed to that night all those years ago.

Lines and circles.

Blood staining my carpet.

Aric.

Conor . . .

I struggled against his hold with everything I had, fear slowing my heart and sending tremors through my body when a laugh rumbled in his chest. I thrashed and opened my mouth to scream once it was free, Dare's name on my tongue, when a low voice I knew like the caress of the wind sounded behind us.

"Lily O'Sullivan." He laughed darkly when Johnny turned us to face him, letting the laugh end with a contented sigh. "I think this might be the greatest moment of my life."

Even in the dark and with a bandana covering most of his face, I knew him.

His stance. Those demanding eyes. The other half of my soul . . . he was there.

"I was coming to find you," Johnny said, his breathing rough from dragging me.

"I can see that." Dare casually raised his arm, enough for me to notice the gun in his hand. Tilting his head to the side slowly, he asked in a mocking tone, "Are you scared, Princess? It won't hurt."

The venom dripping from his words was so unlike anything I'd ever heard from him, his hatred for me tearing at my chest.

"Don't do this," I pleaded, the ache in my heart continuing to pour through each word. "I know . . . I know about your fiancée. Dare, I'm so sorry."

I knew the moment I slipped up.

Felt it in the way Johnny nearly crushed me.

Saw it in the way Dare's head jerked back.

"What the fuck did you just say?" Dare gritted as he took slow steps toward me. Glancing at Johnny, his eyes narrowed on him. "Drop her."

As soon as Johnny's arms disappeared, Dare's hand closed around my throat and he lifted his gun to my forehead.

But once we were in that position, I saw it.

What Dare was seeing, but not understanding.

The woman he was pressing to the window who looked so similar—yet different—to the one he'd been loving.

Using the barrel of the gun, he pushed the hood back to reveal more of my face, the disbelief in his eyes increasing as he did.

"Johnny, light." Before Johnny could respond, Dare bit out, "Fucking light. Shine a light on her eyes."

I flinched against the cool glass, instinctively closed my eyes when the light from Johnny's phone appeared directly in front of me, and cried out when Dare roughly forced my head back, the window creaking from the blow.

"Open your eyes!"

I blinked rapidly against the blinding light until I could hold my eyes open and had to blink again and again once it disappeared. When I could look at Dare again, hurt, disappointment, and an overwhelming confusion lingered in his eyes.

He shook his head with a quick jerk and said, "One chance to explain what you just said."

It took me a few moments to realize what he was asking, and then I was nodding. One chance . . . and I had no doubt that was exactly what he was about to give me. "You've taken everything from me."

He looked shocked for countless seconds before his eyes turned murderous. Tightening his fingers around my throat, he growled out his demand, "What was that?"

"I gave you my heart blindly," I choked out. "And continued to love you even after I found out who you were—who *we* were to each other."

The cruel look was replaced with a horrified understanding, and his hand let up marginally.

"You silently demanded my soul, and I didn't care that it would end like this, because it was beautiful while it lasted. So I let you take and take and take until there was nothing left of me to give," I cried.

He shook his head roughly, like he was trying to clear my words from his mind. "Have you lost your mind, Princess?"

"Dare, you know me," I cried out.

"Stop," he demanded. "Your family has taken everything from me." His finger slid from its resting place against the barrel of the gun to the trigger, and my tears fell faster.

"Dare, please—"

"Just kill the bitch," Johnny demanded from beside me, his voice filled with a crazed excitement.

"For Gia and my dad, I will celebrate the day I ended your life," Dare promised.

"Please. I love you," I whispered, choking on my sobs. Holding his dark stare, I reached up to place my shaking fingers on the inside of his bicep. "Until the very end."

I knew the moment it hit him. The gun relaxed slightly against my forehead and all the air seemed to be sucked up around us by the man holding me. "Elle?" he asked on a breath.

A pained cry left my chest. Unable to nod, unable to confirm, I just prayed he could see somewhere in the ice-blue eyes I was the girl he loved.

"If you want to live, let her go immediately," Kieran warned in a lethal tone.

Dare tensed but didn't turn.

"Bruise her, and I'll kill you slowly," Kieran promised, this time his voice was closer.

"Elle?" Dare repeated.

"I'm sorry. I'm so sorry for everything. I wanted to tell you," I added quickly, my soul crying out when he abruptly shoved away from me, as if I'd burned him.

He ripped the bandana off his face, his expression pained as he roughed a hand through his hair.

"Fucking Holloway whore, I knew it," Johnny growled. "Shoulda killed you when I had the chance."

My pleading, broken stare hadn't left Dare, but I knew the moment Johnny's words reached Kieran . . . I felt it.

The hall was loud with Johnny's curses and my quiet cries, but the house had never been more silent. It was as if death had passed by, leaving an ear-shattering silence in his path.

Johnny shot toward me then immediately staggered back, his roar breaking the heavy silence that surrounded us.

He pulled a blade from his shoulder, a sadistic laugh sounding in his chest. "Hasn't anyone ever told you not to bring a knife to a gun fight, Nightshade?"

Kieran's expression and tone as he focused on Johnny were calm . . . lethal. Pure assassin. "I'll skin you alive for hurting her."

Dare slammed into Kieran's body when Kieran lunged for Johnny, sending them both into the wall beside me—Dare's gun sliding across the floor as fists and curses flew.

"You let me think she was dead," Dare seethed, landing a punch to Kieran's side. "After everything I did and everything you pulled me back into, you've been fucking me over for—"

"You stole what was mine," Kieran growled, finally showing his rage. "You stole every reason for living because yours was taken from you."

"She *ran* from you."

I wanted to scream at them to stop. I wanted to beg Kieran to drop the knife he'd just slid from his boot. I wanted to warn Dare of what Kieran's next move would be.

But I was being forced to watch the entire thing in Johnny's embrace with the bloody knife pressed to my throat as he slowly backed me away.

"You should've died a long time ago," he whispered into my ear, his breaths rough.

My heart lurched when Kieran swiped his blade along Dare's calf, Dare's roar of pain filling the hallway as he twisted Kieran's hand backward and slammed it repeatedly against the wall until the knife clattered to the floor.

Johnny's grip tightened when an anguished cry tumbled from my lips, pressing the blade closer to my throat.

He hushed me, the soft sound that could easily be so comforting held so much warning.

Dare reached for the knife, but Kieran raised his fists above his head, bringing them down hard on his back. Dare stumbled away, releasing Kieran from his caged position against the wall and swiping his gun from the floor to aim at the man I'd spent a lifetime loving.

His chest rose and fell sharply as he stared Kieran down. "I wanted you to know the pain of losing your world. I wanted you to feel it every day. But it wouldn't have affected you because she was never yours."

Kieran just stood there with an expression so calm it was unnerving, but his body was tensed and his hand was slowly moving toward one of his pockets.

Dare's head tilted marginally, a jolt seeming to go through his body when he realized I wasn't where he'd left me. He turned fully, rage and fear warring on his face as he took a hesitant step in my direction.

"Johnny," he began, his voice placating. "Johnny, what are you doing?"

"Told you not to trust her," Johnny snarled. "Told you there was something about her."

Dare and Kieran were now matching us step for step. Dare's focus was on Johnny's shaking hand that held the knife to my throat, his limp growing more prominent with each step from where Kieran cut him.

Kieran kept to the wall, nearly disappearing in the shadows as he soundlessly stalked us. The easiest way to track him was the moonlight catching on his exposed blade from where it streamed in from the many windows on the wall opposite him.

"Think it's convenient we find out she's alive, and not two seconds later she's crawling into your bed."

My chest heaved with a sob and my body tried to bend under the weight of my grief. "Dare, n—" My head was wrenched back, a strangled cry catching in my throat when the blade pressed in to the point where it became painful.

"This is why Gia's gone," he yelled, forcing my face in Dare's direction for emphasis before roughly releasing my hair so he was leading me by the blade alone. "Remember her, Dare? Or is a little Holloway pussy all you needed to forget?"

Dare's lip curled and he rolled his neck, but he kept limping forward, his gun hanging loosely at his side. "Let her go, Johnny."

"Remember what it felt like to watch her die for the sake of this girl. Remember what it felt like to hold her while her blood ran cold."

A cry ripped from my lungs, tearing through the hall when the blade pierced my skin.

"Johnny!" Dare started to rush toward where we were, only to stop, his expression panicked.

Johnny's chest vibrated against my back. "I missed that sound. Isn't it nice?" he asked loudly, his voice wavering on a growl. "Know you're there, Nightshade. If you're smart, you'll stay back. Fiancée for fiancée. Or did you forget why we're here, Dare? You realized yet that every time she left you she was back here fucking him?"

Dare's chest heaved and his armed hand raised slightly. "*Let her go.*"

"Now that I think about it, you probably like blades against your throat being the assassin's whore, don't—"

"Fucking let her go!"

Johnny snarled in pain and his body jerked, the blade twitching against my throat before it fell away along with his hand that now had a knife sticking out of it. I stood there in stunned confusion before I pushed away from him with a strangled sob, my legs automatically taking me to comfort and safety . . .

I staggered backward when Dare suddenly aimed at me, a crippling acceptance washing over me in the split second that seemed to last forever and pass within one last beat of my heart before he fired, sending my world into deafening silence.

Because I knew it would end this way, and I'd been foolish to think it wouldn't.

I hated that we didn't have more time and that we'd been raised to hate each other.

But given the chance, I'd do it all over again.

Chapter 44

I LIED

Dare

My chest moved roughly with each ragged breath. Time passed achingly slow as I waited, gun still aimed on my best friend, my eyes now on the girl just in front of him.

She stood still, her wounded eyes fixated on me as she swayed slightly, as if in a daze.

A jolt went through her body when Johnny collapsed to the floor behind her, and I slowly lowered my gun, but was unable to move.

I needed to check on Johnny, but I knew there was no reason. I knew where I'd shot him, and I could see the dark blood rapidly spreading out from beneath his head.

I needed to go to the girl in front of me, but didn't know how to. She'd buried herself so deep in my heart, but her presence there suddenly felt toxic. She was everything I loved and everything I hated. I wanted to worship her and watch the life drain from those cold blue eyes.

I had absolutely no fucking clue who she was.

I watched numbly as Kieran knelt in front of Johnny to unnecessarily check his pulse, moving quickly to grab the knife he'd thrown into Johnny's wrist before taking Johnny's gun and sliding it toward me. The same one Johnny had aimed at Ell—*Lily* when she'd started running from him.

Johnny had always been destructive, but I'd spent our lives controlling his anger.

And I'd just killed him for it . . . over the girl I'd brought him here to kill.

Rage burned deep in my chest when Kieran grabbed El—when he grabbed *her*, turning her so she was no longer facing me and lifting her head to examine her neck. A string of mumbled curses left him, his voice sounding off from the ringing in my ears, before he wrapped his arms around her and pulled her back toward the wall.

As soon as he hit it, he slid down to sit on the floor with her in his lap.

My finger twitched along the barrel of the gun and my jaw ached from how hard I was clenching it.

I wanted to rip her away from him.

I wanted to punch him again for everything he'd forced me to do over the years.

I wanted to destroy him for ever touching something so perfect.

And I wanted to hate her.

But fuck if it didn't hurt seeing them like that.

She looked back at me, her hands pressed against Kieran's chest as she tried to stand.

"So this is you?" I asked, breathless. "This is it? It wasn't just *him* you were trying to keep from me, it was *this*. And you knew the whole time."

"No," she said when she finally stood—with Kieran's help because he still refused to let her go. "No, not the whole time."

"How long then?" I yelled, my voice reverberating down the hall. "A year? Year and a half?"

"No," she cried out. "I—" She turned to look at Kieran pleadingly, but he stood like a statue with his hardened glare set on me.

"She's trying to get away from you," I growled. "Clearly you never noticed the last couple years since she's been fucking terrified of you, but this is what it looks like."

"Stop!"

But I didn't know who she was talking to because Kieran had set her aside and taken a step toward me. My finger twitched closer toward the trigger, but before he could take another step, Elle situated herself between us and shoved Kieran back.

"*Stop.*"

For long moments she stared up at him, her hand pressed firmly to his chest like she could keep him from moving . . . and somehow she did.

Turning, she looked at me with the most pained expression. "I was terrified of what Kieran would do to you if he ever found out. I was terrified of what the two of you would do to each other when I realized who you were. I *hated* my life here . . . but I've never been afraid of him. I've already hurt him enough, don't make this worse."

"Hurt him?" I asked on an incredulous laugh. "You've been fucking lying to me, Elle," I growled and dragged a hand through my hair. "Lil—I can't even say your goddamn name."

"I've never lied to you, you would know if I had. I told you as much of the truth as I could."

"Half-truths are still lies. Omissions are still lies."

Through the moonlight coming in through the windows, I could see the tears pooling in her eyes as she stepped away from Kieran. "I warned you," she choked out. "Even before I knew who you were, I knew I wouldn't be able to tell you about my life because the worlds we've grown up in need to remain hidden. *My life* had to since I was supposed to be dead. And you told me to lie to y—"

"I thought you were running from a shitty life," I explained. "A boyfriend, a husband, something. I thought there was something else you were hiding that I was still trying to figure out. A kid—*fucking something* other than you being Lily O'Sullivan."

"What difference does it make?"

I flung my arms out and yelled, "It makes all the difference. I look at you . . . Christ, I see your eyes and so much hatred builds up inside me."

She grabbed her stomach, a strained sob bursting from her.

"I have spent my life hating those eyes. I have spent the last four years waiting to unleash hell on those eyes. I have spent the last few weeks dreaming of watching the light die in those eyes. *Your* eyes."

Her head shook slowly, her chest heaving with her uneven breaths. "I'm not Mickey."

"That's all I'll ever see."

She bent slightly, her mouth opened in a silent cry as Kieran pulled her back.

"Put your gun away," he ordered softly.

I shot him a look as I turned toward Johnny, and stopped when I saw Beck's little brother standing a dozen feet away with a gun in hand.

"Conor," Kieran bit out. "Put your gun away."

Conor looked between Kieran and me a few times before reluctantly doing as ordered, his tense stance relaxing when I holstered mine as well.

Bending to grab Johnny's, I slid it into the back of my pants then fought against the pain in my leg as I walked over to where he lay.

"Anyone else on the property will be rushing in here in the next few seconds to find out what that gunshot was. You should go."

I slanted him a glare and curled my lip, but I didn't respond as I bent to roll Johnny onto his side. I swallowed thickly, forcing back any emotion that rose because the people in the hall with me didn't deserve to see it.

I wasn't sure I deserved to feel it.

Grabbing his waist, I pulled him closer and gritted my teeth as I hefted him up, struggling to get him on my shoulder and back to standing when my leg was still threatening to give.

"Dare—"

"Don't," Kieran murmured, silencing her. But seconds later he was there next to me, helping me up.

"Get your hands off me," I said through gritted teeth, turning so Johnny's body was away from him. "You fucking *begged* for my help. You pulled me back into a world I spent years getting out of. And I hate you for it."

He didn't respond or give any indication he'd even heard me. And I didn't care.

I started walking down the hall, my steps slow and unsteady, my jaw clenched as I passed where Conor was trying to hold Lily back.

"No. No, Dare, don't do this," she called out. "You promised. You promised me *after*."

I knew what she meant as soon as the word left her lips.

"I love you," she breathed. "Until the very end."

"After, Elle. After."

Without looking back at her, I murmured, "I lied."

Chapter 45

EVERY LAST BREATH

Dare

I didn't know why I was here.

I wasn't working. I couldn't. And the people who needed me were all gathered together, grieving.

But I could only handle their grief for so long when I was the reason Johnny was dead . . . when part of me knew he'd been pushing and pushing for it, but another part hated myself for what I'd done.

And despite it all, the ache in my chest was from so much more than my best friend no longer being in this world.

It was for Gia.

It was for a failed years-long revenge.

It was for the loss of something so life-altering and consuming that each breath felt weighted and excruciating.

So call me a masochist for coming here. I knew she wouldn't be here . . . but I didn't know how to stay away.

This place was where she would always be real.

I slid out of my car, my eyes lingering on the hood as I shut the door. Memories flooded me as I headed to the side entrance of Brooks, the entire time trying to tell myself to turn back around and get in my car.

Go home. Go to the house. Just drive until I could never find my way back.

I pushed out a pained breath and lifted my head, already knowing what I wouldn't find at the booth she'd always sat in. Not that it made it any easier.

I somehow managed to walk over to the empty booth and folded myself into the seat, letting my head drop into my hands as soon as I was settled.

My body tensed when I heard someone sit on the other side, but before I could look up, a deep voice said, "You know, your information saved Teagan."

I lifted my head to find Beck watching me without a hint of anger or mockery, and cocked an eyebrow. "What?"

"Lily told me everything," he began, taking notice of the way I flinched at her name. "She told me she's been coming here for breakfast for two years. Your notes to her. The street fair . . . all of it."

"That's great, Beck. Today's not—"

"Breakfast with Teagan. Lily's been having breakfast here with Teagan, one of her best friends since she was a kid, for two years."

"Is that the girl . . . ?"

"Who Mickey was gonna have stolen?" he asked, his expression darkening. "Yeah. She's married to this abusive fuck, Finn. Him and his dad want to take over Holloway. Taking Teagan and selling her was Mickey's way of shutting them up."

I sat up at Beck's information. My mind raced, but all of my thoughts remained unspoken as I tried to sort them out. "Why are you here, Beck?"

"I came home this morning and found my best friend looking like her life had been ripped from her. The last time I saw her like that, her brother had been killed right in front of her. Kieran should've been there for her after that, and he wasn't. And as much as I hate to say it—and I fucking hate it—the guy she needs isn't him anymore. But it's up to you if you're going to be there or not."

A sad huff tumbled from my mouth. "Have you forgotten who she is? I've spent the last four years hating her and blaming her for Gia—"

"That right?" Beck growled, leaning over the table to get in my face. "If you want to blame and hate someone, it should be Mickey. Lily didn't even know about your fiancée until a couple weeks ago." Standing from the booth, he took a folded-up piece of paper from his pocket and tossed it at me. "*You've* been the source of her nightmares for four years. *You* were *in the room* and the reason Aric was murdered. She's shared your hate and blame, and she somehow looked past that."

"What is this?"

"It's why I'm here. I fucking hate that the two of you were together. I hate what that did to Kieran. But she's my best friend, and I know what you mean to her. She knew you were going to kill her, and she still wanted to spend time with you until you did."

I glanced at the paper like it had the power to destroy me, then slowly reached for it.

"She wrote that before I picked her up at your place yesterday morning. Made me promise I'd find a way to give it to you today. I think she somehow knew what happened last night was coming."

Of course she'd known. She knew we'd already come looking for her once and she'd never stopped reminding me that there was an end to what we had.

I grabbed Beck's arm before he could walk away, and ignored the way he tensed in preparation for a fight I didn't have the will for anymore.

"Finn," I murmured, my eyes finally sliding from the paper in my hand to Beck's hardened stare. "My informant in Holloway about *her.*"

A dark look crossed over Beck's face, his jaw clenching before he nodded and stalked away.

Once he was gone, I opened the letter, still unsure if I wanted to read whatever she'd written but unable to make myself stop.

It was like tipping the glass back to get the last drop of whiskey. Compulsory and irresistible.

And if this was the last drop of Elle, I wanted to devour it.

So I did . . . again and again until I had her words memorized, and I was left wondering if it would ever be enough.

Dare

> *I never expected you.*
>
> *I never expected a love greater than any other man or woman has ever known, or the pain that came with loving you. Our love has been full of fear and lies . . . but I wouldn't change a minute of it because without it, I never would've known true passion.*
>
> *I love you, Demitri Borello. If you asked, I would figure out a way to rewrite history to be with you. But our pain and your hatred go far too deep.*
>
> *A fire will die if there is no oxygen for it to consume. Ours has already stolen every last breath we can sacrifice to it.*
>
> *I'll love you until the very end.*

Firefly

Chapter 46

DESTROYED

Lily

I tilted my head when I heard a chair being dragged across the room to where I was, but I didn't bother looking over my shoulder to see who it was.

There was only one person who was that loud.

Beck let out a sigh when he plopped into the chair next to mine to look out the windows.

"I miss the window seat," I mumbled.

Mickey was refusing to let us move back into the guesthouse, even though my life was no longer in danger. Then again, I think this was his way of showing us that he still had control over us.

Of showing *me* that he had control over me.

"You know, now that I know everything . . . now that I know how bad it was for you with Kieran . . . I've been looking back on our lives a lot. I can't remember ever finding you staring out a window before four years ago."

"I never felt like a prisoner before four years ago."

"You hadn't felt like you'd lost Kieran," he countered.

I stilled and after a second nodded.

"Lil, I can't watch you go through another four years of this.

How long are you gonna wait for him to come back before you realize he's not?"

I turned to look at him for the first time, pain spearing my chest. "It's been three days. I waited for Kieran for four years. And I don't—I don't know how to stop waiting for him. You don't understand what we had."

"Do you see how much pain you're in?"

"How much pain are you in?" I shot back. "How many years have you been waiting for *her* to stop selling herself, Beck?"

His face fell and jaw clenched, but he didn't respond.

"You punish yourself by being there every night and ensuring she'll continue to hate you, but I know deep down you're still waiting. You'll always be waiting for her. I don't tell you to stop what you're doing. I am trapped in this place, controlled by a man I despise, and all I can do is look out a damn window. So let me look and hope and wait."

He dipped his head in a reluctant nod and squeezed my arm with his large hand. "Can I look out the window with you, Lil?"

A soft, sad laugh left my lips as I settled back in my chair. "Yeah, Beck."

We sat in silence for a long time, thoughts swirling through my mind of Dare and Kieran, of Gia and the girl Beck would always wait for, of Einstein and Johnny, of Teagan . . . so many heartaches, and it wasn't even the beginning.

"Maybe these are the lives we're meant to have. Maybe this is our atonement for being born to monsters or choosing to step into this world no one sees. We can't have love, but we'll always chase it. And as soon as we touch it, grasp it, feel the warmth of it . . . it's destroyed."

"Do you really believe that?" he asked, his tone curious instead of mocking.

I rubbed at my aching chest and looked at my best friend. "I wonder if I'm beginning to."

"So if he came back . . ."

"I would let my heart be destroyed a thousand times if it meant a thousand more days with him."

Chapter 47

SOMETHING MISSING

Dare

I walked into the girls' apartment, my steps slowing and eyes narrowing in suspicion when I found the twins in the living room with Libby.

We'd all moved back to our own places a few days after Johnny's death. I doubted anyone was coming after my family . . . if anything, Kieran would come after me. And I wouldn't be able to blame him when he did.

But that hadn't stopped the near-constant calls from everyone. They wanted to know if I was okay. They wanted to know what our next move was. They had dozens of questions I didn't have the answers to.

I'd turned my back on the girl I needed to breathe.

I'd killed my best friend and buried him next to Gia.

I was a fucking coward because I still couldn't look Einstein in the eye.

And I had a feeling I'd just walked in on my own intervention.

Libby stood when she saw me, relief washing over her face as she rushed to me. "Talk to her. Please."

Not my intervention . . .

"Libby, get over your shit with Mom and talk to her yourself."

"Einstein," she said, frustration lacing her tone. "She's not okay, Dare."

I stared at her for long seconds, my chest heaving with a dry laugh. "Of course she's not okay. Johnny hasn't even been dead five days. We buried him this morning. What do you expect—?"

"She hasn't eaten in . . ." She turned to the twins, but neither answered. "I don't know when she last ate. She won't sleep. She's obsessing over work to distract herself, but it's going to kill her. Didn't you see her today?"

My mouth opened but no response came out, because in avoiding looking her in the eye, I'd avoided looking at her at all.

Libby's mouth formed a tight line, and with two large steps to close the distance between us, she pressed her hands to my chest and shoved me back. "You're not the only one hurting," she hissed, moving to shove me again. "You're not the only one who lost someone. Your family needs you, you can't just check out because you were too stupid to see the signs and got your heart broken."

I grabbed her wrists when she tried to push me again. "What do you want me to do? You're all grieving someone I killed. *Einstein* is mourning the loss of her boyfriend who I fucking killed, Libby."

"I want you to fix it. I want you to keep this family together the way you always have. Johnny was sick. He was insane. No one blames you, Dare, but you can't just leave us when we need you."

"I would never leave any one of you, but that's . . . fuck, Libby." I dropped her arms and stepped back, my shoulders sagging. "I'm tired. I'm so goddamn tired. I've been trying to keep the entire family together since I was thirteen because it's always been, 'Dare will know what to do.' I *never* knew what to fucking do. That role shouldn't have been put on me then, and I don't want it now. People are still dying, and we're still neck deep in things I don't want us in, and at some point I want all that to end. I don't want to be Boss. I'll never be Dad, and it's exhausting trying to be."

"I don't want you to be Boss," she mumbled, her eyes darting to the floor.

A weighted breath puffed from my chest. "For someone who rebels from this life so much, you seem to push me toward it."

"I wouldn't call it *rebelling*, per se," she said with a shrug. "More like fleeing with flare."

The corner of my mouth twitched up and my eyes rolled. "You're an idiot." Stepping toward her, I hooked my arm around her neck and pulled her in for a hug. "All right, let me go check on the genius."

Maverick stood, his face somber. "I'll come."

"No, I've got it. I don't want her to feel like we're ganging up on her." Rubbing the back of my neck, I sighed. "Besides, I've been avoiding this talk."

I walked through the apartment to Einstein's room and almost didn't knock on the door when there was absolute silence on the other side.

I turned, not surprised to find Libby and the twins just a few feet behind me.

"She's awake. Trust me, just go in," Libby said, not bothering to whisper.

And when I opened the door, I found out why.

Einstein was sitting at her desk with her noise-cancelling headphones on. All three of her screens were up and running, her fingers twitching over one before she threw her headphones off, music screaming out of them, and shoved from the desk to run to the bed.

She didn't even notice us standing in the door as she snatched her tablet up and hurried back to the desk.

But I saw her.

She looked haggard.

She looked sick.

And it was my fault.

Maverick tried to push through, but I held up a hand to stop him then slowly entered the room.

I rapped my knuckles along her desk as I moved closer so she would feel the vibration and know I was there, and saw her jerk just before I tentatively reached out to touch her shoulder.

She threw the headphones onto the desk again and whipped her head up to look at me, her eyes crazed. "Dare, look at this," she said breathlessly, her glazed stare moving back to the screens.

"Einstein—"

"See what he's doing? He's got a tail following Kier—"

"*Einstein.*"

"—and he's gonna pin him for taking that girl—"

I grabbed her shoulders and forced her to look at me. "*Einstein!*"

Her chest moved up and down rapidly as she stared at me, her cheeks sunken in and eyes hollow.

"You've gotta stop," I said softly, gently. "You need to eat something and sleep."

She tried to gesture to the computers. "But can't you see what's—"

"I don't care. I care that you're going to kill yourself if you don't *stop.*"

Her eyes darted around us, her head shaking so fast I wasn't sure she knew she was doing it. She stood so quickly that I lost my hold on her. "There's something else," she whispered, then bent, snatching wildly at crumpled papers on the floor before throwing herself back in her chair. "Look at this. Mickey's changing his pattern—"

I grabbed her out of the chair, wrapping my arms around her as tight as I could manage. "I'm sorry," I whispered, my words twisted with grief. "I'm so fucking sorry, Einstein. I'm sorry."

I repeated my apology until she buried her face in my neck, her body heaving with her sobs.

"I tried—I tried to figure him out. I tried to fix him, and I couldn't fix him," she cried. "I tried . . . I did. There was something missing and I couldn't find it, but I tried. I tried so hard."

Tears stung my eyes and my chest burned with pain. "I tried too. But you can't fix someone like that. You can't change them."

"I could've," she insisted.

I glanced over my shoulder when I felt someone come up behind me and saw Maverick anxiously shifting his weight and looking at Einstein helplessly. After a pleading glance at me, I turned and transferred her to his arms.

His eyes shut like he was in pain as he cradled her close, stepping back to lower them onto the bed with his back against the headboard.

As Einstein sobbed against his chest, I had a feeling Maverick's pain was stemming from hers rather than Johnny's death.

And I didn't know what to make of it.

I started to look for Libby, but my eyes caught on one of Einstein's screens as Diggs stood there, quietly shutting everything down.

"Wait," I said softly, studying what she'd been trying to show me before I gave him a nod.

I stepped back, my heart seizing when I glanced down and saw a picture of Lily peeking out under a few papers.

It was the picture Einstein had snuck to try to find out who Elle was.

That smile . . .

Goddamn firefly.

"I could've been what he needed to help him out of the dark," Einstein murmured, her voice dragging.

I turned, my gaze snapping to Einstein. "What'd you just say?"

Maverick slanted a glare at me, and Einstein lifted her head, her bloodshot eyes blinking slowly. "Johnny. He said it was dark in his head and sometimes he didn't know how to find a way out."

Maverick whispered something to her, and no sooner had her head rolled back to his chest than her eyes closed and her breathing evened out.

"You good?" I asked.

"I'm not going anywhere," he said softly, burrowing down against the headboard.

I watched for another second before pulling my attention to Diggs and Libby, my brows pulling together. "Let's go talk."

As soon as we got out into the living room, I said, "I need to go take care of what Einstein was trying to warn me about. When I get back, we'll figure out a plan to put all this Holloway shit to bed for good. If Einstein wakes up before I get back, make her eat. Now *that* . . ." I gestured back toward Einstein's room, but Libby spoke before I could continue.

"Let him be there for her."

"Johnny's been in the ground for about four hours," I reminded her.

"He's not doing anything," Diggs mumbled, shoving his hands in his pockets as he turned to go sit on the couch.

"Maverick's been in love with Einstein forever, Dare," Libby said, her voice soft. "You ever notice he's near her if they're in the same room, even when Johnny was? And he was always there for her whenever Johnny went dark, but he's not acting on anything. He knows she loved Johnny."

I ran my hands through my hair and over my face, groaning as I did. "Where was I when all this happened?"

Libby shrugged. "Holding everything together."

Chapter 48

APOLOGY

Dare

Even after six years working together, it never stopped being fucking creepy the way he was able to materialize from the shadows.

He didn't say anything, just stood there with his arms tensed at his sides, waiting to see what my first move would be.

"Mickey's having you watched. Closely."

"I know."

I rolled my eyes. Of course he did. "If you already know why, tell me now so I don't waste my time." I took his silence as his response, and said, "He thinks you're the reason behind Teagan getting away."

"I am."

"Well, he fucking knows," I bit out.

Kieran folded his arms over his chest and let loose a slow breath. "You made it clear we were done the other night, so why are you trying to warn me about Mickey?"

"We are done," I confirmed. "But Einstein refuses to finish something that isn't completed, which means she's still watching Mickey's every move. And he's about to pin you for messing up his plans the way he was plotting to pin Aric."

"Again, why are you—?"

"I'm warning you because it's the only apology you'll get from me," I ground out. "When all this is over, I'm never letting Lily go again."

Something so evil filled his hardened stare.

I'd seen that look paralyze men with fear before he slit their throats. For some, their hearts had even stopped beating before his blade had come in contact with them.

Just like Deadly Nightshade.

He clenched his teeth as he swore, "I will make your death slow and unbearable if you try to take her."

I huffed a laugh, though I knew he meant every word. "She's not yours anymore. I know you love her, so you shouldn't want her to be forced to continue a life where she's miserable."

It was low . . . I knew it the second the words slipped from my mouth. But it didn't take away from the shock of seeing Kieran look like I'd just annihilated him.

I rubbed at my jaw and let loose a sigh. "Look, stop giving Mickey a reason to have you followed, and don't get in my way. You brought me into this, and now I'm ending it."

There wasn't a response from where he stood, silently seething. Not that I expected one.

"Have Beck bring Lily to my house when Mickey goes into work on Monday."

"You've lost your goddamn mind if you think I'm delivering her to you."

One of my eyebrows ticked up. "You're not. You're getting her somewhere safe where Mickey can't find her. He only knows about the main house—he doesn't know where I live. He's going to be ready to tear the world apart when he sees what I've done. Think about what he'll do to Lily when he realizes his last chance at keeping his blood in power of Holloway has turned her back on Holloway completely." I turned to leave when Kieran's expression fell but paused when he spoke.

"And this is coming from someone who wanted to kill her just last week."

I didn't try to deny or explain it, because he already knew it all. Just like he must've known it took me nearly this long to realize her name and those eyes would never be able to keep me from her.

"I'll beg you to slit my throat before I hurt her."

His mouth curled into the cruelest grin, and his eyes flashed. "You won't have to."

Chapter 49

DEAL

Dare

For a moment, I wondered if this was what Kieran felt like. Waiting in the shadows, watching people go about their lives, completely unaware to your presence. But then I saw him tense. Only the slightest change in the way he was holding himself, his hand slowly creeping toward his pocket as his eyes scoured the room. And then I wondered how a human being could be so damn silent.

His murderous eyes passed over me, the only indication he saw me was the pent-up breath he slowly released as he slipped the knife from his pocket, his head dipping in the slightest nod.

"Go get the men who were supposed to pick up Finn's whore," Mickey muttered as he sat at his desk and logged onto his computer. "They talked to someone, and I want to know who. I want to know where that girl is, and I want to make sure this colossal fuck-up won't happen again."

Kieran's gaze snapped in my direction—the only warning he could give me—a second before he threw the knife at me, the blade imbedding in the wall just inches from where I stood.

I might've cursed if Mickey wasn't already up and looking my way, his eyes cold and his lips twisted into a sneer.

"It won't," I assured him. When he reached for the gun at his hip, I raised mine higher. "I wouldn't."

I waited as Libby, Einstein, the twins, and a few of the older members stepped out from their places within Mickey's office to surround him and Kieran, enjoying his growing frustration as our numbers grew.

"You have a lot of places to hide in here," I said with a grin.

Mickey's office building located in Raleigh seemed to fit him. It was loud, overstated, and dripped with dirty money. His office was even worse. It was like his own personal shrine for how amazing he thought he was.

But for a mob boss, it had been all too easy for his enemy to slip into the building and into his office.

"Security isn't that great," I added.

"You all have some pretty big balls showing up in costumes, kid," he said with a laugh.

My grin widened. He and I both knew the bandana was a Borello tradition, just as he knew exactly who was standing in front of him.

Still, I lowered the piece of fabric so it hung around my neck. Shrugging when I did.

"Computer," I muttered to Einstein, never taking my attention from Mickey. I took a step closer to him when she hurried to sit in the chair he'd just been occupying, her fingers flying over the keyboard. "Like I was saying . . . that colossal fuck-up won't happen again, because your warped dream of selling and buying stolen women is over."

Although his animalistic sneer didn't fade, panic slowly rose in his eyes.

Einstein kicked away from the desk, rolling back in the chair and leaving the computer open for view.

I walked forward until I was standing on the opposite side of his desk, behind the computer, forcing Mickey to face the screen and giving me a clear view of his expression.

"That feed on the left? That's your shipping container. You know, the one you bought to hold the kidnapped women until the auctions." I leaned forward to whisper, "I don't think you're getting a shipment of girls anytime soon, Mickey."

Every one of the men Mickey hired to find and kidnap women was rotting in that container.

Johnny, Kieran, and I had been slowly picking them off over the last six months—made easy because Mickey only kept in contact with them over texts. And we had all their phones. The men tasked with taking Teagan had been the last hired and the last to go.

"That still on the right? It's a few of the men leaving the police station after spilling about your little plan since you tried to blackmail them into going in on it with you. At least, that's what they said . . . and I destroyed all copies of their contracts."

"I will end you," he seethed. "I will murder everyone you've ever loved while you're forced to watch, and then I will tear your heart from your chest and shove it down your throat."

I waited a few seconds then muttered, "That was dramatic. Did you get that?"

Einstein nodded as she lowered her phone. "Yep."

"Christ, Mickey. Now I have you on video threatening my life. And I bet the computer hid my gun. Funny how that works."

"Police in eight," Maverick called out from where he stood behind Einstein.

I tilted my head and sucked in a breath. "*Funny.*"

"What do you want?" Mickey demanded, wrath burning in his eyes.

"A few things. For starters, don't be a sick fuck. I've visited every person who signed a contract with you for this trafficking ring. Not one of them will go to bat for you. Every contract, bill, and statement has been wiped from your servers, and the physical copies are now in my possession. If I hear you're trying to start this up again, I'll take you down with a smile on my face."

He ground his teeth, the muscles in his jaw flexing. "And?"

"Our feud is over. If you ever come after a Borello member or a *Borello*, I will kill you, and it won't be quick. That includes anyone you hire or any Holloway."

"What else?" he spat.

"Do you agree?"

"Yes, I agree, you piece of shit."

"Then you're about to be arrested," I said with a shrug. "You're smart, and you have a lot of money that was supposed to go toward your psychotic plan. I'm not dumb enough to think you don't still have people in your pocket that can get you out on bail and sweep all this under the rug as a bad case of envy and false accusations. But that doesn't change what's happening right now."

"I underestimated you."

With my gun still aimed at his chest, I stuck out my hand. "We have a deal?"

Mickey grit his teeth and forced himself to stand tall, straightening his suit as he did. With a hard nod, he muttered, "Deal."

I released his hand and nodded toward his office door. Once my crew started that way, I turned to head toward the door, smirking at Kieran. He was barely concealing his rage.

"We're even. He's your problem now," I whispered as I passed by him.

His breaths grew more pronounced, his chest heaving, but I didn't care.

He'd fucked me over, and this was my last retaliation.

The plan for six years had always been to stop Mickey. Four years ago the plan had changed to end his life as well.

The only apology Kieran would ever get from me for taking Lily was the warning on Mickey, and for taking all the blame—or credit, depending on how you looked at it—in stopping the trafficking ring. Now Mickey's suspicions of Kieran would end, and Kieran's life wasn't in danger.

But unless Kieran planned to kill Mickey before the cops showed up, he was stuck with him—stuck being Mickey's assassin. And that was the worst kind of retribution because Kieran didn't know how to stop working.

I'd trapped him the way they'd all trapped Lily.

With my back pressed to the door, I grabbed the bandana and looked at the only two men left in the room. "Lily Borello . . . it fits her, don't you think?"

I lifted the bandana over my face and slipped out the door, my smirk widening into an uncontrollable smile as chaos erupted behind me.

Chapter 50

EMBER

Lily

I reached for the back of my neck, trailing my fingers over the tingling that began at the top of my spine. My mind so lost in my heartache and memories as I stared out the window of the foreign house Beck had left me in that I didn't notice the familiarity in that buzz or the way the air seemed to shift around me until he spoke.

"Truth or dare."

I sucked in a sharp breath and turned, sure I was dreaming when I saw Dare in front of me. "What are you doing here?"

"I live here."

"You what?" My eyes darted around the room, surprise filling me.

His voice was gruff, his stare grave when he repeated, "Truth or dare."

I opened my mouth to respond with *dare* but after everything we'd been through . . . all the lies . . . I wanted the opportunity to give him every truth I had.

"Truth."

"Did we meet by chance?"

"Yes," I responded, my shoulders sagging. "Teagan found out I was alive and came looking for me. She asked me to meet her the next day at Brooks Street. She didn't know who you were either. She was furious when she realized I was falling for you simply because you weren't Kieran."

He took a few steps closer, his face remaining impassive. "And when you found out who I was, what did you do?"

"Tried to run," I admitted. "It was after our first night together. I woke up and freaked because I knew someone would notice I was gone soon if they hadn't already, and then I saw your back. But then I decided that it didn't matter . . . and then Einstein found me, and I realized you were Demitri instead of just *Dare*. Before I could make it out of the house, she stopped me and made me think. And I knew our names and our families didn't change what I felt."

"She knew who you were."

It wasn't a question, but I nodded anyway.

"Makes sense. She was the only person other than Johnny who knew I was coming for you last week. I needed her there to cut the power because she would've done it a hell of a lot faster than I did. She lost it, tried to get us not to go."

"How is she?" I asked, my heart aching for the crazy, wild-eyed girl.

Dare shrugged but didn't answer.

"And you?"

He stared at me for so long that I started to wonder if he would respond. "I'm empty," he finally said. "I keep waiting for you to show up, or expecting to step into a room and find you there. When Gia died, I threw myself into work—pulling the family out of illegal stuff where I could, and helping Kieran where he needed it. But I don't know how to get through any of this *without* you. I never wanted to see you again, but I don't know how to let you go when all I want is to be able to reach out and feel you, or turn and see you smile."

The way he let the last word hang in the air let me know he wasn't done, and I dreaded what came next because I had a feeling I knew.

But when seconds came and went without him continuing, I shrugged helplessly. "But I'm not the girl you want there," I whispered.

"Dare, I'm sorry for all the pain I caused you. It ate at me knowing how it was going to destroy you when you found out, but I couldn't give up that time with you when I knew we had so little of it. Who we are to each other . . . I would spend the rest of my life trying to find a way to change that, but nothing can. The girl you fell in love with *is* me, but I can never be Elle. She's a horrible excuse for a disguise and a mystery you couldn't solve. Now that it has been . . . she's just Lily. She's only me with contacts and glasses. She's a girl you hate."

His head shook subtly. "I love you in a way I never knew was possible."

A shuddering breath forced from my lungs and my heart began pounding so rapidly at his admission that it was nearly painful.

And I cherished every painful beat because they let me know this was real.

I was sure the first time he'd said those words it was the beginning of the end . . . and hearing them now, they felt like the beginning of forever.

And I'd thought I'd lost him.

Dare closed the distance between us, each step slow and calculated, each step creating a frenzy inside me. When he reached me, he slid an arm around my waist and cradled my face with his hand in a move so natural and without hesitation I wanted to cry.

"I love you in a way that shouldn't be possible," he breathed, his knowing eyes searching my own. "Tell me you lied."

I blinked quickly, trying to understand his urgent plea. "What?"

"Tell me you lied. Tell me there's still a spark or an ember, and I'll find a way to keep it alive until the day I die."

"You got my note."

"Lily," he said on a groan, dropping his forehead against mine.

My breath caught at the sound of my name on his lips. It was a moment I hadn't realized I'd spent years longing for—*needing*. And in that instant, I felt the peace and comfort I'd been searching for.

Dare was my home. He was where I would always belong.

I tentatively reached up to press my mouth to his, my soul rejoicing in having this connection with him again when I was so sure I never would.

"I was wrong," I whispered against the kiss. "If you're here we still have everything."

"You're done lying, and you're done disappearing," he said, his voice nothing more than a rumble. "I'll follow you across the world but no more chasing. I want you to be mine."

A rush of air tumbled from my lips when I searched his eyes. Worry and unrestrained need swirled in their depths. "Can't you see I've been yours?"

"Then give me your days and nights. Give me your forever."

"They're yours if you'll wait for me to light up the after."

Our next kiss was all-consuming.

Match lit.

Fire burning beyond control.

I was lost.

In him. In this kiss. In us.

And I wasn't sure I ever wanted to be found.

Epilogue

SIX MONTHS LATER

Lily

"What's this?" I asked, a smile tugging at my lips when Dare casually slipped a piece of paper into my hand from where he was relaxing between my legs.

His dark eyes flashed to mine, humor and love dancing in them before he fixed his adoring stare on the small bump growing between my hips. His fingers gently traced over my bare stomach, the touch so light I might not have noticed if I hadn't been watching him.

"Open it," he murmured.

Tearing my eyes from him, I opened the folded paper, my smile widening when I read it.

Truth or Dare.

"Hmm . . . truth."

"Boy or girl," he said immediately. "What do you want the baby to be?"

I didn't have to think long. I'd been going back and forth ever since we'd found out, and I had come to the same conclusion every time. "I don't care. As long as the life we both grew up in never touches the baby, I don't care."

When he looked at me again, his expression was grave. "It won't," he promised.

I knew Dare would do everything to make sure of that.

Ever since Dare stopped Mickey's human trafficking ring, we hadn't heard from Mickey . . . or Kieran, for that matter. And no Borello member had been involved in any illegal activity.

Well, except for Einstein and her impulsive hacking.

Some of the older members who weren't happy about the changes had left town, looking for mobs that were still thriving. The others were happy to have the gang put to rest.

Einstein had taken over Dare's bookkeeping so he'd have more time to help the businesses in town and with me. And when the twins weren't helping Dare, they were working at The Jack. We saw them every few days because they were as much Dare's family as Libby, but everyone seemed to be settling into their own routines of normal living.

As were we.

It had taken a while to get used to going where I wanted, when I wanted, but the freedom never stopped feeling exhilarating. We took care of my faked death—again, Einstein and her hacking. Dare took me on spontaneous trips, just so I could breathe air that wasn't tainted by memories of Holloway. He taught me to drive, and I got my license. And I was now managing Brooks Street for Sophia, where Beck came to see me every other week.

He'd given me a few updates on Holloway before understanding that I didn't want to know, but every now and then he continued to update me on how Teagan was doing . . . wherever they had her hidden. He'd let slip that Mickey's charges had been dropped but hadn't brought it up again when he'd seen the fear and worry that had nearly consumed me, knowing that Mickey might come looking for me to lock me up in that prison again.

Not once had Beck mentioned Kieran, and I wasn't sure if I was thankful for that or not. For the most part we just sat there, and I tried to ignore the deep sadness and betrayal that lingered in his eyes when he looked at me.

Not that it stopped him from coming.

Dare pressed another scrap of paper into my palm, forcing me to bite my lip in an attempt to contain my smile. "Another one?"

His teeth flashed with his brief smile before he went back to tracing patterns on my stomach, and when I opened the piece of paper, I couldn't believe what I was seeing.

The note was in my handwriting, and was from the morning I'd slipped out of the house, sure I would never see him again.

~~Truth or~~ Dare
Love me forever

"You kept this?"

He dipped his head in a nod, the corner of his mouth twitching into a brief grin. "When I found it, I remember thinking I'd gladly love you forever. A few days later I was packing up everything to move back here and saw it, and I realized what you'd really been asking when you left me this. At that point, I'd already spent nearly every waking moment trying to figure out how to move on from you." He glanced up at me and said, "Took another couple days not only to understand I couldn't, but I didn't want to."

"I know the feeling," I whispered. "It's terrifying realizing you're lying in your greatest enemy's arms. Even more so when you realize you never want to leave because you've never felt safer, and he has the ability to touch your soul."

His eyes darkened with some emotion I couldn't place as he dropped his head to press a tender kiss on my stomach. Reaching up, he pushed another piece of paper in my palm.

A laugh tumbled from my lips, excitement thrumming in my veins at what would be next. But as soon as I opened the paper, my breath caught. After a painful pause my heart started up again and began racing as I read the paper over and over again.

~~Truth or~~ Dare
Marry me

"Dare," I whispered, lowering the paper to look at him. Tears pricked my eyes and my mouth fell open when I saw a large diamond ring resting on my belly.

"The baby and I want to know if you'll spend the rest of your life with me."

Tears slipped down my cheeks as I nodded. "Of course I will."

A wide smile burst across his face as he grabbed my hand and slid the ring onto my finger, that same unknown emotion swirling in his eyes. Some mix of pride and excitement and desire . . .

"Don't ever leave," he begged, his voice soft as he lifted himself higher so he was hovering over me, his lips a breath away from my own.

"Anywhere I go, I'll be waiting for you to find me lighting up the dark."

The corner of his mouth tipped up in a quick, perfectly crooked smirk. "Goddamn firefly."

ACKNOWLEDGMENTS

Cory – I can't thank you enough for how much you helped me with this story. I know I was a lot to handle, and I can't imagine what it was like for you having to listen to me while I endlessly changed this story. Thank you for always being there. Thank you for all your help. Thank you for being the best husband ever.

Molly Lee and AL Jackson – The other half of my #MollySquared and my BB! Honestly couldn't have finished this story without the two of you. Thank you for *everything*. All the plotting. All the encouragement. Just being there. So thankful to have y'all in my life. I love you both so much.

Rachel "Cruz" Elliott – Thank you, thank you, thank you for being the best seestor. You've helped with this entire series so much that I'll never be able to thank you enough.

Sarah Cook – You are seriously one of the strongest women I know. I'm so in awe of you, and have been so moved by you during this time. As you already know, this story is for you. Your light is coming. I know it is. But I love more than anything that you hold fast to the knowledge that Aaron got to spend the rest of his wonderful life loving you.

Jill Sava – What would I do without you? You've helped me so much in the last year, that there are just no words. You're incredible. You're a genius. You're the best at everything you do, and you always go above and beyond. I know, I know. I'll stop crying. Sheesh.

Letitia, Malia, Marion, Karen, and Julie – Thank you for being the amazing women who help me make this series come to life. From the cover to the illustrations to the editing to the formatting. You're all so amazing and I'm beyond grateful for all the hard work you do.

Briar Chapman is going to be the death of me, and I don't care. I'll take every day until that death comes, and I'll welcome it when it does.

Turn the page for an extract from the first Redemption novel

Available now from

HEADLINE
ETERNAL

Prologue

Briar

"Trust me." His voice was low, his tone barely hinting at his plea as he placed the material over my eyes, wrapping it around my head and tying it in a knot. Making it so the darkness and his voice and the terrifying memories were all I was aware of.

His mouth passed across my cheek then my lips . . . lingering there as he spoke. The ache in his whispered words nearly bringing me to my knees. "I'm sorry I have to force you to relive those days, but I'll do whatever it takes to keep you safe."

I wanted to reach out for him when I felt him move away from me; I wanted to cling to him and his voice and his words . . . but memories began to grip and suffocate me. I could no longer move. No longer breathe.

A shuddering breath finally burst from my chest and my body began trembling. My lips automatically began moving out of fear as a song begged to be freed.

My entire being thrashed and rebelled against the memories that flashed through my mind as I stood in the enforced darkness. Memories that felt so real as if they were happening now instead of all those months ago.

My body shook harder, and I nearly screamed, *"How can this be happening to me?"*

But it wasn't real. Not anymore.

I'd lived a life made up of rules and appearances. I was told what to wear, how to act, and when to speak—or sing.

Even when I'd found the man I thought I wanted to spend my future with, nothing felt like it was my own. But I'd been happy with our life and excited for the days to come.

Until they didn't.

Until I was forced into a world I'd been blind to and came face to face with the devil.

A man cloaked in darkness—a man who would set me free.

A man hidden in a world I vowed to destroy with him by my side.

"Briar."

I whipped my head to the left when his voice sounded from across the room, barely loud enough to hear. My shaking grew stronger, and when I felt his dark, dark presence slip behind me, the song I'd been trying so desperately to hold back bled out as a whisper.

"I know him. I know *the man behind me,"* my mind screamed. But those screams couldn't be heard while I was consumed with memories *he* wanted me to surrender to.

His breath stirred the loose hair on my neck, and just before his arms wrapped around me, he spoke in a low, sinister tone that sent chills up my spine. "Fight me."